A native of Dundee, Marion studied music with the Open University and worked for many years as a piano teacher and jobbing accompanist. A spell as a hotel lounge pianist provided rich fodder for her writing and she began experimenting with a variety of genres. Early success saw her winning first prize in the *Family Circle Magazine* short story for children national competition and she followed this up by writing short stories and articles for her local newspaper.

Life (and children) intervened and, for a few years, Marion's writing was put on hold. During this time, she worked as a college lecturer, plantswoman and candle-maker. But, as a keen reader of crime fiction, the lure of the genre was strong, and she began writing her debut crime novel. Now a full-time writer, Marion lives in North-east Fife, overlooking the River Tay. She can often be found working out plots for her novels while tussling with her jungle-like garden and walking her daughter's unruly but lovable dog.

Also by Marion Todd

Detective Clare Mackay

MARION TODD
Dead man's shoes

 CANELO CRIME

First published in the United Kingdom in 2025 by

Canelo
Unit 9, 5th Floor
Cargo Works, 1–2 Hatfields
London SE1 9PG
United Kingdom

A CIP catalogue record for this book is available from the British Library.

Print ISBN 978 1 80436 217 4
Ebook ISBN 978 1 80436 216 7

Cover design by Black Sheep

Cover images © Getty Images, Shutterstock

Look for more great books at www.canelo.co

Printed and bound in Great Britain by Clays Ltd, Elcograf S.p.A.

1

For my cowshed chums who, over the years, have given me so much material.

NOVEMBER

Day 1: Tuesday

Chapter 1

'HR want to know if Sara's changing her name now you're married,' DI Clare Mackay said. She bent in front of the fridge, hunting for her lunchbox. 'If someone's taken my roll again...'

'Sure you remembered it?' DS Chris West said. 'Wouldn't be the first time you'd left it at home.'

'Shoved to the back again.' She lifted another plastic tub out of the way. 'Apparently Sara spoke to someone in HR before the wedding but she's not followed it up. Woman who phoned said they'd chased her a couple of times. About her name,' she added.

Chris rolled his eyes. 'She reckons West is too short. Wants us both to change our names to Stapleton-West.'

Clare suppressed a smile. 'Christopher Stapleton-West.'

'I know. Makes me sound a right posh twat. So that's not happening.'

'Well, make up your minds, the pair of you. Get HR off my back.' She began walking to her office, lunchbox in hand. Chris followed her through and sank down on a spare chair.

She eyed him. 'Haven't you any work to do?'

'Jim's had another report of fly-tipping.' He glanced over her shoulder towards the window. 'It's a nice day. We could take a run out.'

'That's a council matter. Or do they know who it is? Where is it, anyway?'

3

He shrugged. 'Somewhere near Strathkinness. Thought you might be interested. It's your neck of the woods after all.'

Clare bit into her roll and chewed. 'No can do,' she said. 'I've been summoned.'

Chris regarded her. 'Not Penny?'

'Yup.'

A smile played at the corners of his lips. 'You been a naughty girl?'

'I've no idea. One of her staff phoned about an hour ago. I've to be there for two.'

'I could drive you.'

'I thought you had a pile of crime reports to go through.'

'They'll wait.'

Clare checked her watch. There was just time for a quick coffee before she headed out for her meeting. She scraped back her chair. 'Let's grab a coffee, then you can make a start on the reports.'

He sighed heavily and rose to his feet. 'Go on, then. But I want a biscuit with it.'

–

Superintendent Penny Meakin's office was across the River Tay in Dundee's Bell Street station. Clare always enjoyed the drive over the bridge, but today her mind was elsewhere, wondering why she'd been called over. What was so important it couldn't be dealt with by a phone call or email?

She reached the end of the bridge and took the west-bound slip road, making her way through a series of traffic lights which pretty much all turned red as she approached. *Not a good omen*, she thought, pulling up at a crossroads.

The car park at the Bell Street station was always overflowing but, as she sat at the entrance, the engine idling, a man in a suit came out and ran down the steps, heading for his car. She drew forward, waiting for him to pull out, then she drove into his space, nose first. Two minutes to spare, according to the car clock. She climbed out, pulling her jacket round as a stiff breeze caught her hair, and made her way into the station.

Penny's office was on the third floor. As she waited for the lift she heard a familiar voice behind her. She turned to see Bill, a plain-clothes officer who'd been seconded to St Andrews a few times when they'd needed extra manpower.

'Bill!' A smile spread across her face. 'Good to see you.'

'Likewise.' The lift door opened and he gestured with his hand for her to go in first. 'Which floor?' he said, indicating the panel on the wall.

'Three.'

'Oh. Like that, is it?'

'I've been summoned by the Super.'

The lift binged and the door drew back. Bill gave her a smile. 'If you need a friendly face you know where I am,' and he stepped out of the lift.

The door closed again and she felt the lift lurch as it creaked its way to the third floor. A uniformed officer she didn't recognise was manning the desk outside Penny's door and he rose to greet her.

'Superintendent Meakin has asked that you leave your phones here,' he said. 'Work and personal.'

Clare waited for an explanation but he said nothing further, his expression impassive. Reluctantly she reached into her bag and withdrew both phones, clicking her personal one to silent. The officer placed them in a clear plastic bag, pressing the seal closed, and put the bag into his desk drawer. Then he motioned to a row of seats. 'If you'd like to wait here.'

Clare eyed the seats but didn't move. The officer went across to Penny's door and tapped lightly on it. She heard Penny's voice and he disappeared inside. There was a murmur of conversation then he returned, closing the door softly. 'You can go in now,' and he stood back to let her pass.

An uneasy feeling was gathering in the pit of her stomach. There was something very wrong here. This wasn't a secure installation. She'd been in Penny's office many times and never had to give up either of her phones. With one eye on the officer, she walked smartly towards the door and tapped on it. A voice from within told her to enter and she pushed the door open.

Penny was behind her desk and she rose to greet Clare. Clare's eyes swept the room and came to rest on the back of a man in a dark suit. There was something familiar about him. Something that pricked a memory, but it wouldn't come. And then he too rose and turned to greet her, a cool professional smile. Suddenly she was back in the dark days when they'd been hunting two prison officers and their wives. The couples had disappeared and Ben had been sent to oversee the investigation. She remembered the veil of secrecy that had marked their enquiries, how he'd kept so much from her; and, when it was over, he'd offered her a job, heading up an undercover team. But, after an uncomfortable few days trying to decide what to do, she'd turned him down. And here he was again, this time with Penny Meakin. Was he about to offer her another job? With Penny's blessing? Surely not? Men like Ben didn't give second chances.

'You remember DCI Ratcliffe,' Penny said.

'Ben,' he said and he indicated a chair. 'It's good to see you, Clare. You're well?'

It wasn't really a question but she nodded, making the right noises, and reciprocated the greeting. She glanced at the chair then at Penny, who waved her down. 'No need to stand on ceremony.' Clare sank down, perching on the edge of the seat, not quite able to relax.

'Before we go any further,' Penny said, pushing her specs up her nose, 'we must have your assurance you'll treat what you're about to hear in complete confidence.'

Clare's mind was whirling. This didn't sound like a job offer. So what was it? 'Of course,' she said. Penny and Ben exchanged glances.

'Ben has some intel that impacts on your patch. I wasn't absolutely sure how widely it should be disseminated but he's suggested we bring you on board.' She smiled at Ben. 'Perhaps it's better if you explain.'

He nodded and turned his chair to face Clare. 'You've no doubt heard of the so-called Chainlink Choker?'

Clare knew the case, of course. The killer of young gay men, so called by the red tops because he strangled his victims with a chain. She ran through the reports in her head. Were there five now?

'Let me refresh your memory,' Ben said. 'This man picks up his victims, most likely in a nondescript white van, probably offering to pay them for sex which takes place in the back of the van. We think he drugs them – four of the victims have been found with Rohypnol in their system. Probably offers them a drink while he drives around, looking for somewhere quiet to park up and have sex. By the time he stops the van they're pretty much incapable of defending themselves. He rapes them, strangling them with a chain as part of the act.'

Clare closed her eyes as Ben related the full horror of the assaults. None of the detail had made it into the press, except for the fact a chain had been used. Now, hearing it in detail, she felt sick. Those poor young men. Bad enough they felt forced into selling sex, but to end their lives in the back of a manky white van?

'Up till now,' Ben went on, 'he's operated mostly in the Midlands and the north of England. But our intel suggests he's planning a trip to this area.' He fixed Clare with his eye. 'St Andrews was mentioned.'

The lunchtime roll was sitting heavily in her stomach now. She glanced at the jug of water on Penny's desk, but she didn't want to ask for a glass; didn't want to show any sign she wasn't up to whatever Ben was about to say. She felt Penny's eyes on her. She seemed to sense Clare's discomfort and she held up a finger to halt Ben.

'I think we'll have some tea,' she said, lifting her phone. 'Or coffee?'

'Tea's fine,' Ben said, and Clare gave a nod. She took a few silent breaths in and out, waiting until Penny had replaced the phone, then she smiled at Ben.

'How do you know he's coming to this area? If you know who he is…'

He shook his head. 'Our intel's not that good.' He glanced at Penny and she gave a slight nod. 'We monitor the dark web,' he said. 'I've a team who've infiltrated some sites thought to be associated with criminal activity. They scrape it for different keywords and we've had a fair bit of success. For months now we've been following about fifty possible leads for the Choker.'

Clare was frowning. 'I don't see how—'

'It's tedious work,' he explained. 'Forensic detail from the bodies has helped. We think he's a painter and decorator. The labs have found traces of paint and sandpaper on the victims' clothes. So that helps. Odd remarks, too. Sometimes there are comments or questions about traffic, roadworks and so on, betraying a lack of familiarity with the area. That suggests he travels around the country. Probably self-employed, multiple Facebook profiles for decorators. Cheap and cheerful, cash-in-hand. But he went quiet in the summer, which is why it's taken us so long to get to this point.'

'Light nights?' Clare suggested.

Ben nodded. 'Not so easy to dispose of a body when it's light.'

'And you've narrowed it down now?' Clare said.

'We think so. There's one user who has different identities. But he always makes the same spelling mistakes, so we're pretty sure it's the same guy. We've been monitoring him for a few weeks now and last week we hit the jackpot. At least we think we have.'

Clare waited and Ben went on.

'He asked for the best place to pick up gay men around St Andrews.'

Clare's brow creased. 'It's such a busy town. I'm not sure.'

8

'Clearly he won't be cruising the High Street,' Penny said, her tone sharp.

Clare decided not to tell her there wasn't a High Street in St Andrews. 'You're thinking out of town?'

'Most likely,' Ben said. 'But it could be his victims don't have transport. He might pick someone up in the town then drive to park up; and that's where you come in. Local knowledge, yeah?'

Clare pressed her lips together, as she took in what he was asking. Where on earth would she start?

'Unless you don't think you're up to it,' Penny said, her eyes on Clare. She returned Penny's gaze. If she had any misgivings, now was the time to share them. And then she thought about the young men who'd fallen victim to this killer. The dreadful end they'd suffered, most likely in the back of a van, then dumped in the undergrowth like a piece of rubbish. If there was a chance she could help she had to take it.

'I'll do everything I can,' she said to Penny, then she turned back to Ben. 'Do you have a timescale?'

'Could be this weekend,' he said, and Clare tried not to react. 'Post-mortems on the victims suggest he kills at weekends. Our guess is he travels round for decorating jobs, using the evenings to scope out the area. Finishes the job at the end of the week and picks up his victim on Friday or Saturday night. We think…' He paused for a moment, his eyes studying her face. 'We think he may be in the area already.'

Clare sat, taking in the implications. The so-called Chainlink Choker in St Andrews already? It wasn't a big town. But there were thousands of properties. Could they feasibly comb the streets, looking for white vans? Send officers round to knock on doors? How many would she need? Could she beg extra help from Penny? She flashed a look at the superintendent.

Ben seemed to read her thoughts. 'If you're thinking house-to-house,' he said, 'it wouldn't work. There are only two ways we'll catch this man: red-handed or by going over his van with a full forensic team. And how many white vans are flying round the streets just now? Christmas is only a few weeks away. The town will be full of painters tarting up properties, ahead of the big day.'

He had a point. There must be dozens of decorators' vans all over St Andrews. And, even if they found the right one, unless they detained the driver and waited for DNA results, he'd disappear like snow off a dyke. 'So red-handed?' she said.

'It's the only way.'

'It's a hell of a risk.'

Ben took a slug of his tea then set the cup down. 'He's going to kill someone. If it's not here, he'll move elsewhere. But if we go storming in, seizing every van we think could be his, he'll be forewarned. He'll go back on the dark web, find another location and we'll have missed our chance. So we have to play this very carefully.'

She let her head drop, as she took this in. Then she lifted her gaze and met Ben's. 'Tell me what you need.'

Chapter 2

She drove slowly back, the conversation with Ben running round her head. It was the proverbial needle in a haystack. The town was buzzing at this time of year, delivery vans racing through the streets, dropping off early Christmas shopping, plumbers, joiners and, of course, decorators. They were all busy. And perhaps one of them was the Chainlink Choker.

Too often Clare dealt with the aftermath of murder, the bodies, grieving relatives, but this – trying to stop a murder before it happened? This was quite different. It was the job of uniformed officers, really. Crime prevention. Stop crime before it starts. But the idea of a young gay man walking around, going to work, out to the pub, maybe even doing his Christmas shopping, oblivious to what awaited him – she felt sick at the very thought of it. She wanted to put out a warning. Keep away from white vans, from men you don't know. Stay safe, as the cliché went. She wanted to prevent this killer even getting close to a potential victim. But killers found victims and this one would find his next, one way or another. And now, thanks to Ben's intel, they had a chance to get there first.

She was nearing the end of the Tay Road Bridge, heading back to Fife, and she slowed at the roundabout, giving way to a van. *Was that him?* she wondered. The impossibility of the task weighed heavily on her as she accelerated, joining the dual carriageway. Where on earth would they start?

–

'I'm just about to start them.'

Clare made her way to her office, Chris trailing in her wake. 'Start what?'

'Those crime reports. I was going to do them earlier when—'

'Forget that.' She stopped, casting an eye round the room. 'Max?'

'Dunno. He was here earlier.'

'Find him. I want the two of you in my office. And bring coffee.'

His expression clouded. 'What's up? Are you…'

'Just find him.'

She left him standing and walked smartly to her office, flicking the light on as she entered. It was growing dark now, a chill in the air, and she bent to turn up her radiator. After a minute the rhythmic ticking began and she put out a hand, waiting for it to warm. Chris and Max appeared a few minutes later, coffees in hand.

'No biscuits,' Chris said but Clare waved this away.

'Sit down, and close the door.' She reached for her coffee, nodding her thanks, and sipped before setting it down on the desk. Chris shifted on his seat and Max's jaw was tight. She studied their faces, trying to work out how to begin.

'You're worrying me,' Chris said. 'What's wrong?'

'Sorry. There's, erm, there's something I need to share with the wider team, but I want to discuss it with you two first.'

They exchanged glances.

'No problem,' Max said and Chris nodded his agreement.

'Before I go into details,' Clare said, 'I need a cone of silence around this.'

'Sure,' Chris said and Max nodded.

'As you know I had a meeting with Penny Meakin this afternoon. There was a DCI there as well.' She paused for a moment. 'You remember Ben Ratcliffe?'

Chris raised an eyebrow. 'Secret Squirrel Ben?'

'The undercover officer, yes.'

'He after you for a job?'

'In a way.' She saw Chris's face fall. 'Don't worry. I'm not leaving. But he has asked for our help.'

Max sat forward in his seat. 'Sounds interesting.'

'Oh it's that, all right. And it's top priority. You've heard about this Chainlink Choker, operating in the north of England?'

Chris's face darkened. 'Killing gay men, yeah. Don't tell me they think he's from up here?'

'No, but they reckon he's heading this way, possibly this weekend.'

'How do they know?' Max asked.

'Best not ask. Let's just say it's reliable intel.'

'So what can you tell us?' Chris said.

'They think he's a painter and decorator, probably self-employed.'

'White van man?' Max said, and Clare nodded.

'Forensic examination of the corpses suggests he kills at weekends. Ben reckons he's in the area already, likely doing a decorating job.'

Max's brow furrowed. 'I don't get it. If he's based in England what's he doing up here? The cost of petrol and his time – it doesn't make sense.'

'Not for his decorating business,' Clare agreed. 'But he's killed five times in the north of England. So clearly all the forces down there will be on the lookout. He's probably had to keep a low profile. Could be he saw the chance of a job somewhere else. Much easier to find your next victim if no one's looking for you.'

They fell silent, Chris and Max taking in what they'd been told. Eventually Chris found his tongue.

'So what's the plan?'

'Ben has asked me to suss out likely places gay men would go to have sex.'

'Like dogging spots?' Chris said.

'I think so. But I can't remember the last time we booked someone for public indecency. Does it still happen these days?'

Chris suppressed a smile. 'You're asking me?'

'You are a detective.'

He laughed. 'I've absolutely no idea.'

'Then that's what we need to find out.'

'I'm sure we can find them,' Max said. 'But what then?'

'Undercover ops. Catch him red-handed. So we'll need bodies at all the likely spots over the weekend.'

Chris exhaled. 'That's a lot of manpower.'

'It is. But Ben and Penny will help out with extra officers. It's our job to decide where to put them.'

She sipped at her coffee while they digested this then she set the cup down again. 'I need to be 100 per cent sure I can trust everyone to keep this confidential. No going home to partners and talking about it. So' – she hesitated – 'is there anyone I can't trust? Anyone you've the slightest doubt about? 'Cause, if there is, I need to shift them elsewhere for a couple of weeks.'

They exchanged glances and both shook their heads. 'As long as they know the score,' Chris said, and Clare nodded.

'Let's have everyone in for eight tomorrow morning. But not a word to anyone meantime, especially significant others!'

–

'You're quiet,' Clare's partner, DCI Alastair Gibson, said as she picked over her food.

She smiled. 'Just work.'

'Anything I can help with?'

She twirled spaghetti on her fork and for a moment she said nothing. He was a DCI and she could trust him absolutely. She knew that. But how could she demand confidentiality from her officers if she wasn't prepared to do likewise? 'Best not.'

He held her gaze. 'I heard you were in Bell Street today.'

'Mm hm.'

'Penny?'

'Yeah.'

'You would tell me if there was something wrong?'

She put down her fork and reached out to take his hand. 'I would. And there isn't. Penny – she's given me something to do. I just can't talk about it.'

He squeezed her hand. 'No problem.' He held it for a moment then let it go, scraping back his chair. 'You take that over to the fire and finish it there. I'll make some coffee.'

Day 2: Wednesday

Chapter 3

The incident room fell silent when Clare entered and she wondered briefly if Chris or Max had forewarned them. But she could trust her sergeants – she knew that – and now every eye in the room was on her as she took her place at the front.

She waited until Jim, the desk sergeant, had closed the door then she looked round. Chris and Max stood at the back, the uniformed officers perched on chairs and she quickly checked all the faces, assuring herself she had their attention.

'We've been asked to assist in an operation of national importance,' she began. 'As I speak, teams in other stations are being briefed and will join us later today.' She paused to let this sink in. Robbie and Gillian, two of the uniformed officers, exchanged glances, while Sara half turned to see Chris's reaction. 'What I'm about to tell you does not go outside this room. That means parents, friends, significant others – not a single word to anyone. If that's a problem, the door's over there.' She glanced at Jim, standing ramrod straight, his back to the door, then she swept her gaze round the room.

There were murmurs of 'Yes, boss,' and 'No problem.'

'Good. So here's the situation.'

She explained about the Chainlink Choker and the proposed operation to intercept him. They listened in silence and, when she'd finished, no one spoke. Sara was the first to raise a hand.

'What's the plan, boss?'

Clare smiled. 'That's what we have to decide. I doubt any of us have been involved in this kind of operation before. But I plan to throw everything at it.'

Robbie caught Clare's eye. 'How much do we know about him?'

Clare settled herself on a desk at the front. 'Post-mortem exams on the victims suggest they were killed in a van used to carry painting and decorating materials.'

'So he's a painter?' Gillian asked.

'Or he has access to a van that belongs to one. But let's work on the basis he's a self-employed decorator, travelling round to different jobs.'

'And they think he's heading up here for the weekend?' Gillian went on.

Clare hesitated. 'He may be here already.'

They stared at her, no one speaking. Robbie was the first to find his voice. 'Should we start checking on decorators working in the area?'

'How, exactly?' Clare asked. 'Think about it, guys. There must be dozens of them in north-east Fife just now – everyone getting their houses done up for Christmas. We couldn't possibly have SOCO go over every van, or wait while their DNA's checked. And if we did find our man he'd disappear as soon as he realised what we were looking for.

'So—' Robbie again.

'We have to catch him in the act.'

'Bit late,' someone said. 'Doesn't he strangle them as they're having sex?'

Clare nodded. 'That's what the PMs suggest. DCI Ratcliffe's team have been checking ANPR cameras for any vans that crossed the border in the last week.'

'That's a huge job,' Chris said.

'Yeah, I know. And there must be over twenty border crossings between Scotland and England, most of them minor roads.'

'With no cameras,' Chris went on.

'Exactly. He could easily be here, in the town, without having passed a single camera. They'll keep checking, though,' she added.

'What are you thinking?' Max said.

'Two approaches. First of all I want as many officers as we can lay our hands on out in the town, checking the number of every van that's parked outside a house. And bear in mind it might not have any markings.'

'He'd be an idiot to use a van with his name plastered over it,' Sara said.

'Exactly. Max, I'd like you and Sara to divide the town up and allocate officers. Every van is to be put through the system. If you find one with a registered keeper in the north of England I want to know.'

'You want us to bring them in?'

Clare shook her head. 'No. We wouldn't be able to hold them, pending tests. But Ben is seeking a warrant to put a covert tracker on any vehicle we suspect could belong to our perp.' She looked round at them. 'All of this has to be carefully done. If he sees any police activity at his van we'll lose him. So we'll use unmarked cars where possible and trackers will be fitted by plain-clothes officers. If you're in uniform and see a van from the north of England, call it in and we'll send someone round in casual clothing.'

Gillian raised a hand. 'You said there were two approaches.'

Clare smiled. 'This one's a bit trickier. DCI Ratcliffe's after our local knowledge – places gay men might go to have sex. Somewhere they wouldn't be disturbed.'

Chris shook his head. 'It's a needle in a haystack job.'

'I know. But we have to try. So let's be systematic. I want those of you who know the area best going through it on a map, identifying every possible location.'

They exchanged glances and Clare nodded. 'It's a big ask, guys. But if we have a chance of stopping this man we have to take it.'

'What about Safenites?' Robbie suggested. 'They do a lot of outreach work around the town. Might be worth speaking to them.'

Clare knew the charity. It had set up in the town a year ago and she'd been impressed with the work they'd done, looking after young men and women who'd drunk too much.

'They hand out condoms, flip-flops, that sort of thing,' Robbie went on. 'And they advise on health stuff, STD-testing and the like. They might know something.'

'Good shout, Robbie. Can you get in touch, please? No details, mind. Just say we're looking to provide some support.'

Robbie noted this down and she went on. 'The DCI thinks if our man's looking for a victim it'll be Friday or Saturday night. Once we've identified any likely sites we'll put covert surveillance in place.'

'That's a lot of officers,' Chris said. 'Think how many places there might be.'

'I know. But it's coming out of Ben Ratcliffe's budget, and I can't think of a better use for it.'

Max raised a hand. 'What time will the extra officers get here?'

'Ben thought early afternoon. If you can be ready with the street plan…'

Max indicated he would do this and Clare smiled round. 'As I say, not a word outside this room. If there's any chance we can stop another young man being murdered we have to take it.' She glanced over to Chris and Max. 'Anything else?' They shook their heads and she ended the briefing.

Chapter 4

By mid-afternoon the incident room was buzzing as officers from other stations started to arrive. Max was poring over a street map of the town which he'd divided into areas with a red marker pen. A clutch of officers stood round, making notes on the areas they'd been allocated.

Chris was in one of the interview rooms, poring over an OS map Jim had produced from his store cupboard.

'Any luck?'

'Yeah, I think so. Just need to get a pen.' He reached over to a desk behind him and picked up a Biro. 'I mean, it's not perfect,' he said. 'The map might not show everything. There could be new buildings, sheds – anywhere a van could be concealed.'

'Okay.' Clare sat down beside him. 'What's your best guess?'

He jabbed the map with his finger. 'We should probably start with Tentsmuir Forest. Lots of places to park up along the roadside, especially after the car park closes.' He glanced at Clare. It would be a long time before either of them would forget the bloodied corpse of a local solicitor. He'd been found in his car just off the road that ran through the forest. But she noted it down anyway. There was only one road in and out so it would be easy enough to station someone there, checking for vans late at night.

'Anywhere else?'

'There's an old RAF meteorological station. Other end of the forest. It's a bit of a ruin, actually. Lots of graffiti and a mess inside. But the structure's pretty sound and it's screened by trees so they could park behind it and be hidden from sight.'

Clare peered at the map. 'Where is it exactly?'

Chris moved the map closer to Clare, indicating a section. 'See Shanwell Road South? Just here…'

'Yeah.'

'If you follow the path along, away from Tayport' – he traced his finger along the map – 'you come to these unmarked buildings – just off the track.'

'And that's the meteorological station?'

'Yeah. One of these. Strictly speaking you can't take a car along there. It's wide enough, but it's part of the Fife Coastal Path and there's a gate further back. Sometimes it's padlocked but often not. You could easily drive a van along and pull off the track. No one would know you were there.'

Clare sat back, considering this. 'Would it be possible to reach it from the other end of the forest? Going in past the riding stables?'

Chris hesitated. 'Probably. There are lots of paths through the forest but they mostly have barriers across to stop vehicles. Not impossible, though.'

'Okay. We'll cover that from the Shanwell Road end. That it?'

'One more.' Chris pushed the map across the desk, adjusting the angle. 'Morton Lochs. It's another part of Tentsmuir Forest, accessed from the road between Tayport and St Michael's cross-roads.'

Clare knew the road well. When she'd first come to St Andrews she'd been hunting a killer, finally running him to ground in a house off that road. It had been one of those moments when she'd wondered if it would be her last. But by some miracle she had survived and the killer was now serving twenty-five years.

'It's a popular spot for nature lovers,' Chris went on. 'Appar-ently good for dragonflies. There's a car park as well,' he added. 'Busy enough in the summer. But, this time of year, at night it would be pitch black. Ideal for our man, I'd have thought.'

Clare studied the area round the lochs. It was heavily wooded with evergreens. 'I agree,' she said. 'I can't see many folk heading along there when it's dark.' She moved the map back to the other locations Chris had identified. 'Looks like it's mostly around Tentsmuir Forest.'

He nodded. 'Lots of tree cover.' He was quiet for a moment, considering this. 'It's maybe worth having a word with the rangers over there. See if they've noticed any vans at night.'

Clare scraped back her chair. 'Good idea. Give them a call please.'

'I could – if I didn't have my crime reports to finish.'

'Like you've even started them.'

He sighed. 'I'll give them a call.'

–

Clare was preparing to go home when Robbie tapped on her office door.

'The lad from Safenites is on his way. Should be here in ten minutes.'

She thanked Robbie and asked him to prepare an interview room. Ten minutes later Robbie appeared again to tell Clare he'd arrived.

'What's his name?'

'Sean Davis.'

She rose from her chair and went to meet him.

He was tall, dressed in a black fleece and grey cargo trousers reinforced at the knees. She shook his hand and felt the calluses. No stranger to hard work, then. She thought he was in his forties or early fifties but he had the look of a man tired of life.

She led him to the interview room, making polite conversation as they went.

'Thanks so much for coming in,' she said when he'd settled himself in a chair and he acknowledged this with a nod.

'The officer who phoned – he was asking about Safenites.'

Clare smiled. 'That's right. I gather you're a volunteer. Can I ask about the kind of thing you do?'

His face clouded. 'Is there a problem?'

'Oh no,' Clare said, anxious to reassure him. 'We just wanted to find out a bit more about risks young people might be exposed to.' She was choosing her words carefully, keen to avoid giving any detail of their investigation.

His face cleared. 'Ah okay. Sorry. Mainly it's when they're off their face. Drink and drugs,' he added. 'That's when they're likely to stagger in front of a car, lose their keys, purse – and some folk, well, they take advantage, you know?'

'It's good work,' Clare said, 'and it's a great help to us. Manpower,' she added. 'There's never enough to do all we'd like.'

He acknowledged this but didn't seem keen to say any more and she wondered if he was nervous. Maybe he was having a bad day. 'We're doing a lot of work these days,' she went on. 'Educating youngsters about consent. For sex, I mean.'

He nodded. 'We see the odd one. Girl obviously drunk and some lad trying to lead her down a lane.'

Clare was racking her brains. She was getting nowhere with this man. Maybe it was a waste of time. She tried again. 'Is there much of a gay scene in the town?'

His eyes widened a little at this. Clearly a question he wasn't expecting. 'Much the same as anywhere else, I suppose. Why do you ask?'

'We're planning a campaign,' she said, thinking as she was talking. 'Trying to stop sexual exploitation.'

Sean nodded. 'Good idea. I'm not sure how I can help, though.'

'We're looking to identify places a vulnerable person might be taken. Say if someone had a car.'

His brow furrowed. 'You mean in the town?'

'Not necessarily. Anywhere they wouldn't be disturbed. Maybe a bit out of town.'

He shook his head. 'Sorry. I wouldn't know. I don't live here.'

'Oh?' Clare couldn't keep the surprise out of her voice. 'But I thought…'

'I live in Dundee,' he said. 'But when I applied to join Safenites they said they'd plenty of helpers over there. St Andrews was trying to start up a branch so I agreed to come over here at weekends. Friday and Saturday nights. Sorry,' he added. 'Looks like I've wasted your time.'

Clare smiled. 'Not at all. But if anywhere does occur to you…'

Something flashed across his eyes and he shook his head. 'If you don't mind my saying…'

'Yes?'

'You'd be better tackling the problem at its source.'

She studied him, not quite understanding. 'Can you explain?'

'Drugs,' he said, an edge to his voice. 'Drink as well but those drugs – they're a scourge. You sort that out, you won't have to worry about kids being taken advantage of. They wouldn't be vulnerable if they weren't hooked on that muck.'

Clare opened her mouth to say she agreed but he cut across her. 'It's been worse since that new club opened up. A lot worse.'

Her brow clouded.

'Retro's,' Sean said. 'Opened a few weeks ago. Up from the Petheram Bridge car park.'

Clare remembered. It had been built on a sloping site, south of the car park, to the fury of locals who'd feared noise from late-night revellers. But it was the third site the owners had applied to use and this one, on the edge of town, was the furthest from houses. Eventually the application had been approved. As the name suggested it promised music from as far back as the 1960s, with themed nights throughout the Christmas party season.

'You think there's a drug problem at Retro's?'

His face darkened. 'I know there is. So, if you want to protect youngsters from being exploited, I'd suggest you start there.'

Chapter 5

It was almost six by the time the ranger at Tentsmuir Forest called Chris back.

'He said they get the occasional car, steamed-up windows – you know. But since the solicitor's murder there aren't nearly as many.'

Clare sat back in her chair. 'Honestly, Chris. This feels like an impossible task. Any luck with the van registrations?'

'Not yet. And they've covered most of the town.'

'Better spread out, then. Say a fifteen-mile radius.'

'That's a big area.'

'It's a big investigation. And one we can't afford to mess up.'

–

Clare's sister, Judith, called as she was drawing out of the station car park.

'Bad time?'

Clare flicked the phone to speaker. 'Just heading home. How are you?'

'Oh fine. You know. Busy.'

'James and Clara?'

'They're good, thanks. James has a support worker at nursery now and he's started speaking to her. Just in a whisper but it's progress.'

Clare smiled at this. It was lovely to see James making progress. He'd been a silent, solitary toddler, able in so many ways but, somehow, social communication was beyond him. 'That's wonderful, Jude. It must be such a relief.'

Her sister sighed. 'It's early days. But it's good to hear he's starting to speak when he's out of the house.'

'Give it time,' Clare said. 'That's a big step for him. And how's my niece?'

'Don't even ask. That girl takes Terrible Twos to a whole new level.'

Clare laughed. 'And work?'

Jude hesitated. 'Actually I'm a bit pushed for time. Work's fine but I'm worried about Dad.'

'Oh?' Clare was suddenly alert. She was acutely conscious her parents were ageing but so far they'd both been in good health, enjoying retirement. 'What's wrong with him?'

'Nothing major. At least nothing I'm aware of. But I was round the other day on my way home from work and I knew something was wrong the minute I walked through the door. Mum was fussing round him and he was snapping at her.'

'Why, though?' Clare asked.

'Something to do with the bathroom ceiling. He'd taken it into his head to paint it. Anyway, he hadn't put the ladder up properly and when he started to climb the steps it gave way.'

'What? Was he hurt?'

'No. But the paint went everywhere and he was so upset. Mum was trying to say it didn't matter. That it would clean up and, if it didn't, well, that was what insurance was for. But he just kept calling himself a stupid old man.'

'Oh, Jude.'

'I know. I stayed a bit longer than I'd intended. Had my tea with them. Then I helped Mum clear up and she told me he'd had a fall.'

Clare listened, a knot in her stomach. Her lovely dad, suddenly so much older. Had she not noticed? Had this been happening while she was so busy with work?

'Black ice,' Judith went on. 'That cold snap a couple of weeks ago? He was going along to the shop for his paper and his feet just went from under him.'

'Was he hurt?'

'Nothing broken, thankfully. A few bruises, Mum said. But it seems to have shaken his confidence; and he's starting to fret about things in the house. Things he'd normally be doing but he's worried he'll make a mess of them.'

'But he's always been so capable,' Clare said. 'Maybe once he gets over the fall.'

'Clare – he's getting older. They both are. So I was thinking – I'd like to get them some help.'

'You mean like a home help?'

'God no! Mum would hate that. I just meant bring in someone to paint the bathroom, cut the grass in the summer – that sort of thing. Frank and I were talking. We think we could afford to pay someone to do a few of these jobs. But if you pitched in too, we could really make their lives a lot easier.'

'That's a great idea,' Clare said. 'Thanks so much for thinking about it. Just let me know how much and I'll set up a standing order.'

–

She drove home, her mind on her dad. Of course he was getting older but, somehow, she'd thought he'd be around for ever, older, but hale and hearty. She was ashamed of herself for not seeing the changes in him; for not realising her parents were needing a bit more support. She made a mental note to take a trip through, just as soon as the hunt for this killer was over.

The smell of garlic greeted her as she pushed open the front door of Daisy Cottage, struggling against what proved to be a stuffed toy. No doubt the work of Benjy, her English Bull Terrier. She bent and wrestled the toy from under the door – the remains of a blue triceratops – and fired it down the hall. Benjy raced after it and she closed the door, letting her work bag fall at her feet.

The DCI was stirring a pot of chilli. 'Just waiting on the garlic bread.'

'I can smell it. Home-made?'

'Of course.'

She rolled her eyes. 'How many cloves of garlic?'

'Best not ask.' He indicated a half-drunk glass of wine. 'Pour you one?'

'Definitely.'

Over dinner he spoke about the conference he'd hosted at Tulliallan, the Scottish Police College. 'We focused more on TikTok this time,' he said.

Clare tore off a piece of garlic bread, licking the butter from her fingers. 'Is there much criminal activity on the platform?'

'It's more the potential,' he said. 'It sells youngsters an impossible view of the world. All those so-called influencers. They're paid to advertise products and some of them have a huge following.'

'I think Zoe follows a few of them,' Clare said, loading her fork with chilli.

'Your admin assistant?'

'Yep. Mainly cake creations. But some of the make-up stuff as well.'

'Maybe I could chat to her about TikTok sometime,' he said. 'Get her view on what she watches.'

Clare shrugged. 'Sure. Pop in any time.' She picked up her wine and drained the glass. He indicated the bottle but she waved it away. 'Need a clear head this week.'

He eyed her and she knew he was thinking of her visit to Penny's office the day before. She met his eye and something unspoken passed between them; and then she smiled.

'So what is it they do, these influencers?'

He took the hint and picked up his fork again. 'Mostly it's nothing to concern us. They get sent free stuff and they video themselves sampling it, saying if it's good or not. Some of them are sneaky with it, adding in a bit of sponcon.'

'A bit of what?'

'Sorry – sponsored content. They do their make-up tutorial – or whatever it is – but they film it so there's another product in the background.'

'Like what?'

'Anything. A can of juice with the name visible, a branded T-shirt on a hanger – anything that shows they're using an identifiable product.'

'And they get paid for that?'

'They do.'

Clare took a glug of wine. 'I'm in the wrong job.'

'You and me both.'

She bit into the garlic bread, chewing for a minute before she spoke again. 'That's hardly criminal, though. What's your involvement?'

'Oh there's no shortage of criminal activity, if you know what to look for.'

'Such as?'

He shrugged. 'Videos telling you how to defraud businesses, for one thing. Do you remember the supermarket vouchers scam? A year or two ago now.'

She shook her head, mouth full of chilli.

'Some loophole that meant a voucher could be used more than once. Whoever discovered it shared the voucher and barcode on TikTok. That one voucher was used hundreds of times before the supermarket stopped it. Admittedly that was a glitch, but there are plenty of TikToks teaching people the same kind of thing.'

'But if it's reported…'

'As fast as one's taken down, another pops up.'

Clare helped herself to more chilli from the pot and dipped the remains of her garlic bread in the sauce.

He talked on and she smiled and nodded, making the right noises, her thoughts drifting back to her dad. The realisation he was growing older, his confidence ebbing away. Her heart ached for him and she was ashamed of herself for not having seen what was happening. She ought to have told Al – discussed it with him over dinner. But there was something so very personal about acknowledging this change in her dad, and she wasn't ready to share it with him. Not yet. Not until she'd come to terms with it herself.

She elected to take Benjy on his last walk, glad of a few minutes to herself. He scampered off as she reached the end of the drive, dashing here and there, his nose to the ground, following some animal scent. It was a clear night, the air cool against her cheeks and she walked on, stopping a minute later to let him investigate a gap in a stone dyke. Overhead a carpet of stars was laid out before her, a tiny part of the universe flaunting its majesty and suddenly she felt very small indeed.

Day 3: Thursday

Chapter 6

'I want to visit that new club,' Clare said as Chris shrugged off his coat.

'Retro's?'

'That's the one.'

'Why?'

She related her conversation with Sean Davis the night before. 'He seems to think they have a serious drug problem.'

'Not exactly a priority,' Chris said. 'Not while we're hunting this Choker guy.'

'I know. But I'm thinking it might be an opportunity to find out if they attract a gay crowd as well. We might pick up something useful.'

–

Retro's was a cream-coloured flat-roofed building sunk into the hillside behind the Petheram Bridge car park. It wasn't dissimilar in style to nearby university buildings and Clare thought the sympathetic design probably had a hand in the development being approved. The club name sat above the chrome and glass doors, in a sprawling font, the outline of a martini glass to the side. In the cold light of day, without what Clare guessed would be neon lighting, it looked cheap and gaudy, but no doubt it was more appealing at night. It was dark behind the glass doors but a BrewDog lorry was parked to the side, a man in jeans and a fleece hefting crates onto a sack barrow.

Clare indicated the man. 'That's our way in.'

Chris followed her up the wide stone steps that led round the side of the club. A fire door stood open and Clare rapped on the side.

'Hello?' She motioned to Chris to wait for a moment, her head cocked for any sound within. When there was no reply she walked in, Chris at her back. There was a strong odour of spilt beer and she wondered if clubs ever got rid of the smell. 'Hello,' she called again.

They followed the corridor along, past a storeroom filled with kegs and crates, through another fire door which, again, was propped open. There were more doors off to the left and right, the last of these ajar, light flooding the corridor. She nodded to Chris and they made their way through the door and found themselves to the side of a bar decorated in black and chrome. Under the harsh overhead lighting the effect was stark and it reminded Clare briefly of school discos – that moment at the end of the night when teachers would put the lights back on, instantly breaking the spell the disco had cast on the assembly hall. A woman in a navy tabard was polishing tables and she glanced up briefly as Clare and Chris entered then returned to her dusting without a word.

Behind the bar a mirrored wall was lined with an array of bottles, a row of fridges below. A figure in navy tracksuit bottoms was bent over one of the fridges, loading it with bottles of wine. Clare averted her eyes from his bum crack and knocked on the bar top. 'Sorry to bother you.'

The figure sat back on his heels and looked up. He was a stocky man in his twenties, his blond hair close cropped, complexion pasty. He took them in, up and down before speaking.

'We're closed.'

Clare held out her warrant card. 'Just need a quick word.'

He sighed audibly. 'Mind if I finish this? Only, one lorry's just been and there's another at the door.'

'Carry on,' Clare said. 'We're in no rush. We'll take a look around.'

His expression wasn't encouraging but he went back to stocking the fridge. After a minute he stood up with a grunt and carried the empty crate through the door to the corridor, disappearing from sight.

Left alone, they took in their surroundings. A DJ's booth stood on a raised area to the side of the bar and she wandered over to see a pair of turntables with what she guessed was a mixer in the middle. She tried to see what was written beside the rows of knobs and levers but the writing had faded with wear. Clearly not a new setup.

The dance floor was a decent size with neon tubes built into the floor tiles, making her think of the film *Saturday Night Fever*. In keeping with the retro theme, she guessed.

'Sorry 'bout that,' a voice behind her said and she turned to see the barman, wiping his hands on his trousers. 'Had to check the delivery. It's not always right. So – was there something?'

Clare smiled. 'Just a social call. Any problems at all, we're here to help.'

'Oh aye. Thanks.'

'I didn't catch your name.'

'Danny.'

'Danny?'

'Glancy. Danny Glancy.'

'You're the barman?'

He shrugged. 'Barman, dogsbody. Whatever needs done.'

'Is the owner here?'

Danny shook his head. 'She'll be in later.'

'She?'

'That's right.' There was an edge to his voice suggesting patience was in short supply.

'Does *she* have a name?'

'Rhona Glancy.'

'Your wife?'

'Mother, actually.' A vacuum cleaner started up in another room and Danny looked back at the bar. 'I'm kinda busy.'

'That's fine,' Clare said. 'We just wanted to say hello.' She looked round the club again. 'Very smart. You've done a good job here.'

He made no reply and she indicated the record decks. 'Old school?'

'Yeah. Punters seem to like it. Having someone doing it, you know? Instead of stuff on a laptop.'

'Who's the DJ?'

'Carson. Used to do a club in Ibiza.' He inclined his head. 'Pretty good. Knows how to work a crowd.'

'What's his first name?' Clare asked.

Chris rolled his eyes. 'I can't believe you asked that,' he said, his voice low.

Danny suppressed a smile. 'Just Carson.'

Clare felt her cheeks colour and she moved quickly on. 'Is there much of a gay scene?'

There was a twitch at the corner of Danny's mouth. 'Not much call for that,' he said. 'Reckon they've got their own clubs.'

She feigned surprise. 'Really?'

'Yeah, really. Look, I've a ton of stuff to do so—'

'Of course. We'll get out of your way.' She made as if to move then stopped. 'Just one more thing.'

He sighed audibly. 'Yes?'

'There seems to be a lot of drugs circulating in the town. Is it much of a problem for you?'

He met her eye. 'Not that I've seen.'

'You sure? No one trying to pass pills around?'

'Like I say. I've not seen anything. If I did, they'd be out. We've our licence to worry about.'

'So you do.' She watched him carefully, looking for any sign he was hiding something but he stared straight back.

'So, if you don't mind…'

She smiled. 'Thanks for your time, Danny.'

They made their way back through the corridors to the side door and out into the cool November air.

'Honest to God,' Chris said, as they walked down the steps to the car park. 'You're such an embarrassment. You do know it's about a hundred years since DJs used their full names.'

'Shut your face.'

'You really *are* ancient, aren't you?'

'More to the point,' she said, clicking to unlock the car, 'what do you make of our Danny?'

'I'd say he's a bit of a homophobe.'

'Agreed. He might as well have a sign up saying *No Gays*.'

Chris looked back at the club. 'Good place to pick someone up, though.'

'Hmm, maybe. But I reckon our Danny wouldn't be above chucking someone out if he didn't like the look of them – or who they were snogging.'

'Suppose. So what now?'

Clare sat thinking for a minute, drumming her fingers on the steering wheel. 'Could you run a check on Rhona and Danny Glancy please? If she's the licensee she'll likely not have any previous. But I wouldn't be so sure about him.'

She released the handbrake then pulled away. As she approached the roundabout, a dark saloon car passed them, tinted glass making it hard to see the occupants. She slowed to a halt, watching in the rear-view mirror as it headed straight for Retro's. Then she signalled right, circled the roundabout and drove back into the car park. The dark saloon had pulled into a disabled space right in front of the club. Clare held back, letting the engine idle, her eyes on the car.

'Clare?'

She was watching as a tall man emerged from the driver's side. From her viewpoint further down the car park it was hard to pick out his features, except for his hair, the white-blond man-bun catching the morning sun. His skinny jeans accentuated his slim frame, in contrast to another two men who squeezed out of the back seats with some difficulty, each of them making two of the tall man. He glanced back at them then nodded towards the club and the trio set off, the pair walking a little behind the driver.

'Trouble?' Chris said, leaning across for a better view.

'Possibly. Get that number, would you? It wouldn't surprise me if this is the source of the drugs Sean Davis complained about.'

—

'We might have a missing person,' Jim said, as Clare made her way to the station kitchen.

'Oh yes?'

'Only since last night, though.'

She opened the fridge and took out her lunchbox. 'That's not very long. Is it someone vulnerable?'

'It's a young man. Early twenties.'

A sense of unease overtook Clare but she told herself to think logically. Twelve hours, even twenty-four was no time at all, especially for those in their teens and twenties. Maybe a student on a bender.

'Is he a student?'

Jim shook his head. 'IT programmer.'

'Who reported him missing?'

'Sister. They share one of those modern houses over at Guardbridge.'

'The new estate?'

'No. Tall ones just off the roundabout.'

Clare knew them: a row of townhouses, with industrial-looking roofs. They caught her eye every time she drove past. The design was modern but the contemporary elements blended well with the local sandstone. 'What's the story?'

'She expected him back about ten last night,' Jim said, 'but he never came home. Phone rings out then it goes to voicemail. She's left messages but he's not called back.'

'Do we know where he'd been?'

'Working. Seems he was at that new club. The one you and the lad went to see this morning.'

Clare's brow creased. 'Retro's?'

'Aye. That's the one.'

Her mind went back to the visit, to their conversation with Danny Glancy. He hadn't mentioned anything about a missing person. But maybe he didn't know. 'What's the name?'

'Theo something,' Jim said. 'Hold on, I'll bring up the report.'

The kitchen door opened and Chris ambled in, a Mars bar in his hand. '*Hola, amigos.*'

Clare ignored the greeting, yet another reference to his Mexican honeymoon. 'We've a missing person. Works at Retro's.'

'Bit of a coincidence,' Chris said. 'Got a name?'

Jim peered at the screen. 'Theo Glancy.'

Clare and Chris looked at each other.

'Same surname,' Chris said. 'How old is he?'

Jim scrolled through the report. 'Twenty-seven.'

'Brother, then?' Chris suggested.

Clare nodded. 'Could be.' She stood thinking for a minute. 'What's an IT programmer doing working at a club?'

Chris shrugged. 'If the family own it maybe he was doing a bit of work for them. Or if he's freelance he might use the club as a base. How long's he been missing?'

'Since last night,' Jim said. 'Expected home about ten.'

'Probably met someone at the club and he's gone home with them.'

Jim frowned. 'Sister says he'd have rung.'

'Okay,' Clare said. 'Keep me posted. That it?'

'Aye, mostly. Another report of fly-tipping.'

'This is getting out of hand. Have you spoken to the council?'

'Not yet. I'll give them a call.'

Ideally Clare would like to have sent a couple of unmarked cars out over the next few nights but she didn't want anything interfering with the hunt for the Chainlink Choker. Her thoughts went back to the report of the missing man – a coincidence, surely? She had to hope so.

Chapter 7

'These sound promising,' Ben said when Clare relayed the locations Chris had suggested.

'I can send someone round to scope them out,' she said.

'No, that's okay. We'll organise the surveillance. Anything else?'

Clare explained they were checking van registrations in the town. 'Nothing turned up in St Andrews so we've increased the area. They're checking towns and villages within a fifteen-mile radius.'

'They know not to approach the drivers?'

'Of course. If we find anything I'll let you know straight away.'

'If that's everything.'

She hesitated. Should she mention the missing man? She glanced at her watch. He hadn't even been gone twenty-four hours. Best not confuse things at this stage. She assured Ben she'd let him know if anything else came up and ended the call.

Max poked his head round the door. 'Good time?'

'As good as any. What you got?'

He sank down in a chair, opposite. 'A few vans registered in Edinburgh, one in Aberdeen. The rest are Fife or Dundee.'

'Where have you covered?'

'All of St Andrews and a few of the villages south of town. I've sent a couple of teams over to Cupar and thought I'd send the rest to the East Neuk. Tay Coast as well if there's time.'

Clare thought of Tayport, close to Morton Lochs and the old RAF station. 'Could you make sure you do the Tay Coast please?'

'No problem. Any reason?'

She explained about the locations Chris had suggested. 'It doesn't mean he's doing a job around Tayport. But if someone's mentioned either of these locations he may head over there for a recce.'

Max rose. 'I'll get the East Neuk guys back. Send them up to Tayport.'

'Covert, mind,' Clare said. 'If he is recceing the area we don't want him scared off.'

Max laughed. 'You should see the state of them. I wouldn't put the bins out in some of the stuff they're wearing. Taking undercover to a whole new level.' He went off to divert the teams to the Tay Coast and Clare turned to her Inbox.

–

The call came in about four o'clock.

'Dog walker,' Jim said.

'Locus?'

'Off the A91. Opposite side to the Old Course.'

'Can you show me?'

They walked quickly to the incident room, moving to the large map on the wall. Jim indicated a section of the road beyond a new roundabout. 'Where the speed limit changes to forty,' he said, tapping the map. 'There's trees along this side, and a field beyond. Dog was off the lead and he disappeared into the trees. The owner called him back but he wouldn't come so she headed in after him.'

Clare stood, taking in the map. 'Just off the road?'

'Aye.'

'Can we access it from the back? Through the field?'

He considered this. 'It's possible. But I'd try to go in off the road if we can. The trees aren't thick and the verge is deep enough for parking.'

'Okay. Any chance it's natural causes?'

'Doesn't sound like it. Gillian attended.' He hesitated. 'She said there were marks round his neck.'

Clare closed her eyes. Had they missed the boat? Was this the Choker's latest victim? She'd been so fixated on having everything in place for the weekend but now it looked like they were too late. She was conscious of Jim waiting and she forced herself to think. 'Erm, can you find Chris please? Tell him to get over there. I'll join him as soon as I've spoken to Ben Ratcliffe.'

Ben answered on the first ring and Clare got straight to the point. 'I'm sorry, Ben. We've found a body.'

There was silence. An agonising silence while she waited for his reaction. 'Tell me,' he said eventually.

'No ID yet, but we had a report of a missing person this morning.'

'This morning?' There was no mistaking his tone. Should she have phoned him sooner? Most mispers turned up safe and well a day or two later.

'Yes, late morning.'

'What sort of missing person?'

She took a breath in and out. 'Young man in his twenties.'

'And you didn't think—'

'He'd been missing less than a day. It was too early to panic.'

'And in the meantime we could have had patrols on roads heading out of town, checking van registrations. This is the closest we've been. There's every chance we could have identified that van. Jesus Christ, Clare! We had actual intel he was here and you've let him just drive off.'

She was taken aback at his tone and for a moment she didn't know what to say.

'I—'

'Never mind,' he said, cutting across her. 'We'll discuss that later. Just give me the details. What time was it phoned in?'

'I'd have to check the report. But I think about eleven.'

'By?'

'Sister. They share a house a few miles from here.'

He was quiet for a moment. When he spoke again his tone was brisk. 'Right. Give me the location. I'll be over in the next hour.'

She sat on after he ended the call, her cheeks burning. Ben was one of the few senior officers she genuinely rated. He was organised, efficient and had a good instinct. He'd trusted her with this investigation and she'd let him down. Her thoughts went back to the meeting with him and Penny. He'd definitely said to prepare for the weekend. And it was only two days since they'd spoken. Should she have phoned him the minute that missing person report had come in? Would there really have been a chance of spotting the Choker's van as it headed back to England? She sat for a minute, turning this over in her head then she rose stiffly, as if the weight of the world was on her shoulders.

Jim was on the phone when she appeared at his side. 'Chris is on his way over there,' he mouthed and she nodded, heading for the door.

A bitter wind whipped across the car park and Clare jumped into the car, turning up the heater. The sky was darkening to the north and she wished she had her big coat. It would be cold standing at the roadside. Out to the east a sliver of moon was rising, heralding a cold, clear night. That was something, at least. Less risk of bad weather degrading any evidence. She slowed for a car at the West Port roundabout then carried on, her mind running over what they knew about the Choker's previous victims. Gillian had mentioned marks round the victim's neck. It seemed unlikely it was a coincidence.

She was approaching one of the newer roundabouts in town now, the winter sun low in the sky. Out to the east it glinted on the windows of the iconic Old Course Hotel, making them burn bright orange; but her attention was drawn to the line of vehicles parked on the verge, beyond the roundabout. Checking her mirror, she slowed down and bumped her car up on the grass.

Chris came to meet her, ducking under the blue-and-white tape marking the outer cordon, pulling off the hood of his forensic suit. Her eyes strayed over his shoulder to the trees where she could see movement.

'Doc's been,' he said. 'Not that he was needed. Life definitely extinct.'

'SOCO?'

'On their way.'

'And it's suspicious?'

'Afraid so. Clear marks round his neck. Ligature, I'd say.'

'Any sign of it?'

Chris shook his head. 'Nah. It's a pretty clean scene, to be honest. Not much evidence of a struggle.'

'He drugs his victims,' she said, shaking her head. 'It has to be him.'

A flash of headlights lit up the scene. Chris turned to see Ben's car, then he looked back at Clare. 'Absolutely nothing you could have done,' he said. 'We were told the weekend and we were working towards that.'

She tried to smile. 'Thanks, Chris. Unfortunately that's not much comfort to our victim's family. Do we know who he is, by the way?'

He nodded. 'Fits Theo Glancy's description. There might be a wallet but I didn't want to touch anything before SOCO arrived.' He glanced up at the sky. 'They'll need lights.'

'He in there?' Ben's voice said. Clare went to greet him but he was looking towards the trees.

'I can show you,' Chris said, walking across. 'If you want to get suited up.'

Ben turned on his heel, striding back towards his car. Clare watched him go. 'I'd better have a look as well.'

Five minutes later, Chris led them under the blue-and-white tape, towards the inner cordon, stepping carefully on metal plates Gillian had put down, although Clare doubted they'd find any footprints through the fallen leaves and twigs.

He lay on his front, his head to the side, face and blond hair spattered with mud. Craning her neck across the red-and-white tape that marked the inner cordon, Clare thought she could see a dark patch on the back of his head. With the light fading, it was hard to be sure if it was mud or the result of an injury. But there was no mistaking the dark red welt encircling his neck.

'He's been strangled, all right,' Ben said. He leaned forward, taking in the tangle of brambles and nettles. 'Hard to see if he struggled. There's so much debris.'

'You want an entomologist out?' Clare said. 'If he wasn't killed here, it might help find the primary site.'

'Not yet. Let's see what SOCO think when they arrive. Meantime, we need this scene protected.' He glanced up at the sky. 'No rain, at least. Should be okay until the tent's up.'

A flicker of car headlights through the trees heralded the arrival of the SOCO van.

'Come on,' Ben said, retracing his steps. 'I need to call Penny. Can you brief SOCO please?'

He ducked under the outer cordon and headed back to his car. Clare removed her mask and began peeling off her forensic suit.

'Could have been worse,' Chris said. 'And I repeat. You've done nothing wrong here.'

'I've done nothing right, either.'

'No change there,' he said, but the joke didn't land and Clare went off to greet Raymond Curtice, the SOCO she worked most closely with.

'Ah, Clare,' he said, reaching into the back of the van for his kit. 'What's the scoop?'

'Young man. Strangled. We're not sure if he died here or was dumped.'

'Condition?'

'Looks pretty recent. We've not been through the inner cordon but it would be handy to know if there's any ID on him; and how long he's been dead. Even a rough idea.'

'Soon as I can.' He glanced across to Ben, standing with his back to them, phone clamped to his ear. 'Is that—'

'Our DCI. Ben Ratcliffe,' Clare said.

'Isn't he the one from that kidnapping case a year or two back?'

'Yep. That's him.'

'Correct me if I'm wrong, but he doesn't do run-of-the-mill stuff.'

'You're not wrong.'

'So this—' He indicated the cordon, Gillian standing at the entrance, the scene log clutched to her chest.

'It's strictly confidential,' Clare said. 'But it's possible our victim was killed by that serial killer – the one operating in the north of England.'

Raymond began stepping into a white forensic suit, putting a hand on the van to steady himself. 'The Chainlink guy?'

'Yes.'

He met her eye. 'Oh, Clare.'

'I know. What's worse is Ben had some intel he'd be up in this area. But he's always killed at the weekends. So we thought we had a few days.' She looked back towards the cordon. 'Got that one spectacularly wrong.'

Raymond pulled the hood up, tucking in his hair. 'Clare, these people – they're not right in the head. You can't predict what they'll do. And you can only go on the intel you have.'

She shrugged. 'I dunno. Maybe if I'd moved a bit faster that young man wouldn't be lying there, covered in mud.'

'Chances are he would. How many forces have been hunting this guy? And they've not found him. You have a tiny team here by comparison, so don't you dare beat yourself up.'

She forced a smile. 'Thanks, Raymond. Who knows – he might have slipped up – left some evidence at the scene.'

'And if he has, we'll find it.' He glanced towards the trees. 'Doesn't look like he went to much trouble to conceal the body. It's not exactly thick in there.' He gave her a smile. 'I'd better get on. But I'll be in touch.'

She left him to his body. Ben had ended his call and she caught his eye. 'I've asked Raymond for an approximate time of death.'

He nodded. 'Not much we can do here. Let's head to your office. I want to know more about that missing person report.'

Chapter 8

Raymond called as Clare was pulling into the station car park.

'Couple of things,' he began. 'Can't give you an exact time of death but I'd say at least twelve hours and not more than forty-eight. Rigor's fully developed but no putrefaction yet. You probably saw he wasn't covered up. So, bearing in mind the temperatures we've had, I'd say most likely last night. But it's only an indication.'

'He was working last night,' Clare said. 'Early evening, I think.'

'Makes sense.'

'And the other thing?'

'There was a wallet in his hip pocket. Bank cards and an out-of-date driving licence all in the name of Theo Glancy. Looking at the photo on the licence, I'd say it's most likely his.'

'Thanks,' Clare said. She hesitated. 'I know I always ask this…'

'But you're after DNA from the killer, yes?'

'Soon as you can. We need to know if it's the same killer. And – this bit's confidential – if you find any traces of materials a painter and decorator would have used…'

Raymond was quiet as he digested this, then Clare heard someone calling his name.

'I'll let you get on.'

'Thanks; and I'll push this one to the top of the list.'

–

Clare found Jim in the kitchen, washing a mug. 'Can you get me the number for the sister please? Address too.'

His face softened. 'It's him then? The lad Glancy?'

'Looks like it.'

'Suspicious?'

'Definitely.'

Ben Ratcliffe appeared at the kitchen door. 'Think we could all do with a coffee.' He glanced at Clare. 'Let's take them into your office.'

She led him along the corridor, wondering what he was going to say. Might he decide to make this official? *Unsatisfactory performance*, it was called. Maybe she should phone her Federation rep. Get some advice.

She switched on the light and put her coffee down on the desk. Then she pulled out a chair for Ben. Overhead the strip light flickered intermittently before bathing the room in its harsh light.

'That needs replaced,' Ben said, and Clare nodded.

'I keep meaning to report it,' she said, her voice flat. She was overwhelmingly tired now, the events of the day having caught up with her, and she just wanted this uncomfortable meeting to be over.

Ben sank down on the chair and took a long drink of his coffee. Then he replaced the mug on the desk. 'So, thoughts?'

Clare was taken aback. She'd expected him to lay into her again for not telling him about Theo straight away.

He saw her face and raised a hand to reassure her. 'Look, I'm sorry. I sounded off at you and it wasn't fair. I just couldn't believe we'd missed our chance.' He shot her a look. 'If I'm being completely honest, I wanted to be the one to bring this guy in.' He shook his head. 'Wrong attitude. I shouldn't have taken it out on you.' He attempted a smile. 'None of this is your fault, Clare. We had good intel suggesting it would be the weekend. You've been doing everything I'd have done in your shoes. And I'd have bet against him dumping the victim just off a busy road.'

She felt relief wash over her. 'Thanks.' She considered his words. 'That road – it is quiet later on. Traffic dies down. It's possible he could have bumped the van up on the verge, lights off.' Her brow creased. 'How long would it take? Open the doors, check for cars, heft a fully grown man out and throw him into the trees?'

'Depends how strong he is. From what I saw the victim's slightly built. If our man's used to carrying ladders, rolling up carpets – maybe a minute, start to finish.'

'And if it was late at night the road could easily have been deserted.'

'Hmm. Where's the nearest camera?'

'Bus station,' Clare said. 'About half a mile away.'

'We need their footage for last night.'

She noted this down. 'I'll get one of the lads onto it. But if he didn't go that way—'

'Any other cameras?'

'Not really. There are so many different ways he could have gone. But I'll put out a shout for dashcam footage.'

'Yeah, do that.' Ben picked up his coffee and drained the cup. 'Who's the next of kin?'

'Not sure.' Clare pulled the keyboard across her desk and logged into the missing person report. 'The sister's name's Ruby. But I'm pretty sure there's more family.' She explained about her visit to Retro's and the conversation with Danny Glancy. 'Apparently the club's owned by the mother – Rhona, I think he said. So, unless our victim has a significant other somewhere, I'm guessing it'll be her.'

Ben drummed his fingers on the desk. 'Start with the sister. She'll know where he went, what he did. Probably know more than the mother; and we'll need an FLO. Any suggestions?'

'Wendy Briggs,' Clare said without hesitation. She'd worked with Wendy on a few cases where a family liaison officer had been needed. Wendy had the knack of finding the right level and she had a sharp pair of eyes.

'Good shout.' Ben scraped back his chair. 'I'll let you get on. I said I'd update Penny. And I'll have to stand down the surveillance teams.'

'I wonder...'

'Yes?'

Clare's brow creased. 'I suppose we are sure it's the Choker this time...'

He put a hand to his chin. 'I mean it's not official yet. We'll need DNA for that. But it certainly seems that way.'

'I just think – you've gone to all this trouble, putting together teams. Maybe we should keep going. Just in case it's not the Choker.'

'Clare...'

'Oh I know. I'm probably trying to make myself feel better. But if we disband the teams now, stop checking white vans and it turns out not to be him...'

He stood thinking for a minute. 'It's a good point. Okay. We'll keep it going – at least until we have the DNA results back. I'll square it with Penny.'

Chris tapped at Clare's door shortly after Ben had left and she wondered if he'd been hovering, waiting for Ben to go. She relayed the conversation. 'So we keep going until forensics confirm the Choker's the killer.'

'Helluva coincidence if it's not him,' Chris said.

'Yeah, I know. But it's his op. His call.' She rose and picked up the coffee cups. 'Come on. Let's get round to the mother's. See if we can catch her before she goes to the club.'

Chapter 9

Rhona Glancy lived in Priory Gardens, a quiet cul-de-sac off Canongate about a mile from the station. Clare drove slowly along while Chris checked the numbers until he indicated the Glancys' house and she drew into the kerb behind a blue BMW.

The house was built in a mock-Tudor barn style with festoon curtains bordering the front room window. A red Ford sat in the drive in front of a garage. An older model, she thought.

Chris quickened his pace. 'That's an XR3i,' he said. 'It's a classic.' He turned to Clare, his face alight. 'There's only about four hundred left.'

Clare glanced at it then nodded at the front door. 'Very nice. But we've bad news to break.'

The doorbell rang out and for a minute Clare wondered if there was no one at home. She hadn't wanted to break bad news at Retro's but maybe there was no option. She rang again and this time there was the sound of voices from within. A minute later Danny Glancy opened the door. He stared at them, no sign of recognition.

'Yeah?'

Clare held out her warrant card. 'We met earlier today,' she said. 'DI Clare Mackay and DS Chris West.'

'Oh,' he said. 'Yeah, course. There's nothing wrong, is there?'

A woman's voice asked who was at the door and Clare looked over Danny's shoulder.

'Is that your mum?'

'Yeah. Erm, I'm supposed to be heading to the club now. Get it ready for opening. So…'

'If we could come in, please.'

He stood his ground for a moment then he moved back to let them enter. The woman's voice came again, asking who it was. 'Polis,' he called back, closing the door behind them. He flicked a thumb at a door to the right. 'In there,' and he made as if to leave.

'I think you should join us,' Clare said. He studied her gaze, his brow creased, then he led them into a square sitting room dominated by a chunky leather sofa and an enormous wall-mounted TV. In one corner a slim black woodburner stood, loaded with logs, ready to be lit. Clare's eye was drawn to the window framed in the 'frilly knickers' curtains, as her mother would have said, a busy pattern with swags scalloped along the pelmet.

'And who might you be?' The voice had an edge, the impatience evident. Clare whirled round and saw a set of bi-folding doors, pulled back, giving onto an open-plan kitchen-dining room. It was brighter than the sitting room thanks mainly to rows of downlighters studded into the ceiling. A set of deer antlers was mounted on one wall, an incongruous note among the gleaming white kitchen units and light wood furniture. There was certainly no accounting for taste.

Two women sat along the side of a square oak dining table, a pile of papers in front of them. The one nearest Clare had a neat red bob, the start of dark roots showing at the crown. This must be Rhona Glancy. She was fifty, maybe, tidily dressed in a cream polo neck and fine brown needlecord trousers tucked into ankle boots. She was heavily made up, her lips pillar-box red, but beneath the pan-stick foundation was the leathery complexion of a drinker. She arched a microbladed eyebrow at Clare, her expression not encouraging.

The other woman was partly screened by Rhona, and Clare moved slightly so she could see her. She wanted to judge if this might be someone who could look after Rhona, while they waited for a family liaison officer to arrive.

She was about to ask the woman her name when she turned and met Clare's eye.

'Inspector,' she said, her gravelly voice familiar. It took Clare a minute to make sense of this. There was no mistaking the bleached blonde hair, the sunbed tan and the trademark animal-print clothes.

Big Val Docherty was sitting at Rhona Glancy's dining table. Big Val, who definitely operated on the wrong side of the law, but far enough away to avoid Clare successfully charging her with anything. Big Val was here in the Glancys' house, looking over some papers with their murder victim's mother. The question was, why?

'Val!' Clare couldn't stop herself.

Val made no reply. Rhona's gaze moved from Clare to Val then back to Clare again.

'Would one of you like to tell me what's going on?'

Clare recovered herself. Whatever Val was doing here, now wasn't the time. 'Mrs Rhona Glancy?' she said, turning back to the red-haired woman.

'Yeah. And I gather you're an inspector. Maybe tell me what you want.' She indicated the sheaf of papers. 'As you can see, we're a bit busy, here.'

'I'm afraid we have some bad news,' Clare said. A noise from behind reminded her Danny was there, hovering.

'What news?' Rhona said. 'Something up at the club?'

Clare took a deep breath. 'This afternoon a body was discovered on the outskirts of St Andrews. We have reason to believe it may be your son Theo. I'm so sorry.'

Rhona stared, her lips parted, eyes blinking, as though trying to process this.

'Theo?' Danny said. 'Our Theo?'

Clare half turned so she could see him. 'We think so. Obviously a formal identification will be necessary, but we do think it's Theo.'

Val was on her feet now and she moved behind Rhona, bending over to encircle her in a pair of beefy arms. But Rhona barely seemed to notice. 'It must be a mistake,' she said. 'Theo – he was at the club last night. Helping with the books.' She glanced at Danny. 'He was fine, wasn't he?'

Danny nodded but said nothing. The colour had drained from his face and Clare moved to pull out one of the dining chairs. 'Maybe you should sit down,' she said. 'Chris here could make us some tea.'

'Aye,' Val said, her voice gruff with emotion. 'Tea'll be good.'

Danny took the chair Clare offered and moved to sit next to his mum, taking hold of her hand. She was crying quietly now and Val gave her arm a squeeze, then she lumbered towards the kitchen to help Chris.

'You do the tea, son. I ken where the biscuits are.'

Chris stole a glance at Clare, who struggled not to react. Never in all her life did she think she'd see Chris and Val Docherty bonding over tea-making.

A few minutes later Chris placed a tray of mugs down on the table, Val a plate of biscuits. She added a lot of milk to two of the mugs and put one in front of Rhona. 'Have a drink of tea, hen,' she said.

Rhona raised her eyes and she shook her head. 'Don't want tea.'

Danny took her hand in his, holding it there for a moment. 'It'll be good, Mum. Just a sip.'

Clare felt an unexpected lump in her throat at this hulk of a man speaking to his mum so tenderly. She added milk to one of the mugs and sat opposite the three of them, motioning to Chris to join them. He eased himself down and Clare opened her mouth to begin.

But Danny forestalled her. 'Where is he? Our Theo? Where is he?' His voice was husky and Clare saw his lower lip was quivering. She hesitated. There was nothing to indicate any of Theo's family had been involved in his death but she knew how important it was to hold the details back. It wouldn't be the first time a guilty person had betrayed knowledge of a crime scene – information that hadn't been known outside the investigating team.

'We hope to have him over to the police mortuary by the end of the evening,' she said. 'Once he's there we'll need someone to identify him. Ideally two of you.'

Tears were pouring down Rhona's cheeks now, sobs overtaking her. Danny moved to hold her and she buried her head in his shoulder. Val's lips were set in a thin line.

'What happened?' she said, her voice low. 'To the lad – what happened?'

Clare eyed her, then she looked back at Rhona. 'We are treating this as a suspicious death.'

'Suspicious?' Val said. 'How so?'

It was a curious turning of the tables, Clare thought. Val – who they believed had been responsible for more than her fair share of human misery over the years – was almost cast in the role of victim here. Part of Clare wanted to ask how it felt, but her focus was the Glancy family. Val was just a bystander, as far as they knew. Come to that, why was Val there? She'd find out, but it wasn't important for now. What mattered was supporting Rhona and Danny, and eliciting any information that could help. If they could find out where Theo had met his killer they might be a step closer to catching him.

'I can't say any more until after the post-mortem,' Clare said, her voice low.

'But you know,' Val persisted.

'As I said, the post-mortem will help establish the cause of death.'

Val held her gaze but Clare refused to be drawn. She let Rhona sip her tea for a few minutes, then she tried again.

'Would you feel up to telling us a bit about Theo?' she said.

'Can't this wait?' Danny snapped.

'Obviously if Mrs Glancy doesn't feel up to it—'

'Rhona,' she said. 'None o' that Mrs Glancy stuff. Rhona's fine.'

Clare smiled back. 'Rhona. I gather Theo was working at the club last night?'

Rhona pulled a paper hankie from her sleeve and blew her nose. Then she dabbed her eyes with a finger, wiping away the tear stains. 'Aye,' she said. 'I was having problems with my spreadsheet. Damn things confuse me. Theo – he works with computers, you know? He's a clever lad. And so good at helping. He said he'd sort it out for me. So he came down and worked in the office.'

Clare took out her notebook. 'What time was that?'

Rhona glanced at Danny. ' 'Bout six, maybe?'

'Nearer seven,' Danny said.

'And how long was he there for?'

Danny thought for a moment. 'Back o' nine. Half past, maybe. He was still there when the DJ started his set at nine. But he'd gone by half past. The fizzy drinks gun was playing up and it spurted on the floor. I went for a cloth and he was away.'

'So that was…'

'Like I said, maybe just on half past.'

Clare noted this down. 'I'm afraid we will need to examine that computer. But we'll have it back to you as soon as possible.'

Rhona shrugged but said nothing and Clare turned back to Danny.

'Do you know what his plans were? After he left the club?'

He looked at his mum but she shook her head. 'Home, I guess,' he said. 'He's got a house in Guardbridge with our Ruby. Bought it between them.'

'He wouldn't have had a date, maybe?' Clare said.

Danny snorted. 'Theo? No chance. Never saw him with a girl.'

'Or a boy?' Clare ventured.

Danny's eyes narrowed. 'He wasn't like that,' he said, and he squeezed Rhona's hand again. 'So don't go saying he was.'

Clare sensed Chris shift in his seat and she pressed on. 'Did he have any friends he saw regularly?'

'Nah. Bit of a loner. Ask Ruby. Spent most nights on his computer. Gaming, like.'

'Online?' Chris said, sitting forward.

Danny stared. 'You think that's what happened? One of those wee dweebs online's got upset 'cause Theo's killed his dragon? Seriously?' He shook his head. 'Bunch o' nutters.'

The sound of the front door opening and closing interrupted them and they all turned to see a young woman in her mid-twenties. She had begun to speak but stopped when she saw Clare and Chris, her eyes suddenly full of concern.

She was casually dressed in leggings, an oversized sweat-shirt and shiny black trainers, her cheeks flushed, and Clare wondered if she'd come from the gym. But her long blonde hair was dry, styled with perfect waves. Her make-up was immaculate and her lips sat in a pout, suggesting she was no stranger to Botox. She jingled a set of car keys in her hand as she took in the scene before her; and then her expression changed.

'Is this Theo?' she said, her voice quavering. 'Have you found him? He's not in trouble, is he?'

Danny stood and crossed the room, taking his sister in his arms. She allowed him to cradle her for a minute then pushed him away, the colour gone from her cheeks. 'What?' she said. 'What's happened? What's he done?'

'It's no' that,' Danny said. 'They think…' He swallowed and tried again. 'They think Theo's dead.'

She stood, taking this in for a moment, her mouth opening and closing as if she was trying to speak. 'No,' she choked at last. 'Not Theo. Oh please, no.'

Chapter 10

Whether it was the arrival of Ruby or the news of Theo's death gradually sinking in, Clare couldn't decide but, finally, the Glancys began to unbend and talk about him.

'Always good at the school,' Rhona said, dabbing her eyes. 'No' in trouble like these two.' She indicated Danny and Ruby. 'He stuck in. Got his exams and went to college.'

'What did he study?' Clare said, keen for Rhona to share as much as possible.

'Computing. It was always computers with Theo.'

'He built his own,' Ruby said. 'While he was at school. He was always ordering stuff off eBay – cables and disks. Most of it – I hadn't a clue what it was. But he kept at it until one day he said he'd done it.' She shook her head. 'There was nothing he couldn't do.'

'Proudest day of my life, his graduation,' Rhona said. 'He wore the gown and all that.' Her eyes were pink from crying, her voice husky. 'My laddie. Clever as all those other kids.'

'Better,' Danny said, and Rhona nodded.

'Where did he work?' Clare asked.

'Worked for himself,' Rhona said. 'Freelance, he called it.'

'Was he busy?'

'Oh aye. Built lots of websites for folk. And he did repairs as well.'

'He was turning work away,' Ruby said. 'He had a name for doing a good job.'

Clare smiled at this. 'Did he often help at the club?'

Rhona shrugged. 'We had a few teething problems, getting it off the ground. Theo – he was good at all the admin stuff.' Her face fell. 'The club.' She looked at Danny, her eyes full of tears. 'We should be over there now – setting up for tonight.'

'You'll no' open tonight,' Val said and, again, Clare wondered what Val was doing here. She shot her a look and Val met her gaze. 'I've – an interest in the place.'

'Financial?'

'Let's just call it an interest.' She turned to Danny, sitting with his arm around Ruby. 'Head over there, son. Pay the staff off and stick a note on the door.'

'We should put something on the website,' Ruby said, her voice dull. She had finally run out of tears and she seemed exhausted by it. 'Theo would know how…'

'A note on the door'll be fine,' Val said. She fixed Danny with a hard stare. 'Get it done, then get back here.'

Danny rose and gave Ruby's shoulder a squeeze. 'Back soon,' he said, and he left the room. He returned a minute later. 'Anyone seen my jacket?'

Rhona rolled her eyes. 'You'll have left it at the club again.'

'Aye, most likely.' He turned on his heel and they heard the front door slam. Chris's eyes strayed to the window as Danny gunned the XR3i, backing it out of the drive.

'Nice car he's got,' he said. 'The Escort.'

Rhona followed his gaze. 'He was always into his cars, Danny. He spends hours tinkering with it.'

'Did Theo drive?' Clare said, thinking of the out-of-date driving licence.

Rhona shook her head. 'I bought him driving lessons when he was seventeen. Did it for the other two as well. But Theo – he was nervous, like. Didn't take to it. Then he said he didn't want to do it any more.'

Chris rose and moved across the room to a large photo frame on the wall. It was the kind with multiple apertures and he stood for a minute or two, studying the photos. Rhona followed his gaze.

'That's our Theo at the top,' she said. 'Holding the certificate. School prize for computing.'

Chris turned and smiled at Rhona. 'You must have been very proud.'

'Oh, I was,' she said. 'He worked hard for it.'

Chris looked back at the photos, standing for a minute, then he returned to his seat. Clare glanced at him, wondering if there was more to the photo than he was saying. But it would keep. She turned back to Ruby.

'And you live in Guardbridge? You shared with Theo?'

Ruby nodded. 'We always got on well, me and Theo; and it's not so far away if we wanted to see Mum.'

They talked on for a bit, then Clare said, 'Did Theo still have a bedroom here?'

'Nah. Turned it into a gym last year,' Rhona said.

'Are there still some of his things – in other rooms, maybe?'

'No. When I cleared out the room I put his school and college stuff into boxes and Ruby ran them along to their place.'

'They're still there,' Ruby said. 'We've a third bedroom we use to store stuff like that. I can show you if you like?'

'Actually, that would be really helpful. If you feel up to it? The more we know about Theo the easier it'll be to find out what happened to him.'

Ruby looked across at her mum. 'Will you be okay? If I take the inspector to the house?'

'I'll look after her,' Val said, one eye on Clare, as if daring her to interfere.

Ruby moved round the table and hugged her mum. 'I'll come back after.'

Rhona put a hand out and patted her daughter. 'Quick as you can.' Then she turned back to Clare. 'When can I see him?'

'As soon as possible,' she said. 'Hopefully tomorrow.'

Rhona gave a slight nod and Clare rose from her seat. They followed Ruby to the door but, as she stepped out onto the drive, Val appeared at Clare's shoulder.

'This lad Theo,' she said, her face a bit too close to Clare's. She could smell the stale breath, see the tiny broken veins on Val's cheeks, the yellow tinge to her eyes. She drew back a little and Val went on.

'He was a good lad,' she said. 'If it had been Danny, well that woulda made sense. Always getting into scraps, that one. But Theo – there was no need for anything to happen to him.'

'We're throwing everything at it,' Clare said, 'as we do with any murder.'

Val appeared to be weighing this. 'I wouldn't like to have to take matters into my own hands,' she said after a moment.

Clare took a breath in and out. She'd known Val long enough to realise this wasn't an empty threat. 'I would strongly advise against that,' she said.

'Well, you would, wouldn't you?' She looked beyond Clare to Ruby, who was now sitting in a racing green Mini Cooper, exhaust vapour condensing in the early evening air. Then she turned on her heel and left them at the door.

'Come on,' Clare said. 'Let's get over to Guardbridge.'

They followed Ruby down the road and joined a queue of commuter traffic, crawling out of town. It took almost twenty minutes to drive the five miles to the house Ruby and Theo had shared. They pulled in after Ruby, who nosed her car in front of a charcoal-grey garage, triggering the security light. She stepped out of the car and motioned to Clare to park alongside.

'Neighbours are in Tenerife,' she said, when Clare stepped out of the car. 'You'll be fine there.' She fished in her pocket and took out a set of keys, turning one in the lock. She held the door for Clare and Chris to follow then went into the house, lights flicking on as she moved up the hall. The sitting room was bright and airy, the colour scheme cool greys and whites, the furnishings simple but classic. The odd statement piece added interest and it wouldn't have looked out of place in a glossy magazine. Clare thought briefly of the hotchpotch of furnishings at Daisy Cottage, some inherited from old relatives, odd pieces she'd bought herself and the DCI's furniture, brought from his house when he'd moved in with her. How on earth had two twenty-somethings created such an attractive living space?

'This is lovely,' she said, indicating the room.

Ruby looked round without enthusiasm. 'I suppose it is. Doesn't much matter now.' She moved to a large chrome fridge and pulled it open, taking out a bottle of wine. 'I need a drink,' she said. 'Want one?'

Clare thought there was nothing she'd like more than a cool glass of Chardonnay. It had been a very long and difficult day. But the wine would have to wait. 'No thanks.' She watched Ruby as she poured herself a large glass of white wine. She had the sense there was something on her mind. Maybe the wine would loosen her tongue. 'A chat would be good, though,' she said. 'We'd like to hear more about Theo. Maybe stuff he wouldn't necessarily tell his mum.' She watched Ruby carefully as she said this. Ruby put the glass to her lips and sipped. She held it there for a moment then she drank steadily, draining it in one.

'Don't normally drink that much,' she said. 'It's so bad for my skin. But it's not every day...' She topped up her glass and replaced the bottle in the fridge. 'Would you like to sit down?' She indicated a long grey sofa and they followed her lead. Ruby waited until they'd sat, then she perched on a black leather Stressless chair, swinging it left and right, her hands clutched round the glass. 'What do you want to know?'

'How had Theo been lately? Anything different? Was he worried about anything? Any changes in his routine?'

Ruby shook her head. 'He didn't really have a routine. He'd do his computer work in the study. And I'd do mine in here.' She glanced across to a desk in the corner of the room, a sleek iMac on top.

Clare suddenly realised she didn't know what Ruby's job was. When she'd first seen her she'd thought Ruby might be a beautician or, thinking about the clothes she was wearing, a personal trainer. But if she worked from home... 'What is it you do?'

'I'm an influencer.'

Clare hesitated and Chris leaned forward. 'Clare doesn't know much about social media,' he said, smiling. 'That's the first time I've seen her lost for words in a long time.'

Clare recalled her conversation with the DCI the night before – TikTok and influencers. But she played along, sensing Ruby relax at this. 'He's right, I'm afraid. I can only just manage my emails.'

'I make money by doing videos of products,' Ruby explained. 'Companies send me stuff to try – make-up, skincare products, even new hairdryers. I make videos of me trying them out.'

'And they pay you to do this?'

'They do now,' Ruby said. 'I've half a million followers on TikTok alone, never mind Insta and other platforms. When I started I only got the free stuff. But now I have so many people watching my videos I can pick and choose; and the companies pay me to do it.'

'Does it pay well?'

Ruby waved a hand round the room. 'It pays for this lot. So, yeah. I'd say so.'

Clare sat thinking for a moment. 'Do you get those – what are they called?'

Chris regarded her. 'You might have to give us a bit more.'

'People who are abusive. Online, I mean.'

'Trolls?' Ruby said. 'Yeah, a few. But I block them. They don't know where I live. I never post anything about Guard-bridge. Most of them are just saddos without a life.'

Privately Clare thought some of the people Ruby referred to as saddos could be dangerous. You never knew when a threat of violence was a genuine one. Was that what had happened here? 'Have you had any threats recently?'

Ruby's eyes widened. 'You think that's why Theo was killed? Someone's gone after him to get to me?'

Clare shook her head. 'I've no idea, Ruby. We'd have to see the kind of threats you get. But it is worth bearing in mind.' She looked round the room. 'Do you have a burglar alarm?'

'No. Maybe I should.'

Clare thought about Theo. He was almost certainly the Chainlink Choker's latest victim; and, if he was, Ruby was in no danger. But she couldn't be sure and she couldn't tell Ruby that, without Ben's say-so. 'Until we know a bit more about what happened to Theo it might be better to stay at your mum's.'

Ruby looked at the glass in her hand. 'Probably shouldn't have had this.'

Clare smiled. 'We can run you over there,' and Ruby nodded. 'So you haven't noticed anything recently? Anyone hanging around? Any strange phone calls? Anything that upset Theo? There must have been a reason you reported him missing,' she went on. 'It was only a few hours, after all.'

Ruby was quiet for a moment. Clare waited. She was good at this part. Sooner or later a witness would find the silence unbearable and Ruby was no exception.

'About Theo,' she said. 'There's something you should know.'

Again, they waited.

'Theo was gay. Mum and Danny – they wouldn't understand. They're so outdated in their views. Theo and I were close, growing up. Danny was five years older and he didn't want to hang around with us. But me and Theo – we were like pals. I've known almost as long as Theo did that he liked boys. But he couldn't tell Mum or Danny. So he kept it to himself.'

Clare's heart sank. Had Theo gone online, looking for somewhere to find other gay men? Had he unwittingly stumbled into the path of the Choker? If so, they might learn something here – something about how the Choker operated. 'Did Theo have a regular partner?'

Ruby hesitated. 'Not that I knew.'

Clare eyed her. There was something she wasn't saying. 'Had you seen him with anyone recently?'

She nodded. 'There was this one guy – at the club.'

'Name?'

Ruby shook her head. 'Sorry. Theo didn't say.'

'What did he look like?'

She thought for a moment. 'I'm not sure, really. I saw him at the club, but the lighting, you know – it's not easy to tell. I'd say mid-twenties, quite slim.'

'Hair?'

'Blond, I think; and his eyebrow – he had a piercing.'

'When did you see him with Theo?'

Ruby's brow furrowed. 'I'm not sure. Maybe last week. I mean I'd seen him a few times with other men. But I think he was with Theo last week.'

'Did Theo bring him back here?'

Ruby shrugged. 'He might have. I knew there had been men here before. I get hotel deals, you see? Hotel groups, they send me vouchers and I make videos of the rooms, the bar, restaurants, the spa. So maybe once a month I'd be away. Theo would ask when I was coming back, and I'd joke he wasn't to have any wild parties. But I always knew if he'd had someone here.'

'How could you tell?' Chris asked.

'Well, his sheets would be in the wash, for a start. And sometimes there would be food in the fridge. Stuff he didn't eat. Olives, for one thing. Theo hated them. But I'd come back and there would be some olives, cubes of cheese – that kind of thing. Beer, too. Theo always drank wine or vodka, never beer, but there would be cans in the recycling.'

'Did you ask him about it?' Clare said but Ruby shook her head.

'I reckoned if he wanted me to know he'd tell me. But he wasn't daft. He knew I'd see what was going on. Sometimes I'd tell him to be careful.' She shook her head. 'Seems I didn't say it loud enough.'

Clare suddenly felt they were close. She had to ask the right questions, here. 'Did you think Theo might have been meeting someone yesterday? This man from the club, maybe?'

Ruby took a breath in and out. 'Yes,' she said, her voice small. 'I'm pretty sure he had a date. I'd arranged to try out a spa, down in Edinburgh. And he asked when I'd be home.' Her brow creased. 'I don't know why I said it but I told him he should be careful who he brought here.'

Clare and Chris exchanged glances. 'What did you mean by that?' Clare said.

Tears began to course down Ruby's face and she reached over to a box of tissues on a glass coffee table. 'I was worried about something happening to the house – someone going mad and damaging it, or stealing stuff. But I never thought anything would happen to Theo.'

'That's completely understandable,' Clare said, trying to soothe Ruby. 'This is your home. It's quite natural you want to protect it.'

She shook her head. 'But I should have been protecting my brother. He relied on me, and I let him down.'

Chapter 11

Chris went to fetch a bundle of evidence bags from the car while Ruby and Clare studied the kitchen.

'Anything unusual in the recycling?' Clare asked. Ruby opened a door to a utility room. 'Don't touch anything unfamiliar,' Clare warned. 'Just point it out.'

Ruby stood, looking at the different coloured bags for plastics and paper waste. She shook her head. 'I think all that was there yesterday before I left for the spa.'

'What about the fridge?' Clare asked.

Ruby pulled the door open and scanned the shelves. 'I can't see anything.'

Chris returned, laden with bags and white forensic suits. He handed one to Clare and a look of alarm crossed Ruby's face.

'It's just a precaution,' Clare assured her. 'But we will have to take away any electronic devices Theo used.'

'Not my iMac, though?' Ruby said. 'I need it for my social media.'

Clare considered this. There was nothing to indicate Ruby was involved in her brother's death. Not at this stage, at least. And if they did have to examine the iMac in the future, she was pretty sure the Tech Support staff would be able to find anything suspicious, even if it had been deleted. 'Could you download any threats you've had?'

'I'll give you my account logins,' she said. 'As long as I can keep using them.'

Clare smiled. 'That would be brilliant. We'll restrict access to the bare minimum. But it would allow us to see anyone who's made threats or anything like that.'

'You might regret that,' Ruby said. 'I get thousands of notifications every day.'

Clare nudged Chris. 'I'll give it to Chris here. He loves social media.'

Chris rolled his eyes but Clare ignored this. 'If you could show us Theo's bedroom and study, we'll leave you in peace.'

'And the room where his school and college stuff is,' Chris added.

'You can take that if you like,' Ruby said. 'I don't really want it.'

She pointed them to the three rooms and made to leave when Clare stopped her. 'Do you mind if I ask one more question?'

'Sure.'

'What interest does Val Docherty have in Retro's?'

Ruby's lips thinned. 'It's not for me to say.'

Clare gave her what she hoped was a sympathetic smile. 'We need to know everything, Ruby. So...'

She met Clare's gaze. 'You can't say you got this from me.'

'Understood.'

'Val owns Retro's. Mum's the licensee but she didn't have the capital. She's run bars before and she's good with the punters. Has a good way with them and she understands what works and what doesn't. She's known Val for a few years, off and on. Mum and Val met at a funeral about a year ago and they got talking. Mum said how St Andrews was crying out for a club and Val said why didn't Mum open one. Mum said she didn't have the money and Val offered.'

Clare took this in, wondering if it had any bearing on Theo's murder. Val had upset a fair few folk in her time. If Theo hadn't been killed by the Choker, might it be something to do with Val? Someone looking to settle a score? 'Does anyone else know about Val?'

Ruby shook her head. 'Far as I know it's just me, Mum and Danny. Mum told us to keep it to ourselves.'

Clare thanked Ruby and they headed for Theo's study, pulling on forensic suits before entering. It was a small room with a window screened by a pale grey roller blind. As they entered a light came on automatically and she stood taking it in. A light wood desk stood against one wall with a bank of sockets and USB ports on the wall behind. A laptop sat on the desk flanked by two monitors. To the side of the desk a narrow bookcase held a selection of CD-ROMs.

'I thought everything was downloads these days,' Clare said.

Chris ran an eye down the cases. 'Some vintage stuff here. These old games are pretty popular. Classics, back in the day.'

'Hark at you, Grandad.'

'He's even got a ripped copy of *Spectre Supreme*. How the hell's he done that?'

'Focus, Sergeant.'

'You have no idea how exciting that is, Inspector.'

'So's the prospect of getting home before midnight. So let's get on with it.'

They worked away, Clare going through the desk drawers while Chris checked the CD-ROM cases, with the occasional delighted remark. After forty minutes Clare rubbed the back of her neck. 'I think we're done here.'

'Yeah.' Chris got to his feet with something approaching regret.

'Tell you what,' Clare said. 'Maybe Ruby will let you come round to play one day. If you're very good.'

They moved on to the bedroom, which was as tidy as the study. Clare handed Chris a large bag. 'You do the bed,' she said. 'We'd better get those sheets off to the lab; and check the laundry basket in case he changed it.'

He sighed. 'Why do I always have to do the bed? Why can't you do it for a change?'

'Perks of the job,' she said, and she began going through Theo's bedside cabinet.

It took them another hour to check his bedroom but there was little to suggest anything suspicious. It was looking more and more likely Theo was the victim of a random attack, probably by their serial killer.

'We done?' Chris asked and she nodded.

'Think so.' She indicated the sack of bedding. 'I'd rather Ruby didn't see this. Might upset her. I'll go and speak to her while you pop it in the boot; and grab those boxes from the spare bedroom as well.'

She found Ruby at her iMac, scrolling through TikTok posts. She looked up when Clare appeared.

'Suppose you think I'm heartless,' she said. 'But if I ease off my followers will find someone else. These things change in a heartbeat so I have to keep at it.'

Clare hesitated. 'I'd avoid saying anything about Theo,' she said. 'I mean you might want to let your followers know you've suffered a tragedy. But no details, please. It might prejudice the investigation.'

Ruby stared at Clare, her eyes full of bewilderment. 'I can't believe we're having this conversation. Theo – he was such a – a good person. Really good, you know?'

'He sounds lovely,' Clare said.

'You will get them, won't you? Whoever did this? You'll get them?'

'We'll do everything we can.'

Ruby said nothing for a moment. She ran her tongue round her lips. 'But what if it's not enough?'

–

They dropped Ruby at her mother's house and headed back to the station.

'We'll put these in the store overnight,' Clare said. 'It's time we both went home. I'll just send a message round the team about tomorrow. Eight o'clock sharp.'

Chris went to call Sara to let her know he was on his way home and Clare took Theo's bagged possessions to the store. Then she checked her Inbox, sent a message round the team and switched off her computer.

The roads were quiet, glistening with frost. Her car flashed up a black ice warning and she moderated her speed.

The DCI was in the attic when she put her key in the door. She was greeted by a volley of barks from Benjy as he raced down the stairs to meet her. A minute later a dusty DCI appeared, wiping his hands on his trousers.

'What on earth have you been doing?' she asked, shrugging off her coat.

'Checking on the Christmas decorations. We shoved a lot of my stuff up in the attic when I sold the house. I wanted to be sure I could reach them.'

She yawned. 'It's November!'

'And Christmas is less than four weeks away. It'll be here before you know it. Did you order the turkey?'

'Yes,' she lied.

'You're a dreadful liar, Clare Mackay. I phoned the farm this morning to check.'

She shook her head. 'It's like living with my mother.'

'But with extra sex.'

She laughed. 'Don't even start. I am so tired I could sleep on my feet.'

He pulled her towards him and kissed the top of her head. 'Come on. Soup and crusty bread do you? Or would you like something more substantial?'

She wandered through to the kitchen and pulled open the fridge. 'Is that all you had?'

'Yeah. I was at Penny's lunch thing at headquarters. Interesting thing came up, actually.'

'Get you! I never get invited to her lunch things.'

'To be honest, you didn't miss much. It was a working lunch for the social media forum. Good spread, though – outside caterers. But I did have an interesting chat with Penny. I can fill you in if you like.'

She eyed him. 'I thought Police Scotland had no money?'

'Some external fund.'

'Ah. In that case, soup and crusty bread sounds wonderful.' She glanced at him. 'Could we do your Penny thing tomorrow? I'm absolutely bushed.'

He smiled. 'Sure. I'll put the soup on to heat.'

'And then, Al Gibson, I am going to my bed.'

Day 4: Friday

Chapter 12

'Your murder,' the DCI began, plunging the cafetière.

Clare poured milk on her cereal. 'What about it?'

'Is it connected to Ben?'

She was quiet for a moment, weighing up whether she should tell him. And then she thought, *This is a DCI. He's going to hear it from someone sooner or later, so it might as well be me.* 'Yeah.'

He poured out two mugs of coffee and pushed one across the table. 'Does that mean—'

'I've no idea what it means, Al.' She added milk to her coffee and stirred it, slowly. 'Oh, what the hell,' and she launched into an account of her meeting with Penny and Ben.

He listened, watching her carefully as she went on to describe the murder scene. 'And that's not all,' she said. 'That new club – Retro's – the licensee is Theo's mum, Rhona. But it's Big Val Docherty who owns it.'

The DCI weighed this for a few moments. 'In that case, the murder might be something to do with Val. Someone hitting out at her. I'd maybe stick a cop on the mother's house overnight. What about the other two? Ruby and – what's his name?'

'Danny,' Clare said. 'He has a flat over in Dundee. City Quay, I think. But they're both staying with the mother just now.'

'Good plan,' he said. 'The kind of people Val upsets wouldn't think twice about killing someone to make a point.'

'But if it's our serial killer…'

'You think it is?'

She sighed. 'Given Ben's intel, it is the most likely scenario.'

'And your watch over the weekend?'

'It still goes ahead – assuming Penny agrees. I mean, if the Choker did kill Theo he'll be long gone. But if he didn't…'

'Then he might still be looking for his next victim.'

'Exactly.' She drained her cup and scraped back her chair.

'You leave that,' the DCI said. 'I'll clear breakfast up. You get into work.' He stretched across the table and took hold of her hand. 'And be careful. This is a particularly nasty individual.'

His words ran round her head as she drove into work. The moon was still faintly visible but out to the east the sky was growing lighter. The sun would be up soon. The roads were thick with white frost and she drove carefully, the temperature warning on the dashboard blinking again.

The station was buzzing and she made her way to her office. The overhead light was still flickering and she dropped her bag, heading for the kitchen in the hope it would have stopped by the time she'd made her coffee.

Jim appeared as she was pouring water into a mug. 'Message from the pathologist.'

Clare put down the kettle. 'Oh yes?'

'Post-mortem's scheduled for midday. He thought you might want the next of kin to ID the body first.'

'Good idea. Can you let Wendy know, please?' She checked her watch. 'Let's say I'll pick them up about nine thirty.'

'No problem. I'll tell the mortuary staff as well. Erm, ten fifteen?'

'About then.'

He made to leave but she caught him. 'Could you put in a request for a sparky please? The light in my room's driving me mad.'

Jim went off to his tasks and Sara appeared. Clare indicated her mug. 'Kettle's just boiled.'

'Lovely.' Sara rubbed her hands together. 'It's so cold out there.'

Clare glanced at her. There was something different. 'You look nice,' she said, tentatively.

Sara smiled. 'I've got new lashes.'

Clare peered at her and saw her eyelashes did look longer. 'Lovely. Erm, are they like false ones?'

'Not the kind you peel off at the end of the night. They're little individual ones. Not as obvious. They're still temporary but they last longer.' She smiled. 'You should try it. I can recommend my salon.'

'Maybe.' She thought for a moment. 'Sara, do you use Instagram?'

'Sometimes.'

'So you follow people?'

'Yeah. If I'm interested in what they post. It's mostly friends' holiday snaps, new puppies – stuff like that.'

'What about influencers?'

She laughed. 'Not really. Think I'm a bit old for that.'

'Me too! Only – you know our murder victim?'

'Theo Glancy?'

'Yes. His sister – she seems to make a really good living as an influencer. At least that's what she says. Nice house – beautifully furnished.'

'And you're suspicious?'

Clare spread her hands. 'I genuinely don't know. Is it possible?'

'I'd say so. Not millions, or anything like that. But if you hit that sweet spot it can really take off. You want me to check her out?'

'Would you? I want to be sure the money isn't coming from somewhere else.'

Sara reached into her pocket and took out her phone. 'I was about to put this in my locker. But I'll look now. What's her name?'

'Ruby,' Clare said. 'Ruby Glancy. Long blonde hair.'

Sara tapped at her phone and began scrolling. 'There's a few that might be her,' she said, her eyes fixed on the screen. She held the phone out for Clare to see. 'Have a look at these.'

Clare scrolled through the thumbnail photos, stopping at the fourth one down. 'Can I make this bigger?'

'Tap it. That'll take you to the profile then you can expand any of the photos.'

Clare tapped the thumbnail and a screenful of photos appeared. Ruby with a full face of make-up, Ruby holding up a sleek black mascara tube, the brand name in gold lettering, Ruby demonstrating a hair curler – the photos went on and on. She handed the phone back to Sara. 'What do you reckon?'

Sara peered at it, flicking through the images. 'She's good,' she said after a minute. 'Lots of content, posts several times a day. I'll just check – crikey. Almost six hundred thousand followers.'

'And that's a lot?'

'That's huge, boss. Some TV personalities don't have that many.'

'So she could make a living from it?'

'Definitely. She must be really good.'

Clare thought of Ruby, sitting in front of her iMac just hours after learning her brother had been murdered. She had been upset about Theo but she was clearly a sharp businesswoman. 'Thanks, Sara.'

She wandered back to her office, Ruby's Instagram account on her mind. How on earth did someone of her age amass such a following? She must really be good at – whatever it was she did. She was relieved to see the strip light had stopped flickering and she settled down to check her Inbox before starting the briefing. As the emails updated, her phone began to ring. Raymond.

'Hi,' she said. 'This is an early call.'

'I'm afraid I have some bad news.'

–

78

The incident room was buzzing as Clare entered and it took a few moments to bring it to order.

'For anyone who wasn't here yesterday,' she said when they had quietened down, 'the body of a young man in his twenties was found in the trees on the road to Guardbridge. SOCO attended and I had hoped we'd know today if there was DNA on the body that matched the Choker's previous victims.' She paused for a moment. 'I've just spoken to Raymond. They've had a flood at the lab. Burst waste pipe so the whole place will have to be deep cleaned.'

A collective groan went round the room and Clare nodded.

'Yeah, I know. The only good news is our samples are unaffected. They're in a secure store but there's no way they can access them or use any of the equipment.'

'Any idea how long?' Chris asked.

'Sorry. Your guess is as good as mine. Raymond did say he hoped no more than a few days. It certainly won't be today and most likely not tomorrow.'

'But we are assuming this is the Choker's work?' Max asked.

'Can't say one way or the other,' Clare said. 'Ben's going to ask Superintendent Meakin if we can carry on with the watches in case it's a different killer. I'm hopeful she'll agree.'

'But if it *was* the Choker,' Max said, 'he'll be long gone, won't he?'

Clare nodded. 'I'd put money on it. So I need a few of you checking ANPR and CCTV on the main routes south. Any vans heading away from St Andrews with a north-east of England registration are to be followed up.'

She glanced at her notepad. 'In the meantime, back to basics. Who was on the bus station CCTV?'

Robbie raised a hand. 'I requested it yesterday.'

'Can you chase please? And Chris – ask the press office to put a shout out for dashcam footage.'

He nodded at this. 'Already done. Speaking of the press, Jim's had them asking for a comment. They must have seen SOCO's tent.'

Clare sighed. 'I'll ask the press office to draft something about a sudden death but no details.' She made a note of this then looked round for Sara. 'We've Theo Glancy's laptop and phone to go down to Tech Support today, and the night club computer. Also Theo's bedsheets need to go to SOCO. Raymond said they've set up a temporary office to receive evidence. If you call reception they'll tell you where to go.'

Sara indicated she would do this and Clare studied her notes again, wondering if she'd covered everything.

Gillian caught Clare's eye. 'When will we know about tonight, boss? The surveillance?'

'Hopefully within the hour. So keep in touch.'

She ended the briefing and nodded to Chris. 'I'm taking Rhona and Danny to ID the body this morning. I want you with me, watching their reactions. I'll ask Wendy to stay at the house with Ruby. If Ruby has remembered anything else, particularly about Theo's private life, she might be more likely to talk when Rhona's not there.'

'She'll have to know he was gay,' Chris said. 'Rhona.'

'I know. But I need to pick the right moment.' Her phone buzzed and she fished it out of her pocket. 'Raymond's sent some photos of clothes identical to the ones Theo was wearing. It'll help corroborate their identification.'

'What about the PM?' Chris said. 'You'll be pushed for time if you want to run the Glancys home.'

'Dammit. I hadn't thought of that.' She shook her head. 'I'll give Neil a call. See if he can push it back to one.'

Chapter 13

Rhona Glancy had clearly felt an effort was required. She was dressed in a black trouser suit and a dark red blouse. But her make-up, in contrast to the previous day, was minimal. A touch of mascara and the palest of pink lipsticks. Whether it was the lack of heavy foundation, Clare wasn't sure but she thought Rhona had aged overnight. The alertness and energy she'd displayed when Clare and Chris had arrived to break the news of Theo's death had gone now. Her shoulders sagged and her eyes were pink with crying.

Danny was sitting on the couch and he glanced up as they entered, but said nothing, his face expressionless.

'Ruby's making tea,' Wendy said, but Rhona waved this away.

'I want to see my laddie.'

Clare nodded. 'We'd like Danny to come as well if that's okay? Better to have someone with you.'

Danny gave a slight nod but he still said nothing.

'If you're ready.' Clare indicated the door. 'It's a cold morning. You might want a coat.'

Rhona picked up a coat which had been draped over a dining chair. Then she nudged her son. 'C'mon. And get yourself a jacket.'

Danny forced himself up and off the couch, as though the effort caused him pain. 'Told you. I left it at the club. I'll go in for it later,' he added.

They climbed into the car, Rhona's head down, as though afraid someone would see her. Clare waited until they were settled then she pulled away. At the end of Priory Gardens she signalled right to turn onto Canongate and she felt a hand on her shoulder.

'No,' Rhona said, her voice thick with emotion. 'Go the other way.'

'Rhona, I don't think—'

'I don't care what you think. I want to see – where it happened. I need to see it.'

'Mum,' Danny began.

'Go left, Inspector. Or I'm getting out right now.'

Clare let her foot rest on the brake for a moment, then she cancelled the signal and turned the car left. Minutes later they were heading out of town, passing the Old Course Hotel. She slowed a little as the white SOCO tent could be seen, partly obscured by the trees. In contrast to the flurry of activity the night before there was just one van on the verge now and Clare thought it wouldn't be long before the tent was dismantled.

'That it?' Rhona said, her voice husky.

Clare signalled to pull in, drawing as close to the kerb as she could, one eye on the rear-view mirror. She left the engine idling and twisted round to face Rhona and Danny. 'Yes. Just in the trees.'

Rhona clicked off her seat belt. 'I want to see.'

Clare put out a hand to stop her. 'I'm afraid that's not possible. Not yet. If we go tramping over the ground we might destroy some evidence.'

'What sort of evidence?' Danny growled.

'At the moment we don't know. That's why we have specialist teams working there. They'll spot things the rest of us might miss.' She put a hand on Rhona's arm. 'They won't be there much longer. As soon as it's clear to pay a visit we'll let you know.'

She held Clare's gaze. 'There should be something – something to mark it.'

'We'll get some flowers,' Danny said. 'Leave them at the trees so folk know.'

She nodded at this and reached behind her to pull the belt on again. Clare waited until she was safely belted then she pulled back out into the road.

As they passed through Guardbridge her eyes strayed to Ruby and Theo's flat, looking for any suspicious activity. But there were no lights, no one hanging around – only Ruby's car parked in front of the garage where she'd left it the previous night.

They drove on into Leuchars and Clare saw her first Christmas tree, taking pride of place in a house window. She made a mental note to do some Christmas shopping very soon. The idea was at odds with the grim nature of their journey but, as every officer knew, it was important to leave the job at the station door. Easier said than done, though, she thought as she caught a glimpse of Rhona's face in the rear-view mirror, twisted in misery.

The mortuary car park was almost full but Clare managed to squeeze into a space at the end of a row. She turned off the engine and gave Rhona and Danny a smile. 'Okay?'

Rhona sat, not moving, one hand gripping the other. Danny clicked off his seat belt and gave her arm a squeeze. 'C'mon,' he said. 'I'll be with you.'

Clare waited until Rhona released her seat belt then she nodded to Chris. They climbed out of the car and opened the rear doors for the pair. Clare noted Rhona's high heels. 'Mind your step,' she said. 'Some of that frost's not lifted yet.'

Danny took his mother's arm and they followed Clare and Chris into the mortuary building. She signed them in and the attendant led them to a small viewing room. Clare settled them down and explained they would be viewing Theo through a glass screen, for now.

Rhona nodded. 'Seen it on the telly.'

'But before we do that, I have some photos to show you.' She took out her phone and navigated to the images Raymond had sent. 'These are photos of clothing identical to that worn by the man we believe to be Theo. If you recognise them it would help confirm his identity.'

Rhona's brow creased. 'You'd be better showing them to Ruby. She's more likely to know what he was wearing.'

Clare gave her a smile. 'We will do. But for now, maybe you could look at them?' She held out her phone and Danny moved closer to his mum so they could view the photos together.

'These jeans,' Clare began, 'they're the same brand as the ones found on the body.'

They peered at the photo then Clare flicked to the next, which showed a branded leather patch on the back of the waistband.

'Hollister,' Danny said. 'Theo had a pair.'

'Would you know his waist size?'

Danny looked at Rhona but she shook her head. 'Smaller than me, anyway,' he said. 'And I'm a thirty.'

Clare gave Chris a slight nod. Theo's jeans had been a twenty-eight, according to Raymond. 'And this jumper…'

The image showed a black cable-knit jumper, the cuffs edged with a white stripe. Danny and Rhona exchanged glances but Rhona's expression was blank.

'No idea. I've not seen it before but he liked clothes, Theo. Probably got lots of stuff I've not seen.'

'That's fine,' Clare said. 'And the last one is his jacket.'

It was more a jerkin than a jacket, dark blue with *Nike Air* in large white lettering and the trademark Nike Swoosh on the back. Pretty distinctive, Clare thought. Surely they'd recognise that? Theo might have a dozen jumpers but his family must have seen this jacket before. Rhona stiffened and Clare saw Danny put a hand over her arm – not under her elbow, as if to support her, more like a restraining gesture. It was an odd reaction, she thought, but maybe he was worried Rhona was about to kick off. She flicked a glance at Chris and saw he too was watching the pair carefully. For a few moments, no one spoke, then Clare saw Rhona look up at Danny, her eyes full of fear.

'Does this look like Theo's jacket?' she said at last when it seemed neither of them would speak.

Danny cleared his throat. 'Yeah. That's Theo's.'

Rhona's eyes were still on him but she said nothing.

'It's his jacket,' Danny said again, his eyes meeting Clare's. There was something in his expression, but she couldn't work it out. It was as if the shutters had come down. She glanced at Chris again but he just shrugged.

Rhona took a tissue from her pocket and blew her nose. 'Can we see him now?' she said.

'Of course.'

Chris slipped out of the room to let the attendant know they were ready. He was back a minute later and motioned them over to the window. Rhona gripped Danny's arm tightly and Clare stood at the other side, ready to grab her if needed. She watched them carefully but there was no mistaking Rhona's reaction. She began to shake and Clare put a hand at her back. Tears coursed down her face and she gulped as sobs overtook her.

Danny's jaw tightened and he stood staring straight ahead at the lifeless body of his brother, his face devoid of emotion.

After a minute Clare spoke softly. 'Is this the body of your son Theo Glancy?'

At first Rhona seemed not to hear, then she nodded, sobbing audibly. 'Yes,' she managed, between sobs. 'That's my bairn. My Theo.'

Clare held onto Rhona, fearful her legs might give way, and she looked across to Danny, standing utterly still. 'Danny? Can you confirm that please?'

He didn't move, didn't look at her. He continued staring through the glass. 'Aye,' he said, after a moment. 'That's Theo. That's my wee brother.'

The formalities complete, Clare led Rhona gently to another room with comfy chairs and a drinks machine. She settled Rhona in a chair, Danny at her side, and indicated the machine. 'Would you like a tea? Or a coffee?'

Rhona shook her head. 'I want to go home,' she said. 'Please. Just take me home.'

Clare tapped out a message to Wendy letting her know Theo's identity had been confirmed, adding:

> Rhona's pretty upset, Danny saying nothing

Wendy replied a moment later saying she'd let Ruby know and have the kettle boiled for their return.

–

The journey back was completed in silence, the only sound an occasional sniff from Rhona. They pulled up outside the house and, as they emerged from the car, Ruby appeared at the door, her face tearstained. She walked down the path to meet her mum and the pair stood in a tight hug for a few moments.

'Maybe we should get inside,' Clare said. 'It's a cold morning.'

Ruby led her mum into the house, Danny at her back. In the kitchen, Wendy was pouring out mugs of tea and she set these down on the dining table.

'So, what happens now?' Rhona asked, when she'd had a few sips of tea. 'We'll need to organise a funeral.'

'It's early days,' Clare said. She hesitated. This next part was never easy. 'We need to carry out a post-mortem exam on Theo's body. To ascertain the cause of death.'

'You know, though, don't you?' There was an edge to Danny's voice. 'You already know.'

Clare glanced at Chris. They'd have to know sooner or later. Neil Grant would likely confirm his main findings by the end of the day. What difference would a few hours make?

'This isn't confirmed, but we think Theo died from asphyxiation.'

Danny's eyes narrowed. 'What – like strangled?'

'Not manually,' Clare said. 'We think something was put round his neck.'

Rhona gulped, her eyes brimming with fresh tears.

'It would have been quick,' Clare said, not actually sure if this was true or not. But she wanted to spare Rhona as much as possible. 'He wouldn't have known much about it.'

Rhona eyed her. 'Really?'

Clare nodded. Privately, she thought the blow to the back of the head would have stunned Theo, making him less aware of what was happening. But she didn't want to share this with the Glancys. Not yet. They didn't know enough about what had happened to Theo, so the less they gave away – even to his grieving relatives – the better.

'So your post-mortem thing,' Danny said. 'We can have Theo back after that?'

This was difficult. Until they had a clearer idea of who might be responsible, she couldn't say for sure when the body would be released. 'It might be a bit longer,' she said. 'But we will keep you fully informed. And Wendy here will be around for any questions you might have.'

Ruby put a hand across the table. 'I need to go home, Mum. Do some stuff. But I'll come back.'

Rhona shook her head. 'I don't want that. Whoever did this to Theo, they might come after you next.'

Danny stiffened in his chair. 'I'll go with Ruby. I need to nip home as well. But we'll be back. And we'll go in daylight. Honestly, Mum. It'll be fine.'

'And I'll be here,' Wendy said. 'Maybe you could tell me a bit about Theo while the others are out. I'd like to hear about him.'

Rhona threw her a grateful look. 'Aye. I'd like that.'

They left soon after, Danny and Ruby following them out. 'Be careful, both of you,' Clare said.

'I'll go in with Ruby,' Danny said. 'See she's okay.'

Chris stood watching as they climbed into Danny's XR3i. He gunned the engine and a plume of blue smoke belched out of the back.

'Time that car was serviced,' Clare said, and Chris threw her a look.

'It's a classic. You have to expect a few niggles.'

Clare unlocked the car and they climbed in. She started the engine and sat, letting it idle as their breath steamed up the windscreen. 'Anyway,' she began.

'The jacket?'

'Yep. Are we agreed? It's Danny's jacket? The one he thought he left at the club?'

Chris nodded. 'Has to be. They both reacted to it. But for some reason Danny's keeping that to himself.'

'And he grabbed Rhona's arm to stop her saying anything.'

'So, let's think it through,' Chris said. 'Theo's at the club, yeah? For some reason he takes Danny's jacket. Maybe he forgot his own, or left it somewhere. Either way, it's a cold night so he helps himself to Danny's.'

'But if Theo was killed by the Choker, the jacket doesn't matter. We don't think the Choker knows his victims so he'd likely have killed Theo, whatever he was wearing.'

'Agreed,' Chris said. 'So why would Danny lie about the jacket? Does he have a target on his back?'

'Could be. The question is who has a motive for killing Danny?' And then she remembered. 'That black car, Chris – the day we went to the club.'

He fished in his pocket for his phone. 'I forgot about that. I did check it out, then Theo's body was found and it went out of my head.'

'Who's the registered keeper?'

'Guy called Viggo Nilsen. Address in Dundee.' His brow creased. 'Name rings a bell. I'll check with some of the Dundee lads. See if they know him.'

'More to the point,' Clare said, 'let's ask if this Viggo and Danny have history. I'm starting to think we might have another killer on our hands.'

Chapter 14

Clare dropped Chris at the station, then she headed back to Dundee for the post-mortem, arriving as Neil was beginning. She made her way to the observation room and took out a pad and pen, ready to note anything significant.

'No damage to the clothing,' Neil was saying into his voice recorder. He began cutting the clothes off the body which was now face up on the table, lividity evident on the front where the blood had settled. An assistant bagged and labelled the clothes while Neil removed the protective bags from Theo's hands, examining them closely.

'No evidence of defensive injuries,' he said into the recorder, and he carried on describing Theo's physical characteristics as he scrutinised the body for anything notable. After a minute he waved Clare across. She quickly donned a gown and mask and stepped down to join Neil and his assistant.

'Couple of things,' he said. 'His neck, obviously. I'd expect whatever caused the bruising resulted in his death. I'll know for sure once I've finished but it looks that way.' He moved round to the other side of the body and raised it up by the shoulder. 'Here,' he said, indicating the back of the head, the dark patch Clare had noted last night. The hair was matted with what Clare thought was a mixture of earth and congealed blood. 'It's possible he was stunned first – hammer or something like that. It would be easier to pull something round his neck if he was dazed.' He stood back to let his assistant take photographs.

'When will you know for sure?' Clare asked.

'End of the day.' He looked down at Theo's body. 'Anything else you'd like us to check?'

'I think Raymond's already taken samples from the body but it would be good to know if he had sex the day he died; and if there's any Rohypnol in his system.'

'No problem.' He nodded at his bench of tools. 'It's joinery time. You might want to step back.'

Clare retreated to the observation area, well aware of the smells that would soon fill the room as Neil went through the grim task of opening the abdomen and removing the organs. It was an undignified end to a life but necessary if they were to find the person responsible for Theo's murder.

At half past two she tapped on the glass and indicated to Neil she was leaving.

'I'll be in touch,' he said and he returned to his grim task.

She escaped thankfully, drawing in deep lungfuls as she walked to her car. Her phone had been on silent during the post-mortem and she saw three missed calls from the DCI and a voicemail from Ben. She clicked to play Ben's message and put the phone to her ear.

'*Penny's agreed to one night's surveillance,*' he said. '*I've sent a message round the teams. There's no time for them to have a proper break but I've suggested they go off now and return at five for a briefing.*'

She sent a quick reply thanking Ben then she flicked her phone to hands-free and returned the DCI's call.

'I had a thought,' he said. 'Your operation tonight.'

Clare pulled out onto the Marketgait and headed back towards the Tay Road Bridge. 'What about it?'

'I know you have a few locations covered, but had you thought about Magus Muir car park?'

'Where?'

'You know it,' he said. 'But maybe not by that name. It's on the road running south from Strathkinness. Over the crossroads, as if you're heading for the Craigtoun Road.'

'Oh, I know where you mean. I think there's a bit where you could tuck a car behind the trees.'

'Or a van,' he said.

Clare's mind was working overtime. The teams had all been allocated to the three locations. Every other spare officer was busy with Theo Glancy's murder. She was stretched for manpower as it was. 'Are you at Bell Street?'

'Yeah.'

'I don't suppose…'

'You after more bodies?'

'If possible.'

'Leave it with me,' he said. 'I'll try for Bill and Janey, plus another few.'

'Couple of cars as well, if you can – maybe three. Unmarked.'

'I'm on it.' He ended the call as Clare steered her car up the slip road to the Tay Road Bridge. The sky was clear again, heralding another cold night. She hoped the officers on surveillance would remember their thermals.

She made it into the station just before three o'clock and dumped her work bag in her office. Something was niggling away at her and then she remembered and she lifted the phone to call Ben.

'The previous victims,' she began.

'What about them?'

'Did any of them have wounds to the back of the head? Or other injuries?'

'Hold on.'

She waited and a minute later he was back on the line. 'No. Nothing like that. A couple had scratches, the odd bruise but that's all.'

She hesitated. 'Theo Glancy – I don't think he was killed by the Choker.'

'Because of the head wound?'

'That and the fact that he was killed on a weeknight.'

Ben was quiet for a moment. 'It could have been opportunistic. Maybe the Choker finished his decorating job early, saw Theo walking in the dark and took his chance.'

'And Raymond said something as well,' Clare went on. 'About the Choker not having made much of an effort to conceal the body. Weren't the other bodies better hidden?'

She waited again while Ben tapped at his keyboard. 'Yes and no,' he said. 'He didn't bury them – nothing like that. But he did choose out-of-the-way spots, I'm guessing to delay detection.'

'I think it's a different killer.'

'Clare – I know you feel bad about this one. But it's far more likely to be the Choker.'

'With respect, Ben, I disagree.'

'And that is your right. Look, we've authorisation for tonight. Let's see how that goes then we can reassess.'

She sat on, phone in hand, after he'd ended the call, thinking about Theo Glancy. Was she wrong? Was he the Choker's latest victim after all? They wouldn't know for sure until Raymond's lab was back up and running. In the meantime, if she was right, there was a chance one of the teams would spot the Choker.

–

They arrived just before five and squeezed into a packed incident room.

'Right,' Clare said, raising her voice to get their attention. 'Let's make a start.' She waited until the chatter had died down then went on.

'We have three teams at the moment and, with luck, a few more officers will arrive from Dundee.'

She saw Chris and Max exchange glances.

'Another possible location has come to light,' she explained. 'But let's deal with the ones you've been allocated first.' She moved to the Ordnance Survey map which Jim had pinned on the wall. 'As you'll see, so much of the land round here is flat and exposed. But we have Tentsmuir Forest to the north and there are several locations there to be covered.'

She glanced round the room. 'Where's the Blue Team?'

A group of officers raised their hands and she turned to face them. 'You'll have three cars, covering the main road to the beach car park. I'd like two of the cars dotted along the road, backed into the trees, lights off. Take some *Police Aware* tape and wrap it round so the cars look abandoned. Sergeant Douglas will sort that out for you.' She stopped for a minute to let them make notes, then pressed on.

'Car three will be just before the barrier. There's a cottage near the riding stables, yes?'

They nodded, indicating they knew the location.

'The owner's agreed we can park a car there. You'll have a clear view of any vehicle approaching. The car park barrier will be down by dusk, so our man might head along by the stables. But that is a guess so stay alert.'

She scrutinised their faces. 'Any questions?'

They shook their heads and she went on to the Red Team. 'You'll be at the Tayport end of the forest, concealed before and after the old RAF meteorological station. The station itself is in a mess so it's unlikely our man would use it. But he may try to park behind it, out of sight of the road. So I want one car beyond the station and two before it. Choose your locations so you can block his escape route if necessary. All clear?'

The officers from the Red Team nodded and Clare moved on.

'Yellow Team, you'll cover Morton Lochs car park, up a track between St Mike's crossroads and Tayport. There's a little group of trees at the start of the track, just off the B945. I'd like one car in there but you'll probably have to be out of it to see any vehicles approaching so I hope you're wearing your winter vests!'

There was a ripple of laughter at this and Clare pressed on. 'Second car should be in the car park itself. Unfortunately there's nowhere to hide so chuck some mud around it and use the *Police Aware* tape. Keep your heads down and you should be okay. Third car, beyond the car park please. There's a through road to the forest so be ready to block it off. The good news is there's a dense bit of trees so you'll have no problem concealing yourselves.

'DCI Ratcliffe has given us night vision cameras to capture number plates,' she continued. 'But they don't work well with car headlights so rear-view shots only. Once you have an image, check the registered keeper and advise the other two cars. Any car from out of the area is to be checked and all vans need searched, no matter where they're registered. Okay?'

The officers nodded and she gave them a smile. 'And for God's sake look after those cameras. The DCI says they cost an arm and a leg.'

She scanned the room. 'Let's not forget: this man is dangerous. Be in no doubt of that. I don't want any heroics. If you think you have him, park broadside to prevent him escaping and deploy stingers. Air Support will be on standby in case he legs it. They'll have thermal imaging technology so even if he heads deep into the forest there's a good chance we'll find him. But ideally you want to disable the vehicle and cuff him.'

She looked round at them. 'Any questions?'

They exchanged glances but it seemed she'd covered everything. 'Best get going, then. I want you all in position before dark. Make sure you have stingers in every car and plenty of tape to wrap round the cars. Radio silence, unless and until a vehicle has passed you. We'll be manning the phones back here, checking car registrations as you send them in.' She smiled. 'Good luck, guys. Let's try and nail this bastard.'

The officers began heading for the door. Clare watched them leave and, as the last few drifted out, Bill and Janey, two plain-clothes officers from Dundee, appeared. They'd helped out a few times in the past and Clare knew they could be trusted.

'Your hunky DCI sent us,' Janey said, and Clare suppressed a smile.

'He has his uses.'

'Another couple of cars following,' Bill said. 'Six or seven cops in them.'

'Thank you so much,' Clare said. 'Honestly, I need every officer I can get my hands on.' The door opened and a clutch of officers appeared. Clare recognised some but not all. She thanked them and explained the nature of the operation.

'It's highly confidential,' she said. 'Not a word's to go outside this room, understood?'

They acknowledged this and she went on. 'The teams that have just left are covering three possible locations, but this afternoon I was apprised of another one our man might use.' She led them over to the map and pointed out Magus Muir car park. 'The location's pretty straightforward. One road we can block off at both ends. And there's a farm track not quite opposite where you could conceal a car, and another track at the north end of the road. As far as the south end's concerned, there are some cottages beyond the car park. I haven't had time to contact the owners but if you head over shortly you should find somewhere you can park up.'

She explained about the night vision cameras and Bill nodded. 'Used them before,' he said. 'Nice bit of kit.'

'What about stingers?' Janey asked.

'Definitely; and the *Police Aware* tape will be useful if you can't find a decent hiding place.' They chatted on for another five minutes, discussing the operation, then Bill rose from his seat. 'Sooner we get out there the better.' The others followed him out.

Clare watched them go, listening until the last one had left the station. Suddenly it was so quiet. Sara, Gillian and Robbie were on standby to check vehicle registrations and had gone out to grab some food before the long night ahead.

'We could have fish and chips,' Chris said, cutting across her thoughts.

'Isn't Sara bringing you back something?'

'Nah,' he said. 'It's Friday. Officially our night off eating sensibly.'

She laughed. 'In that case – I'm about to phone Ben. He's heading over soon. Let me check if he wants anything then you can fetch it.'

'You buying?'

'Don't I always?'

'Privilege of rank, Inspector.'

Chapter 15

They sat in the incident room, Clare positively refusing to allow the smell of fish and chips in her office.

'This is really good,' Ben said, squeezing a sachet of brown sauce over his chips.

Chris shook his head. 'Who does that?'

Ben looked at him. 'What?'

'I mean it's probably a disciplinary offence to criticise a DCI, but brown sauce on a fish supper? It's the stuff of nightmares.'

Clare laughed. 'From the man who dunks Wagon Wheels in his coffee.'

Her phone buzzed with a message from the Blue Team. 'Tentsmuir lot's in position,' she said. 'Cars concealed with a view of the road.'

Ben wiped his hands on one of the green paper towels Clare had brought from the kitchen. 'How many teams are there?'

'Four in total. Red's at the old RAF meteorological station, Yellow at Morton Lochs.'

'And the other lot?'

'They've called themselves the Dream Team,' she said, and Ben smiled. 'They're at Magus Muir car park, half a mile south of Strathkinness.'

Ben nodded at this and dipped a chip in the sauce. 'My lot's covering the main routes away from these locations. Set further back – in case he gives your lads the slip.'

Clare's phone buzzed in her pocket. She picked up a paper towel and wiped her hands before clicking to take the call.

'Hi, Clare.' Neil Grant's voice came through the phone and she switched on the speaker. 'PM report will be with you tomorrow. But I can give you the basics now if you want.'

'Please. Just let me get a pen.' She reached over to one of the desks behind her and picked up a pen and notepad. 'Okay, fire away.'

'First of all, the blow to the back of the head was done before he was killed. It most likely stunned him. There were no defensive injuries; but it didn't cause death. That was constriction of the airway.'

Clare noted this down and Neil went on.

'It was smooth,' he said, 'the garotte. I had a look at the PMs for your man's other victims. They were different. The chain markings were quite clear. This isn't the same.'

'Diameter?'

'Not a lot. Maximum five millimetres.'

Ben leaned across towards the phone. 'It's Ben Ratcliffe here,' he said. 'Any idea what it could have been?'

'Some kind of cable, maybe. Not woven like string.'

'Plastic rope?' Clare suggested. 'Like a washing line?'

'Maybe. If you have anything in mind, the lab could match it against the markings.'

'Thanks, Neil. Anything else?'

'Yeah. I'd say he regularly had anal intercourse.'

'Around the time he was killed?'

There was a pause. 'On balance, probably not. He'd showered, but we took swabs and there were traces of semen. Most likely a few hours before he died.'

Clare noted this down. It made sense. Ruby was away. He'd have had the house to himself. Maybe he'd invited someone over, they'd had sex, he'd showered then headed to the club.

'I've sent the samples over to the lab,' Neil said. 'But I gather it's out of commission for a couple of days. I'll type up what I have in the meantime and put it on the system.'

She put down her phone. 'That proves it. I don't think the Choker killed Theo. The garotte's different and he hadn't had sex around the time he died.'

Ben shook his head. 'I hear what you say but there could be any number of reasons he's deviated from his usual routine.'

'It's true,' Chris said, breaking off a piece of fish. 'Saw this programme – on killers.'

They waited while he chewed.

'It's like our sex perverts,' he went on. 'How they start by watching people through windows, pinching underwear from washing lines. Then they move on to exposing themselves, getting more extreme every time. I reckon the Choker's the same. He's had it too easy lately so he's pushing his luck. Seeing how far he can go without being caught.' He picked up a green paper towel and wiped his hands. 'Deep down, he probably wants us to catch him. Wants someone to admire how clever he's been.' He eyed Clare's fish supper. 'You not eating that?'

She shoved the box across the table. 'I must have been out the day you did your psychology degree.'

'It's the lowest form of wit, Inspector.'

Clare's phone buzzed with another message and she swiped to read it. 'Red Team's in place at Tayport. They've managed to conceal all the cars with a good view of the track.' As she spoke another two messages came in confirming all the teams were in place.

'So now we wait,' Ben said.

The incident room door opened. Sara, Robbie and Gillian appeared. Sara eyed the chips boxes. 'You're all going to die before you're fifty,' she said, shaking her head.

'But we'll die happy,' Chris said.

She aimed a fake slap at him and sank down in a chair. 'I'm so full! We had wraps from that Turkish deli. Absolutely delicious but I've eaten far too much.' She glanced at her watch. 'Anything yet?'

Clare shook her head. 'But there is something else you could do while we wait. Can you check all the Glancys for precons please? Or even any charges that didn't make it to court. And I'd like known associates for the whole family – the mother and sister as well. We're looking for anyone who might have a grudge against them. Co-accuseds, neighbour disputes – anything at all.'

Sara rose from her seat. 'I'll boot up some laptops.'

'And keep alert for those vehicle registrations,' Clare added. 'We need quick results on that.'

–

It was half past eight before the first calls started to come in.

'Red Fiat 600 at Tentsmuir,' Sara said, tapping at the keyboard. A minute later she lifted her phone. 'No go. Keeper lives in Glenrothes.'

Gillian took the next call from the team at Tayport. 'Blue Golf,' she said. This too was registered locally.

The yellow team at Morton Lochs were next. 'Boss,' Robbie called. 'Looks like someone's set up shop selling drugs. The team want to know if they should bring them in.'

'Absolutely not,' Clare said. 'Photos of the number plates, head shots if you can get them, but covert, mind. We'll pass it to the drugs guys tomorrow.'

There were no calls at all from the Dream Team at Magus Muir car park and only one van at Tentsmuir. 'The driver opened up the back,' Sara said, reading the message. 'Mostly gardening tools – hedge cutters, leaf blowers – that kind of stuff.'

By one o'clock none of the teams had reported any vehicles for over an hour and Clare stood them down. 'Sorry,' she said, putting her phone on the desk.

'It's fine,' Ben said. 'It was worth a shot.' He rose stiffly and yawned. 'Thanks, though. It was well organised.'

Clare forced a smile. 'I'd really like to give it another go tomorrow. I'm sure Theo's death is unconnected,' but Ben shook his head.

'Penny was quite clear. One night only.'

She watched him go then wandered back to her office, wondering if she was wrong. Maybe Theo *was* the Choker's latest victim. If Chris was correct – that he was becoming bolder, more daring – how many more young men would die at his hands before he was apprehended? It didn't bear thinking about.

She tapped out a message telling the day shift she'd be in for nine and thanking the surveillance teams for their efforts. Then she shut down her computer, switched the phones through to the nearest station at Cupar and locked up.

She drove home, her eyes going automatically to any vans she passed. They were all in darkness, the windscreens frosted. They clearly hadn't been driven for a good few hours.

A volley of barking from Benjy heralded her arrival and she opened the door quickly, shushing him. He scampered past her for a sniff and a pee in the garden then trotted back inside, following her through to the kitchen. The house was chilly after the heated car seat, only the faintest glow from the embers in the woodburner, and she felt the air cold on her nose. She stood for a minute, wondering if she should make a hot drink, then decided against it. She led Benjy back to his basket, tucked a blanket round him and climbed wearily up to bed. The DCI was snoring gently and she shrugged off her clothes, slipping in beside him. He turned to face her, put his arm across and pulled her into the warmth of his body.

Day 5: Saturday

Chapter 16

'Right,' Clare said, calling the day shift to order. 'A quick update. Last night's surveillance went smoothly. The car registration checks were quickly handled and we did pick up evidence of a drug deal. Details of the cars involved have been passed to the drugs team over in Dundee.'

There was a murmur of approval at this.

'But,' she went on, 'all of the vehicles the teams spotted were local, including just the one van. Superintendent Meakin won't authorise another night's surveillance.' She took a moment, choosing her words. 'Current thinking is Theo Glancy's the Choker's latest victim and that he's already left town.'

This was met with silence, officers exchanging glances.

'So, until SOCO are back in their lab I'm afraid that's it.'

Gillian raised a hand. 'Wasn't this one – Theo, I mean – wasn't it different from the previous victims?'

Clare wanted so much to share her misgivings with the team. But Penny had made herself quite clear and she didn't dare undermine her. 'I think,' she began, 'I think it's possible the Choker has changed his MO. For what it's worth, I'd be prepared to give it another night's surveillance. But it's not my decision.'

She saw their faces, saw the disappointment. They were so invested in this case. Like Ben, they were desperate to be the ones to bring the Choker to justice. But it wasn't to be.

'Sorry, guys.' She forced a smile. 'In the meantime, we've had a report of drugs being passed around at Retro's club. We can't go in heavy handed when the owner's just lost her son. But let's do some digging. See what we can find out. It's possible our victim's brother, Danny Glancy, is involved in some way.'

She shared her suspicion that Danny had lied about the jacket. 'While we're working on the assumption Theo is the Choker's latest victim, I suspect Danny may have different ideas.'

'You think someone wants Danny dead?' Sara asked.

'I'm not sure, but it's possible Danny thinks so.' And then she remembered Viggo Nilsen – the way he and the two other men had gone striding towards the club; almost as though they had a score to settle.

'Have any of you come across a tall thin lad called Viggo Nilsen? He possibly has a couple of thick-set guys with him – close-cropped hair. Chris and I saw him at Retro's the other morning, accompanied by two big lads. I'd like to know if he has any connection with Danny or Val.'

'He's a Dundee lad,' Robbie said. 'I haven't come across him but the guys over there might know something.'

Chris said he'd call Dundee and Clare went on. 'We need to find out if there are any links between Danny and Viggo. And there's something else.'

They stopped making notes and waited.

'Retro's is owned by Val Docherty. As you know, we've questioned Val in the past about other matters but she's never been charged with anything. Frankly, I'm suspicious, especially when I hear there's a drug problem at the club. So let's see if we can find any connections at all between Danny, Viggo and Val.'

Robbie raised his hand. 'Danny has a flat in Dundee. Nice block in the City Quay, overlooking the river. Secure parking, lift. Wouldn't be cheap.'

Clare considered this. 'I'll request a warrant to investigate his finances. I'd like to know how he can afford a posh flat. Being dogsbody at Retro's wouldn't pay an expensive mortgage. Can you get his work history as well please?'

Robbie noted this and Clare ended the briefing. She caught Chris's eye. 'Get onto Dundee. I want everything they have on Viggo Nilsen.'

Chapter 17

Chris tapped on Clare's office door then he came in, holding out his phone. 'Got Bill for you. You probably want to hear this for yourself.'

She took the phone from him and clicked to put it on speaker. 'Hi, Bill.'

'Chris says you were asking about Viggo Nilsen.'

'That's right. Do you know him?'

'Aye. We know him, all right. Never been able to pin anything on him but he's a bad lot.'

'Anything special?'

'Girls, drugs, just the usual.'

'Does he have folk working for him?'

'A fair few.'

'Chris and I saw him with a couple of big lads. Well-built, shaved heads.'

'I mean, a few of them are like that. But word is he's using the McCarthy twins. Bruce and Brad. Couple of wall punchers.'

'Nice.'

'Very!'

'I think he may be pushing drugs at our new club, Retro's.'

'That's the family of the lad that died, isn't it?'

'That's them. Thing is, the club's owned by Val Docherty.'

Bill let out a low whistle. 'Now that's interesting.'

'Yes? Could Viggo be supplying Val?'

'Not a chance. It'll be a cold day in hell when those two throw their lot in together. If Viggo's trying to muscle in on

Val's territory, I'd be ready for trouble. That has the makings of a very nasty turf war.'

Clare thought for a minute. 'Bill, if you hear any whispers will you give me a shout?'

'Aye, no problem. I think we'd all be glad to see Viggo behind bars.'

Clare thanked Bill and handed the phone back to Chris.

'What do you reckon?' he said, pocketing the phone.

'I reckon Sean Davis was right about someone dealing drugs at Retro's. The question is which of them was Danny working for – Viggo or Val?' She drummed her fingers on the desk. 'I'm going to give Ben a call,' and she reached for her own mobile.

–

'If you're phoning to ask for another night's surveillance...' he began.

'Just hear me out,' Clare said and she explained about seeing Viggo and the McCarthy twins at the club the day before Theo's body was found. 'There's no love lost between Viggo and Val,' she went on. 'Bill reckons it's a turf war in the making; and we're pretty sure Theo was wearing Danny's jacket the night he died. The MO is different from the Choker's usual. Ben, the Choker did not kill Danny. I'm sure of it.'

He said nothing and Clare sensed he was coming round.

'And that means the Choker may still be planning his next victim. Ben, we have to try again. In fact, if you won't sanction it I'll scrape together as many officers as I can myself.'

'Hold on,' he said. 'Don't do anything. I'll speak to Penny.'

She exhaled, relief washing over her. 'Thank you,' she managed. 'Seriously. Thanks, Ben.'

She sat on, looking at her phone, wondering how long it would take Ben to persuade Penny; and then she thought she'd go mad if she sat in her office any longer.

Chris was in the kitchen, waiting while the kettle boiled.

'Is Danny Glancy back at Rhona's?'

He stopped, kettle in hand. 'Not that I've heard. You want to head over there? Or we could see if he's at his flat?'

She glanced at her watch. Even if Ben gave the go-ahead, there was still plenty time to alert the surveillance teams. And if Danny was at his flat he might be able to tell them something – something he wouldn't admit to in front of his mother.

'Let's do it.'

Chapter 18

As they drove down the A92 towards the Tay Road Bridge, Clare saw a bank of fog rolling in from the North Sea. It was a low channel of cloud gradually swallowing the city of Dundee. Only the top of the hill known to locals as The Law remained visible, along with the jacked-up legs of an oil rig, berthed in the harbour. Above the fog the sky was a grey-blue, a watery sun doing its best against the elements.

'Weird, isn't it?' Chris said as Clare slowed for the roundabout that led to the bridge. The headlights came on automatically as they were plunged into gloom. Moisture began settling on the windscreen and the wipers flicked intermittently across. Suddenly a car loomed up in front and Clare braked sharply.

'No lights,' she muttered, shaking her head. 'No wonder there are accidents.'

As they neared the end of the bridge, the city came into view.

'It's in the City Quay,' Chris said, nodding in the direction of the oil rig.

'Number?'

'Thirty-two.'

She swung the car to the right, entering the City Quay area, and drove down the side of a harbour, bordered on three sides. The last time she'd been here was for a meal at the hotel opposite. She'd sat with the DCI, watching a few hardy souls slipping and sliding over the inflatable water park. But today it was deserted.

'Shut for the winter,' Chris said, following her gaze. 'Left here.'

Clare turned as directed and drove on, past the rusting *North Carr* lightship and the nineteenth-century frigate HMS *Unicorn*. 'I went to a concert on the *Unicorn*,' she said, slowing for a speed bump.

'Some poncey classical stuff?'

'Worse. Jazz.'

He laughed. 'I forgot the DCI was a sophisticate.'

'I nearly fell asleep.'

'I'm with you on that. Next right.'

She followed his directions, turning right, then left again, and she stopped for a moment, looking towards the river. The land on the Fife side sat higher, the road bridge sloping gently upwards across its mile-and-a-half length. It was one of her favourite views. But today there was nothing to see. The river and what lay beyond was lost in the fog.

A gentle peep from behind brought her focus back to the road and she drove slowly along while Chris scanned the buildings for thirty-two.

'Anywhere here,' he said. 'That's it across the road.' He looked ahead then turned back to check behind him. 'Can't see the XR3i.'

'Isn't there a garage round the back?'

'Oh yeah. I think there is.'

Clare pulled into a space and stepped out of the car, feeling a chill from the freezing fog. It was thick now, only the first few spans of the bridge visible, giving it the look of a road to nowhere.

Chris followed her gaze. 'Apparently it's called Steve.'

She stared at him. 'Eh?'

'The bridge. Some online poll a few years ago – to give it a nickname.'

'And they chose Steve?'

'Yup.'

'I don't believe a word of it.'

He shrugged. 'Look it up. It's absolutely true.'

She shook her head and began walking towards Danny's block. Ahead of them, the oil rig stood, its legs and drilling-derrick tall and forbidding in the encircling gloom. Clare stopped again, staring up at it. 'I hadn't appreciated how enormous these things are,' she said, and Chris nodded.

'Mate of mine's a roustabout. Says there's nearly a hundred guys on his rig.'

Clare shivered. 'On a day like this I can't imagine being stuck on one of these, miles offshore.'

Chris began walking again. 'Good money, though.'

She followed him to the main door and they stood looking at an array of buttons built into the wall. Chris lifted his finger to press the buzzer for Danny's flat but Clare pulled his hand away, indicating a glass panel to the side of the door. 'Someone coming out,' she said.

A woman in a parka and jeans pulled the door open. Clare gave her a smile and stood back to let her out, catching the door before it slammed shut.

'Better he doesn't know we're coming,' she said.

A small lift stood towards the back of the hall but Chris shook his head. 'It's only three floors.'

Clare sighed. 'You really need to do something about this lift thing, you know.'

'It's good exercise,' he said, and Clare followed him towards the stairwell. He took the stairs two at a time. 'How do you want to play it?'

'I'm going to be honest with him. Tell him we know Theo was wearing his jacket and ask who might have wanted to harm him.'

'Might be an idea to appeal to his protective side. If we can persuade him to stay with Rhona and Ruby for a few days at least we'll know where he is.'

'I wouldn't hold your breath. I can't see Danny listening to us. But he might give something away if we get him talking.'

They reached the third-floor landing and Chris pulled open a door, scanning the numbers on the wall. 'This way.'

They walked quietly along until they were outside Danny's front door. There was a spyhole but no bell and Clare rapped on the door. She stood, her ear cocked for any sound within but they heard nothing. She tried again. 'Danny? It's DI Mackay.'

A noise behind made Clare whirl round. The door opposite Danny's flat opened and a young man in a grey tracksuit smiled at them. 'Looking for Danny?'

'We are,' Clare said. 'Have you seen him?'

He shook his head. 'Not for a few days. I took a parcel in for him. But he's not been back. Maybe if you see him you'd let him know?'

Clare assured the neighbour she would tell Danny about the parcel and he closed his door.

'So what now?' Chris said.

Before she could answer, her phone began to ring. Ben. She tapped at the screen, and put it to her ear. 'Ben?'

'She said no.'

'What?' Chris's eyes widened but she ignored this. 'Why? Did you tell her—'

'Hold on,' he said, 'if you'll give me a minute to explain.' He paused, as if checking she wasn't going to interrupt then he went on. 'Penny said no, but I'm saying yes. It means the whole thing comes out of my budget but I think you're right so I'm taking the hit. Have your teams ready to go for six p.m.'

She ended the call and began walking, Chris trailing in her wake.

'You want to fill me in?'

She pulled open the door to the stairwell and began running down the stairs. 'Let's get back to the station. We've a night's surveillance ahead.'

Chapter 19

'Message from Raymond,' Jim said, as Clare entered the station.

'Oh yes?'

'He hopes to be back in the lab tomorrow – Monday at latest – and he'll prioritise your results.'

'Excellent. Is that it?'

'Aye. But I gather tonight's back on again?'

She grinned. 'It is indeed.'

–

The teams began arriving just before six.

'Same arrangements as last night,' she told them, 'except you'll swap cars. Remember: every vehicle number's to be checked and every van searched.'

–

The car registrations started arriving just after eight, Sara and Gillian checking them while Robbie continued trawling through the bus station CCTV, muttering about eye strain.

'Of course, he might not be a painter and decorator,' Chris said, twiddling a pen in his fingers.

Clare stared at him. 'You have read the forensic reports on the other victims?'

'Sure. Yeah, they all have traces of decorating materials. But all that tells us is they had contact with that kind of stuff when they were killed. Doesn't mean it's his van.'

'Then whose van would it be?'

'Maybe he's a pal who's a decorator. Lets him borrow the van. Maybe says he's helping someone move house, or he's stuff to take to the dump. I dunno. There's umpteen reasons someone needs a van at the weekend. Could be he slips the friend a few quid, fills it up with petrol so the friend doesn't ask questions.'

Clare was quiet, considering this.

'So, if he's not a painter and decorator, he might be here for a completely different reason. He might even be on holiday. Could have hired a van,' Chris went on.

She shook her head. 'If that's the case, we've been looking at this all wrong.'

'Yup!' He rose from his seat. 'I'll make us a coffee,' and he wandered off to the kitchen. Clare sat on, mulling this over. Her mobile trilled, cutting across her thoughts. Wendy. She rose from her seat and headed back to her office.

'Thought you'd be home by now,' Clare said, when she was back at her desk.

'Yeah. Should have been. But Val arrived so I thought I'd hang around.'

'Problem?'

'I'm not sure. She came to talk about the club. So she said.'

'What about it?'

'Wants to open again. Says they're losing money.'

'I suppose they are,' Clare said. 'What did Rhona say?'

'She wants to stay at home, keep an eye on Ruby. She worries about her social media stuff.'

'She has a point. So what's Val going to do?'

'Says she'll run it for a couple of weeks. Give Rhona a bit of time.'

'Hah!'

'I know. Not like her, is it?'

'She does have a stake in it,' Clare conceded.

'There's something else, though,' Wendy said.

'Go on.'

'Val asked for a mug of tea. I guessed this was to get me out of the way. She took Rhona into the sitting room and waited until the kettle was coming to the boil. So I cracked on I was going to the loo. Left the sitting room door open. They were whispering but I think Rhona told Val about the jacket.'

'You sure?'

'Pretty sure. I heard her saying something about *a big Nike Swoosh on the back*.'

'That's the jacket, all right,' Clare said. She picked up a pen and wrote *Val* on her notepad. 'Is she still there?'

'No. She's gone to make a few calls. See if she can get enough staff to open tonight – recoup some of the money they've lost by being closed.'

Clare sighed. 'As if money matters at a time like this.'

'Money always matters to Val,' Wendy said.

Clare opened her mouth to tell Wendy about Viggo and the McCarthy twins when her office door burst open and Chris stood there, phone in hand. 'We might have him,' he said. 'The Choker. Think they've spotted his van.'

Chapter 20

They gathered round the map Jim had pinned to the wall, Chris tapping the B-road that led to Magus Muir car park. Clare had to fight the urge to jump in the car and drive there herself. It was less than two miles from Daisy Cottage, for God's sake!

'We've a car here,' Chris said, indicating a stretch of road south of Strathkinness. 'It's parked up a farm track, hidden behind trees. Two cops were in the car, ready to block the road. The other two guys were in the trees, further down.'

'White van?' Clare asked.

'Yeah.'

'Has anyone run the reg through the computer?'

'Don't have it yet.'

She studied the map. 'Did it go into the car park?'

'They couldn't see. Another car came down the road, obscuring their view. But the guys parked further up, beyond the car park, said it didn't pass them.'

'Does Ben know?'

Chris nodded. 'He's in radio contact with them. The road's blocked at both ends now and they're moving in.'

'How long ago?'

Chris checked his watch. 'A minute. Two at most.'

Clare couldn't stand it any longer. This was Ben's op. She couldn't interfere but not knowing what was happening was unbearable. 'Can you get one of them on the phone, Chris? It surely doesn't matter about radio silence – not now they've cornered him.'

Chris scanned the list of teams Clare had pinned on the notice board. 'I'll try Janey.'

Clare stood trying to imagine the scene. It was dark, of course. If the road was blocked at both ends the cars would be able to move without headlights. But every second mattered. Right now the Choker could be putting something round his victim's neck. The trees were thick there too, especially on the opposite side of the road. Even if they found the van, saved whoever the intended victim was, the Choker could slip away into the woods. The sky was cloudy tonight. No moon. They could so easily lose him.

She didn't dare phone Ben – distract him from the op. But those woods were so dense; and Ben had asked for her help. If there was one part of Fife she knew it was the woods around Daisy Cottage. She had to make sure he had it covered. She picked up her phone and tapped out a message asking if he had a helicopter on stand-by. He replied immediately.

> Yes. Night vision cameras too.

'Got Janey,' Chris said and he flicked the phone to speaker.

'Moving in.' Janey's voice was low. 'Guys at the far end are in the car park now.'

There was a pause. 'Dammit,' she said. 'Car park's empty. Where the hell's he gone? He definitely didn't go past our car.'

'Any houses up there?' Chris said into the phone.

'Yeah, but the other car's parked ahead of them.'

Suddenly Clare remembered something. 'Janey,' she said, raising her voice, 'there's another farm gate. Opposite side of the road.'

'They've seen it,' Janey said. 'Someone's shouting. I think we've got him.'

The noise from the phone indicated Janey was running and Clare heard shouting in the background. Clearly there was no longer any need to remain quiet. But had they got him? The wait was agony. If they did have him, they'd have saved lives. No doubt about that. This man was dangerous. But, if not…

'It's a white van,' Janey said, breathing hard as she ran. Clare could hear the elation in her voice.

'Don't let him get away.' It was an unnecessary remark but she couldn't help it. Hearing them closing in but not being there to direct operations was agonising. The incident room was silent now, the only sound Janey's breathing coming through the phone.

'They've got him!'

'Definitely?' Clare said. She had to be sure.

'Yes. I can see it. Nearly caught up with them. Bill's just cuffed him.'

All eyes in the room were on Clare, waiting for her reaction, waiting to be sure it was okay to celebrate. She looked round at them, processing the events of the last few seconds. She realised she'd been holding her breath, and as she blew out air the tension left her body.

A cheer went up around the room and Chris thumped her on the back. 'We did it! We got him.'

Clare waited for the noise to die down then she leaned forward to speak into the phone.

'Oh Jesus.' Janey's voice came first. She had stopped running now.

Clare's mouth was dry. Had the celebrations been premature? Were they too late? Had he already killed whoever was in that van? 'Janey?'

'The van,' she said. 'In the back.' She was catching her breath.

Clare sent up a silent prayer for whoever was in the back of that van. 'Janey?' she said again.

'It's not him,' Janey said. 'He's fly-tipping, Clare. Back of the van's full of rubble.'

Clare closed her eyes, a sick feeling developing in her stomach. 'You're sure?' She didn't know why she said it. Of course Janey was sure. She just couldn't believe it.

She heard a shout in the distance and a confusion of conversation.

'Janey? What's happening?'

Janey was running again and Clare could hear the sound of a car engine. 'Janey! For the love of God, tell me what's happening?'

But the only sound was Janey's breath as she kept on running; and then the call cut out.

It was five long minutes before she came back on the phone, the roar of a car being driven at speed in the background. Janey was on the move.

'Sorry,' she began, still breathing hard. 'Not as fit as I used to be. And I had to call Ben.'

'Where are you?'

'We're mobile – heading west from the Strathkinness crossroads.'

Clare moved back to the map and traced her finger along the route. 'Heading for Pitscottie,' she said. 'What's going on?'

Janey explained they'd been busy checking the fly-tipper's van, making sure he didn't escape. 'Then we heard a shout and the cops blocking the road came on the radio. They'd seen another white van driving slowly up from the crossroads. Like it was heading for the car park. It saw our car blocking the road and it birled round.'

'Nothing suspicious about that,' Chris said. 'If the road was blocked they'd have to turn round.'

Clare began to relay this but Janey cut across her. 'Yeah, I heard. But it was the speed that alerted our guys. He'd been driving pretty slowly up the road, as if he was looking for the car park. When he saw our car parked broadside he did the quickest three point turn the cops had ever seen – shot off down the road. Definitely dodgy.'

'Get the number?'

'Only part of it. He switched his lights off and by the time our guys turned their car he'd gone left at the junction so they couldn't see it. But the van's missing a tail light.'

'I'll put a call out.'

'Ben's done it,' Janey said. 'He's sending a car to Pitscottie.'

'From Cupar?'

'Think so.'

Clare stared at the map. 'They might make it. It'll be tight, though.'

'If he turns around, we'll stop him,' Janey said. 'The road's blocked off at Strathkinness as well so if he gets past us he won't get much further.'

There was nothing else to do but wait. And then Janey came back on the phone and Clare's heart sank. 'That's us at Pitscottie now. No sign of him.'

Clare swore under her breath. What the hell could they do now?

'There's at least four different ways they could have gone from there,' Chris said. 'Even if we pull the other cars off their watch points, we wouldn't be in time to cover them all.'

Clare's mind was whirling. He was right. She knew that. She couldn't believe they'd been so close; couldn't believe he'd slipped through their fingers. Damn that fly-tipper. He had no idea the damage his selfish act had done.

'What do you want us to do?' Janey said.

'Sit tight for now. I'll see how many cars Ben can get his hands on.'

'You want the partial registration? Might help.'

'Please.'

'P15,' Janey said. 'Sorry that's all there is. The cop who spotted it thought it looked like the word *piss*. He wasn't 100 per cent sure but he thought that was it.'

'Does Ben have it?'

'Yeah.'

Clare thanked Janey and ended the call. 'I'd better phone Ben,' she said and she sank down in a chair. Mindful he might be busy on the radio, she tapped out a message saying she would call when he was free to talk. But the message wasn't read and, after a few minutes, she put her phone back down.

'So what now?' Chris asked.

She shook her head. 'I have absolutely no idea.'

Chapter 21

'I can't stand this,' Clare said, pacing the room. It was after nine now and still no sign of the van.

'I can't stand you pacing,' Chris said. 'You're like an expectant father. Sit down, for God's sake.'

She sank down into a chair opposite, picked up a pen and began drumming it on the desk, drawing a look from Chris.

'Could you not?'

She looked down at the pen, as if unaware of what she'd been doing. 'Sorry. I hate feeling so useless.'

'You could do us some coffees,' Chris said, but she ignored this.

'Okay.' She sat forward. 'Let's talk it through.'

Chris and Max drew their chairs closer to the desk. 'We're back at the woods,' Max began. 'Car's parked across the road.'

'An unmarked car,' Chris said.

'Right,' Max said. 'The Choker – if it was him – he wouldn't have known it was a police car.'

Clare nodded at this. 'Go on.'

'So maybe he thinks something else is going on.'

'Like what?' Chris said.

'Anything. A drug deal, dog fighting, guns – who knows? Either way, he sees the road's blocked so has to go another way.'

Chris shook his head. 'I don't buy it. Soon as he saw the car across the road he'd have realised it was us. The guys who sell drugs, fight dogs – they don't block roads. They want to keep a low profile. I reckon seeing the car spooked him. He'll be miles away by now.'

'Not necessarily,' Max said. '*We* know organised crime groups don't block roads, but would the average person in the street? Think of the rubbish some of the red-tops print – banging on about police no-go areas, places the emergency services won't go without heavy police back-up. He probably watches *Line of Duty* when he's not murdering young guys. Remember, he knows nothing about the area. He might have seen the car across the road and thought he'd stumbled on something really dodgy; and, if he'd seen any of our guys, they were all pretty scruffy. Cars, too. I doubt his first thought would have been police.'

'You're right,' Clare said. 'Organised crime groups are not nice people; and they don't take kindly to being spotted. I reckon most folk stumbling on something dodgy on a dark November night would be out of there as fast as they could. Especially if they thought someone might come after them.'

'Okay,' Chris said. 'So, if it is the Choker, what's he doing now?'

'Let's wind back,' Clare said. 'Why was he heading up that road in the first place?'

'Magus Muir,' Max said. 'Quiet road – car park's hidden by trees – perfect spot for a bit of murder.'

'So he has his victim in the van,' Clare said, 'maybe already drugged. Then he sees our car blocking the road. He panics and turns the van around.' She looked at the two sergeants. 'What does he do next?'

'He might head for one of the other spots we're covering,' Chris said, reaching for his phone. 'I'll just warn them about the broken tail light.'

'No point,' Clare said. 'He went in the opposite direction. Where might he go?'

'From Pitscottie, pretty much anywhere,' Chris said. 'It sits on a crossroads.'

'Plenty of woods around there,' Max said.

'Yeah, maybe.' She frowned. 'I wonder if seeing something going on at Strathkinness would put him off isolated spots? It might have freaked him out.'

Chris nodded. 'Yeah, could be. And it's not like he needs to be in the middle of a dark wood. Nobody's going to see in the back of an old van.'

'And the victim would be incapable of crying out,' Max added.

'He could park anywhere quiet,' Clare said. 'So where's the best place to park a white van at night?'

'I'd go for an industrial estate,' Chris said. 'Loads of vans parked up there at night.'

'He's heading west,' Max said. 'So…'

'Cupar Trading Estate,' Chris said. 'It's perfect. It'll be deserted at this time of night and a white van parked up with lights off wouldn't attract any attention.'

'Sometimes,' Clare said, getting to her feet, 'just sometimes, I remember why I let you be my sergeant.' She nodded at the door. 'Come on. We've a serial killer to arrest.'

Chapter 22

'Shouldn't you tell Ben?' Chris said, pulling on his seat belt.

Clare checked over her shoulder and reversed out of the parking space. Max, waiting behind in another unmarked car, followed her out of the car park and into the street.

'I'm not interfering with his operation,' she said. 'Anyway, if I told him he might tell me not to get involved.'

'And you're getting involved because?'

'Let's put it this way – if we don't find anything, we were never there.'

'You sound more and more like me every day.'

'Shut up and get on the phone. See if Bill and Janey are free to follow us over. But subtle, mind. I don't want this on the radio in case we're wrong.'

As they crested the rise at the West Port, a crowd of students began stravaiging across the road, singing tunelessly. One, a young man wearing a top hat, walked backwards, his arms waving like sails on a windmill.

'He must be the conductor,' Chris muttered, as Clare blasted the horn. The students jumped, then, seeing the car had slowed, made theatrically slow progress towards the pavement.

'If I wasn't in such a rush,' Clare said, her expression darkening.

Finally the road cleared and Clare put her foot to the floor. She glanced left as they shot past the bus station.

'Robbie had any luck with that CCTV?'

'Hundreds of vans,' he said.

Clare shot him a glance. 'Seriously? On a Wednesday night?'

'He might be exaggerating.'

'Just a touch.'

They were passing the Old Course Hotel now, almost at the point where Theo Glancy had died. SOCO's tent was gone, their investigations complete. There were a few bunches of flowers and someone had placed a placard against a tree. *RIP THEO*, it read. A string of fairy lights was draped around it making the base of the tree seem like a shrine. The lights made her think of Christmas. It would be a tough one for the Glancys.

'Rotten time of year to lose someone,' she said.

'Yeah. Especially like that.' He sighed. 'And, if Danny was the intended target—'

'Needle in a haystack,' Clare said. 'If what we hear about Danny's correct, there's no shortage of likely candidates.'

The Strathkinness junction came into view and Clare glanced left, looking up the road. There was nothing to be seen, of course. The village was over a hill, a couple of miles to the south but she wondered what was happening. The operation had changed now – no longer covert. 'I wonder what Ben…' She stopped as her phone lit up, the ringtone cutting through the air.

'That'll teach you,' Chris said. 'It's him. Want me to answer it?'

For a moment she hesitated. 'Go on, then.'

'I'm at your station,' the voice boomed over the speaker. 'One of your PCs told me you'd gone after the Choker.'

They were approaching the roundabout at Guardbridge now and she pressed down on the brake.

'Inspector?' he said, suddenly formal.

'Sorry,' she said. 'I've an idea where the Choker may have gone. There wasn't time to let you know.'

Clare skirted the roundabout, heading up the road towards Cupar. She saw Chris's eyes go to the chip shop, the lights bright against the November darkness, but Ben was speaking again.

'You've an idea where he's gone and you're haring after him without any back-up? A man we think has already killed five times?' His tone was sharp. 'We'll discuss this later. Just tell me where you are and where you're heading.'

'We're leaving Guardbridge, heading west,' she said. She explained about the trading estate. 'We'll be there in five minutes – ten, tops.'

'I'm on my way,' Ben said. 'Wait for me.'

'Sorry, Ben. Can't do that. We need to get into that van. Max is following behind. He'll block off the entrance to the estate while we go round, looking for the van. But if there are any cars available…'

'Hold on.' She heard him radioing then a minute later he came back on the phone. 'Most of Cupar cars are out at Magus Muir. They'll send what they can. And, Clare?'

'Yes?'

'No heroics.'

Ben ended the call and Clare pressed down on the accelerator. Every minute could be a minute nearer losing whoever was in that van. Chris's phone buzzed and he swiped to read the message. 'Bill and Janey passing Guardbridge now,' he said.

Clare nodded but said nothing.

'How much of a start do you reckon he has on us?' Chris said.

She slowed for a roundabout then accelerated towards the village of Dairsie, ignoring the speed limit sign. 'Ten minutes. What you thinking?'

'The Rohypnol. How long does it usually take – to make the victim helpless?'

'Depends,' Clare said. 'Anything from twenty minutes to an hour or two.'

'Okay. I reckon – Jesus, Clare!' He stuck out his feet, bracing himself as Clare took a corner too fast.

'Sorry.' She ran a hand through her hair. 'Go on.'

He drew his feet back again and carried on. 'I reckon the victim would still have been pretty lucid by the time they saw our car at Magus Muir. The Choker does a swift one-eighty and heads for Pitscottie. The trading estate's another ten, maybe fifteen minutes. Might even be longer. Once he'd shaken Janey off he probably slowed down to avoid drawing attention to himself.'

'So by the time he gets to Cupar—'

'His victim's starting to get sleepy,' Chris said. 'Probably incapable of getting himself into the back of the van. Van's likely got a bulkhead—'

'So he'd have to get out, go round to the passenger door and help him out,' Clare said, picking up the thread. 'And maybe he's losing consciousness so he has to lift him.'

'Exactly.' Chris was nodding. 'He has ten minutes on us, but there could have been a bit of a delay while he worked out where to go so he might not be that far ahead.'

Clare was quiet for a moment. 'You don't think he'd be freaked out by seeing the cars at Magus Muir? Abandon his plan – drop whoever he's picked up by the side of the road?'

'That kind don't get freaked out,' Chris said. 'He probably gets off on the adrenaline rush. And he can't just drop him off. He might remember the van registration. Give us a description of the Choker. He has to see it through.'

'Then let's hope we've made the right call.'

Chapter 23

'It's just coming up,' Chris said. He glanced at the speedo. 'Maybe slow down a bit.'

'I know!'

'And signal to let Max know.'

'Godsake, Chris! Cut it out.' She checked her mirror then flicked the signal. The sign for the entrance to the trading estate loomed up and she pressed down on the brake. 'Happy?'

'Delirious.'

'Thing is, though…' She pulled off the road and came to a halt, leaving enough room for Max to park behind. 'There's another estate further along the road. Not as big, but he might have gone there.'

Chris stepped out of the car and Clare followed. He stood looking west along the A91. 'I know it,' he said. 'Sara likes the garden centre. She's had me in looking at lawn mowers as well.' He shook his head. 'I reckon this one's a better bet. More buildings to hide behind.'

Max appeared at Clare's shoulder. 'What's the plan?'

Clare looked back at the junction. The road was so wide here. Impossible to block it off. 'We need more cars,' she said. 'But we haven't the time.'

A flashing orange indicator caught Clare's attention and she saw another car approaching from the direction of the town. Was this the Choker? Had he missed the turning and doubled back? There was no time to conceal themselves; but as the vehicle came closer relief swam over her. A police car. She raised her arm to flag it down. It stopped beside Clare's car and an officer she didn't recognise jumped out.

'Another car on its way,' he said. 'Two or three minutes.'

'Right,' Clare said. 'I want this junction blocked off and the whole estate searched. White van possibly with P15 as part of the reg.'

'I've a thermal imaging camera back at the station,' the officer said. 'Might help find the van if the engine's still warm.' He picked up his radio. 'I'll get it brought along.'

Clare took in the estate, her eye sweeping over the different roads. They were all dead ends so there was no way out for the Choker but there were so many places he could have hidden his van; and they didn't have time to wait for the camera. She heard the sound of another vehicle approaching and seconds later she saw one of the cars from Magus Muir pulling into the estate, Bill at the wheel.

Janey leaned out of the passenger window. 'Ben's right behind us. He must have put his foot to the floor.'

Clare could have hugged Janey. Suddenly it seemed possible. Maybe they could arrest the Choker before he harmed whoever was in his van. 'Right,' she said. 'Let's divide the roads up.'

The Cupar officers explained the layout of the estate. 'If it was me,' a red-haired PC called Will said, 'I'd head for the old sugar beet silo. Dead quiet down there. Plenty places to tuck a van in behind.'

'We'll take that,' Clare said. She turned to see another car swinging into the estate. Ben. He jumped out as Nita arrived from the opposite direction. For a brief moment Clare's heart swelled with pride. There was nothing finer than seeing officers dropping everything for an emergency. But time enough for that when they'd caught the Choker. If they caught him.

Ben listened to the plan and he nodded. 'Good work,' he said. 'I'll stay here with my car. The rest of you, slowly does it and lights off, unless you absolutely can't see a thing.'

They went to their cars. Clare waited until the others had headed off, then she swung her car onto the narrow road that ran along the top of the estate, parallel to the A91. They passed a car dealership and she slowed while Chris checked for white vans.

The road veered round to the left and the lights from the car showroom faded.

'Back of the garden centre,' Chris said, indicating a fence on the right.

She glanced over to the fence but said nothing, her eyes darting all round as she crawled along. It was cloudy now, no light from the moon, and she strained to see the road ahead. It sloped downwards slightly and she stuck her feet on the clutch and brake pedals to minimise engine noise, stopping at every building to look for vehicles. And then she braked sharply. A white van backed into a gap between two buildings. Chris was out of the car, moving noiselessly, crouching low as he approached. Clare saw him put his hand on the bonnet then shake his head. He took out his phone and switched the torch on briefly, just long enough for them to see the registration was wrong. He ran back to the car and poked his head in the door.

'You keep driving. I'll shine my torch behind for you to follow. Easier to check vans if I'm on foot.' He darted off without waiting for an answer. Clare crawled along behind, following the light from the torch. Chris stopped periodically to check more vehicles then back to the road again. The bulk of the iconic concrete silo loomed up, the dark outline unmistakable, despite the lack of light.

And then they saw it. It was parked nose in behind the silo. End of the road. A good hiding place, Clare thought. But not good enough. She slowed right down, swinging the car round to block the road and climbed out, padding softly over to the van, her breath condensing in the night air. Chris shone his phone torch on the number plate and she knew they'd found it. As he approached from the rear, Clare tapped quickly at her phone, dropping a pin to let Ben know her location. There was no time to send a message and she hoped he'd realise why she'd sent it.

Chris motioned for Clare to approach the passenger door while he checked the driver's side. She crept round and looked in the window. No one there. And then she heard sounds coming from inside the van. They ran round to the back, Clare trying to remember if it was possible to lock this type of van from inside. But there was no time to check. They had to get in. Chris wrenched it open and Clare moved forward, her phone raised, ready to shine the torch on the interior. Suddenly the phone flew from her hand as a figure leaped from the back of the van, a foot striking her on the chest. She fell back, in time to see the figure side-step Chris and melt into the darkness.

She gasped, catching her breath, and felt a pain in her chest. 'Go after him,' she wheezed, and Chris took off into the darkness. She scrambled to her feet, squinting to find her phone; and then she remembered she could send an alert from her watch. Clutching her chest, her fingers trembling, she tapped in the passcode and hit the *Find Phone* icon. She heard the ping and began feeling around on the ground, hitting the alert again and again until the sound took her to where it had fallen. She scooped it up and tapped at it, entering the passcode. Nothing happened. She tried again and still she couldn't get in. Dammit, she thought. Was this one of the phones that only gave you three chances? She took a deep breath in and out, wincing at the pain in her chest, and tried again, slower this time. The phone came to life.

She could hear shouts in the distance as word about the Choker spread. A flash of headlights told her a car was approaching but there was no time to wait. She had to find out what – or who – was in the back of that van. She clicked the camera icon and switched to video. A grainy screen appeared and she pointed it towards the van, tapping the flash. She clicked to start the video, her heart thumping, and the back of the van was illuminated as the flash came on.

Chapter 24

'I'm entering a white Transit van, found parked at the trading estate in Cupar,' she said into her phone, the camera trained on the figure lying face down in the back of the van. Suddenly it was bathed in light from Ben's car. He jumped out and indicated Clare's phone.

'Is that recording?'

'Yes. I'm just—'

'Stay there. I'll check him. But keep recording.'

Without waiting for an answer, he stepped into the back of the van, Clare standing at the door, still videoing. He bent over the lifeless figure, two fingers at the neck. 'Got a pulse,' he said. 'Pretty strong. No obvious sign of injury,' and he took out his phone to call for an ambulance.

The call done, he directed Clare to video the whole interior of the van. At the far end, up against the bulkhead, were the decorator's tools: pasting table, assorted brushes, tins of paint and a collapsible ladder. A set of paint-stained overalls was neatly folded to one side next to a plastic tub filled with bottles of clear liquid – white spirit, Clare guessed, although it could have been whatever he'd drugged his victims with. The rest of the floor was covered in a double sleeping bag and two grubby cushions. In the centre of this a man lay face down, his jeans and boxers pulled down to his knees. And next to him, dangling from a hook on the side of the van, was a long steel chain.

'Zoom in on that,' Ben said, indicating the chain. He jumped down from the van to give Clare a clear view, bumping into her as he landed. She cried out as the pain shot through her chest again.

'You're hurt,' he said. 'What happened?'

She dismissed this. 'I'm fine. Took a hit to the chest, but I'm okay.'

'I'll ask the paramedics to look you over.'

'No!' Her voice was sharper than she intended, the effort of raising it a painful one. 'I mean, he's priority. We need him alive.' She nodded at him, one arm clutched round her chest, the video still running. 'If you have that camera, get after him. Chris went round the back of the silo. I'll wait for the ambulance, then I'll join you.'

Ben ran back to his car to retrieve the thermal imaging camera and Clare ended the video. She heard him radioing for the helicopter, then the car door slammed and he executed a swift turn, heading back up the road. Suddenly she was alone with the unconscious figure. Or was she? She couldn't imagine the Choker coming back to the van, creeping up behind her and reclaiming his victim. No, he'd be as far away as his legs could carry him. But there was something about the darkness, so dense and all-consuming it made the hairs stand up on the back of her neck. And then she thought of this man, lying in the back of the van, half undressed and drugged, and the instinct to protect him lit a fire in her aching chest.

'Come on if you dare, you bastard,' she said into the inky darkness. 'Bring it on!'

A siren split the night air, distant at first, but coming ever nearer. 'Almost here,' she whispered to the unconscious figure in the van. 'Just hang on.'

She ran to her car to retrieve a pair of nitrile gloves then she went back to the van, pulling open the driver's door. The keys were gone but the interior light let her see the controls. She turned on everything she could find and the hazard warning lights lit the sky with their rhythmic flashing. The siren was close now and she saw the ambulance. She put up a hand to shield her eyes from the lights and waved her other hand to ensure they'd seen her. The ambulance drew up next to her car and she went to meet the paramedics.

'Adult male, unconscious, possibly drugged with Rohypnol or similar. Pulse regular.'

They nodded at this and Clare stepped back as they went about their checks. She tapped her phone to call SOCO.

'Absolute priority,' she said. 'I need a team to go over the interior of a transit van; and a possible murder weapon, associated with previous killings.' The call done, she watched as the man was wheeled up a ramp into the back of the ambulance. 'Any ID?' she asked.

A tall paramedic began checking the man's pockets and she withdrew a wallet from his jacket.

'Let me get an evidence bag,' Clare said, and she rushed over to her car, holding her chest as she went. When she returned a minute later the paramedic was regarding her with a critical eye.

'You hurt?'

'Just bruising.'

'Want us to check you over? If it's a cracked rib you could end up with a collapsed lung. Not recommended!'

She saw their point. 'I'll head over to A&E after this. I'm more concerned about him.'

'See you do,' the paramedic said, dropping the wallet into the evidence bag. 'I don't want your death on my conscience.'

A few minutes later, their checks completed, they slammed the ambulance doors and the driver climbed into the cab. The siren burst into life once more, almost deafening Clare, and they pulled away, leaving her entirely alone.

Suddenly she felt vulnerable there in the darkness, and her fingers went to her radio, seeking reassurance. Was the Choker hiding somewhere? Watching her? Had he doubled back, planning on jumping into a police car to make his getaway? She was being ridiculous. She knew that. 'You've been watching too many scary films,' she told herself. All the same...

She went quickly back to her car and checked the boot and back seats before climbing in and locking the doors. Only then did she pull on a clean pair of gloves and take the wallet out of the evidence bag. A Bank of Scotland card was in the first pocket and she eased it out to check the name. Mr F Coverdale. She breathed a sigh of relief. They had a name; and, if he recovered, he might have vital information that would lead them to the Choker.

But where was the Choker now?

A rap on the window made her jump and she winced at the pain in her chest. She'd definitely have to get it looked at. With the interior light on she couldn't see outside.

'Who is it?'

'Me – Max.'

She clicked to unlock the doors and he climbed into the passenger seat, shivering. 'Mind turning on the engine? It's freezing out there.'

Clare started the engine and turned up the heater. 'What's happening?'

'They think he's headed for the river. Could be anywhere really but Nita brought night vision goggles from Cupar and she definitely saw a figure heading west along the river bank. Ben's got a team on both sides and they're making their way back along the bank towards here. Based on when Nita saw him, he won't have got away. I reckon they'll force him back this way.'

'How far away's the copter?'

'Another ten minutes, Ben says. Dog handlers have arrived, though.'

Clare sat thinking. 'Are they all down there?'

'At the river? Think so,' Max said. 'The road's still blocked off so he can't get out that way. Ben's pulled the other teams off their surveillance so we've pretty much got this place surrounded.'

Clare looked beyond Max, out of the window. The estate was like a rabbit warren of roads and yards, buildings, containers

– there were so many places he could hide. He could be running from one hiding place to the next. And if he was hiding under something solid, the thermal image cameras wouldn't pick him up.

She navigated to the maps icon on her phone and switched it to satellite view, staring at it for a few minutes. Then she tapped the screen. 'We're here,' she said. 'That's the top of the silo.' She held the phone out for him to see and he nodded. 'And that' – she moved the screen to the left – 'is the other side of the silo.'

Max peered at the screen and Clare went on.

'These rectangles – they must be trailers. I saw some of them as we drove round here. He could easily hide under one of them.'

'And the cameras wouldn't pick him up,' Max said.

'Nor would the copter.'

Max glanced across to where the trailers were parked. 'You want to head over there?'

'I've a better idea.' She picked up her phone and dialled Ben's number.

She could tell he was on the move when he answered. 'You okay?' he said.

She ignored the question. 'How many dogs are there?'

'Three.'

'Good. Can I have one up near the silo please? There's somewhere I think we should check.'

Chapter 25

The dog was called Pasha and Clare heard him before she saw him, the hoarse panting an unnerving sound in the cool night air.

'You got anything belonging to the target?' the handler said. Clare vaguely recognised him. Dean, she thought. Yes, that was it. Dean Cochrane.

She led him round the side of the van and opened the driver's door. 'Let him have a sniff in there.'

Pasha jumped up and began sniffing the seat and Clare took the opportunity to scan the cab. Her eye fell on a half bottle of Smirnoff and she made a mental note to have SOCO analyse it.

'There's a set of overalls in the back,' she said when Pasha had sniffed every corner of the cab. 'But I'd really like SOCO to go over the van first.'

Dean waved this away. 'This'll do. Where's the search area?'

'It's just beyond the silo,' Clare said. 'My guess is he wasn't quick enough, heading for the river. I reckon he'll have heard the commotion and doubled back this way. There's a load of trailers parked the other side of the silo. If I was him I'd hide under one of them.'

'No problem. Ready?'

'Just let me cover his possible exit routes,' Clare said. She took out her radio and began directing officers. 'Bill and Janey, take the entrance to the trailer area. Chris, I want another two with you to the east of the trailers. Radio when you're there and we'll send the dog in.'

The wait seemed endless but finally they were all in position. Using her phone torch, Clare led Dean and Pasha round the silo. Her eyes had become accustomed to the darkness now and she saw the outline of the trailers. Pasha began straining at the lead and she nodded to Dean. He strode off into the darkness, Pasha's nose to the ground. Clare held her breath. If she'd guessed wrongly and taken officers away from the Choker's original escape route, he might slip past them. Admittedly they had his van now. And, unless it was stolen or hired in a false name, it would give them an identity. That meant a photo and, with nationwide coverage, there was every chance they'd catch him. But this operation – it was the biggest she'd ever commanded. Obviously, Ben was in charge; and he'd be the one answerable to Penny if they didn't catch the Choker. But it was Clare's advice – her instinct for what this man might do – that had guided tonight's operation. So far she'd guessed correctly. They'd tracked him to this quiet spot. They'd found his van and hopefully saved the victim's life. But could they apprehend the Choker?

The wait seemed endless, the only sound Pasha's hoarse breathing and Dean's footsteps as he ran to keep up with the dog. She waited for barking, for the sound of voices, the shouts and instructions that would tell her Pasha had found his target. But the shouts didn't come. Five minutes passed, then ten and still nothing. The moon had disappeared behind clouds now and, even with headlights from vehicles peppered across the estate, the dark felt all encompassing. Finally she heard footsteps and saw the light from Max's torch.

'No go,' he said and Clare's heart sank. 'Pasha's on the trail but he's leading Dean down to the river and he's not keen without lights. The bank's too uneven.'

'We can't let him go,' Clare said, her voice shrill. She jerked her head towards the darkness. 'He's out there, Max. All these officers – surely they can find him?'

The light from another torch approached and she recognised Ben's gait as he joined them. 'I'm calling it for tonight. It's too dangerous with him heading for the river.'

'But…'

'No buts. There's a collection of houses and barns further east. We have a car down that end if he makes it that far. And we'll have roadblocks on all possible routes. Cupar are organising that now. But there's a little footbridge over the river. Judging by Pasha's behaviour, we think he's gone over that.'

'What's on the other side?' Clare asked.

'Farmland. I've sent a car round to the farm and it'll stay there until first light when we can resume the search. In the meantime we've covered all possible escape routes. His only alternative is to go into the river. And in these temperatures…'

She saw the light from another torch coming closer and a few seconds later Chris joined them. 'Roadblocks are in place,' he said. 'They'll stop and search every car. Anyone who can't produce ID will be detained while they're checked out.'

'And the farm?'

He nodded. 'Car's there now and the farmer's aware.'

'Good. Right. Anyone who's not at a checkpoint straight home. We begin again at six a.m. And you' – he looked pointedly at Clare – 'are off sick for the next few days. At least until you're checked out.'

Clare put a hand to her ear, affecting deafness. 'Sorry,' she said. 'I didn't catch that.'

'S'okay,' Chris said, leading her towards the rough grass. 'I'll tell you.'

'Traitor.'

–

The duty doctor at the St Andrews hospital was waiting at reception when Clare and Chris arrived. He was slim and dark, with thick hair swept back from his face. He greeted them and his eyes travelled to Clare's arm clutched round her chest.

'I'm guessing you're the chest pain,' he said. He led Clare to a small room and helped her off with her coat. She explained what had happened and he lowered the bed, waiting for her to ease herself down. She loosened her top and he pressed gently, apologising when she winced with the pain.

'You're going to have some wonderful bruises,' he said, helping her to sit up again. He sounded her chest, asking her to breathe in and out as he listened through his stethoscope. After a few minutes he indicated he was finished and he helped Clare off the bed and onto a chair.

'I think your ribs are bruised,' he said. 'Pretty badly, judging by the marks on your chest, but I don't think they're cracked or broken. I'd X-ray them now but the department's shut for the night. I suggest you head over to Ninewells and get an X-ray there to be on the safe side.'

Clare sighed. She was tired, sore and she wanted nothing more than to get home to Daisy Cottage and fall into bed. 'Is it really necessary? It'll be mayhem up there. I'll sit for hours and chances are they're not broken anyway.'

He inclined his head. 'You're right, of course; and the treatment's the same whether they're bruised or broken. On balance, an X-ray's probably not needed.' He turned to the keyboard on his desk and began tapping at it. A moment later the printer came to life. He reached across and withdrew the printout, handing it to her. Clare scanned it quickly. *Rib fractures and chest injuries.*

'Study that,' he said. 'If you experience any of the warning signs listed, or the pain worsens, you must seek medical help.' He rose from his chair. 'If you wait here I'll fetch some painkillers. And I'll write up a prescription you can take to the pharmacy tomorrow.'

Chris was waiting at the end of the corridor. He indicated a side door. 'Nurse says we can slip out here.'

Five minutes later, Chris crunched into the drive at Daisy Cottage.

The DCI, no doubt alerted by the headlights, came out and walked round to open the passenger door. 'Out you come,' he said, his tone matter-of-fact. But his eyes betrayed the concern he felt.

Clare eased herself out of the car and accepted his arm. The duty doctor had given her a painkiller, with a warning it would make her very sleepy, and she was feeling the effects now. She walked slowly, leaning on the DCI, mumbling her thanks to Chris. She could hear Benjy barking somewhere but she couldn't work out where he was. 'Jeez,' she said, 'these painkillers – it's like Benjy's somewhere else.'

'He is, you numpty,' the DCI said, closing the front door behind her. 'I didn't want him jumping up and hurting you so he's shut in the kitchen.'

She smiled at this and made for the sofa. 'I'll just—'

'No you don't,' he said, taking her arm and steering her towards the stairs. 'Chris says they gave you a pretty strong painkiller. If I don't get you up these stairs now you'll end up sleeping on the sofa.'

'Fine by me,' she slurred. But she allowed herself to be propelled up the stairs. It was cool in the bedroom, the bed turned down, and suddenly she was outstandingly tired. She kicked off her shoes and sat down gingerly.

'You might want to go to the loo,' he said. 'Before you get too sleepy.'

But it was too late. Clare was lying down now, tucking her feet beneath the duvet. The pain didn't seem so bad and she reached down, feeling for the rest of the covers. But they were out of reach.

The DCI bent and gently pulled them over, kissing her softly on the forehead. 'Sleep tight,' he whispered.

She opened her lips to reply but the words wouldn't come. The tablet the doctor had given her seemed to have furred her thinking and she felt herself slipping further and further into a deep and dreamless sleep.

Day 6: Sunday

Chapter 26

'Why the hell didn't you wake me?' Clare snapped and the DCI held out his hands as if defending himself.

'You were dead to the world. Anyway, it's only half seven. You have a serious injury and Chris said you were on compulsory sick leave. Maybe you should lean on your team. Let them do their jobs, eh?'

She eased herself up on her elbows, grimacing at the pain. 'It's because I'm injured that I'm so invested,' she said, putting an arm round to cradle her ribs. She swung her legs out of bed. 'I wanted to be there, Al. Don't you get it?'

He stared at her for a minute then he turned and walked out of the room. Clare rolled her eyes. She hadn't time for a row. She needed to know what was going on. Her phone was on the bedside table and she glanced at the display. Thirteen per cent.

'Dammit,' she said, cursing herself for not plugging it in. But she couldn't even remember getting to bed. In fact she couldn't remember much after getting out of the car at Daisy Cottage. She looked round for the charger and saw the cable trailing on the floor. Clutching her ribs as tightly as she dared, she reached down for it, stifling a groan. She plugged it in and dialled Chris's number. It went to voicemail so she tried again. Then she tried Ben.

'Not now,' he said. 'We're doing the changeover from the night shift,' and, with that, he ended the call.

She stared at the phone for a moment then hauled herself to her feet and wandered through to the bathroom. She had slept in her clothes and now she undressed gingerly, trying to move as little as possible. It took twenty minutes for her to shower and dress in fresh clothes. By the time she wandered downstairs the DCI was making bacon sandwiches, the sound of Jazz FM tinkling in the background. Benjy had been sitting at his feet, his face upturned for any stray bits of bacon. Then he saw Clare and trotted over. She put down a hand to pat him and he began licking it. The DCI glanced up.

'Fancy a sandwich?'

'I'd love that. And, sorry – for being a bitch. You didn't deserve that.' She leaned across to plug in her phone, still low on charge, and grimaced as her ribs protested.

He took the cable from her and plugged it into a socket on the wall. 'It's fine.'

She eased herself down on a chair and glanced at the phone. 'Dammit, I missed Chris – while I was in the shower.' She clicked to return the call.

The DCI put a plate of sandwiches on the table. 'Help yourself. Coffee's on.'

'Chris? What's happening? Where are you? I've only just wakened.' She clicked to put the phone on speaker and set it down on the table. She looked pointedly at the radio and the DCI took the hint, turning it down low. Then he brought a cafetière over to the table and plunged it.

'We're pretty sure he crossed the river last night,' Chris said, the phone buffeted by the wind. 'There's a little footbridge just downstream of the trading estate. Pasha's taken Dean over there and they're working their way across the farmland.'

The DCI put two mugs down on the table and poured the coffee. Then he sat opposite Clare and began to eat.

'Looks like he made for the farm,' Chris said, his breath coming fast. 'There's a roadblock beyond it so he's either hiding somewhere or he's heading for one of the villages – Kemback or Dura Den.'

'How many officers are there?'

'Maybe twenty or thirty. If he's still here we'll get him.'

Suddenly a volley of barks came through the phone. She could hear shouting now. 'Chris?'

There was no reply, just the sound of him breathing hard. He must be running.

'Chris?' she said again.

And then the call ended.

Chapter 27

The wait was interminable. Clare ignored the DCI suggesting she eat something.

'At least drink your coffee,' he said and she put the mug to her lips and sipped at it. Then she set it down and stabbed *Redial* repeatedly on her phone.

'Maybe you should leave it a few minutes,' he said. 'Sounds like they're right in the middle of it. They won't want any distractions.'

She threw him a look. 'So that's what I am? A distraction? And there was me thinking I was the station DI.'

He made no reply and rose from his seat, carrying his mug and plate over to the sink. Then he began washing up as Clare kept hitting *Redial*.

Finally the call connected, Chris's breath the only sound for the first few seconds.

'What's happening?' she said. 'Have you got him?' She could hear barking and shouting and for a few seconds he didn't reply.

'I think I can see him,' he said eventually. 'He's across the next field and he's running. Dean's let the dog off the lead.'

The DCI whistled to Benjy and opened the back door to let him into the garden. Benjy, his head resting on Clare's knee, eyed him then slowly padded towards the door.

'Can you still see him?' Clare said into the phone.

'No. The land dips here. I'm trying to get higher up.'

And then there were more shouts, Dean's stentorian command, and she held her breath, hardly daring to hope. It was a full two minutes before Chris spoke again. The shouting was closer now, Dean firing off instructions, telling someone to lie still. There was screaming, the sound of a man in pain and she hoped it was the Choker. Hoped Pasha had bitten him good and hard. She wanted him terrified!

Chris was breathing faster now and she thought he must be running. And then the words she'd waited so long to hear came over the phone.

'We've got him! At least I hope it's him. Dean's cuffed him and Ben's checking him for ID.'

'Make sure it's him,' Clare said. 'If Pasha's found a rough sleeper the Choker's still out there.'

There were lots of voices now, instructions being fired off, Dean praising Pasha and through all this the sound of someone squealing in pain. She waited and finally she heard Chris's voice cutting through the chaos. 'Dean's pretty sure the man Pasha found has the same scent from the van. Obviously we'll need DNA but it looks like it's him.'

She felt tears pricking her eyes, a mix of emotions – the pain in her ribs, the frustration of not being there to see him arrested and the sheer relief of knowing they had him.

The DCI and Benjy came back into the kitchen, the little dog straight to her side. 'You okay?' the DCI said and she nodded.

'I think they've got him.' She reached across the table and took a tissue from a box, wincing as she blew her nose, the effort causing a spasm of pain. 'It's just the relief.'

He smiled. 'I know,' and he bent and kissed her gently on the head.

–

'Chris says his name's Leon Maddox.' Clare squinted at her mobile. 'Fifty-two, lives in South Shields. They've taken him to hospital but hopefully he'll be fit to be interviewed.' She looked round for her work bag, no memory of where she'd left it the previous night. 'Could you give me a lift? I don't think I'm up to driving yet.'

'You're not seriously going in?'

'I have to,' she said. 'Too much going on.'

'You'll get nowhere near him. It'll be Ben's interview.'

'I know. But I'm hoping I can watch.' The tension of the last hour was easing and she realised it had been almost eighteen hours since she'd eaten. She picked up one of the sandwiches, cold now, and bit into it. 'Thanks,' she said. 'This is great.'

'Still don't think you should go in. You're not fit.'

She put the sandwich down and prodded her ribs. 'I'm surprisingly okay. As long as I keep popping the pills, I'll be fine. And besides, there's the lad from the van. Given I found him, I'm hoping Ben will let me speak to him.'

He shook his head. 'Lean on your team,' he said again. 'Chris and Max are perfectly capable.'

She gave him an apologetic smile. 'I know. But last night...' She hesitated, recalling the events at the trading estate. 'After Maddox burst out of the van, I was hurt, so Chris went after him. Then Ben turned up and he went after him too. Everyone was out, combing the estate, blocking him off further up the river – it was all happening, you know? Lots of noise and bustle. And I couldn't do anything to help. My ribs were screaming, and someone had to stay with the victim. I'd taken a video of the van, showing where he was found and...' She stopped for a moment, then gave herself a shake. 'There was a chain, you know? Hanging from a hook. Most likely the chain he used – was going to use on that poor man.'

The DCI moved to sit beside her. He picked up her hand and held it. She sat, enjoying the sensation, grateful for the comfort. 'Anyway, they all disappeared and I was left alone with the victim. Just the two of us. He was out for the count. I couldn't tell if he knew I was there or if he could hear me. But – the way we found him – so undignified. He was just like a piece of meat. Left on a slab for Maddox to do whatever he wanted with. So I made a promise to myself – to this man as well – whoever he was. I promised I'd nail this guy. So I want to be there when he's conscious. I want to be the one to tell him we caught this monster.'

He smiled back at her. 'Of course you do.' He rose from his seat. 'Finish that and I'll run you to the station. I'll find a pharmacy that's open and drop your pills in as soon as I have them. Just promise me you'll take it easy, yeah? It's a big shock to the system, something like this.'

She sat on for a few minutes, enjoying the sandwich, Benjy gently nuzzling his head against her leg. For once he didn't jump up, didn't bring her the remains of the newspaper or his soggy chew-toy. The DCI turned and saw the little dog, his eyes never leaving Clare.

'He knows you're not right,' he said, and Clare smiled.

'Sometimes,' she said to Benjy, 'you're not the worst behaved dog in the world.'

His tail thumped the carpet and she rewarded him with the remains of her sandwich.

Chapter 28

Jim came forward to meet Clare as she entered the station.

'Heard you took a kick to the ribs,' he said, his face full of concern. 'How are you?'

She grinned. 'I have wonderful painkillers.'

He shook his head. 'I didn't think you'd take the day off. Ben – the DCI – he says I've not to let you anywhere near the station for the next few days.'

'You leave Ben to me,' Clare said, heading for her office.

A minute later there was a tap on the door and Jim appeared with a mug of tea and a piece of chocolate brownie.

'Zoe?' she said, and he nodded. 'You know what she's like – any excuse to get the baking bowl out.'

Jim left her to it and she turned to her computer, sipping the tea while it came to life. As her Inbox loaded, the door opened and Chris came in.

'So you're here, then.'

'Full marks for observation.'

'Even though Ben said to stay at home.'

She clicked her tongue in irritation. 'If one more person—'

He held up his hands. 'I'm just the messenger.' He picked up the brownie and made to break a bit off.

Clare tried to swipe him then groaned as pain shot through her ribs. Chris gave an exaggerated sigh and put the brownie back down.

'Calm yourself,' he said. 'I'll leave the cake.' He pushed it across the desk. 'So, how are you?'

She inclined her head. 'I'll live.' She bit into the brownie and chewed for a minute. 'Go on, then. What's he like?'

'Maddox?' He shrugged. 'I dunno. Pretty nondescript. Fifty, maybe. You'd probably walk past him in the street. He doesn't scream *serial killer* at you. He does scream, though,' he added. 'Quite a lot, once Pasha had a hold of him.'

She laughed, an arm cradling her ribs. 'I can't believe I missed it all. Is he off to hospital?'

'Yeah. He took a bite to the arm, obviously. Pretty superficial but they've given him a tetanus jag to be on the safe side. The paramedics were more concerned about him being out all night. Possible hypothermia.'

'But we can interview him?'

He sank down on a chair and yawned. 'Probably not today. Ben says he's playing it by the book. He's not come this far to mess it up.'

Clare nodded. 'Makes sense. What about the lad in the van?'

'He's doing okay,' Chris said. 'Think he'll get out today. Ben's gone up to the hospital to take a statement.'

She was quiet for a moment.

'He's Ben's witness,' Chris said, anticipating her next question.

'But I found him.'

He shook his head. 'Honestly, I wouldn't push it. His evidence could help put Maddox away for a very long time. I wouldn't go near him without Ben's say-so.'

'Suppose.'

'On the plus side, Raymond called. They're back in the lab so he's rushing through the samples from Theo's body.'

She smiled and took another bite of brownie. 'That's something, at least. I don't suppose Raymond gave you a time for the results?'

'Nah. Late afternoon at the earliest.'

'Oh well.' She sat thinking for a moment. 'Any sign of Danny Glancy?'

'Nope. Wendy says Rhona's up the wall with worry.'

Clare finished the brownie and licked the chocolate off her fingers. 'Then where the hell is he and what's happened to him?'

Chapter 29

'He's called Finn Coverdale,' Ben said when Clare swiped to answer his call.

'How is he?'

'I've just left him. Not too bad, considering. More embarrassed than anything.'

'Was he able to tell you what happened?'

'Mostly. He met Maddox online. I gather he's in the habit of using dating sites and not averse to casual encounters. Maddox told him he had a van and Finn suggested the Premier Inn car park. Largo Road, he said.'

'I know it. Quite near the station. There might be CCTV.'

'Thanks,' Ben said. 'We'll check that.'

'Whose idea was it to head for Magus Muir?'

'Maddox. But he said to Finn they should drive around for a bit – get to know each other first. Then he handed him a bottle of vodka and told him to have a swig.'

'Rohypnol?'

'Almost certainly. Finn said Maddox turned the heater up and he thought that was why he started to feel sleepy. Anyway, they got to the junction north of Magus Muir and, as we know, Maddox did a swift about-turn.'

'Did Finn ask why?'

'Maddox said he thought it might be a dog fight or that kind of thing. Finn said he still occasionally gets hassled for being gay so he guessed Maddox didn't want to take any chances.'

'So they headed for Cupar?' Clare said.

'Yes. He turned left to avoid the speed bumps in Strathkinness and Finn suggested the trading estate in Cupar. He said a white van parked there wouldn't attract any attention. But by this time he was feeling pretty woozy. He could hear Maddox's phone giving directions and that's the last thing he remembers until he wakened up in Ninewells.'

'Poor guy,' Clare said. She hesitated. 'I would like to speak to him as well.'

'That's fine. I have his statement so I won't need him again, unless Maddox's interview throws something up. But you might want to leave it until tomorrow. He was pretty worn out by the time I'd finished with him.'

Clare thanked Ben. 'Will do. How is Maddox, by the way?'

'He'll live, unfortunately. They're keeping him in overnight but I've a couple of officers outside his room. As soon as he's released he'll be taken into custody and I'll interview him.'

'I don't suppose I could…'

'No. Stay away from him. You're welcome to observe the interview, if that helps – unless of course you fancy taking that sick leave I suggested…'

'Well, I'm back now.'

'So you are. I knew I was wasting my breath.'

She thanked Ben and put down the phone, her mind back at the trading estate the previous night. How close had Leon Maddox been to killing Finn? Another five minutes and they might have been too late. It didn't bear thinking about.

–

Raymond was true to his word and he called Clare just after half past two.

'Wow,' she said. 'That was quick.'

'We've a huge backlog but we're prioritising and yours somehow made it to the top of the list.'

'I owe you big style,' she said.

'Yeah yeah. So you always say. Anyway, I heard you arrested the Choker.'

'Not me,' she corrected, 'but, yes. A rather lovely police dog called Pasha detained him for us.'

'Ouch.' Raymond laughed. 'Better him than me. So I'm guessing his DNA will be heading our way as well.'

'I'd have thought so,' Clare said. 'But he's in hospital just now.'

'I'll get to it as fast as I can. We've a load of samples from the van last night as well so it might take a few days. But it would be good to know you have the right man.' He hesitated and she heard him tapping at a keyboard. 'As for the results for Theo Glancy, I can confirm they don't match the Choker's previous victims.'

'So it's a different killer?'

'As to that, it's not my job to say, but the good news is we do have a match.'

'Someone on the system already?'

'Yep. Name of Finn Coverdale.'

'What? Say that again.' Had she misheard?

'Finn Coverdale. Do you know him?'

She gave Raymond a quick explanation then went in search of Chris. He was in the kitchen, making tea and toast. 'Want some?'

She waved this away. 'The DNA on Theo Glancy...'

'Yeah?'

'Finn Coverdale – the same man we found in Maddox's van last night.'

He stared at her. 'Eh?'

'Yep. He's on the database.'

'He has previous, then.'

'Reset of alcohol, apparently.'

He began buttering the toast. 'So what does that mean?'

'I'm not sure. Ben interviewed Finn this morning. Said he was pretty tired after giving his statement about last night. He suggested we leave it until tomorrow. I'll have to call him back. Let him know about this.'

'Makes sense, though,' Chris said. 'About the interview. If he's not fully fit, any statement he gives could be challenged in court; and another thing,' he went on. 'You know what it's like getting a duty solicitor. It's bad enough in office hours but on a Sunday afternoon? Ben did well to get one up at the hospital. I bet we'd struggle; and if you do suspect Finn of involvement in Theo's death he'll need legal representation.'

She said nothing.

'You know I'm right. You just don't like it when I am.'

She rolled her eyes. 'I feel so helpless. I missed out on this morning and now I can't even interview one of the last people to see Theo alive.'

Chris finished buttering his toast and threw the knife in the sink. 'Tell you what we can do…'

'Yeah?'

'We could check in on the Glancys. Let them know we're making some progress with Theo's death. See if there's any news of Danny boy.'

–

Clare stared out of the window as Chris made his way through the streets. 'I should let you drive more often.'

'Anytime you want your ribs bruised.' He slowed as they approached the turn into Priory Gardens.

Rhona was standing at the window. Clare gave her a smile then she unclicked her seat belt and made to open the door.

'I'll do it,' Chris said. 'Just let me get round.'

She waited, grateful she didn't have to pull the handle. Chris opened the door and she swung her legs round to step out of the car, leaning on the arm he offered.

'It's like taking my granny shopping,' he said.

'I'd smack you one but it would hurt too much.'

'I know.'

They walked up the drive past Ruby's Mini, Clare noting Danny's XR3i was still missing. The door opened as they approached, Wendy on the threshold.

'Heard about the Choker,' she said. 'Great work. But, Clare, your ribs – how are you?'

Clare shrugged. 'I'll live.' She lowered her voice. 'How are things?'

'So-so. Rhona's not saying much but I reckon she's struggling. Ruby – well, she's getting on with her social media stuff. She's upstairs doing it now. But she keeps an eye on her mum.'

'Danny?' Clare asked and Wendy shook her head.

'I could be wrong, but I don't think either of them's heard from him. Rhona keeps going to the window and Ruby checks her phone all the time.' She stood back to let them in. 'I'll pop the kettle on. Leave you to chat.'

'Maybe ask Ruby to join us,' Clare said and she tapped softly on the sitting-room door. Rhona was sitting down now. She looked up as they entered but made no effort to rise. The smell of cigarette smoke hung heavy in the air. A half-drunk mug of something sat on a small table next to an ashtray full of dogends. There were dark circles beneath Rhona's eyes and Clare wondered when she'd last slept.

Rhona looked at them, her eyes searching their faces. 'Any news?' she said eventually.

'A little,' Clare said. 'Do you mind if we—' She indicated the chairs and Rhona jerked her hand in assent. Clare eased herself down, taking the weight on her hands, an action that didn't escape Rhona's notice.

'Hurt yourself?'

She forced a smile. 'Yeah. A bit.'

The door opened and Ruby came in, her eyes full of concern. She looked from Clare to Chris then at her mum. 'What's happened?'

Rhona eyed Clare. 'That's what I'd like to know.'

Clare took a moment, choosing her words carefully. She wasn't sure how Rhona would react to what she had to say.

'There's something I need to tell you about Theo.' She saw Ruby's eyes widen, thought maybe she was sending Clare a signal. *Don't tell her. She can't take it.* But Rhona had to know so she pressed on. 'We believe Theo was gay,' she said, watching Rhona carefully for a reaction.

Rhona regarded her steadily. 'That's it?' There was an edge to her voice. 'That's what you came to tell me?' She sighed heavily. 'You think I didn't know?'

'You knew?' Ruby said, her tone almost accusing.

Rhona shook her head. 'I'd be a pretty crap mother if I didn't.' She turned back to Clare. 'Why are you telling me this? Has it something to do with what happened?'

'I'm not sure,' Clare said, 'but we think we've found the man Theo was with the day he died.'

Rhona's eyes narrowed. 'He a suspect?'

For a moment Clare wasn't sure what to say. She'd been so focused on catching Leon Maddox over the past couple of days – every spare bit of manpower had been thrown at that; and it had been worth it. If his DNA matched samples taken from the previous victims, they had stopped a ruthless killer. But now, here in this smoky room with Rhona – a mother who had lost a precious son – she was struggling to get her head back into the case.

'We don't think so,' Chris said. 'But we'll know more when we interview him.'

Rhona considered this. 'Where is he?'

Chris glanced at Clare and she guessed he was thinking the same as her. Was there any harm in telling Rhona where Finn was? She couldn't see a reason to withhold the truth.

'He's in hospital,' she said.

'Oh aye?' There was a note of suspicion in Rhona's voice. 'He pick on the wrong one this time?'

'It's nothing like that,' Clare said. 'We think he was the innocent victim of an attack.'

Rhona said nothing and Clare went on.

'If he's able to tell us anything that might help, we will let you know. In the meantime, has Danny been in touch?'

Rhona's jaw tightened and she reached for her cigarettes and lighter. 'No,' she said, avoiding Clare's eye. 'He'll be busy.'

Clare watched her for a moment, waiting until she had lit up and had her first draw at the cigarette. 'If you do know where Danny is, it would be better if you told us.'

She shrugged. 'Like I said, he'll be busy.'

'Is it possible he's gone after someone?' Clare said. 'Someone he thinks might be responsible for Theo's death?'

Rhona drew deeply on the cigarette again and blew out a column of smoke. 'Honestly?' She met Clare's eye. 'I have no idea where he's gone. I wish to God I did.'

Clare turned to Ruby. 'Would you know where he is?'

Ruby shook her head. 'I've been trying his mobile but it rings out.'

'Friends?'

'Tried all the ones I have numbers for. No one's seen him since you found Theo.'

'What about social media?'

'He doesn't do much, to be honest. Maybe a bit of Facebook. But he's not posted for days.'

Clare studied her. She didn't think Ruby was being evasive but she barely knew the girl. 'Do you think he'd have gone after someone if he thought they knew anything about Theo?'

She met Clare's eye then slowly she nodded her head. 'Yeah. I think he would. But I don't think he'd know where to start.'

'Did he know Theo was gay?'

Ruby took a moment to answer. 'I'm not sure. He probably suspected but didn't want to admit it to himself.'

They were getting nowhere. Wendy appeared with a tray of mugs, taking the half-drunk one away, and Clare tried again.

'How are things at the club?'

Rhona took a final drag then stubbed the cigarette out in the ashtray. 'Still shut,' she said. 'It can stay shut for all I care.'

Clare and Chris exchanged glances. 'I thought Val was planning to open last night,' Chris said.

'Aye. But she's – she's been busy.'

An uneasy feeling was gathering in Clare's stomach. 'Have you spoken to her today?'

Rhona shook her head but said nothing.

'And you've no idea where she is?'

Again, Rhona said nothing.

Wendy shot a glance at Clare, and she guessed they were thinking the same thing. Val and Danny both disappearing – it couldn't be a coincidence. Had the two of them gone after Theo's killer? Taken the law into their own hands? If they had, it wouldn't be Val who suffered the consequences. It never was. Sitting here in this room, the grief as thick as the smoke, Clare wanted desperately to spare Rhona any more heartache. She tried again.

'Rhona, you've suffered a dreadful tragedy. I wouldn't like anything else to go wrong for you.'

Clare saw the rise and fall of Rhona's chest and guessed she was trying to control her emotions.

'Has Danny gone after someone?' Clare asked again, softening her voice.

Still Rhona said nothing, her eyes on the floor.

'Rhona?' Clare persisted, her tone as gentle as she could make it.

Rhona lifted her head and Clare saw her eyes were brimming with tears. 'As God is my witness, I've no idea where Danny is. If I did, I'd send someone to fetch him back.'

Clare's heart went out to her. She put up a front, all right – a brassy exterior – fully equipped to deal with drunk punters, sort out fights and anything else that came her way. Most folk wouldn't mess with Rhona. But this – this double whammy of grief and worry? It had damn near broken her. They had to find Danny – and soon. But Rhona's expression was blank now. The shutters had come down.

They left soon after, Ruby seeing them to the door.

'If you do hear from Danny, or Val,' Clare said, 'you must let us know.'

Ruby's expression darkened. 'As far as I'm concerned the less I see of Val the better.'

'You don't like her?'

She shook her head. 'She pushes Mum too hard. The club – it was Mum's dream and she runs it well. Or she would have done if this hadn't happened. But Val – because she put the money up she thinks she can tell Mum what to do. If she'd just leave Mum alone she'd be fine. But Val's always pushing, pushing; and Mum, she doesn't need it. She didn't need it before – and she certainly doesn't need it now.' She met Clare's eye, her expression steely. 'I have no idea where Val is and, as far as I'm concerned, if I never see her again that'll suit me fine.' She glanced at her watch. 'I need to get back upstairs. I've a TikTok to record.' She opened the front door, waiting for Clare and Chris to leave.

'Just one more thing,' Clare said.

She stopped, one hand on the door. 'Yes?'

'Keep an eye on your mum. I think she's struggling.'

Chapter 30

They climbed back into the car, Chris helping Clare to put on her seat belt.

'I do feel like your granny,' she said.

He appraised her as the engine came to life. 'I can see the resemblance.'

'Shut up and drive.'

'Back to the station?'

'Please. I want to speak to everyone.'

–

Ben's extra officers had mostly gone back to their stations but a dozen or so were still in the incident room, typing up their reports.

'I won't keep you long,' Clare said, easing herself down on a desk at the front. 'I just wanted to thank you for your efforts over the past few days. You're honestly the best officers I've ever worked with. It's due to you all going over and above that our man is now in custody.'

There was a murmur round the room acknowledging this and she waited until it had died down before going on. 'For anyone who doesn't know, his name is Leon Maddox.'

Nita, one of the Cupar officers, looked up.

'Nita?'

'He got any previous, boss?'

'I'm not sure,' Clare said. 'He's from South Shields so I don't think we'd have come across him.'

Nita pulled a laptop across the desk. 'I'll just have a look. Something about that name...'

Clare nodded her thanks and went on. 'SOCO are back up and running and they've confirmed DNA taken from Theo's body doesn't match Maddox's previous victims.'

'So it's a different killer?' Robbie said.

'Yes. But we have a bizarre coincidence.' She hesitated. 'It seems the man found unconscious in the van last night was also Theo Glancy's last sexual contact. His DNA was found on Theo's body.'

They exchanged glances and Max was the first to find his voice. 'Is he a suspect?'

Clare spread her hands. 'As to that, it's too early to say. I can't interview him without a solicitor and he's still in hospital. But he might not be involved. It's possible whoever killed Theo mistook him for his brother, Danny.'

'Where does Danny fit into this?' Gillian asked.

Where indeed, Clare thought. 'It could be something to do with drugs.'

There was a buzz round the room and she went on.

'Sean Davis, one of the Safenites volunteers, claims drugs are circulating at Retro's night club. The Glancys run the club but it's owned by Val Docherty. We've long suspected Val of involvement in drugs but never been able to prove it. So it's possible she's the source. The Glancys haven't seen Val since yesterday, and Danny's disappeared as well now but we don't know if the two are connected.'

'Could someone else be trying to take over supplying the drugs at Retro's?' Robbie asked and Clare nodded.

'Could be. Chris and I saw Viggo Nilsen and two big lads we think are the McCarthy twins at the club on Thursday morning. According to Bill there's no love lost between Val and Viggo. So Viggo and the twins turning up at Val's club is definitely suspicious.' She stood thinking for a minute. 'If it was Viggo supplying the drugs, it could be Val's given Danny a smack to teach him a lesson. To be honest, guys, there's any number of possibilities. So finding Danny is the priority.'

'He's maybe lying low,' Gillian said. 'If he thinks one of them's after him.'

'Quite possibly,' Clare agreed.

'Boss…'

Clare looked round the room to see who had spoken. It was Nita again.

'The *Fife Newsday* website ran a series of features on cold cases, a few years back. Unsolved murders in Fife. One of them was Charlie Thomas. Young lad of nineteen found in Falkland Estate – must be thirty years ago. It's still unsolved. So I looked it up on the network and guess who was arrested but released without charge?'

Clare stared at her. 'Leon?'

'Yep. The article doesn't say why he wasn't charged but we must have something in the archives. Want me to check?'

'Please. I'm sure we'll have enough to charge him with the murders but it's always good to have a bit extra.' She looked round the room. 'Meantime, let's find Danny and Val.'

They drifted back to their laptops and Clare slipped off the desk.

'Boss?' Robbie was staring at his laptop. 'Might have something.'

Clare walked over and he turned the screen so she could see.

'It's dashcam footage,' he said. 'Came in yesterday.' He picked up the mouse and dragged the scroll bar back. 'We've a couple of files.' He clicked the mouse and the footage began. Robbie slowed the speed and Clare leaned in to watch. 'This is the roundabout at the North Haugh,' he said. 'Down from Retro's.' He clicked the mouse again and moved the footage on, frame by frame. 'And this is the bus stop, further along the road.'

'Is that—'

'Theo Glancy,' Robbie said. 'Same hair, and he's wearing that jacket with the Nike Swoosh. The car headlights pick it up because his back's to the road. Bit of luck, really. Looks like he's reading the timetable.' He clicked again, this time moving to another file. 'This is from another car. We can't be sure their clocks are synced but it looks like it came along maybe five minutes later.'

'He's not at the bus stop,' Clare said. 'Did the bus come?'

'I've not checked but I don't think so.' He advanced the footage beyond the bus stop and two figures came into view. 'That,' he said, pausing the clip, 'is Theo. I reckon he missed his bus – or maybe it didn't turn up – and he's started walking to Guardbridge.'

Clare peered at the screen. There was no mistaking the distinctive jacket, picked out again by the car headlights. 'So who's that?' A tall, stocky figure in dark clothing was walking behind Theo, maybe twenty or thirty paces. There was something in his body language; something that suggested he wasn't just walking – he was following. 'Can you zoom in on him?'

Robbie increased the magnification but the image became blurred and he zoomed out again until the focus was sharp enough to study the figure. Allowing for the gap between them, Clare thought he was taller than Theo – certainly more heavily built. 'Is that a hood?' she asked.

'Might be.' He turned to Clare. 'Do you think that's him? Theo's killer?'

Clare eased herself off the seat. 'If it's not, he might be a witness. He might have seen Theo talking to someone. Get the best copy you can and fire it over to the press office. I'll give them a call and tell them to expect it.'

'I've still a couple more files to go through,' Robbie said. 'Might get a better one.'

Clare nodded. 'Good work, Robbie,' and she was rewarded when his face lit up.

'I've still to look into Danny's employment history,' he went on. 'I've been head down, going through the footage.'

'Leave Danny,' she said. 'I'll get Chris onto it.'

She found him in the kitchen chatting to Max. 'Jobs for you two.'

Chris's face fell. 'I was just going to have some lunch.'

'Working lunch, then. I'd like you to take over looking into Danny Glancy – jobs, money – anything at all, especially any possible links to drugs. He must be paying for that flat somehow.'

'Thought Robbie was on that?'

'He was. But I've taken him off it.'

Chris raised an eyebrow and Clare guessed he was thinking of the time Robbie had been seriously ill with depression. She shook her head. 'Nothing like that. He's fine. But he's spotted something – or rather someone – on a couple of dashcam files. It looks like Theo was followed along that road.'

'Got a photo?'

'Not a clear one, but Robbie's sending it over to the press office now. He's more files to check so we might get a better photo. Might even be able to identify him.'

She turned to Max. 'I'd like you on the CCTV in Danny's block. Might show us when he was last there. Also some of these blocks have garages. I'm not sure if they're underneath the building or round the back but I'd like to know if his car's there. It's pretty distinctive – Chris will fill you in.'

She left them to their tasks and went slowly back to her office, her mind on Robbie. It had taken months for him to recover, once he'd accepted he needed professional help. Clare had blamed herself for not being alert to the warning signs and had resolved to make officer welfare a higher priority. But it wasn't easily done. They'd been so stretched lately. Maybe if they did find Theo's killer, she could fit in some one-to-ones with the team. Stop another case like Robbie before it started.

–

It was just after three when Suzy Bishop, the press officer, rang.

'Had a photo through from one of your officers. He said you'd explain.'

'Oh, Suzy. Sorry. I meant to phone you but it completely slipped my mind.'

'I take it you want this photo out to the press?'

'Please. Just that we're anxious to contact this man.'

'No problem,' Suzy said. 'What about the figure ahead of him?'

'Oh, that's our victim. I thought Robbie was going to crop him out. Could you—'

'Leave it with me. How are you, by the way? I heard you took a bit of a kicking?'

Clare gave Suzy a brief account of events at the trading estate.

'DCI Ratcliffe's given us a brief statement about that,' Suzy said. 'Good work all round.'

They chatted on for a few minutes then Clare ended the call with a promise to catch up over a drink. She worked on for a bit, feeling more and more weary. Her eyes were tired squinting at the screen and she decided to call it a day. She was about to shut down her computer when Chris burst into her office.

'Finn Coverdale,' he said. 'He's been snatched off the street.'

Chapter 31

'He'd been discharged from hospital,' Chris began, 'and he was making his way along Ninewells Drive when a car screamed up. Couple of big lads got out and bundled him in the back. A group of medical students were on their way home and they witnessed it.'

'Did they get the car registration?'

'No. It was over too quickly. By the time they realised what was happening the car was heading away.'

'Any description?'

'The men or the car?'

Clare clicked her tongue in irritation. 'Either.'

'Big men, hoodies, dark clothes. Saloon car, nothing distinctive.'

'Not red?'

Chris shook his head. 'They said it was dark.'

Clare sat drumming her fingers on the desk, her mind racing. 'Did they see which way it went?'

'They couldn't be sure. The road was busy – lots of head-lights. They thought it maybe turned up Ninewells Avenue. But they're not certain. Could have gone down.'

Suddenly Clare remembered Robbie's footage of the man following Theo. Big, with dark clothing. Was that something? Could it be the same man? They were almost certain Theo had been killed in error – that Danny had been the real target. So why would anyone grab Finn off the street?

'It's Danny,' Chris said. 'Has to be.'

Clare frowned. 'But how would he know Finn had anything to do with Theo? We only found Finn last night and the DNA only came back this afternoon. Even Ruby didn't know who he was.'

'But she saw him at the club,' Chris said. 'Chances are Danny saw him as well. He worked the bar, don't forget, and I bet he wasn't happy about Theo seeing men. Remember what he said about not having gay nights at the club.'

'I still don't see how Danny would know who Finn was.'

Chris shrugged. 'I don't know – any number of ways. Maybe Finn paid for drinks with a bank card. Or Danny asked him for proof of age. He could have followed Finn. Found out where he worked.'

Clare shook her head. 'Okay, I know I'm being thick here but how would he know Finn was in hospital?'

Chris leaned across and pulled Clare's keyboard towards him. He opened up a browser and began to type. The *Fife Newsday* website filled the screen and within a few seconds he'd found a report of a young man taken to Ninewells Hospital after being found unconscious in a van at Cupar Trading Estate.

'Unconfirmed reports suggest the man is twenty-eight-year-old Finn Coverdale of St Andrews,' Chris read.

Clare stared at the screen. 'How the hell did they get hold of his name?'

'You know reporters. Danny most likely saw that article and made the connection. He probably phoned the Acute Medical Unit, pretended to be a relative. Could be whoever he spoke to said Finn would be getting out soon. Danny lifts the phone, calls a couple of big lads with a car and tells them to hang about near the hospital. Finn's name's quite unusual. Most likely got his photo from Facebook.'

Clare lifted her phone. 'I'll warn Wendy. Then I'll get back onto Suzy. Danny Glancy wanted urgently in connection with an abduction.'

Her next call was to Penny Meakin. 'Finn Coverdale's been abducted,' she said.

'You're sure?' Penny sounded sceptical. 'Not just lads larking about?'

'Not from what the witnesses said.'

'Right.' Penny's tone was business-like. 'What are you thinking?'

'We suspect our victim's brother, Danny, is involved. He's known to be a bit of a hothead and the FLO got the impression he was out for revenge. Finn was seen with Theo at least once at Retro's. Danny might think he knows something.'

'Makes sense,' Penny said. 'What do you need?'

Clare opened her mouth to reply and then stopped. What *did* she need? And where would they start looking in a city the size of Dundee? He could be anywhere. Back to basics, then.

'I'll start with Danny's known associates,' she said. 'I've a couple of officers on that anyway. If they've found anything I'll pass it on to someone at Bell Street. Erm, who can I use?'

'Anyone in mind?'

'Bill and Janey,' Clare said, 'and if you can spare Benny and Cheryl.'

She heard Penny tapping at her screen. 'Looks like Benny's on leave. I'll ask Cheryl to suggest someone else. Given your current state of health, you'd better stay put in St Andrews. Set up a Zoom call and invite whoever you need.'

She thanked Penny and went in search of Chris. 'I'm going to do a video call with Dundee in...' she checked her watch, '...let's say twenty minutes. I'd like you and Max to sit in. Check with Robbie, Gillian and Sara please. See if they've found anything at all on Danny Glancy and bring what they have to the meeting.'

Max appeared. 'About that garage.'

'In a minute,' Clare said. 'First, I need you to schedule a Zoom call with Dundee. I'd like Bill, Janey and Cheryl, please. Hopefully another detective but check with Cheryl. Penny's asked her to drum up another body. Twenty minutes. You can share the garage info then.'

Twenty minutes later they gathered in the incident room, the Zoom call hooked up to a large screen on the wall. The four officers from Dundee appeared as Max clicked to admit them to the call. Cheryl introduced DS Hamish Tough.

'Hammy,' he corrected.

'Good to have you on board, Hammy,' Clare said. She got straight to the point. 'You've heard about our abduction?' They nodded and she went on. 'We've very little on the car. Dark saloon, two large men, dark clothes, hoodies. They abducted Finn from Ninewells Drive, near the roundabout, so it's unlikely they've been picked up on any of the hospital CCTV.'

'Direction?' Bill asked.

'Not known. Possibly up Ninewells Avenue but they could easily have gone down. Either way it's impossible to know where they went. The car could even have false plates.'

'Anyone in the frame?' Hammy asked.

'At the moment we're working on the theory our murder victim's brother, Danny Glancy, is behind it. He disappeared pretty quickly after his brother's death and hasn't been seen since. Chris and I visited his flat but he didn't answer the door and a neighbour had taken in a parcel. Either he's not answering or he's not there.'

'Should we force entry?'

Clare was quiet as she considered this. 'To be honest, I'm not sure. He's the victim's brother, so we need to be sensitive to that. I don't want to cause the family any more upset. They're just the kind to go crying to the press.'

'Could flag it as a cause for concern,' Janey said. 'Worried he's come to some harm. Weren't you working on the theory he was the real target? Brother killed by mistake?'

'Yes,' Clare said. 'That's a good point. We could force entry.'

Chris moved forward so he could be seen on screen. 'I might be missing something but surely the mother or sister have spare keys.'

Clare gave herself a shake. 'Sorry, guys. My head's not in the game. Let's try that first.'

Max rose from his seat. 'I'll give Wendy a quick call.'

She waited until Max had left the room then she went on. 'One way or another I'd like two of you in Danny's flat. Force entry if you have to but hopefully we'll get a set of keys. What you'll find is anyone's guess. Could be that's where Finn is, or there might be evidence he's been there – I've no idea. But eyes alert.'

'You want us in PPE?' Hammy asked.

'Not at this stage. Take it with you and, if there's any evidence of foul play, give me a shout.'

'Who do you want in the flat?' Bill asked.

She glanced at Chris. 'Let's say Chris and Hammy. I'm going to stay here but I want you on the radio as you enter.'

Max came back into the room. 'Rhona has a set,' he said. 'Jim's sent Sara over for them now.'

'Thanks, Max. Erm, you were looking into Danny's building, weren't you?'

'Yes. There's CCTV in the foyer. Covers the front entrance right up to the stairwell and lift.'

'Is there a back door?'

'There is. It's not covered on camera but the lift, stairs and mailboxes are. I've requested the footage from Saturday onwards.'

'And the car?'

'Still waiting to hear.'

'We can look for the car when we check the flat,' Chris said and Clare nodded her thanks.

'What do you want us to do?' Janey asked.

'Known associates. I've a list my officers were working through. Can you get the Dundee lot on that please, Janey? Max, I'd like you to handle his St Andrews connections. I suspect, with him living in Dundee, we're more likely to find something there, but we can't leave anything to chance.'

'Anything from Finn's phone?' Bill asked.

She slapped her head. Why hadn't she thought of that? She really wasn't on top of things.

'I'll take that,' Bill said. 'I take it Penny will okay us triangulating it?'

Clare nodded. 'She will. Thanks, Bill.'

She glanced at Max and Chris. 'Have I missed anything?'

They shook their heads and Clare ended the call.

Sara appeared a few minutes later with the spare keys to Danny's flat and a scrap of paper bearing the alarm code. 'You be careful,' she said, handing them to Chris. 'They're a rough lot, those Glancys.'

'Okay, Mum,' he said, earning himself one of Sara's looks.

'She's right,' Clare said, walking back to her office. 'Just be careful.'

–

Half an hour later, Max appeared at Clare's office door. 'I've been down to Retro's.'

She beckoned him in. 'Is it open?'

He came in and sank down. 'Opened again last night. Instructions from Val, apparently.'

'Any sign of her?'

Max shook his head. 'Nope. Seems she sent a last-minute message round the staff saying they were to open from Saturday night. But nobody's actually seen her.'

Clare sat, mulling this over. 'Who was there?'

'Just the barmaid – Tammi. She said the rest would be in later.'

'Is that it?'

'Not sure,' he said. 'Might be something and nothing. I asked her about Danny – who he hangs about with, anyone she's seen him with at the club. She said there was this one man.'

'Name?'

'She doesn't know. But she thought he was foreign.'

'Well, that narrows it down!'

'I know. But it's a start.'

'Description?'

'Tall, blond hair, tied back in a man bun. Good looking, she said, but he doesn't smile much.'

'Sounds like Viggo. You checked with Rhona or Ruby?'

Clare's phone began to ring and she snatched it up, clicking the speaker icon.

'We're at the flat,' Chris said. 'Or at least we're in the building. Hammy's waiting by the stairs and lift in case he appears. I'm heading out to the garage to look for the XR3i.' Clare heard the sound of a door squeaking then Chris's voice became echoey. 'I'm in the garage now,' he said. 'No sign, as far as I can see.' She heard his breathing as he walked along, checking cars. After a few minutes he came back on the phone. 'It's not here.' She heard the wind buffeting his phone and another squeak from the door. 'That's me back in the hall. We'll head up to the flat.'

'One in the lift, one on the stairs,' Clare said.

'Way ahead of you. Hammy's taking the mobile death trap. I'll take the stairs.'

In spite of the seriousness of the situation, Clare allowed herself a smile. Chris and lifts did not mix. 'What is it, three floors?' she said. 'Surely you can manage that.'

'High enough for the plunge to be a problem.' His breathing became faster as he climbed the stairs and for a minute he said nothing. 'That's us at the flat door,' he said, a minute later. Clare heard the sound of a key in the door. An insistent beeping began. 'Hold on.' There was a muttered exchange between Chris and Hammy then the beeping stopped. 'Alarm,' Chris said. 'I doubt he's here.'

Clare heard Hammy say he'd check the bedrooms. 'Try the fridge,' she said.

After a few moments Chris spoke again. 'Not much here. Milk's out-of-date — so's this pasta meal.'

They listened as the two officers moved round the flat. 'Kettle's cold,' Chris said. 'Oh, there's a laptop here. You want us to take it?'

'No,' Clare said. 'We don't have a warrant. Official line is you're here with Rhona's consent.'

'Fair enough.' She listened as they continued moving about the flat.

'Newspaper here,' she heard Hammy say.

'Date?'

There was a pause then Chris said, 'Yesterday's.'

'Anything else at all?' Clare said. 'Any letters? Receipts? Check the bin.'

Chris sighed heavily into the phone. 'Why do I always end up raking in bins?'

'Because you're so good at it. So?'

She heard rustling and some low muttering then he spoke again. 'Receipt here.'

'For?'

'Looks like that paper, sandwich and a bottle of Coke. Yeah, yesterday.'

'Just the one sandwich?'

'Yeah.'

She was quiet as she tried to make sense of this. Danny had been in the flat on Saturday – just twenty-four hours ago. Nowhere near long enough to be considered a missing person. But Rhona was worried – Ruby too; and now someone had picked Finn Coverdale off the street. The more she thought about it the more she believed Danny had gone missing for a reason, and that reason could only be Finn.

She heard Hammy's voice in the background, then Chris spoke again.

'Nothing else,' he said. 'No sign of a disturbance – nothing to suggest Finn's been here.'

'You've checked the bathrooms? No blood on towels or anything like that?'

'Nothing.'

Clare thought for a moment. 'I'm going to ask Ben for a warrant to search Danny's flat officially. That'll let us take the laptop. But can you see if there's a spare set of car keys anywhere? If we do find his car there might be something that tells us where he's gone.'

She waited again, listening to the sounds of them searching the flat.

'Got them,' Chris said after a few minutes. 'In a dish on the coffee table. Erm, that it? Anything else you want us to look for?'

'Maybe ask the neighbour – the one who took in the parcel. See if he's seen Danny.'

'Will do. What do you want us to do now?'

'Check with Bill and Janey. They might need an extra pair of hands. And put a shout out for Danny's registration. I want to know if it passes any cameras.'

Chapter 32

Penny authorised the warrant for Danny's flat, and copies of Finn and Danny's phone records. But, by eight p.m., with no sign of either man, Clare sent the teams home and handed over to the night shift in Dundee. They promised to phone her if there was any news and she shut down her computer. It was only when she hunted through her bag to find her car keys that she remembered the DCI had driven her to work.

Max appeared at her office door. 'You need a lift?'

She gave him a smile. 'Yes please. It'll save me phoning Al.'

They went out the side door towards Max's car. As she followed him across the car park she realised she didn't even know what kind of car he drove. She was surprised when he stopped to unlock a light blue Saab.

'This is your car?'

He flushed. 'Had it for years. Can't bring myself to part with it.' He opened the door and looked down at the low-slung seat. 'Is this going to be okay?'

Clare laughed. 'I'll get in all right. Not sure if I'll get back out again, though.'

Max waited until she'd eased herself onto the seat and swung her legs in. Then he closed the door and went round to the driver's side. He checked Clare was safely belted in and drove out of the car park, taking care not to accelerate or brake too sharply.

'Has Chris seen this?' she asked as they drove along.

He glanced at her. 'The Saab? Think so.'

'He was very taken with Danny Glancy's car. An XR some-thing.'

'XR3i,' Max said. 'Bit of a boy racer's car.'

'Whereas this?'

He beamed. 'This is a touch of class.'

'Have you had it from new?'

'Crikey, no. Couldn't have afforded it at the time. It's nearly twelve years old.'

'You don't fancy something newer?'

For a minute he didn't speak. 'Left here?'

'Yes. Then it's a straight road.'

They fell silent, Clare wondering if she'd touched a nerve with the car. She was on the point of changing the subject when Max spoke again.

'It belonged to my father-in-law. I fell heir to it when he died.'

'What?' It was out before she could stop herself. 'Sorry,' she said, and she felt the colour rising in her cheeks. 'That was rude of me.'

His eyes were focused on the road ahead. 'No. I should have mentioned it.' He flicked a glance at her then back at the road. 'I'm not married any more, in case you were wondering.'

'I'm sorry,' was all she could think to say.

'It's fine. I don't mention it because – well, it wasn't the happiest time for me. My wife…' He broke off and checked his mirror before pulling out to pass a cyclist.

Clare waited, unsure if he wanted to continue.

'We weren't married for long,' he said, eventually. 'She – turns out she preferred the best man.'

Clare stared at him. His face was impassive, eyes straight ahead. Even in the dim light of the car she could see his jaw was tight. 'Your best man?'

'Mm-hm. Josh. My best friend from school. Stacey and I – we'd been married for six months when she told me. Her father had just died and she'd inherited a bit of money. I think it made it easier for her to leave. She bought me out of the house, paid a fair price; and said she didn't want the car. I was fond of her dad and I loved the car. So she said I could have it. Said it was the least she could do.'

Clare's throat was tight with emotion. Max, her lovely, kind DS – a man who would do anything for anyone – to be treated so dreadfully by his wife and his best friend. 'I don't know what to say.' Her voice was husky and she cleared her throat.

He signalled left and braked gently, turning in to the drive at Daisy Cottage. Then he pulled on the handbrake and gave her a smile. 'Don't worry. I don't really talk about it. Suppose I'm a bit embarrassed. Couldn't even keep my wife for six months. But it doesn't matter now. If I'd still been married I'd never have met Zoe.'

Clare patted him on the arm. 'You've found a good one there,' she said. 'But Zoe's found a better one.'

His smile broadened. 'That's a kind thing to say.'

She clicked off her seat belt. 'Absolutely true, Max. And don't you forget it.'

He opened his door and was about to climb out to help Clare when the front door opened and the DCI appeared. He glanced at the Saab then came out in his slippers.

'Come on, old woman,' he said, extending his hands. 'Grab hold and I'll pull you out.'

She swung her legs round and took hold of his hands. 'I'll *old woman* you! Just you wait till I'm fighting fit again.' She walked to the door, one hand still holding his, then she stood on the threshold, watching Max back out and pull away. As the tail lights disappeared round the hedge she thought about him, going home from work one night to be met by his wife, her suitcases packed – maybe the best man – Josh, was it – waiting in the car. What a homecoming. Poor Max. Admittedly, he'd found happiness with Zoe, her admin assistant. But he must have endured months of unhappiness.

They went in and the DCI closed the door. She watched him for a moment, thinking of his own divorce – again, his wife's choice. How painful it must have been. But, like Max, they had found each other and she was as happy with him as she'd ever been.

Somewhere distant Benjy was barking. 'Shall I let him out?' he said. 'I wasn't sure if you'd be up to it.'

'In a minute.' She turned and stood, taking him in. 'Do you think you could manage a very gentle hug?'

Day 7: Monday

Chapter 33

They gathered in the incident room, just before eight, Clare electing to sit, rather than stand by the board.

'Let's start with phones,' she said. 'Anything?'

Bill shook his head. 'Both Danny and Finn's phones are going straight to voicemail. We have the warrant for their phone records but nothing back yet. We've also got the warrant for Danny's flat and his finances,' Bill added. 'Again, nothing from the bank. But at least we can carry out a legal search of the flat now.'

Clare considered this. They weren't exactly drowning in manpower and Chris and Hammy had already looked round the flat. 'Let's leave that for now,' she said. 'But keep on at the bank and phone companies.' She turned to Max. 'What about the CCTV in Danny's building?'

'Got the footage this morning,' he said. 'I'll make a start as soon as we're done here.'

Clare glanced at her pad. 'Known associates?'

'We've quite a list for Danny,' Chris said. 'Janey's team are working through it now.'

Her eye was caught by Chris, hand on his chin. 'Something on your mind?'

His brow creased. 'I'm sure I've seen Danny somewhere before, but it won't come.'

'No precons?'

'Nope.'

'Accused of something that didn't come to trial?'

'I don't think it's that.' He gave himself a shake. 'It'll come.'

'Let's move on, then,' Clare said. 'Finn Coverdale – any sign?'

'Nothing,' Max said. 'The Dundee lads have been knocking on doors, checking premises – anyone handy with their fists, but nothing so far.'

'Finn's known associates?'

Chris shook his head. 'Nothing.'

'Does he work?' Clare asked.

'Waits tables in The Coffee Stop.'

Clare knew the café. It was in North Street, near the ruined cathedral. 'Chris, we'll take a turn along there. See what they can tell us. Erm, what about the press release?'

'The man who followed Theo?' Max said. 'A few phone calls. Sara and Robbie are following them up. They'll let us know if there's anything.'

Clare exhaled heavily. 'So, a big fat zero. Come on, guys. We've lost Finn and Danny. They must be somewhere. If Danny is behind Finn's abduction, someone's helping him – the two big lads who snatched him, for a start. If we have to pull people in and threaten them with charges then do it.' She sat thinking for a moment. 'What about Big Val?'

Chris's brow furrowed. 'Having a job finding her as well.'

'Godsake! Is there anyone connected to Theo Glancy we haven't lost?'

Chris scribbled a note on his pad. 'I'll keep trying.'

'See you do.' She looked round at them. 'Is that it?'

No one had anything else to contribute and Clare headed for her office, telling Chris they'd call into The Coffee Stop at nine thirty.

–

A heavy fog had descended on the town, chilling Clare to the bone as they walked from the car to The Coffee Stop. She lagged behind Chris, missing the brisk pace that kept her warm on the coldest of days. The lights in the café shone brightly through the gloom, the windows framed in multi-coloured fairy lights. Clare's heart sank as they pushed open the door and heard the tinny sound of Christmas music.

'It's November,' she hissed.

'It's four weeks away,' Chris said. 'You ordered that turkey yet?'

She ignored the question and looked round the café. There were several tables free and she chose one near a radiator, settling herself with her back to it.

'I'm buying then?' Chris said.

'Thank you. I'll have a hot chocolate with everything.'

'Anything to eat?'

She peered over at the glass-fronted counter, trying to make out the different cakes. 'You choose,' she said. 'No raisins, though.'

Chris ambled over to be greeted by a man in his thirties. He wore a blue apron with the outline of a coffee cup embroidered on the bib, the long ties knotted at the front. He took out a notepad, scribbled down Chris's order and said he'd bring it over. Chris resumed his seat, looking round the café.

'Not been in here before.'

'I have,' Clare said. 'Remember that house fire? I met the householder here the day after it happened.'

He nodded. 'I got a bravery award for that.'

'You're lucky you didn't get a kick up the backside,' Clare said in a tone of mock severity. 'Going into a burning building!'

'Just because you don't have one.'

'Eyup,' Clare said. 'Here he comes.'

The man in the apron approached, a tray in his hands. He set down the hot chocolates, a shortbread biscuit in the shape of a Christmas tree for Clare and the largest chocolate muffin she'd ever seen for Chris. 'Enjoy,' he said, preparing to leave.

'Actually,' Clare began, 'do you have a minute?' She took out her ID badge. He studied it, his brow clouded. Then he scanned the café.

'Our busy time starts soon,' he said. 'I've still a bit to do.'

Clare smiled and indicated a chair. 'It won't take long.'

He perched on the edge of the chair, his eyes flitting from Clare to Chris. 'Is this about Finn?' he said, pre-empting Clare's questions. 'He messaged yesterday to say he'd been taken to hospital but he'd be back today. I hope he hasn't taken a turn for the worse.'

Clare ignored the question. 'We're having a bit of trouble getting in touch with him. Do you have contact details for any family or friends? Colleagues? Maybe a staff WhatsApp group?'

The waiter laughed. 'There's not enough of us for a group. But I can check his staff record. See who his next of kin is.'

Clare smiled. 'That would be really helpful. What about friends? Do any of them come into the café?'

His eyes widened. 'I honestly haven't noticed. I mean it's quiet just now but, come ten o'clock, we'll be really busy – and it'll stay that way until four. That's what Finn works – ten till four.'

'Are you friends on social media? Facebook – Instagram? Anything like that?'

'Erm, probably. I think so.' He reached into his pocket and took out his phone. A minute later he held it out for Clare to see. 'We are friends. But he doesn't do much, really. Scroll through his posts if you like.'

Clare took the phone and studied the profile picture. It was the one from the online news article. *The perils of social media*, she thought. She scrolled down but nothing jumped out at her – mostly posts shared from other pages. She handed the phone back to the waiter and fished in her pocket, taking out a card. 'If he does get in touch, please let me know. It's very important.'

He pocketed the card then he rose from the chair, taking the tray with him. A minute later he was back, empty-handed. 'Sorry, but Finn never did give us a next of kin. I asked about it, reminded him a couple of times and he always said he'd bring in the details, but he never did.'

Clare thanked the waiter and they sat on, drinking their hot chocolates, Clare munching on the buttery shortbread. She eyed Chris as he attacked the muffin. 'You know how many calories are in those things?'

He shrugged, brushing chocolate crumbs from his lips. 'Way I see it' – he took a drink of hot chocolate – 'I might die young, but I'll have had a lovely life.'

She nibbled at her shortbread. 'I'm not sure it works like that.' Her phone buzzed with a message and she took it out, scanning the screen. 'Max,' she said.

'Oh yeah? God, this muffin's fabulous. Can we come here again?'

She drank the last of her hot chocolate and rose from her seat. 'Come on. Let's get back.'

They walked slowly back to the car, Clare reading Max's message as they went. 'CCTV at Danny's flat,' she said. 'Has him entering the building from the back door on Saturday afternoon and leaving again about eight in the evening.'

'So he was driving,' Chris said. 'If he came in through the back.'

'I guess so. Probably stopped to buy the stuff on the receipt then headed for the flat.' She glanced at the screen. 'Still no sign of his car.' She stood thinking for a minute. 'I wonder if he has a lock-up somewhere.'

Chris clicked to unlock the car. 'Quite possibly. Full of stolen goods – or drugs. But, if it is, he'd be daft to have it in his own name. He'll have slipped some lad a few quid to be the tenant.'

'You're probably right.' She eased herself down and into the car. Chris climbed in beside her and started the engine. 'Funny about the next of kin,' he said.

'Not necessarily. He could be estranged from his family. Or maybe he grew up in care and didn't want to say.'

'Suppose. So, what now?'

What indeed, Clare thought. 'Let's get back to the station. See if there's anything from that warrant.'

Chris switched on the fog lights, then he pulled out, using the wider part of North Street to execute a U-turn. He peered into the gloom as the wipers flicked back and forth. 'I reckon this is here for the day.'

Clare stared out of the window as they drove slowly along. The streets were quiet save for the odd figure, Puffa jacket zipped up against the chilling fog. Even the buildings looked dismal, a fine drizzle dampening the sandstone. It was a cheerless morning and it matched her mood. They were making no progress. She had no idea who was responsible for Theo's death. The only possible suspect was the man who'd been walking behind him, minutes before he was killed. A large man in dark clothing. There were a lot of them about.

And then there was Finn. Were they right to assume he knew nothing about Theo's death? They'd been working on the theory Danny was the intended victim. But what if Finn and Theo had argued – an argument that had got out of hand? So often the simplest explanation was the correct one. Was it a mistake to overlook Finn? Maybe Danny had seen something in the way Finn had been at the club and that was why he'd gone after him. Hadn't Ruby said she'd seen Finn with other men – not just Theo? She considered this as Chris crawled on through the streets, visibility down to a few metres.

He pulled into the car park, nosing into the first vacant space. 'Want a help out, granny?'

She flicked a hand at him. 'Just you wait till I'm back to normal.'

'You've never been normal,' he said, jumping out of the car. He walked round to Clare's door, waiting to offer a hand if needed. Then he locked the car. 'Come on – it's freezing. Let's get inside.'

Chapter 34

'They've found Danny's car,' Max said, his head round Clare's office door.

She looked up from the paperwork she was wading through. 'Where?'

'Cinema car park, north of Dundee. The lad who called it in thought it had been there at least a day.'

'So it could have been there since Saturday,' Clare said.

Max nodded. 'Quite possibly. There's a twenty-four-hour McDonald's so cars parked overnight wouldn't particularly stand out.'

'What made him call it in?'

'Seems he's a bit of a petrol head and Danny's car caught his eye.'

'Any CCTV?'

'Yeah. Cameras on a few of the buildings. We've requested the footage so we'll soon know how long it's been there.'

'Do we know if he went to the cinema? Or the McDonald's?'

'Not yet but, again, we've asked for the footage.'

'Thanks, Max. Anything else?'

'Yes. Ben called. Leon Maddox is being discharged from hospital. He plans to interview him probably this afternoon. He'll confirm nearer the time, if you want to watch.'

'Good. Hopefully he'll cough.' She sat thinking for a minute. 'Think I'll give Penny a call and ask for a warrant to search Finn's house.'

'Do we need one?'

It was a good point. 'Probably not,' Clare said. 'There's enough evidence his life's in danger. But it's Penny's call.'

Fortunately Penny agreed with Max. 'Get in there, but don't make a mess,' she said. 'Remember he's a victim.'

Clare put her phone down and went in search of Chris and Max. 'Penny's okayed a search of Finn's house. We don't have keys so check with a neighbour, under plant pots – the usual. If you can't find a key get hold of a locksmith. Take anything that might help – laptop, phone numbers on a pinboard – you know the drill. But no mess,' she added. 'Penny was at pains to stress he's a victim.'

'Is it a potential crime scene?' Max asked, but Clare shook her head.

'I'd be surprised if whoever snatched him took him back to his own house.'

'They might have snatched him, taken his keys and gone over his house,' Chris said. 'If they thought he had something.'

Clare stared at him. 'Like what?'

'I dunno. Drugs – money – maybe he was up to his old tricks, receiving stolen property.'

'Normally I'd agree,' Clare said. 'But we think Danny's behind this, don't we?'

Neither of them spoke.

'Don't we?' she repeated.

'I'm not so sure,' Max said. 'If Danny's behind this, why's his car been in a cinema car park for the past couple of days? Maybe there's no connection between Theo's death and Finn's abduction. Maybe we should be looking for something that links Theo's death and his brother's disappearance.'

Chapter 35

Chris and Max set off for Finn's house, promising to let Clare know ASAP if they found anything. She headed back to her office but Jim forestalled her.

'That's the phone records in for Finn and Danny. Gillian and Robbie are going through them now.'

'Thanks, Jim. Get them to check against any known associates. See who they've been in touch with over the past few days.'

She had just reached her office when her phone rang. Her mother's number. It wasn't like her to call without warning. She always texted to check Clare was free to talk. She swiped to take the call.

'Mum? Is everything—'

'Oh, Clare!' Her mother's voice was high-pitched – higher than normal. 'It's the car. We've had an accident.'

Clare's throat was tight, suddenly, and she swallowed. 'Accident? What's happened? Are you all right? Is Dad okay?'

'Yes, oh sorry. I should have said. We're both fine. But, your dad – he's in a bit of a state.'

Relief swam over Clare and she sank down in her chair.

'It was that damned fog,' her mother went on. 'We were going into town to do a bit of Christmas shopping. We stopped at the shop along the road because he wanted some chocolate. I stayed in the car and, while he was inside, another car parked in front of us. He was in the shop for ages. They have this new system now.' Her mother rattled on and Clare resisted the urge to tell her to get to the point.

'So when he eventually came out, he was in such a rush. Moaning about the shop and how it was fine before they changed things around. I thought he'd seen the car in front but...'

Jim appeared at Clare's door and she made a gesture indicating she was stuck on a call. He nodded and Clare mouthed, 'Five minutes.'

'He put his seat belt on and checked over his shoulder,' her mother was saying, 'then he pulled away. I really did think he'd seen the car in front so I didn't say anything until it was too late.'

'So he rammed the car from behind?' Clare said.

'Yes. And the number plate fell off. That sound,' she said. 'It was awful.'

'But no one was hurt?' Clare tried to make her tone soothing, hoping to calm her mother down.

'No. But that's not it. Oh – it's so hard to explain.'

Clare sighed inwardly. This clearly wasn't going to be a five-minute phone call.

'It's how he was,' her mother said, finally. 'How he reacted.'

Clare thought of her dad: so gentle and kind. Surely he hadn't lost his temper – got into a row with the other driver.

'He was just lost,' her mother said. 'He didn't know what to do. He sat there saying, "Oh God, oh God," over and over again. In the end I got out and spoke to the other driver myself. She was quite young but she was very understanding. I think she saw your dad through the windscreen – saw how upset he was.'

'You exchanged details?'

'Oh yes. That's all sorted. I told her we'd pay for the damage. I'm going to call her later. But I don't know what to do with your dad. He's so upset.' She hesitated. 'Clare, could you come through? Please?'

She promised her mother she'd call later and put down the phone. The conversation with her sister came back into her head. Judith had said her father had lost his confidence and this accident wouldn't have helped. Was there anything she could do? In the middle of an investigation it wouldn't be easy to find the time. But her mother clearly needed help and she couldn't leave it all to Judith.

Jim was waiting for Clare when she emerged from her office, thoughts of her father running round her head.

'The lad Glancy,' Jim said. 'McDonald's confirm he used the drive-through. Bought a burger. Paid cash.'

'Time?'

'Saturday evening, just before nine.'

Clare nodded. 'Fits with him having left his flat after eight. Could they see where he went after that?'

'No. But the cameras further along should have picked him up. Gillian's going through the footage now.'

Clare thanked Jim then went to the kitchen to make herself a strong coffee. What on earth was she going to do about her dad? It wasn't like he was ill – or was he? Was there something he was keeping from the rest of the family? Either way her mum was so upset she'd have to do something. But with her ribs, she wasn't fit to drive yet; and she didn't want to tell her mum she was injured. She worried enough about Clare's job as it was.

She was pouring boiling water into a mug when Chris's name flashed up on her phone.

'Hiya. What you got?'

'Nothing, actually. No laptop or tablet. House is tidy. No sign of a disturbance.'

'Any paperwork?' Clare asked. 'Bills or other stuff?'

'Not that we've found. He most likely does it all on his phone.'

She thanked Chris and clicked to dial the DCI's number.

'Hello, you,' he said. 'Everything okay?' The relief at hearing his voice was enormous and she hesitated, wondering where to start. He picked up on the hesitation. 'What's wrong? Are you okay, Clare?'

'I'm fine,' she said, keen to reassure him. 'It's my dad,' and she relayed the conversation with her mother. 'I just can't spare the time to go through there. I mean it's not like he's ill.'

'You can't drive, either,' the DCI said. 'Erm, I could take you through this evening. Spend a couple of hours and be back for bedtime.'

She considered this. 'From what Mum said, I think I'd need a bit longer. Maybe it could wait until this case calms down.'

'That could be long enough,' he said. 'I know you don't want to hear that but you have to be realistic.'

She sighed. 'Yes, I know. But Mum – she sounded so—'

'Look, what about this: I've a meeting through at Tulliallan. I'll go on to your parents' after that. Make up something about needing a sitter for Benjy. I'll bring your dad back for a few days. That way you can chat to him in the evenings; and it'll be a change of scene for him. Take his mind off what's happened.'

Clare was quiet for a moment, weighing this up. Would it work? He'd most likely drive her crazy being around all the time. But at least she'd be in her own home. She could go to work and she'd only be a few miles away if he needed her. In the circumstances it was the best she could do. 'Al, you're a lifesaver. Thank you!'

'No problem. I'll call your mum now. Say I'm going to be in Glasgow and could your dad come through for a few days to help us out.'

'Give me five minutes to warn her.' She cut the call and tapped out a message. Her mum replied a minute later saying that sounded perfect, and Clare tucked the phone into her pocket.

Chapter 36

Chris and Max returned to the station and took over trawling through Finn and Danny's phone records. There were countless posts on the Force Facebook page suggesting who the man following Theo might be and she asked Sara and Robbie to follow these up. The DCI had texted to say he was at Tulliallan and would be at her parents' house in a couple of hours. It occurred to her he was spending a lot of time at the police college. She had a vague recollection of him saying something interesting had happened but she'd been so tired he hadn't pursued it. Once this investigation was over, she'd make time to chat properly.

She began working through the backlog of emails, only looking up when Gillian tapped on her door. Clare gestured her in and she sat down, perching on the edge of a chair.

'Danny Glancy,' she said. 'I've got CCTV footage of him parking at the far end of the car park, in front of the ice rink. He stays in the car for about twenty minutes, probably eating his burger. Then he gets out, locks the car and disappears up the side of the building.'

Clare turned to her monitor and opened up a map of Dundee, moving it so Gillian could see. 'Up here?' she said, tapping the screen.

'Yeah. After that I lose him. I haven't gone any further through the footage but I think the car's in the space where it was found. Maybe he didn't come back.'

Clare zoomed in. 'That's Camperdown Park behind, isn't it?'

'And to the side.'

'So he's gone into the park – to meet someone?'

'Probably,' Gillian agreed. 'I can't imagine why else he'd go in there, unless it was for a quick pee.'

Clare thought for a moment. 'There aren't cameras in the park, are there?'

'Not at that bit.'

'So whoever he's gone to meet must have known that.' She shook her head. 'Why would he do that? His brother's just been murdered, wearing Danny's own jacket. He must have had an inkling he was the real target. Why go up the side of a building and into a park? It would have been pitch black.'

'Beats me. You want me to keep going with the footage?'

'Yes. For an hour or two at least. Speed it up a bit to save time.'

Clare rose from her seat and followed Gillian to the incident room. Chris was bent over a laptop and as she approached he sat back, rubbing his eyes. 'Think we can be pretty sure how Danny pays for his posh flat. He has a lot of calls and messages, all different numbers. They're mostly on WhatsApp so I can't see what the messages say.'

'So he's dealing?'

Chris nodded. 'Looks that way. I've been cross-checking each of the numbers but it's not flagged up anyone on the system.' He glanced at his laptop screen. 'I'm up to about six on Saturday. Should be done soon.'

'What time was the last call?'

Chris scrolled forward several screens. 'Saturday night. Easily a dozen or more missed calls from ten until one in the morning. Before that' – he peered at the screen – 'there's a couple of WhatsApps about half-eight. Can't see what was said, though; and there's an exchange of text messages about eight.' He was quiet for a moment as he scrolled through the messages. 'I'll just check this number.'

Jim appeared, his face flushed. 'Finn Coverdale,' he said. 'They've found him. He's in an ambulance on his way back to Ninewells.'

Clare rose from her seat. 'Where was he? What's his condition?'

'Riverside Park,' Jim said. 'Between the rail bridge and the airport. He's pretty cold, probably been there a few hours. He'd been knocked about a bit but he's conscious.'

She jerked her head at Chris. 'Leave that. If we hurry we might have time to see him before Ben interviews Leon.'

–

The A&E department at Ninewells Hospital was as busy as Clare had ever seen it.

'Used to be like this on a Saturday night,' Chris said. 'But a Monday?'

'I reckon it's folk who can't get a GP appointment,' Clare said. 'So they tip up here knowing staff will have to see them.'

'Suppose.'

The receptionist told them Finn had been taken to a treatment area to be assessed and she'd let them know as soon as they could go through. There was nothing for it but to wait. Clare scanned the room. A toddler was playing with some kind of chunky console that made a dozen different noises and she sent up a silent prayer he would be seen next. Over in the corner a drunk man was arguing with himself while a young lad with one foot bare moaned intermittently.

'This might not be hell,' Chris muttered, glancing at his phone as it buzzed with a message. 'But I bet we can see it from here.'

Clare checked her watch. The DCI would be in Glasgow now. She hoped her dad would buy the story about needing someone to look after Benjy. Then she remembered Moira, her dog walker, and she tapped out a quick message, letting Moira know she wouldn't be needed for a few days.

The noise from the toddler's toy was grating on Clare's nerves. 'Come on,' she said. 'Let's see if we can muscle in on Finn. He's probably just under observation, anyway.'

After a little persuasion the receptionist agreed to find someone to take them through. A few minutes later a nurse appeared and motioned them to follow. 'He's through here,' she said. 'Waiting to go to X-ray. But it'll likely be a while.'

Finn was lying on a bed at the far side of the assessment area. Clare fought with her face not to react when she saw him. Even from across the room he was almost unrecognisable from his Facebook photo, his eyes so swollen they were reduced to slits. There was an angry wound just above his eye and Clare recalled Ruby saying he'd a piercing on his eyebrow. Had they ripped it out? She shivered at the thought.

'Thankfully his teeth look okay,' the nurse said, leading them over. 'But he's taken quite a pasting.'

'It's an assault, then?' Clare asked. 'Not an accident?'

'Definitely an assault. Defensive injuries to his arms. Cigarette burns as well.'

Clare winced at this and her resolve to find whoever was responsible hardened.

'You'll be wanting his clothes,' the nurse said, lowering her voice.

'Please.'

She nodded. 'We can give him a gown in the meantime.'

Clare thanked the nurse. 'Is he able to speak?'

'He is. Just don't expect too much.'

He lay on the bed hooked up to machines which blinked and gave the occasional beep, his head turned to the side. Clare wasn't entirely sure he'd seen them. It was hard to tell if his eyes were open or closed. Chris pulled over two chairs and they sat down.

'Hello, Finn,' Clare said, her voice as gentle as she could manage. 'I'm Detective Inspector Clare Mackay and this is my colleague Detective Sergeant Chris West. I'm so sorry about what's happened. How are you?'

He raised a hand, a noncommittal gesture. Then he ran his tongue round his lips and swallowed. 'Oh – you know.' His voice was husky and he seemed unable to lift his head from the pillow. His eyes went to a lidded cup with a straw and Chris went to ask the nurse if Finn could have a drink.

He returned a minute later and held the cup out for Finn. He sipped, some of the water running out of his mouth. Clare took a tissue from a box and dabbed gently at his lips, making him wince.

'Sorry,' she said. 'It must hurt.'

He gave a slight nod but said nothing.

'I know you'll be tired,' Clare said, 'and we'll take a proper statement when you're up to it. But, for now, I would like to ask a few questions. Is that okay?'

His voice was little more than a whisper and Clare saw him swallow hard. 'Yes.'

'If you need a break, just let us know.'

He nodded and Clare went on.

'Can you tell us about your relationship with Theo Glancy please?'

A spasm of pain crossed Finn's face and he took a few moments before answering. 'We met online,' he said, eventually. 'Gay dating site.'

'Did you see each other often?'

'Few times. His mum has a club. Sometimes we went there. Sometimes to his flat.'

'Were you in a steady relationship?'

Finn gave a slight shake of his head. 'Theo didn't want his family to know. Said his older brother was a bit of a psycho. Suited me,' he said. 'I was fine with us not being exclusive.'

'When did you last see Theo?'

'Wednesday. I went to his house.'

Clare took out her notebook. 'What time was this?'

He was quiet for a moment, as if trying to remember. 'Just before midday.'

'And how was Theo? How did he seem?'

His brow furrowed. 'Okay, I think.'

'How long did you stay?'

He took a moment as if trying to remember. 'I left about half two – maybe three. Theo stayed on in the flat. His mum wanted him at the club but he said he'd things to do first.'

'Did you hear from him again?' Clare asked and Finn nodded.

'He texted later on. Said he'd had a lovely time and maybe we could do it again at the weekend. I texted back saying that would be great; and that's the last I heard from him.'

His eyes were moist now and Clare's heart went out to him. 'Just one last thing about Theo,' she said. 'Can you think of anyone who might have wanted to harm him?'

A single tear escaped from a swollen eye. 'No,' he said, his voice hoarse with emotion. 'I can't. Theo was lovely.'

A nurse bustled up and checked the monitors. 'Maybe not too much longer,' she said and Clare nodded. She waited until the nurse was out of earshot then turned back to Finn.

'If you're up to it I'd like to ask about yesterday.' She paused for a moment and, when he made no reply, she went on. 'A witness said you were forced into a car as you left hospital. Is that correct?'

He nodded again.

'What happened when the car stopped?'

He took a moment before answering. 'I thought maybe they were stopping to ask directions – something like that. By the time I realised what was happening it was too late. They had such a grip on me. They forced me into the car. I tried to open the door to get out but one of them had a knife – said he'd finish me if I moved.'

'Did you know the people in the car?'

'I couldn't see. They had masks on – like balaclavas.'

'How many were there?'

'Two men,' he said. 'And the driver.'

'Did you see their hands?' Clare asked. 'Their skin colour, maybe?'

He was quiet for a moment. 'Sorry – I don't remember. It was nearly dark. But – one of them had a signet ring – the kind with the flat bit on top.' He lifted his hand, a pulse oximeter on his finger, and he touched the side of his cheek, gingerly. 'I felt it when they hit me. Think my cheekbone's broken,' he said and Clare's expression softened. *Poor lad.*

'Thanks, Finn,' she said. 'Details like that really help. What about their eyes?'

His brow creased as he appeared to be thinking back. 'Sorry,' he said after a moment.

Clare smiled again. 'Not to worry. You're doing really well.'

'Did you see which way the car went?' Chris asked, and Finn shook his head.

'They put something over my eyes. But I think it went up the road. They'd forced me in the left of the car and it did a quick U-turn. Then it accelerated and swung round. I fell into the man beside me. So that must have meant it went left. I think…'

Clare smiled. 'That's great, Finn. Anything else?'

He was quiet for a moment. 'I – I don't think so. The car swung around so much, I lost the sense of where I was.'

'That's understandable,' Clare said. 'How long do you think you were in the car for?'

He considered this. 'Maybe twenty minutes.'

She noted this down. 'What about when the car stopped?'

'I think it was near some houses.'

Clare glanced at Chris. 'What makes you say that?'

'One of the men – he told the other one to wait. After a minute I heard some voices – like people were walking past – outside the car.'

'What sort of voices?'

His brow furrowed. 'Girls I think. Maybe teenagers.'

'And the men,' Clare went on. 'What were their voices like?'

'Scottish,' Finn said. 'Dundee maybe. Not posh – a bit rough.'

'Did they sound young or old?'

'Sorry – I don't know. I mean not really old or really young. Just normal. Sorry,' he said again. 'I know that's not much help.'

'It's a great help,' Clare said. 'What happened next?'

'They got me out of the car. One of them had a tight grip on my arm. Then someone else gripped the other arm. Practically carried me.'

'Were there steps? Stairs?'

'A couple of steps and a flat bit after that. I heard a door creaking and I tried to dig my heels in. I didn't want to go in wherever it was. Thought if I went in I might never…' He stopped for a moment, his eyes closed as he concentrated on his breathing. After a minute he opened them again. 'I tried to cry out,' he said, 'but they put a hand over my mouth. Horrible.' He shivered. 'Horrible taste.'

Clare gave him a smile. 'Do you remember anything about where you were? Was it a house? Or a lock-up maybe?'

'It was warm,' he said after a moment. 'And there was carpet on the floor. There must have been a rip because I caught my foot in it and one of the men said something about the carpet. So I think it was a house.'

'Great,' Clare said. 'You're doing so well.' She glanced across and saw the nurse speaking to a doctor. She held up a hand, indicating they'd be five more minutes and the nurse gave a nod. Then she turned back to Finn. 'Did they remove the blindfold?'

'No. It was on the whole time.'

'And did they say why they'd abducted you?'

He nodded. 'They said I'd to tell them about Theo – what had happened to him. They thought I'd killed him. It didn't matter how many times I said it, they just kept on hitting me. Kicking as well. And then they brought the dog.'

A wave of nausea swept over Clare as she imagined Finn's terror. Forced into a car, blindfolded and bundled into a house to be kicked and punched for something he knew nothing about. But the medics hadn't said anything about a dog bite.

'Did the dog hurt you?'

'No. But I was so scared. Even with the blindfold, I could feel its breath on my face; and the barking was so loud. I didn't know what it was going to do.'

Something stirred in Clare's memory. What was it? She couldn't quite bring it to mind. 'It must have been so frightening,' she went on. 'I'm sorry we have to ask about it.'

He gave her a watery smile. 'It's fine. I wish I could have told them something about Theo. I want whoever killed him to be caught. But I couldn't. I don't know anything.'

Clare thought about the dog. She imagined herself in Finn's place, blindfolded, sensing the dog so close. She closed her eyes for a moment. Finn had felt its breath. But he hadn't said anything about its paws on him. She opened her eyes again. 'Were you sitting or standing?'

'Sitting.'

She moved her chair closer. 'If it's okay, I'd like to ask about the dog.'

He looked at her, his brow creased. 'But I couldn't see it.'

'Don't worry about that. Hold your hand out, if you can. Show me how close you think the dog was to your face.'

He thought for a moment then held his hand out about a foot from his face.

'What sort of seat were you on?'

'Quite low. Soft.'

'Like a sofa?'

He considered this. 'Suppose.'

Clare indicated herself. 'So lower than I'm sitting now?'

He nodded. 'Definitely.'

'Thanks, Finn. Just one more thing about the dog: do you think its head was lower than your face, about the same height or higher?'

He shivered. 'I'd say about the same height, or maybe just lower.'

Clare was quiet for a moment as she noted this down. Then she gave him a smile. 'And how long did this last?'

'I'm not sure. An hour or two, maybe. Then they left me. They told me not to move or touch the blindfold so I just sat, trying to hear what they were saying. They were in another room but I couldn't make it out. My ears were buzzing.'

'What happened next?'

The creases on his brow deepened as if the effort of remembering was almost too much.

'I think I was there all night,' he said. 'I couldn't see because of the blindfold but I knew it was dark. Think I dozed off. When I wakened I was still blindfolded but I could tell it was lighter. Next thing I know they've lifted me up again, one on either side and they're dragging me out.'

The tears were flowing now and Clare saw his hands were shaking. She glanced at the monitor. His heart rate had risen. 'Take deep breaths, and blow slowly out of your lips.' She held his gaze, breathing slowly and deliberately until he breathed along with her, drawing in deep lungfuls. Gradually his heart rate calmed and the fear left his eyes.

'Are you okay to carry on?' Clare asked, her eyes flicking back to the monitor.

Finn nodded. He took another breath in and out. 'I thought they were going to kill me,' he said, his voice a whisper. 'I thought: this is how it ends. And I didn't care, really. Because of Theo. It didn't much matter any more.'

He closed his eyes and his head sank into the pillow. Clare looked at Chris. There was so much more she wanted to ask. But she sensed Finn was tiring. What else did they need to know? What had she not asked?

Chris sat forward. 'Was the dog still there at this point?'

'No. I don't think so. She must have taken it away.'

'She?' Clare's tone was sharper than she'd intended.

'Sorry. Did I not say? The one who brought the dog – it was a woman.'

Chapter 37

'It has to be Val,' Chris said as they headed back to the waiting area. Finn had gone for an X-ray to check for what the staff suspected were broken ribs.

'You think?'

'Stands to reason. Think about it. Theo's murdered and Val threatens to take matters into her own hands – her exact words if I recall correctly. Sunday was four days since Theo died. In Val's world, that's plenty time for her to decide we weren't doing enough. The only link she has to Theo is Finn.'

'And if Danny saw that news website, chances are Val did as well.'

'You can bet on it. She misses nothing, that one.'

Clare glanced at the child who was now banging the toy against the floor. 'I have to get out of here,' she said. 'Can we get a couple of uniforms to stay with Finn please? We'll need someone with him anyway. I'm not risking them trying to get to him while he's in here.'

Chris went out to make a call to the Bell Street station in Dundee. Clare lay back in her chair and closed her eyes. And then Finn's face, battered and bruised, came into her head and she opened them again, scanning the room for anyone who looked as if they didn't belong. They had to protect Finn at all costs. He might not know anything about Theo's death but he'd suffered enough at the hands of Val – or whoever was responsible for the state he'd been found in. Chris reappeared, tucking his phone away.

'Patrol car on the way. They'll stick to him like glue.'

Five minutes later, a couple of officers arrived. Clare took them through to Finn's bay and explained to the staff he wasn't to be left alone. The officers briefed, she nodded to Chris. 'Come on. Let's get out of here.'

As they walked towards the doors that led to the car park, they stood back to let a couple of footballers come in. One was hopping on one leg, an arm round his friend's shoulder. Clare waited until they had passed then she made to go out. Chris was standing, his eyes on the two men. He was lost in thought then he began walking to the car, Clare trailing in his wake.

'You want to catch me up, Columbo?' she said, as they reached the car.

'Sorry,' he said, pulling out of the car park. 'It took me a minute to work it out. The two footballers back there – they reminded me where I'd seen Danny Glancy before.'

'Which was?'

He glanced right as he joined the roundabout. 'Remember that day we were in Rhona's and I went to look at the photos on the wall?'

'Yeah?'

'She assumed I was looking at the one of Theo – winning the prize at school. Remember?'

'Again, yeah.'

'But I was actually looking at one of Danny – him and some football team. Probably a school team. He looked a lot younger. But he's not changed that much. It was definitely him.' He was quiet for a moment, as if recalling the photo. 'Something about it nagged at me, but it wouldn't come. Until tonight.'

'Go on.'

'Couple of years ago, I was playing five-a-side – Tuesday nights. Anyway, one of the lads fell awkwardly. Twisted his knee pretty badly. So I got him in the car and ran him to A&E.' He broke off as he approached a junction, muttering an expletive as a car failed to give way. 'Place was rammed – as usual – much busier than tonight. We took a seat then this lad came in, drunk as a skunk.'

'Danny?'

'No. Viggo! Must have had a fall – blood pouring down his face. He'd a load of paper towels and he was holding them against his head. The woman on reception told him to take a seat and he kicked off. Shouting the odds, saying he didn't want a fuckin' seat, could they not see he was bleeding – yadda yadda. I was going to step in, have a word, but his friend appeared and calmed him down – got him to apologise and led him to a seat.'

'I still don't see.'

'The friend,' Chris said. 'It was Danny Glancy. Seeing that footballer hobbling in – it reminded me.'

Clare's face cleared. 'So Danny and Viggo don't just know each other – they're friends.'

Chris nodded. 'Yep. Your Safenites lad – Sean something?'

'Davis.'

'Yeah, him. He was bang on. We know Viggo's supplying drugs. I bet that's why he was at Retro's the day we saw him. And I wouldn't want to be in Danny's shoes if Val got to hear Viggo was pushing drugs at her club.'

'So where is Val now,' Clare said slowly, 'and has she done something to Danny?'

Chris was quiet for a moment. 'Think I'll see what Hammy knows. He's worked Dundee for years.'

As Chris left a voicemail for Hammy, Clare's phone buzzed and she clicked to open the message.

'Let's get down to Bell Street,' she said. 'It's show time.'

Chapter 38

There was a round of applause when Clare entered the incident room at the busy Bell Street station in Dundee.

'Enough,' she said, waving it away. 'Teamwork.'

Bill came over to greet her, his face full of concern. 'How are you? Heard the doc said bruised ribs.'

'I'm fine,' she said. 'I'm annoyed at myself for being caught like that. He must have heard us outside the van. Soon as Chris opened the doors he flew out and caught me on the ribs.' She winced as she recalled the moment she saw the Choker's feet heading straight for her. 'I should have anticipated it.'

'No way,' Bill said. 'Just bad luck. That was bloody good police work, bringing him in. Think how many forces he's evaded.'

She smiled. 'It's thanks to you and Janey for being so alert. At least we knew which way he was heading.'

The door opened and Ben appeared. He took in her arm, now a semi-permanent fixture across her ribs. 'Is it very painful?'

She moved her arm away. 'It's a bit sore. But I'm better working. Stops me thinking about it.'

'Just see you don't overdo things.' He took a breath in and out. 'So, here we go, then.'

She smiled. 'Good luck. Not that you'll need it.'

He returned the smile. 'I hope not.' He showed Clare and Chris to the viewing room. 'He's being brought up from the cells now. We should be ready to start in – say – ten minutes.'

Clare settled herself on a plastic chair, Chris at her side. A few minutes later the room began to fill, everyone keen to see if Leon would admit to his crimes. Bill and Janey stood at the back, then the door opened and Penny Meakin came in. They all rose to their feet and she waved them back down.

'Especially you,' she said to Clare. 'You must take things very easy over the next few days. Maybe delegate to your nice young sergeant here.'

Chris beamed and Clare threw him a look. 'To be honest,' she said, 'I'm better keeping busy. I'd go mad at home.'

Penny arched an eyebrow but said nothing more. She accepted the chair Chris offered and made small talk until they saw Leon enter the room, accompanied by a uniformed officer. He was wearing a plain grey tracksuit and Clare guessed his own clothes were off to the lab. There was obviously some padding under the sleeve of his left arm, a hospital dressing on his dog bite, she thought, and she hoped it was hurting as much as her ribs were. His face was expressionless and he glanced around the room without much interest. And then he saw the camera high in a corner and his eyes bored into it. Clare's arm went to her ribs again, an involuntary gesture. There was something in his gaze, unflinching, uncompromising that made her very glad he had taken off into the night. Somehow, she knew, if he'd stayed, if he'd faced her down, for all her training in self-defence, in disarming and arresting suspects, she'd have come off worst.

A young woman in her thirties, power-suited, followed them in and took a seat next to him, the duty solicitor no doubt. But still Leon stared at the camera. A minute later Ben and another plain-clothes officer entered. He spoke a few words to Leon, who finally dragged his gaze from the camera and the recording began.

Ben asked Leon to confirm his name and he did so, his voice low. But when he asked if Leon was the registered keeper of the van found at the trading estate, he clammed up.

'Let's work on the basis it is your van,' Ben said, his tone brisk. 'It was found on Saturday night, an unconscious man in the back, under the influence of a substance yet to be determined.'

'Mr Maddox denies any knowledge of the man in the back,' his solicitor said.

'Curious,' Ben said. 'Two of my officers attended. When they approached the van, Mr Maddox burst out, assaulting one officer before escaping.' He turned to Leon. 'Perhaps you could explain that.'

He stared at Ben for a long minute; and, when it seemed he would say nothing, he adjusted his position and cleared his throat. 'I'd been driving,' he said. 'And I got sleepy, yeah? You guys are always telling us not to drive tired so I looked for somewhere to pull off the road – have forty winks. I passed the trading estate and thought if I went right down the bottom I wouldn't get any noise from traffic. So, I drove to that big round tower and parked up. I've a sleeping bag in the back. Thought I'd be comfier there. I went round, opened up and climbed in. Interior light's burst so I didn't know there was anyone in there. Not until I settled down, then I felt him next to me. Scared me to fuck. I've no idea how he got in but I knew I had to get out of there fast. For all I knew he could have been waiting to kill me.'

'You have to hand it to him,' Penny said. 'He's spent his hours in custody profitably. Good story.'

'It's rubbish, though,' Clare said.

'Obviously.'

'We have a team going over your van as we speak,' Ben said. 'So far they haven't reported any damage to the back door lock.'

'Must have left it unlocked.'

'With all your decorating tools inside?' Ben said. 'I find that hard to believe.'

'Like I said. I've been pretty tired. Busy too. It's easy to forget when you're busy.'

'What about the vodka bottle?'

Leon began examining his fingernails. 'What bottle?'

'A half bottle of vodka was found in the cab of your van.'

He shrugged. 'Nothing to do with me.'

'You deny it was yours?'

'Yep.'

'Did you add anything to the bottle?'

'Wasn't my bottle, so I could hardly add anything to it. That lad – whoever he was – it must have been his. Maybe he was planning to drug me.'

'I didn't say there were drugs in it,' Ben said quickly.

Something flashed across Leon's eyes.

'He knows he's slipped up,' Penny said, and Clare nodded.

'Sorry,' Leon said in mock apology. 'I just presumed that's what you meant.'

'You said it was dark in the back of your van.'

'Aye.'

'You didn't see the figure until you'd settled down to sleep?'

'No.'

Ben looked intently at him for a few moments but Leon's gaze didn't flinch.

'Let's wind back an hour or two,' Ben said, picking up his pen and scanning his notes. 'You drove down Largo Road and pulled into the Premier Inn car park, yes?'

Leon's expression darkened. His eyes were steely grey now, a flash of anger behind them. 'Not me.'

'There's CCTV in the hotel car park,' Ben said. 'We've requested the footage and we'll check it against your van registration.'

Leon shrugged. 'Somebody with false plates.'

'And a broken tail light?' Ben said quickly.

Leon's lips tightened but he said nothing.

Ben put his pen down again. 'I believe you met a young man at the Premier Inn car park, that he joined you in the cab of your van. I believe you drove him to Magus Muir car park and—'

'Where?'

'And from there,' Ben went on, 'you observed police activity and executed a swift three-point turn. What did you do after that?'

Leon sat back and folded his arms. 'No idea what you're talking about.'

'No matter,' Ben said. 'We'll wait on the CCTV. In the meantime, a chain was found in the back of your van. What is it used for?'

An expression of mock innocence crossed Leon's face. 'I don't own a chain. Must belong to the lad who broke into my van.'

Ben opened a folder and flicked through the pages, stopping at a photo of the chain, hanging in the back of the van. 'This,' he said, passing the photo across the desk.

'Never seen it before.'

'So we wouldn't find your DNA on it?'

'No idea. If it was in my van it might have picked up my DNA but it's nothing to do with me.'

'He's not going to cough,' Penny said.

'We've still enough to hold him, though,' Clare said.

'We do. Allowing for his time in hospital, we have until nine tonight. If the DNA results aren't back by then we'll charge him with abducting Finn Coverdale. We'll oppose bail and he'll be remanded in custody.'

The solicitor was speaking now. It sounded like she was making a plea for Leon to be released. Clare held her breath.

'Out of the question,' Ben said. 'We have reason to believe Mr Maddox may be responsible for five deaths. I would like to ask him about these.' He reeled off the names of the other five victims, Leon shaking his head as if he couldn't believe what Ben was saying.

'The DNA sample you gave on arrival at this station is currently being analysed at our lab and it will be compared with samples taken from these other victims.'

Leon shrugged but said nothing.

'The other victims were all young gay men who had been sexually assaulted at or around the time they died. Are you in the habit of engaging in casual gay sex, Mr Maddox?'

'You cheeky bastard,' Leon spat. He was almost out of his chair and the solicitor put a restraining hand on his arm.

Ben feigned surprise at this outburst. 'I'm sorry?'

'I'm not a fucking gaytard!'

'That's quite an unpleasant term, Leon. Do you have a problem with gay men?'

Leon's eyes bored into him and, even from behind the glass, Clare felt nervous. She hoped he wouldn't suddenly leap across the desk. He held Ben's gaze for an uncomfortably long time. Ben stared straight back. After a minute or so Ben repeated the question, his eyes never leaving Leon's. Eventually Leon gave an exaggerated sigh and flopped back in his chair.

'No,' he said, slowly and deliberately. 'I do not have a problem with gay men.'

'Are you gay?'

He closed his eyes and exhaled. 'No. I am not gay. I do not visit gay websites; nor do I pick up gay men.' He looked at his solicitor, as if appealing for her to intervene. 'I'm the fucking victim, here. It's my van that loser broke into. He planted the vodka and you're trying to pin it all on me. It's a fucking liberty.'

The solicitor caught Ben's eye. 'I think maybe Mr Maddox needs a break.'

'No!' Leon said, an edge to his voice, his eyes never leaving Ben's. 'I do not need a break. What I need is you people to understand – to know what goes on out there. The filth! The repulsive, disgusting behaviour these people indulge in, hanging about street corners, picking people up on websites – they disgust me. Do you hear? They are disgusting!'

'Who is they?' Ben asked, his calm tone a contrast to Leon's fury.

'Those so-called victims. They think they're all so modern – so liberated, having sex with people they've only just met. These men – they deserve everything that's coming to them. And they're so fucking stupid!' He threw his arms out wide, causing the officer standing by the door to move forward. Ben waved him back, a small gesture unnoticed by Leon. He wanted to give Leon as much rope as he would take and sit back while he hanged himself.

Leon's solicitor drew back slightly. 'I think maybe…'

But he wasn't listening. 'They don't even see it coming. Don't even see what's right in front of them.' He leaned across the desk, his face close to Ben's now.

Clare moved back before she could stop herself and she wondered how Ben was able to remain so cool. He had his back to her but he hadn't flinched. Not once. Leon's voice was low now, and he spoke slowly, steadily, enunciating every word with deliberate care. 'They turn their backs, you see. Complete trust.' He shook his head. 'Silly little lads.' He sat back, his lip curling. 'Masks – gags – they just don't think about the danger! Fucking idiots.' He looked round, as if inviting the officers to agree. 'Some of them even like something round their neck. Heightens the pleasure, so I'm told. Don't see it myself. What about you, love?' He turned to his solicitor, taking her in, up and down. Then he laughed. 'Nah. You're too strait-laced. I bet you won't even do it with the lights on.'

Clare had to hand it to the woman. She met Leon's gaze unflinchingly until he shrugged and looked away.

Ben waited a few moments and when it seemed Leon was spent, he picked up his pen. 'Is that how you did it, Leon? Is that how you killed them?'

He didn't answer at first. A smile spread over his face and he gave a little shake of his head. 'I'm so much better at this than you could ever imagine. I am the king of this stuff.' He let the remark hang in the air for a few moments then he looked towards the officer standing by the door. 'Don't suppose you could fetch me a coffee, son? I could do with a drink.'

'Fucking nutter,' someone behind Clare said. 'Sorry, ma'am,' he added, no doubt directed at Penny.

'No need,' she said, in her usual crisp tone. 'I'm inclined to agree with your assessment.'

Ben asked Leon if there was anything he'd like to add and, when he said nothing, he turned his head towards the recorder. 'Interview terminated at…' He checked his watch and reeled off the time.

Leon stared at him, then back at his solicitor. 'So what? I can go now?'

'I'll give him this,' Clare said, 'he's putting on a great performance.'

'I reckon he's convinced himself,' Penny said. 'Totally delusional.'

Clare wasn't so sure. She thought Leon knew exactly what he was doing.

'You'll be returned to custody,' Ben said.

'If you haven't charged Mr Maddox by' – the solicitor glanced at her watch – 'nine o'clock this evening he'll have to be released.' But her tone suggested she knew this wasn't going to happen.

Ben smiled again. 'I know.' Then he nodded to the uniformed officer to escort Leon back to his cell and he swept from the room.

Chapter 39

They were almost at the station when Hammy phoned back. Clare answered the call and put it on speaker.

'We know Viggo's dealing,' Hammy said. 'But no one will finger him. He's a bad rep – complete nutter. But it's not just drugs. Word is he's pimping.'

'Sex workers?' Clare said.

Chris drew into the car park and shut off the engine.

'Yep. The usual. Gets them addicted to drugs and when they can't pay he gives them an out.'

Clare and Chris exchanged glances. This confirmed what Bill had said.

'And is Danny involved?' Chris asked.

'We – think so. Never been able to prove it. Viggo's got them all shit-scared. Even Danny wouldn't cross him, and they've been pals for years. We bring the women in, stick them in a comfy room, promise protection but they know we can't keep them safe from guys like that. So we give them the usual advice, phone numbers of shelters, but they go straight back out on the streets. What you thinking?'

Chris hesitated. 'Not sure. But we reckon Danny was the real target when his brother was killed. Maybe Danny was trying to edge Viggo out.'

Hammy promised to let them know if he found anything else and Clare ended the call.

'Come on,' she said. 'Bring a couple of coffees into my office. We need to think.' She wandered through, checking her phone as she went. A message from the DCI confirmed he was at her parents' and was currently tucking into her mother's homemade steak pie.

> Your dad's delighted to help out with Benjy
>
> Home in a couple of hours x

'What are you smiling about?' Chris said, kicking open the door.

She hadn't realised she was smiling. 'Just overjoyed at working with you, Sergeant,' she said, tucking the phone back in her pocket.

'Hmm.' His tone suggested he wasn't convinced. 'Anyway, you'll be even more pleased when you see this.' He put down the mugs and reached into his pocket, withdrawing something wrapped in a green paper towel. Clare stared at it.

'No!'

'Yes! Sara's out of the station. Not expected back for at least half an hour.'

He put the paper towel down and it fell open to reveal two of Chris's precious Wagon Wheel biscuits.

'She'll find out, you know.'

'Nah. I've a new hiding place.' A smug look spread across his face. 'She'll never find it.'

Clare drew her coffee across the desk and sipped from it. Then she took a bite of the Wagon Wheel. 'Honestly, I don't know what you see in these. There are much nicer biscuits.'

'I'll take it back, then,' he said, stretching across the desk, but she swiped his hand away.

'Let's go through what we know.'

Chris bit into his Wagon Wheel and chewed for a few moments. 'Okay, Theo is killed but we think the killer was after Danny.'

'Agreed. Do we think Danny realised this?'

'Definitely. You saw their faces when we showed them Theo's clothes.'

Clare drew her notepad across the desk and wrote down, *motive*. 'So why would someone want to kill Danny?'

'Could be Viggo – if they've fallen out. Or maybe someone else trying to muscle in on Viggo's patch? Maybe killing Danny was meant as a warning.'

She considered this. 'I'm not so sure. These guys use knives – guns, occasionally. But there's a risk in trying to strangle someone. Not as easy as sticking a knife in their back.'

'Does logic even come into it?' Chris said, brushing crumbs onto Clare's floor, earning him a look.

'Fair point.' She wrote *turf war* on her notepad then looked up again. 'What else?'

'He's upset someone?'

'I think we can take that for granted. Unless it's a random attack.'

'In which case, we're stuffed,' Chris said. 'The chances of catching a random killer are low enough within the first few days. Almost a week later, we've no chance.'

They fell silent considering this. Then Clare wrote *who?* on her pad. 'So who might have wanted Danny dead?'

'Viggo, obviously. Not that he'd have done it himself. But he could be behind it. Or, like I said, someone trying to move in on Viggo's patch.'

Clare wrote *Viggo* and *rival gang* on her pad. Then she looked up. 'Anyone else?'

'We could look at who was released from prison recently – anyone who has history with Danny.'

'Good point,' Clare said, and she added *ex-cons* to her list. 'That it?'

'Someone with a grudge?'

'Could be. The question is, who?' She sat thinking for a minute. 'Is it worth bringing Viggo in?'

'You've two chances of him talking.'

'Yeah, I know: fat and slim. But if it wasn't Viggo, and we suggested someone was trying to move into Dundee...'

Chris shook his head. 'Guys like Viggo – they never talk to the police. Oh wait...'

She eyed him. 'What?'

He rose from his chair. 'Need my laptop. Back in a minute.'

She took another bite of Wagon Wheel, wondering what was on Chris's mind. He kicked open the door again, laptop in his arms, the cable trailing behind him. He leaned across and plugged it in and clicked to bring it to life. Then he tapped at the keyboard.

'You want to tell me—'

'Ssh,' he said. 'I just need to check something.'

A minute later he sat back. 'I knew it.'

'I'm just gonna wait...' Clare said, dipping the remains of the Wagon Wheel in her coffee.

'That list of phone numbers,' he said. 'The ones I was checking when we heard they'd found Finn.'

'Yeah?'

'There was a text message from a guy called Malky Dennehy.'

'Do we know him?'

'Small time dealer. Not above a bit of violence. Hammy's lifted him a couple of times.'

'And?'

Chris turned the screen so Clare could see the message.

> Lost ma fukn phone so this is ma numbr for next cupla days.
>
> Heard sumthin bout Theo but tell you wen I see you.
>
> Malky

'There's a string of messages,' Chris said. 'Lot of rubbish but if you scroll down you'll see them arranging to meet.' He scrolled through the messages then tapped the screen. 'There. Sent Saturday just before six.'

> Camperdown – behind the ice rink
>
> Anytime after 9

Clare sat back. 'Looks like he took the bait. I'm guessing Malky lured him there to have a pop at him, or for someone else to,' but Chris shook his head.

'You don't think Malky sent this?'

'I know he didn't. I knew his name was familiar. Sure I'd heard it recently. I've just checked the crime reports on the network. Malky was lifted for an assault on Friday afternoon. He was cooling his heels in a cell until he appeared in court this morning. He's out now but he definitely couldn't have sent that message to Danny.'

Clare was quiet for a moment, working it out. 'Okay,' she began. 'Let's say someone steals Malky's phone. Maybe looks over his shoulder while he types in the passcode, then he lifts it. Malky would have reported it stolen…'

'…and the phone company would block the number,' Chris said. 'But the thief would still have access to Malky's contacts.'

'So he stole Malky's phone to get Danny's number…'

Chris nodded. 'I think so. He nicks the phone then he sends Danny a text from a burner, telling him to use this number in the meantime. I'm guessing that wouldn't phase Danny. These guys use untraceable mobiles all the time.'

'And that's how he lured him to Camperdown,' Clare finished. 'Clever.' She met Chris's eye. 'If that's true, we may be looking at a second murder.'

'Looks that way.'

'Viggo or Val?'

Chris shrugged. 'God knows. Take your pick. I could make a case, either way.'

'It must be someone who knows Danny's mates with Malky.'

'And has Danny's number.'

They fell silent, Chris slurping his coffee.

'Is it worth pulling Malky in?' Clare asked, after a minute or two. 'Ask him about his phone?'

Chris shrugged. 'It's not in his interests to talk either, is it? He won't want mixed up in whatever's going on with Danny.'

'Unless we suggest someone's trying to take over Dundee—'

'We could hint Malky might be next?' Chris said, a smile breaking across his face. 'You think he'd go for it?'

Clare considered this. 'He'd have to know it wouldn't get back to Viggo.'

'That's the problem,' Chris said. 'Soon as he's seen getting into one of our cars – even an unmarked one – you can bet Viggo'll hear about it.'

Clare drummed her fingers on the desk. An idea was forming in her mind. 'Think I'll give Ben a call.'

Chapter 40

Clare was on the point of going home when Ben returned her call.

'Sorry,' he said. 'One of those interminable meetings. So, how are you? How are the ribs?'

'Sore! But thanks for asking. Actually, I'm after a favour.'

'Go on.'

'I have a small-time crook I'd like to bring in for questioning. But I don't want it getting back to the guy we think he works for.'

'Name?'

'Malky Dennehy.'

'He's one of Viggo Nilsen's boys, isn't he?'

'Think so. But if Malky's spotted getting into one of our cars he'll clam up.'

Ben was quiet for a moment. 'You'll need someone from out-of-town,' he said. 'Viggo will know all the local cops.'

'Do you have anyone?'

'It's not just that,' Ben went on. 'You'll need guys with the right approach – so it looks like a casual conversation with mates.'

'Will Malky go for that?'

'Yeah. No problem. If I can get hold of the right lads, they'll make it look like they want to buy some smack. It'll even look like they're doing a deal. Anyone watching won't realise what they're up to. They'll crack on they think Malky might go the same way as Danny. Usually they say they can do it the easy way or arrest him as publicly as possible – scare his punters away.

There's a beaten-up old Toyota they use. A real rust bucket. It won't look remotely like an arrest.'

'That sounds ideal. Think you can do it?'

'Depends if the guys are available. Leave it with me.'

Clare put her phone down and glanced at her watch. Half past seven. No wonder she was tired. She shut down her computer and wandered through to the incident room. A few stragglers sat poring over laptops.

'Get off home,' she told them. 'It's been a long day.'

They didn't need telling twice and a few minutes later she was left alone in the station, even the cleaner having gone. She switched the phones through to Cupar, turned off all the lights and set the alarm. The fog had lifted but it was bitterly cold and she pulled her coat round herself as she walked out to the car park. And then she remembered she hadn't brought the car. Her ribs were still too painful to drive. Across the car park she saw Max spraying his windscreen with a can of de-icer and she walked over to beg a lift.

–

Her dad was sitting in front of the woodburner, Benjy on his lap when Clare came into the sitting room. He made to rise but she waved him back down. Unusually Benjy didn't come to greet her but his tail wagged as she approached to give her dad a hug.

'Clare,' he said. 'You're so late!'

She planted a kiss on his head and suppressed a groan as her ribs objected. 'Hi, Dad. Great to see you.' She glanced at the DCI, who was pressing buttons on the microwave. 'Erm, thanks so much for helping out with Benjy.'

The little dog's tail began beating against the sofa at the mention of his name.

'It's no trouble. One of the benefits of being retired.'

She sank down on a chair opposite, shrugging off her coat. 'How is it? Retirement, I mean.'

He looked intently at her. 'You heard I had an accident.'

She smiled and placed her hand on his arm. 'Mum mentioned it. Are you okay?'

His gaze dropped to Benjy, who began licking his hand. 'Oh yes. I'm fine; and the damage wasn't too bad.' He raised his gaze and met Clare's eye. 'It's only a car, isn't it?'

She nodded. 'Yes. It's only a car.' But, somehow, she knew it was so much more than that.

The microwave began to beep and she heard the DCI open the door. A cloud of steam escaped and a delicious smell filtered through from the kitchen. Suddenly she realised how hungry she was. 'I must eat,' she said, patting his arm. 'But we'll talk later.'

By ten o'clock they were all yawning and her dad took the hint. 'I'll go up,' he said. 'Give you two a bit of time together.'

She waited until she heard the creak of the spare room door then she took hold of the DCI's hand. 'Thanks for going through; and for bringing him here. Hopefully it'll be a change for him.'

He leaned over and kissed her softly on the lips. 'You look done in,' he said. 'You get to bed. I'll take Benjy out for a last pee.'

She climbed the stairs, bone weary from the events of the day. Her dad came out of the bathroom, tartan washbag in his hand. 'All done?' she said, and he nodded.

He hesitated, and she felt there was something on his mind. She was about to ask if he was all right when he spoke.

'This,' he began, his hand indicating the house, 'it's so good of you both.'

She smiled. 'Not at all. You're helping us out.'

His face softened and his eyes grew moist. 'Let's not lie to each other, Clare. You don't really need help with Benjy. Do you?'

She opened her mouth to contradict him, then she saw the expression in his eyes – the wisdom born of seventy years on this planet. Her wonderful dad now becoming an elderly man. The role reversal had begun. Soon the child would take care of the parent and they would both recognise how acutely painful such a transition was. The least she owed him was a bit of honesty. 'No,' she said. 'I don't. Mum wanted me to come through but—'

'Alastair told me. You're in the middle of this awful murder case. I thought it would be easier all round if I came to you.'

She watched him for a moment. Maybe he was getting older; maybe he did need a bit more support. But he was no fool.

'It keeps your mum happy,' he said. 'And that's all that matters.'

She pulled him in for a hug, bracing herself for the inevitable pain in her ribs. He must have sensed her stiffen.

'Something wrong? Are you hurt, Clare?'

She pulled back. 'I've bashed my ribs a bit. Nothing serious; and don't tell Mum!'

He smiled. 'We both have our secrets, eh?' Then his face became serious. 'I will say this, though: I've not told your mum yet, but I've decided to give up my licence.'

Clare stared. 'Your driving licence?'

He nodded. 'It's time, Clare. The roads – they're so fast now. It's a younger person's game. Not for someone my age.'

She shook her head. 'Dad, you're only seventy. That's not old at all. Not these days; and it was just a bump. It happens to us all. It doesn't mean you have to give up your licence.'

He put a hand on her shoulder. 'It's time,' he said again. 'I want to stop before I have a real accident – before I hurt someone; and, besides – we have our bus passes now.'

She laughed. 'I can just see you and Mum scooting round Scotland on the bus.'

The front door slammed and Clare felt cold air rush up the stairs. 'Better get to bed,' she said. 'And, Dad?'

He turned, his eyes searching her face.

'I'm so glad you're here. So glad.'

'Me too.'

She waited until he'd closed the spare room door, then she went to her own bedroom. The DCI had lit the bedside lamps and closed the curtains. He'd probably put the electric blanket on as well. She began undressing, slowly, her thoughts on her parents. The years had passed, almost without her noticing, and an uncertain future lay ahead. The lump in her throat felt enormous and suddenly she knew she was going to cry. She sensed the DCI at her shoulder and she turned, burying her head in his chest, weeping silent tears.

Day 8: Tuesday

Chapter 41

Ben called as she was waiting for her computer to come to life. 'All sorted,' he said.

'That's great. When can we expect him?'

'If it goes to plan I'd say early afternoon. Guys like Malky don't surface much before midday. And we do want it to look like they're after a bit of business.'

Clare tried not to let her disappointment show. They had to do it right if they were to get anything out of Malky. Admittedly Finn was safe in hospital – for now. But Danny and Big Val were both still missing and she was no nearer finding Theo's killer. She had to make some progress – and fast. She went through to the kitchen and found Chris and Max, mugs in hand.

'Ben's sorted it,' she said.

Chris poured boiling water into his mug and set the kettle down. 'Oh yeah?'

'Sorted what?' Max asked. He was standing by the microwave, watching as it counted down.

'Malky Dennehy,' Clare began. 'We—'

The microwave pinged and Max opened the door.

Clare stopped. 'Is that your breakfast?'

He gave her an apologetic smile. 'Didn't have time this morning.'

Chris beamed. 'You should get up early, like me.'

Clare snorted. 'That'll be a first. Anyway, get that over your neck,' she said, indicating the porridge. 'I want everyone in the incident room in ten minutes. I'll fill you in on Malky then.'

–

Ten minutes later, every available officer had gathered in the incident room. Max had finished his porridge in record time and set up a video link with Bill, Janey and Hammy in Dundee. Clare positioned herself so she could be seen on camera and by the rest of the room.

'I'll be as quick as I can,' she said. 'But there's a lot to get through. The first thing to say is I expect Leon Maddox to be charged with abducting Finn, plus the other murders in the north-east of England. It's a great result, guys, so thank you all again.'

A ripple of chatter ran round the room and she gave them a moment. Then she glanced at a photo of Theo pinned on the board. 'We're as sure as we can be Theo Glancy was mistaken for his brother last Wednesday night and the killer's intended target was Danny Glancy. Danny disappeared, we think on Saturday night around nine p.m. He was last seen on CCTV, parked at the far end of the Camperdown Leisure Park in Dundee. The leisure park, for those who don't know it, is right next to the park itself and that's a huge area. Lots of trees and no cameras. Danny's car is still there but there's no sign of him.'

Gillian raised a hand. 'Do we think Danny's come to some harm?'

'It's a strong possibility,' Clare said. 'He received a message from Malky Dennehy on Saturday evening asking for a meet.'

She scanned the room to make sure they were all attending. 'Malky Dennehy was in custody at the time that message was sent. So there are two possibilities. Could be Danny wanted to disappear so he set the message up himself using a burner. We're fairly sure he's on Viggo Nilsen's payroll. Maybe they've fallen out and it's not safe for Danny to stick around.

'The other option is someone nicked Malky's phone to lure Danny into the park.'

She waited while they digested this then she went on.

'Either way, it makes sense to bring Malky in – see what he knows.'

A movement on the video link caught Clare's eye. Janey's hand was raised. 'Janey?'

'Guys like Malky don't talk. He's shit-scared of Viggo. They all are.'

'Yeah, I know,' Clare said. 'But DCI Ratcliffe has agreed to provide two undercover officers and a crappy old car. These guys are from out of town and Ben reckons they're expert at making it look like they're doing a bit of business with whoever they pick up.'

'Are they bringing him in under false pretences?' Max said, a note of concern in his voice.

'Nothing like that. It'll all be explained to Malky. He'll know what's happening. But they'll make it look good so if Viggo has eyes on him he'll think it's a drug deal, or something like that. In the meantime, I want Danny's photo circulated.'

Bill raised a hand. 'What about the lad Finn? Can he describe the guys who snatched him?'

Clare shook her head. 'They wore balaclavas. Soon as he was in the car they put a blindfold on him. The only thing he could tell us was one wore a signet ring. It made an imprint on his face when he was punched. Other than that, we think there were two men, plus a driver, and one woman. But that's it.'

'Has he any idea where he was taken?' Max asked.

'Not really. But he thinks he was in the car for around twenty minutes. When it stopped he heard voices passing by, so most likely in the town. He remembers walking up a couple of steps then along a flat piece of ground. A door opened and he was led inside.'

'Sounds like a tenement,' Chris said. 'Or a block of flats with a common close.' He shook his head. 'There are hundreds of them in Dundee – most within twenty minutes of Ninewells.'

Bill raised his hand again. 'But most wouldn't take twenty minutes to get to.' He glanced at Janey and Hammy. 'I'd say Douglas. Other end of the city. At that time of day on a Sunday it wouldn't take twenty minutes to get to the other schemes.'

'More like ten,' Janey said.

'I'd say Douglas, as well,' Hammy said. 'Plenty of semis and terraced houses there, but a few blocks of flats.'

'Can you arrange for a car to do a tour about?' Clare said. 'Given the state Finn's in, he'd probably have made a bit of noise so bear that in mind.'

'You're looking for a block with some flats unoccupied, then,' Hammy went on. 'Maybe end of a street.' He bent his head and Clare guessed he was noting this down. 'Leave it with us. We'll see what we can find out.'

Clare thanked Hammy then she scanned the room. 'One last thing – Big Val Docherty has also disappeared. Val, as you know, has an interest in Retro's – the night club run by the Glancys. She also made veiled threats about looking for Theo's killer.'

'Do we think she's involved in the assault on Finn?' Sara asked.

Clare nodded. 'It's definitely worth considering. Finn said there was a woman present when he was being assaulted. He described her voice as rough and gravelly and it seems she led the questioning. So we need to speak to Val urgently. But – and this is vitally important – I don't want any potential witnesses here at the same time as Malky.' She checked her watch. 'I'm expecting him early afternoon. If you do find anyone you want questioned under caution, they'll have to be taken to a different station.' She looked round the room then across at the screen. 'Any questions?'

There were murmurs of 'No, boss,' and she ended the briefing.

As she made her way back to the office, her phone pinged with a WhatsApp message. Wendy. Just two words.

Val's here.

Chapter 42

'Bring her in,' Clare said to Chris and Max. 'We have an abduction, a serious assault and a missing man. I'm not messing about any longer.'

'Hold on,' Chris said. 'What about Malky? We can't risk Val seeing him in the station.'

Clare glanced at her watch. 'There's time. Ben's guys won't be here for a few hours yet and they'll let us know when they're on their way.'

Chris and Max headed off to bring Val in and Clare sat down to reply to Wendy.

> The boys are on their way to bring Val into the station. They'll arrest her if necessary. I need to know if you think Rhona or Ruby know anything at all about Danny.

Clare's phone rang a minute later. Wendy.

'Just a quick one,' she said. 'Rhona and Val have gone out to the garden so I can't hear what they're saying. And Ruby's upstairs, doing her social media stuff.'

'What about Danny?' Clare asked.

'It's hard to be sure but I'd say they've no idea where he is. Rhona's absolutely broken. Keeps trying his number. I've heard her asking Ruby time and time again. Ruby keeps saying she doesn't know anything.'

'Hmm – you believe her?'

'Ruby? Not sure. She's definitely more together than Rhona. I think she'd be back home by now if Rhona wasn't so desperate to keep her here. She keeps saying she's lost two sons already – she doesn't want to lose Ruby as well.'

Clare considered this. 'Does Rhona think something's happened to Danny?'

'I think she does.'

'Okay. See how she is after Val leaves with the lads. Let me know if she seems different at all – less worried, yeah?'

Clare ended the call and went to ask Jim to prepare an interview room.

Val arrived in high dudgeon, her black leather trousers squeaking in protest as she sauntered towards the interview room.

'We had to arrest her,' Chris said, his voice low. 'She refused to come.'

'Dammit. Better get a move on, then. What about her solicitor?'

'On his way, apparently.'

–

Dermot Callaghan strode into the station twenty minutes later, his calf-coloured brogues tapping against the linoleum. Clare had interviewed Val on many occasions over the years and locked horns with Dermot every single time. But Val always seemed to wriggle out of any possible charges. They all knew she was responsible for her fair share of human misery but Clare had never managed to make the charges stick. She'd last seen Dermot when they'd been hunting a missing baby a few years ago. Clare thought he fancied himself as a sophisticate but today, under the harsh office lights, she saw his hair was tending to grey, his skin tanned and craggy, most likely from too many holidays in the sun. Perhaps the constant demands of being Val's solicitor had become a two-edged sword. She had no doubt Val paid well – she could clearly afford it – but Clare thought it must be increasingly difficult to defend the indefensible. He saw Clare and crossed the office to greet her.

'Mrs Docherty, if you please.'

She gave him a polite smile and led him to the interview room. 'I'll leave you to chat,' she said, her tone light. Val glared in response, then she turned a dazzling smile on Dermot.

'I could do with being outta here in an hour,' she rasped. 'There's a roll and sausage with my name on it.'

Clare closed the door before she could hear Dermot's reply. 'Come on,' she said to Chris and Max. 'Let's have a quick confab.'

'Think she was taken aback when we arrested her,' Max said. 'Did she say anything?'

He shook his head. 'Only a quick comment to Rhona that she'd be back within the hour.'

'Dream on,' Clare said. 'So, how should we play this?'

Chris rubbed the back of his neck. 'I'd say we ask her to account for her movements since Saturday.'

Clare nodded. 'She'll play dumb. Say she's been busy, working at the club and so on.'

'Most likely places with no CCTV,' Max said. 'But, if she was involved in Finn's abduction, her car would be seen crossing the Tay Road Bridge.'

'Good shout,' Clare said. 'Can you put someone on that please? In fact, run her car reg through the ANPR database as well.'

Max rose to do this and Clare picked up a pencil, drumming it against her desk. 'I think we should leave mentioning Danny until the last minute. Let her think this is all about Finn. If she was party to his abduction and assault she'll be expecting questions on that.'

'Makes sense,' Chris said. 'But I honestly can't see us being able to hang onto her. Not unless you charge her.'

'I doubt we'll have enough,' Clare said. 'But let's see how it goes.'

Max reappeared. 'That's Val ready.'

The three of them entered the interview room. Val had removed a camel-coloured furry jumper to reveal a strappy vest top. Her face was scarlet and she had placed a portable fan on the desk in front of her.

'I'm perimenopausal.' She indicated the fan. 'But you'll know all about that,' she said to Clare.

Chris suppressed a snort of laughter, turning it into a cough, and Val grinned. The joke had landed. Clare ignored the exchange and sat down, fiddling with the recording machine. She began with the usual list of those present and reminded Val she was under caution. But before she could go any further, Dermot picked up his fountain pen.

'On what grounds has my client been arrested?'

'We have reason to suspect your client of involvement in an abduction and serious assault,' Clare said.

'Nonsense,' Dermot said. 'My client—'

'Let's start with your movements since last Saturday,' Clare said, cutting across him.

Val's eyes widened in mock surprise. 'No idea. That's three days ago. I'm a busy woman.'

'Indeed,' Clare said. 'You're clearly a huge support to Rhona Glancy just now. Are you staying here in the town? Or travelling back and forth to Edinburgh?'

'Still got my mother's house in Newport,' Val said.

Clare knew the house. It was in a quiet street about ten or eleven miles north of St Andrews in the bustling town of Newport-on-Tay. She and Chris had gone there to bring Val in for questioning about the missing baby. It seemed so long ago, now. 'So you've been staying in Newport since Theo died, yes?'

'More or less.'

'Where else?'

Val shook her head. 'Just Newport.'

Clare pretended to study her notes for a minute, letting a silence hang in the air. When she sensed Dermot shift in his seat, she spoke again. 'It's not as plush as your house in Edinburgh, though. Wouldn't you be more comfortable there?'

Val shrugged. 'It's handy for the club.'

'And Rhona's house?'

'Aye. Poor lassie. She needs a bit of support.'

'Yes,' Clare said. 'It must be a help for Rhona, especially with the club to think about. You're a good friend to her.'

Val preened.

'Tell me,' Clare went on, 'is your relationship with Rhona purely business?'

'Suppose. She's a nice lassie. Good manager. I had a few bob to invest – she needed an investor. But we get on, anyway. Helps,' she added.

'I'm sure it does,' Clare said. 'She must appreciate having you to rely on.'

'Aye.'

'But you've been missing for a few days.'

Val's eyes narrowed. 'Stuff to do.'

'What sort of stuff?'

'Nothing exciting.'

'That's okay,' Clare said. 'I've had enough excitement this week. So where have you been? What have you been up to?'

Dermot raised an eyebrow. 'I don't like the sound of that,' he said. 'There's an implication of wrongdoing in that phrase.'

Clare gave him a polite smile. 'I'll rephrase it.' She turned back to Val. 'What have you been doing since Saturday?'

Val met her eye. 'Paperwork. The club,' she said. 'There's a lot to do; and Rhona's no' up to it, is she?'

'So you've been in your house in Newport-on-Tay since – let's see – since Theo's body was discovered on Thursday?'

'Mighta popped over to see Rhona; and out for a pint of milk – that kinda thing.'

'Where?'

Val stared at her. 'Where do I buy my milk?'

'Yes. And anything else you might have bought this week.'

She inclined her head. 'Newport shops, mostly. Or I might have nipped to Tesco.'

'Tesco in Dundee? Across the Tay Road Bridge?'

'Aye.'

'What about petrol?'

Something flashed across Val's eyes. Clare tried not to react but sat waiting for a reply.

'Might have,' she said eventually.

'Where do you buy your petrol?'

'Varies.'

'How about since Thursday?'

Val glanced at Dermot. 'Do I have to answer that?'

He picked up his pen and replaced the cap, as though challenging Clare to end the interview. 'You don't have to say another word, Mrs Docherty.'

She turned back to Clare, a smirk developing. 'No comment.'

Clare smiled. 'Not to worry. We can check petrol station CCTV. It is a bit odd, though. Not exactly an incriminating question. We all need petrol in our cars.'

There was a tap on the door and Clare paused the interview. Outside Jim was waiting.

'Hammy left a message asking you to call.'

She thanked him and went to use the phone in her office.

'Got a couple of possible properties,' he said. 'One down in Broughty Ferry, the other in Douglas. Both end blocks – completely empty – set for renovation – windows boarded up. We're checking with the council now. It'd be better if we had the keys, rather than putting the door in.'

'Addresses?'

Hammy reeled them off and Clare jotted them down on her notepad. 'What's your gut, Hammy?'

'I'd say the Douglas one. Balunie Crescent. It's pretty quiet round there; and it backs onto a huge park. Plus the Ferry one has a path that slopes down from the street. The lad might have mentioned that. It's the kind of thing you'd notice if you were blindfolded.'

'Any CCTV?'

There was a pause while Hammy tapped at his computer. 'She could pretty much avoid it,' he said after a minute, 'if she knew about the cameras. There's just one on the Broughty Ferry Road – where it meets Greendykes. If she turned up there we'd spot her.'

'And she'd go that way?'

'Aye. If she was heading for Douglas. Mind you, it leads to plenty other places so it's not conclusive.'

'It helps, though.' She asked Hammy to let her know if they managed to access the flats. Then she re-entered the room and started the recording again. 'As I'm sure you're aware,' she said, 'we have CCTV cameras all over Dundee.'

Val gave a shrug but said nothing.

'And so it's easy for us to check if a vehicle has driven on a particular road on any given day.'

Again Val said nothing.

'So if we were to check CCTV, say, between Dundee and Broughty Ferry…' She watched Val carefully but there was no reaction. 'Would we find your car had passed a camera?'

There was a glint in Val's eye but she remained silent. *Douglas, then*, Clare thought.

'Or maybe Douglas,' she said. 'A housing estate in the east of the city,' she added.

Val picked up the portable fan and held it close to her neck, raising her chin. A whiff of stale sweat reached Clare's nostrils and she wondered if Val was rattled. Fiddling with the fan was surely a distraction technique.

'Balunie Crescent,' Clare added.

'Never heard of it,' Val said, but she didn't meet Clare's eye.

Bingo, Clare thought. She excused herself, leaving Chris to carry on, and tapped out a message to Hammy, asking him to prioritise Balunie Crescent and to have SOCO on standby. If this did turn out to be the property used to hold Finn Coverdale there might be DNA from anyone who'd been there. Maybe even from Val.

She re-entered the room and resumed her seat. 'One last thing.'

A look of surprise crossed Val's face, as though she expected the interview to last longer.

Clare waited a few moments, then she said, 'Where's Danny Glancy?' She watched Val carefully, hoping the change of topic would wrongfoot her – hoping she'd give herself away. But she wasn't prepared for the look that crossed Val's face. There was something in her eyes that, in all the times Clare had faced her across the desk, she hadn't seen before: a look of fear.

'You tell me,' Val managed, at last. 'I've not seen the laddie since the day Theo was found.'

'You didn't text, asking him to meet you?'

This time there was no mistaking the surprise in Val's reaction. 'I might have texted him but it was only to ask where the fuck he was. His mother's goin' out of her mind with worry.'

Clare studied her. Was she telling the truth? 'You've honestly no idea where he is?'

Val put down the fan and placed a pair of pudgy arms on the table, her face uncomfortably close to Clare's. She could see the broken veins on Val's cheeks, smell the rancid breath, a mix of stale smoke and alcohol. The whites of her eyes were yellowed and Clare wondered if she was suffering from some kind of liver disease.

'If I knew where he was,' she said, taking time to enunciate each word, 'I'd rattle his jaw for him – putting his mother through all that worry.' She sat back in her chair. 'Mebbe you'd be better employed looking for Danny instead of wasting my time here.'

Dermot put the fountain pen back in his pocket and closed his leather-bound notepad. 'I think we're done here, Inspector. And I suggest you owe my client an apology for wasting her time.' He pushed back his chair and Val upended the fan, clicking a switch to turn it off.

'I'll be off, then,' she said, reaching for her jumper.

'Off to a holding cell,' Clare said, smiling. 'Pending further enquiries.'

Val met Clare's gaze. 'I wouldn't do that if I were you.'

'You're not, though, are you?' Clare said. And she rose from her chair and swept from the room.

Chapter 43

'And the prize for dramatic exit of the week goes to Inspector Mackay,' Chris said, filling the kettle from the kitchen tap.

Clare grinned. 'Couldn't resist it. Sorry to leave you to finish up.'

'Worth every minute. It's not every day you get to see Big Val Docherty's face fall to her feet. She's off to Cupar now. Best she's out of the way when Malky arrives.'

'Good call. How was she, anyway?'

'Absolutely raging. Threatening to sue, go to the papers – she even mentioned *The Sunday Post*!'

Clare laughed at this. The much-loved weekly paper was better known for its human-interest stories and light-hearted features than its cutting-edge news reporting. 'I'd love to see Val on the front cover. All the same…'

'Yeah. We don't have enough to make it stick, do we?'

'Not yet. Let's hope Hammy turns something up. Any news on that?'

'Jim says the council's sending a housing officer up with a set of keys.'

'Who was the last occupant?'

'Some old guy. Died last year. Someone turned up at the council office a few months back and paid six months' rent in cash. Most likely gave a false name. Said it was his uncle's flat but the uncle hadn't been well.'

'And they didn't question it?'

Chris shook his head. 'I think they're just grateful anyone pays rent these days – huge problem with arrears.'

'So it's empty now?'

'Yep. I reckon whoever paid the rent realised the old boy had died and thought it would be a handy place to have.'

'Makes sense. Keep me posted.'

–

It was just after one when Ben called to say his boys had picked Malky up.

'Should be with you in half an hour or so.'

Clare thanked him and went to deal with her Inbox. Half an hour later, Jim tapped on the door to say they were coming in the side entrance. She left her office to meet them and when she set eyes on the trio she honestly couldn't work out which one was Malky. Ben's boys certainly knew how to blend in. They were a scruffy group, right down to their grimy fingernails, and Malky turned out to be the tidiest of the three. He was sporting a Ben Sherman polo shirt, three-stripe Adidas trousers and a navy Puffa jacket. By contrast, Ben's officers were in dirty denims and grubby sweatshirts. They were unshaven with greasy hair and one kept sniffing and wiping his nose on his cuff. She led them to an interview room and, once in the privacy of the small room, their demeanour changed.

'This is Malky,' the sniffer said. 'He's here voluntarily and understands he's free to go at any time.'

Malky regarded him. 'How'm I supposed to get home?'

'You've an uncle in Kirkcaldy, yeah?' the sniffer said.

A look of surprise crossed Malky's face, then he nodded.

'Right, then. We'll hang around here till you're done. Then we'll run you down there, drop you at a bus stop with enough money to get yourself home. Your cover is you came with us to see some girls we thought you could run. You reckoned they were mingers and told us to fuck off. As you were in the town and the Kirkcaldy bus was away to leave, you jumped on and went to see your uncle. Sound okay?'

'Might even be worth popping in at your uncle's,' the other one said. 'Keeps you right, yeah?'

Clare marvelled at how efficient Ben's officers were, particularly as they looked like they'd just crawled out of a not very clean bed. But they had it all covered. 'Thanks, guys,' she said. 'Ask Jim and he'll sort you out with a coffee.'

Ben's officers left Clare and Chris with Malky. He eyed them suspiciously. 'This is no' going on the record, is it?'

'Nothing like that,' Clare said. 'It's unofficial at this stage. Just a chat.' She indicated the chair opposite. 'Take a seat.'

He eyed the seat then sat slowly, perching on the edge. 'What's it about, like?'

'Danny Glancy,' Clare said.

Malky eyed her but said nothing.

'You know Danny, yes?'

'Aye. What about him?'

'Danny's missing and we're concerned he may have come to some harm. Now we're not asking you to confirm this, but we believe you're both… *friends* with Viggo Nilsen. If so, you'll know Viggo's not a man to be messed with.'

'You're no' wrong there,' Malky muttered.

'One of the lines of enquiry we're following is the possibility someone's trying to send Viggo a warning – maybe even take over his patch.'

'And you think that's what's happened to Dan?' Malky asked, his voice rising. 'Someb'dy's taken a pop at him?'

'It's possible,' Clare said. 'But there's something we need to tell you.'

Malky's glance flicked between Clare and Chris. 'What? What is it?'

'Your phone was stolen, yes?'

'Aye. But it's no biggie. Phone company cut it off.'

'That didn't stop someone accessing your contacts.'

His eyes narrowed. 'Eh?'

'Whoever stole your phone got into it and copied Danny Glancy's number. When you were in custody last Friday we believe this person used another phone to send a message to Danny, pretending it was from you – saying this was your new number.'

Malky's eyes widened.

'The message asked Danny to meet you behind the ice rink at Camperdown Retail Park.'

Malky shook his head. 'And he thinks it came from me? I never sent it. I've no' been in touch with Dan since his wee bro' copped it.'

'We know that,' Clare said. 'We think your phone was stolen for the purpose of luring Danny to Camperdown. For what reason, we don't yet know. But the fact is Danny's been missing since Saturday night.'

Malky's hand went to his face. He was shaking his head. 'I cannae believe it.' He stared at Clare. 'My phone? Someb'dy nicked my phone to trick Danny into a meet?'

'That's what we think,' Clare said. She let this sink in for a minute, then went on. 'Do you know where you were when you lost your phone?'

He was quiet for a moment. 'Honestly I'm no' sure. Might've been in the pub.'

Clare picked up a pen. 'Which one?'

'The Specky Cow. Along South Road.'

Chris indicated he knew the pub and Clare went on.

'Who were you drinking with?'

Malky hesitated. 'Few of the lads. Don't think they'd want me to say.'

'Fair enough,' Clare said. 'Do you think any of them would have a grudge against Danny? Or Viggo?'

'Or you?' Chris added.

Malky sat thinking for a minute then he shook his head. 'Nobody would take Viggo on. It's no' worth it. He's a head case.'

'Might Danny have been tempted away?' Chris asked. 'Work for someone else?'

'No' Dan. He and Viggo – they're good mates.'

Clare studied Malky. Was he telling the truth? She honestly couldn't tell. 'If there had been a falling-out between Danny and Viggo, would you have heard?'

Malky eyed her. 'You sayin' that's what's happened? Do you lads know somethin'?'

Clare decided to run with the idea. See what Malky would say. 'It's a definite line of enquiry.'

Malky's hand went to his chin, fingering the day-old stubble. 'I mean – and you didn't get this from me, okay? If Viggo has taken against Danny, well, I wouldnae like to be in Danny's shoes; and I doubt Viggo would make a secret of it. He likes folk to know what'll happen if they cross him.'

'Is it possible Viggo might have gone after Danny?'

Malky shrugged. 'Depends what Danny did. But I've no' heard anything.'

They kept trying – asking the same questions in different ways, trying to get Malky to relax, to open up. But he seemed genuinely at a loss.

Clare looked at Chris. Was there anything else they could learn here? Malky didn't seem to know who might have taken his phone. Admittedly, guys like Danny were always upsetting someone – rival drug gangs picking each other off. It wasn't that unusual. But the message from Malky was something else. That could only have been sent by someone who knew Danny and Malky were friends. The question was who? From what Malky had said, if Viggo had gone after Danny, it would hardly be a secret.

'Of course, there was that bit of bother,' Malky was saying. 'The lassie in Dundee…'

Chapter 44

'Her name was Millie Davis,' Bill said.

Clare's phone was on speaker, Chris and Max gathered round her desk, listening to Bill.

'Seems she met Danny at a club one night. He walked her home, courted her – the usual. She thought she'd found Mr Right. One night he suggests they have a bit of fun—'

'Drugs?' Chris asked.

'Yeah. Coke, most likely. Anyway, one hit turns into another and soon she's an addict. Coke turns into smack and she develops a serious habit. Then Danny starts cooling it on the romance but he's still supplying her with the stuff. She gets desperate and he feeds her a sob story. The usual about owing his supplier money – doesn't know how he'll pay.'

'Let me guess,' Clare said, 'he'll clear Danny's debts if Millie sleeps with him?'

'Got it in one. From there it was a short step to Danny pimping her out. Viggo likely took a cut as well. Millie got her drugs and precious little else. The more addicted she became the less attractive she was for the punters. Eventually Danny tells her to sling her hook. She's no more use to him.'

Clare swore under her breath.

'What happened to her?' Max asked.

'Hard to be absolutely sure,' Bill said. 'A lot of this is informed guesswork. But we think she bought some pretty dodgy smack. God knows what it was cut with but she was found in a filthy flat up the Hilltown, needle still in her arm.'

'Jesus,' Clare said, her head in her hands. 'Why are we even bothering to look for this scumbag?'

'Did it come to trial?' Chris asked.

'Nah. We tried but the Fiscal said there wasn't enough evidence. No one was willing to speak against Danny – Viggo had put the frighteners on them all, even the girls. One of the worst parts of the job,' Bill said, 'telling the parents we won't be prosecuting.'

'How did they take it?' Clare asked.

'The mother was dead within the year. Cancer. The dad reckoned she lost the will to live. Turned her face to the wall. According to the family GP it can make a difference.'

'Any brothers or sisters?'

'Nope. She was the only one.'

'What about the dad?'

Bill shook his head. 'Not heard of him since. We offered him support. The GP put him in touch with a counsellor. But he was so buttoned up. Said he'd deal with it in his own way. Never saw him shed a tear the whole time.'

'Poor man,' Max said.

'Know anything about him?' Clare asked.

'Hold on.' There was a pause as if Bill was looking it up somewhere. 'Got him. Sean Davis. I think he's a sparky. Self-employed.'

She stared at the others. 'Say that again, Bill?'

'Sean Davis. Sparky from Dundee.'

She turned to Chris. 'That's him – our Safenites volunteer. The one who complained about drugs at Retro's.' Her expression hardened. 'I want him found and brought in for questioning. Check his home, business premises – if he has them – car, phone – the works. He is officially a person of interest.'

–

'Clock's ticking on Val,' Jim said.

Clare clicked her tongue in irritation. With Malky's revelation about Millie Davis she'd forgotten Val. 'Any word from Hammy? Actually, forget it. I'll call him myself.'

Hammy answered on the first ring. 'Thought you were SOCO,' he said.

'You've found something?'

'Definitely blood. Whether it's Finn's is another matter. With a bit of luck SOCO will find something.'

Clare thanked Hammy and clicked to dial Raymond.

'Yeah, I know,' he said, by way of greeting. 'I've a team heading over there now. Anything particular you're after?'

'Indications someone was held and assaulted. DNA, prints – I'd like to see if they match anyone on the system, as well as our victim. It would be good to place him at the scene. Plus I have someone in custody but the clock's ticking on that.'

Raymond sighed. 'It always is with you. Honestly – we're stretched here. Still playing catch-up after the leak. Even if the team find bodily fluids we'll not get a DNA result today. Tomorrow if we absolutely push it. We may have something on Finn Coverdale's clothes before then, though,' he added. 'We've detected some bodily fluids that may not be his.' He hesitated. 'So, if that's all?'

Clare's mind was racing. Was there anything else?

'I am pretty busy…'

'Sorry – look, I'll send DNA and prints over for my suspect; and I'll see if I can get someone to okay holding her a bit longer. If you could try.'

'Do my best. Now I really must get on.'

She let him escape and dialled Ben's number. 'I could do with a bit of advice.' She explained the situation with Val. 'She was brought in about half ten this morning. I've officers at a house where we think Finn Coverdale may have been held.'

'SOCO there?'

'Not yet.'

'You're up against it, then.'

'I know. Raymond's said it'll be tomorrow at the earliest for any DNA results and we'll have to release her by tomorrow morning.'

'You want an extension.' It was a statement rather than a question. 'Anyone we know?'

She took a breath in and out. 'It's Val Docherty.'

For a moment he said nothing. 'You think she's involved?'

'I'm sure of it. She threatened to go after whoever had killed Theo, and Finn said there was a woman's voice in the house where he was kept.'

'It's a bit thin,' Ben said. 'I don't think it's enough.'

'Can we ask Penny?' Clare said. 'Honestly, if I let Val go she'll melt away and we'll never get her; and this is serious stuff, Ben: abduction and assault. Finn could have died.'

'Are his injuries that bad?'

'Well – no, to be honest. But bad enough; and he was left in a park on a freezing cold night. Surely the abduction alone?'

'Leave it with me. I'll come back to you.'

And with that she had to be content.

Chapter 45

Hammy called an hour later.

'SOCO's here,' he said. 'Definitely blood spatter. They've photographed it and the lad I spoke to reckoned it was consistent with an assault, rather than some kind of accident.'

'Anything else?'

'Nah. I mean, they're taking loads of samples but chances are they'll find multiple profiles, especially if Viggo's used it for the odd bit of business.'

'Fair enough.' Something was stirring in the back of Clare's mind; and then it came. 'Hammy, what's on the floor?'

'Erm, different stuff, I think. Hold on, I'll see if SOCO will let me back in.'

She waited, hearing the murmur of conversation between Hammy and the SOCO officer.

'No go,' he said after a minute. 'They're working at the door just now. I don't want to get in the way.'

'Can you see in the doorway?'

'Yeah. You looking for something particular?'

'Could you ask the SOCO if there's a rip in the carpet?'

Again, she waited while Hammy asked the question. It only took a minute.

'Affirmative.'

'Good. I want a photograph of that, and can you ask them to take a sample of the carpet fibres please? Our assault victim tripped as he was led in. We might get something off his shoes; and ask them to compare any samples with his clothes. Raymond has them at the lab.'

Hammy relayed the message then he spoke again. 'Anything else, boss?'

She thought for a moment. There was something else – something she'd been trying to remember when she'd interviewed Finn; and then it came. She was right back at the trading estate in Cupar, watching Pasha the dog as he picked up Leon Maddox's scent from his van. It had been so cold, everyone's breath condensing, including Pasha's. He'd barked a few times and Clare had seen spittle fly from the dog's mouth. Did all dogs do that? She thought about Benjy. Did it happen with him? More to the point, had it happened with whichever dog had been used to terrorise Finn Coverdale? She'd asked Raymond to check Finn's clothes for bodily fluids. But would he be able to detect a dog's saliva? And if so, could they extract DNA from it? She couldn't see why not. But if he could, would it be any use?

'Can you ask SOCO to check Finn's clothes for dog saliva as well, please? And, if they can, ask if they can extract a DNA profile.'

'The *dog's* DNA?' Hammy couldn't keep the surprise out of his voice.

'Yep.' And then she remembered something else from Malky's interview. 'Hammy, do you know a pub called The Specky Cow?'

'Specky's? Aye. South Road.'

'Swing by please? See if they've CCTV from last Thursday or Friday.'

'No bother.'

Clare's phone indicated another call was waiting and she thanked Hammy before switching to Ben.

'Sorry,' he said. 'Penny says unless you have anything linking Val to Finn's abduction or assault, she won't extend her detention.'

'Dammit. I really do think she's involved.'

He hesitated. 'You've history with Val, yes?'

'I don't see—'

'Penny's concerned you're letting your determination to nail her cloud your judgement.'

'What? That's—'

'In fact, she suggested arresting Val was a mistake. She thinks you've shown your hand too early – possibly blown any real chance of nailing her.' He paused for a moment before going on. 'She did say maybe you should take a few days' sick leave – let your ribs recover. I believe it's very painful.'

Clare felt her pulse quicken and she took a couple of breaths in and out. How long was it since Penny had been operational? She had no idea what it was like on the streets these days – dealing with folk like Viggo and Val. And how dare she suggest Clare wasn't fit to be at work. She had to admit her ribs hurt like hell. But lots of folk put up with pain and they just bloody well got on with it, didn't they? She tried to ignore the small voice in the back of her head telling her Penny might have a point. Would she have detained anyone else on what amounted to little more than a suspicion? Or had she let her frustration at not being able to nail Val cloud her judgement? Had she actually detained Val in a fit of temper? Just because she could?

Ach, to hell with it, she thought. She'd made a decision, based on possible danger to life. Danny and Val had both disappeared and Danny was still missing. That alone was suspicious enough. She knew she'd done the right thing.

'And you, Ben?' she said, fighting to keep her voice level. 'Do you think it was a mistake?'

'Impossible to say.' His tone was brisk – professional. He wasn't getting involved. 'Bottom line is you have until tomorrow morning to find a reason to keep Val. In fact, Penny suggested we might limit any potential damage by releasing her at the twelve-hour mark.'

'So,' Clare said, throwing caution to the wind, 'she's more concerned about the fuss Val's going to make than the benefit of having her in custody when we *do* find something to hold her on, yes?'

There was silence and Clare wondered if she'd pushed him too far.

'Is there any real prospect of finding something?' he said at last.

'I have SOCO going over a property right now – the property we suspect was used to hold and assault Finn Coverdale.'

'And you think they'll find Val's DNA there?'

She hesitated. 'I don't know,' she said, eventually. 'Possibly not. She's not daft.'

'Then you know what to do.'

–

'Got some intel on Sean Davis,' Chris said. 'Millie Davis's father.'

'Go on.'

'First of all, we ran his vehicles through the ANPR database.'

'How many does he have?'

'Two. A Transit and a Ford Focus Estate. The Transit crossed the Tay Road Bridge every night for a week, leading up to Theo's death.'

'Time?'

'Around seven. Not always the same time but more or less.'

Clare considered this. 'Does he live in Dundee?'

'Yeah. Lawside Avenue.'

'Any premises over here?'

Chris shook his head. 'Not that we can find. He's a unit in the north of Dundee – Cheviot Crescent.'

'Bill said he was a sparky, yeah?'

'That's right.'

'Maybe he was doing homers over here.'

'He's self-employed, Clare. Why would he be doing homers?'

'Could be helping out a friend.'

'Or it could be he was watching Danny Glancy. Checking out where he went, when he was at the club. If you wanted to have a pop at the man you hold responsible for your daughter's death, what better opportunity than when he leaves the club after closing?'

'Good point.'

'And there's this: what do sparkies have a lot of?'

'I dunno. Light bulbs?'

'Honest to God, Clare! Cable. They have a lot of cable.'

She stared at him, taking this in, then she tapped at the keyboard, navigating her way to the post-mortem report on Theo Glancy. Chris came round the side of the desk as she scrolled through the pages.

'There,' he said, leaning over to jab the screen. 'A smooth garotte of between five and fifteen millimetres.'

'Like electrical cable,' Clare said slowly. She turned to face him. 'You think it could be him?'

'He has the motive – opportunity too. He was there on Wednesday night.'

Clare's mind was whirling. Was this it? Had they found their killer? 'What time did he go back over the bridge? We need to check.'

'Way ahead of you. Half past ten.'

'Danny said Theo left the club at – what – half nine?'

'Think so.'

'Okay. Let's say he's killed by nine forty-five. He was found only five or ten minutes' walk from the club.' Her brow creased. 'It wouldn't take forty-five minutes to get to the bridge from there.'

Chris shrugged. 'We don't know where he left the van. Might have been parked up in the town.'

'So he walks back to the van,' Clare went on. 'Maybe he's rattled. He's just killed a man. He probably needs to calm down. Gather his wits before driving back. He wouldn't want to be stopped for dangerous driving – have to give his details to one of our patrols.' A smile spread over her face. 'I think it works.' She checked her watch. 'Any sign of him?'

Chris shook his head. 'I'll get hold of Bill.'

He left Clare, her mind racing. Until now they'd had no idea who'd killed Theo. It was all tied up with Viggo and Val, Malky and Danny – even poor Finn; and she hadn't been able to come up with a motive that made sense. But now, there was a glimmer of hope. If Sean Davis was their man, did that mean he'd killed Danny as well? Realised his mistake and tried again? If so, Danny probably had nothing to do with Finn's abduction. Maybe Danny had been dead since Saturday night. But, if so, why hadn't they found him? Sean – if it was Sean – hadn't gone to much trouble to hide Finn's body. And, if Danny had been killed on Saturday night in Camperdown Park, surely a dog would have sniffed him out by now. So if Danny was dead, where was his body?

–

With no prospect of test results for at least another day, Clare reluctantly gave the word to release Val.

'At least I don't have to do it myself,' she said to Jim, who said he'd call the Cupar station. 'Bit cowardly but I fully expect her to put in a complaint so I've that to look forward to.'

Jim smiled. 'You've had a rotten few days. But Val's luck can't hold out for ever. You'll get her one day. They always slip up in the end.'

She thanked Jim and wandered through to the kitchen to make herself a drink. Chris came in behind her.

'I'll have one if you're making it.'

She shook her head. 'I must be getting soft in my old age.' She began spooning coffee into mugs. 'Heard from Bill?'

He shook his head. 'Not yet. But he'll let us know as soon as he finds him.'

'Fair enough. Not much more we can do, then.'

The kettle came to the boil with a rush of steam and Chris moved forward to lift it. 'I'll do it,' he said. 'No point in hurting yourself.'

'Thanks.' She stood for a moment, watching as he poured water into the mugs. 'I've released Val,' she said after a minute.

'I heard.'

'Penny thinks it was a mistake to bring her in.'

'To be honest, that sounds like a Penny problem,' Chris said, handing Clare a mug. 'Forget it. She hasn't a clue what it's like out there these days.'

She slapped him on the back. 'It's times like this I remember why I let you keep coming here.'

He inclined his head. 'You couldn't live without me.'

'I'd give it a bloody good go.'

Chapter 46

'No one at Sean Davis's premises,' Max said. 'Neighbouring traders say they've not seen him for a couple of days, although he's often there early and away late so that may not mean much. The officers who attended thought there was a radio playing inside but it was hard to be sure. The shutters were down, though, so he's probably left it on by mistake.'

Clare looked up from a stack of crime reports. 'What sort of premises?'

'Flat-roofed unit with steel security shutters.'

'Any windows?'

'No. Bill and Janey had a good look round but not much to see – from the outside at least. We could request a warrant to enter.'

Clare hesitated. She wasn't exactly Penny's favourite person at the moment, after the Val debacle. 'Let me think about that. Erm, tried the house?'

'Yep. Car's at the door but no one home.'

'What about the van?'

Max shook his head.

'Can you check ANPR again please? See when it last passed a camera. And let's send someone to speak to his neighbours – at the house, I mean. See if they know where he might be. Nothing heavy – just we're anxious to speak to him.'

She watched Max go then rose from her seat. It was stuffy in the office and suddenly she was desperate to be out in the fresh air. It was all very well managing an enquiry from her desk but sometimes there was no substitute for seeing things for yourself. She locked her computer and went in search of Chris.

'Fancy driving me?'

He eased himself off the desk he'd been perching on. 'Where we off to?'

'Anywhere, frankly. I just need to get out.'

'We could get chips.'

'I was rather thinking of some police work. You know – the stuff they pay us for.'

He went to fetch keys for a pool car. She waited, easing on her coat, then followed him out to the car park.

It was cold in the car and she rubbed at her arms, trying to keep warm. Chris turned the fan up full blast to clear the windscreen. 'So, where to?'

'I want to swing by Sean Davis's house. I've asked Max to organise someone to speak to the neighbours. But I'd like to get a feel for it myself. And, if he's not at his unit, he might have popped home. Could be Bill and Janey just missed him.'

The windscreen was almost clear now and Chris pulled out into the road. The sun was low in the sky, the moon already rising. 'Going to be another cold one,' he said.

'Yep. Done your Christmas shopping?'

'Yeah. Easy peasy. I only have to buy for Sara. She does the rest.'

'I hope you're doing your share of the Christmas preps, then. Your first as a married couple.'

'We're hosting Christmas dinner,' he said. 'Sara's already freaking out.'

'What are you having?'

'That's the problem. Her mum can't have gluten and her dad's dairy intolerant. Her sister's veggie but her brother hates vegetables. And her Aunty Joan's allergic to nuts! Honest to God, Clare, it's like the world's worst Venn diagram, trying to work it all out.'

She laughed, holding onto her ribs. 'It's a lovely thing to do, though.'

'And her uncle's bringing his cat. I said to Sara could he not leave him at home but he doesn't like to. Apparently the cat cries when he's left.' He slowed for the roundabout at the West Port, his foot idling on the accelerator. 'So I said, could he not farm him out for the day but Sara says they're all coming to us so there's no one to take him. Anyway, no one would have the little shite. He's pure evil, that cat.' He glanced at her. 'Who're you having?'

'My mum and dad and we're having Al's parents as well.'

'Ooh – should I buy a hat?'

'Don't be stupid. They live abroad but they've decided to come home for Christmas.'

'They staying with you?'

'No. They've hired an Airbnb for a couple of weeks. Somewhere in the town. They'll drive over on Christmas Day and get a taxi back.'

'You get on okay with them?'

'No idea. Never met them.'

'Seriously? How long have you two been together and you've never met them?'

'I dunno. We're both busy. Al went out to see them for a week last year. But they're busy too. Lots of friends. Always heading off on another holiday. I've no idea what they're using for money but they seem to have plenty of it.'

Chris was quiet for a moment. 'It's a compromise, isn't it?'

'Marriage?'

'Marriage – relationships – being part of a couple. I didn't realise until now. My folks – they've always been so important to me. And, don't get me wrong, I get on fine with Sara's mum and dad. Mostly. But now we're married, they're supposed to be as important as my mum and dad. Only, they're not, are they?'

Clare thought of her own parents – her dad back at Daisy Cottage looking after Benjy but, in reality, struggling with his reaction to a pretty minor accident. He didn't need to stop driving. She knew that and he probably knew it as well. But, with what Jude had said about him losing his confidence, maybe it was the sensible thing to do. She'd seen them around the town – drivers who should have stopped years ago – and she didn't want her dad to become one of them. Her heart ached for him, for his quiet acceptance that a part of his life was over. Would she ever feel anything even approaching that for Al's parents? She couldn't imagine it.

She gave Chris a smile. 'Just say all the right things and keep their drinks topped up.'

–

'What's the address again?' Chris said as they neared the end of the Tay Road Bridge.

'Lawside Avenue,' Clare said. 'Know it? Or will I stick it into Google?'

'Nah. You're okay. Had a mate used to live up that way.' He signalled left and swung the car round and off the bridge, towards the dramatic V&A building on the waterfront. 'Every single red light,' he muttered, bringing the car to a halt outside the railway station.

They made slow progress towards Lochee Road and Clare wondered if everyone was knocking off early. Maybe the town was busy with Christmas shoppers.

A mile further on, Chris swung the car round to the right and changed down as they began climbing the lower slopes of Dundee Law, known affectionately to locals as the Law Hill. He weaved through the streets, eventually turning into Lawside Avenue, crawling along, checking house numbers.

'I think that's it,' Clare said, indicating a single-storey detached house, the front clad in riven-faced blocks. It was an older property but the charcoal-grey front door and windows looked newer. The garden was mainly given over to gravel with a few stone troughs planted with hardy heathers. A dark blue

Transit bearing the logo *Davis Electricals* was parked in the drive but there was no sign of the Ford Focus.

'So he's been home and swapped the van for the car,' Clare said. Her phone buzzed with a message from Max and she swiped to read it.

'The Transit,' she read, nodding at the van, 'pinged cameras about an hour ago. Forfar Road, Kingsway – makes sense if he was heading here from his unit.'

Chris jumped out and walked up the drive, placing a hand on the bonnet. 'Engine's cold,' he said. 'Mind you, it wouldn't take long in these temperatures.' He went to the front door and pushed the bell, pressing his ear to the door to listen for any sound within. Then he walked round the back of the house, returning a few minutes later. 'House is in darkness.'

Clare eased herself out of the car and followed him back to the house, bending to put her nose to the letterbox. 'Smells okay.'

'You're thinking Danny?'

'Hopefully not. But he has to be somewhere.' She stood up again. 'We could be completely wrong. He might have nothing to do with Danny's disappearance.'

They began walking back to the car. 'Might be worth a look at his business unit,' Chris said.

Clare nodded. 'Got the address?'

'Cheviot Crescent. No idea where but I'm sure we'll find it.'

–

They were sitting in a queue at the roundabout waiting to cross the Kingsway, a dual carriageway running along the north of Dundee, when Clare's phone buzzed again.

'It's Max,' she said. 'Hopefully the Focus has pinged a few cameras.' She swiped to take the call and began speaking but Max cut across her.

'Think we've found the car,' he said. 'Where are you?'

'Old Glamis Road,' Chris said, raising his voice so Max could hear. 'Approaching the Kingsway. Heading for Sean Davis's business unit.'

There was a pause and Clare guessed Max was checking a map. 'Take a left onto the Kingsway,' he said after a minute. 'He's parked at the top of the Law Hill.'

Chris tore along the Kingsway then turned left, weaving through the streets, making for the narrow road that led to the car park at the top of the Law, Max still talking.

'Couple who called it in are waiting further down. There's a kind of turning circle. I think they're a bit freaked out.'

'How so?' Clare asked.

'They'd parked up and were going to look at the view. They noticed his car because he was parked right in front of the war memorial. Parking spaces are at the back. He was kind of blocking the road. When they approached the car they thought he was distressed so the man tapped on the window – asked if he could help. That's when they saw the knife.'

'He threatened them?' Clare said, reaching up to the grab handle as Chris took a sharp right then swerved left.

'I'm not sure,' Max said. 'They were pretty agitated.'

'What are they driving?'

'Red Toyota.'

They were on the upper slopes of the Law now, Chris changing down as the gradient grew steeper.

'There's the car,' Clare said. The turning circle was ahead, a fence screening the city allotments to the left. A red Toyota sat to the back of the circle, exhaust fumes vaporising in the cold night air. Chris pulled in beside the car and jumped out, Clare following. The couple emerged from the Toyota, their faces lined with worry. They were young, early twenties perhaps, and Clare noticed the woman kept glancing up towards the summit of the hill.

Chris gabbled an introduction and the couple gave their names as Gordon and Amy Wylie.

He nodded at this. 'Can you tell us what happened?'

'He was blocking the road,' Gordon said, his arm round Amy. 'Thought I'd mention it – in case he didn't realise he wasn't supposed to park there.'

'You didn't shout or anything, did you, Gordie? We were only going to say—'

'But he – he wasn't right,' Gordon went on. 'He was like, really upset, yeah? Crying and rocking. I tapped on the window. Asked if he needed help.' He glanced at Amy. 'He just stared at us. Like he didn't understand why we were there.'

'And then he reached over to the passenger seat and picked something up,' Amy said. 'And he waved it at us.' Her voice broke and she leaned into her husband's shoulder.

'It was a knife,' he said. 'Pretty big one, too. So we ran back to the car and locked the doors. Amy took a photo of the licence plate and we called it in. I thought we'd better get out of the way so we drove down here.'

Clare looked up the road for any sign of headlights but it was almost dark, save for the glow of a red navigation light on top of a nearby radio mast. 'Is he still up there?'

Gordon glanced round, as if expecting the driver to appear behind them brandishing his knife. 'He's not driven down, at least. Look – Amy's a bit shaken up. Do you mind if we—'

Clare smiled. 'We'll take your details, then you can get home. We can take a proper statement later on, if necessary.' She looked back as lights from another car approaching the hill swept over them and Chris stepped into the road, his hand held up. 'Turn them back,' Clare said, then she saw it was Bill and Janey.

'Another car two minutes behind us,' Bill said, leaning out of the window.

'Can you get details from this couple?' Clare said. 'And block the road off here. No one up or down. Then follow us up – but slowly, mind. Sounds like he's pretty disturbed.'

She left Gordon and Amy with Bill and ran back to the car. Chris was already gunning the engine and he took off up the road as soon as Clare had closed the door, neither of them bothering with seat belts. The road spiralled round the hill, climbing steadily higher until the tapering plinth of the granite war memorial loomed up, caught in the headlights.

'There he is,' Chris said, indicating a silver car parked in front of the memorial. It was facing south, the lights of Dundee a glittering array below, the River Tay a dark ribbon beyond.

'Give him a bit of space,' Clare said and Chris reversed, leaving the car broadside across the road, cutting off Sean's escape route.

He opened the door then turned to Clare. 'You want to wait here? The last thing you need's another kicking.'

But she was already out of the car, walking towards the Focus with a determination that owed more to restoring her reputation with Penny than to good sense. Chris retrieved a torch from the boot and ran lightly to catch up with her. As they neared the Focus, Clare pointed out a narrow viewing platform, blocked for vehicles by a black bollard. 'If he moves the car suddenly, head over there – or up the steps of the memorial.'

Chris indicated he understood. They exchanged glances, then softly they moved round behind the car, Clare making for the driver's door, Chris the other side. Sean was in the driver's seat, his eyes closed. Chris flashed the torch around the interior and they both saw something glint on the passenger seat. Sean's hand was resting on the knife handle and Clare wished they were both wearing stab vests. His other hand was clutching something to his chest but the angle of the torch meant she couldn't see what it was.

She nodded at Chris and took a deep breath in and out. Then she tapped on the driver's window, stepping back in case he went for the door. His eyes opened a little and he seemed to be trying to focus, then he closed them again. She tapped once more but there was no response. She tried again, louder this time, but he didn't seem to have heard.

Chris indicated he would open the passenger door and she waited while he pulled on a pair of gloves. He snatched at the door handle but it was locked. There was no movement from Sean, and Clare tried the driver's door. It too was locked.

'Keep an eye on him,' Chris said. 'I'll get something to put the window in.'

He was back a minute later with an emergency hammer and a thicker pair of gloves. He passed the torch to Clare and swung the hammer at the back seat window. It took a couple of sharp blows then the glass shattered into small pebble-like pieces. Clare's eyes never left Sean's face but he barely flinched as the window went in.

'Careful,' she said, as Chris reached in through the window to open the front passenger door. Clare was at his side now and she wrenched the door wide, reaching for the knife. She pulled it quickly back and out of the car. Chris leaned past her and clicked the central locking button on the dash. Then he ran round to the driver's door, pulled it open and placed two fingers on Sean's neck.

'Anything?'

'Got a pulse but it's slow.' He took out his phone. 'Breathing's shallow. I'll get an ambulance.'

'Better tell them about this?' Clare said, directing the torch on the dashboard. Two discarded boxes of tablets lay there, the empty blister packs beside them. She squinted at the box. 'Zopiclone,' she read. 'Sleeping pills, I think.' There was a half-drunk bottle of water in the cup holder and she wondered how many he'd taken. The boxes held twenty-eight tablets each. Almost certainly enough for a fatal dose. They had to get him to hospital.

Chapter 47

By the time the paramedics arrived, Bill and Janey had sent Gordon and Amy Wylie home.

'I've said we'll go round to take a proper statement later on,' Bill said, and Clare nodded.

The paramedics had Sean on a stretcher now and Clare went to speak to them. 'You saw the zopiclone packs?'

'Yeah,' one of them said. 'We'll give him some flumazenil just now. It usually helps, although' – her eye went to the empty packs – 'if he's taken all that...'

Clare waited until Sean had been lifted into the ambulance then she turned back to Janey. 'Follow them to hospital. I want you and Bill there when he wakes up. He's a suspect in Theo Glancy's murder and he may be involved in Danny's disappearance.'

The paramedics set to work on Sean, Janey and Bill in attendance. Suddenly Clare realised how cold it was and she began to shiver.

'Come on,' Chris said. 'Let's warm up in the car.'

The windscreen had a thin film of ice already and Chris turned the fan on full. 'It'll soon warm up.' He glanced at her and she attempted a smile.

'I'm just so cold.'

'Here.' He began tugging his arms out of his jacket.

'Oh, no,' she said. 'I'm fine really.'

'You are not! It's hours since you had a painkiller and we were out there for ages.' He pulled his other arm out of the jacket and tucked it round her. 'We'll soon get you warm.'

A minute later the windscreen had begun to clear and Chris directed the air towards Clare's feet. 'I reckon you should go home now. It's almost six.'

It was a tempting prospect.

'I'll run you back,' he went on, 'then I'll give Janey a call. See how our patient is.' He pulled on his seat belt then he stopped. 'Why do you reckon he did it?'

'Sean?'

'Yeah. The overdose. Why now? I'd have thought if he was going to do it he'd have done it after his wife died.'

'Guilt for Theo? When he realised he'd killed the wrong man?'

'Or maybe he's done what he wanted now,' Chris said.

'Danny?'

'Exactly.'

Clare was quiet for a moment, the only sound the roaring from the car heater. 'I think,' she began, 'I think we need to get into his business unit.' She nodded her head towards the boot. 'You got any more tools in there?'

–

Cheviot Crescent formed part of the northern boundary of the city, with houses on one side and rich Angus farmland on the other. There was a row of flat-roofed shops at the start of the crescent, with a pub to one end; and in the middle, distinctive by its steel security shutters, was Sean Davis's unit. Chris pulled up outside and they sat in the car for a minute, studying the premises.

'Sturdy-looking shutters,' he said.

'Reckon you can get in?'

'Not without doing a fair bit of damage. But I'll give it a go.'

A car pulled up behind them and Cheryl climbed out, Hammy following. 'Hammy's got a crowbar in the boot,' she said. 'In case you need it.'

'Definitely.' Clare began walking towards the unit and the faint sound of a radio reached her ears. The closer she got the louder the music became.

A woman in a blue tabard came out of a shop next door. 'At last,' she said. 'I hope you're here to turn that bloody racket off. It's not so bad out here but you should hear it in my shop.'

Clare smiled and said they'd do their best. The woman stood her ground, arms folded.

'It's a bit cold for standing,' Clare said. 'If you could give us some space, please.'

She stood on for a moment and Clare thought she might argue the point; then she marched back to her shop, arms still folded. Clare watched her go, then saw her take up position just inside the glass door.

'Let's shift the cars round this side,' she said, indicating the shop. 'Keep the rubbernecks back a bit. In case we do find something.'

Cheryl and Chris went to move the cars while Hammy approached, crowbar in hand. He studied the shutters for a minute.

'Don't suppose there's any chance of getting the keys?'

'Might be the kind that operates with a remote control,' Clare said. 'Could be in his van but I'd rather not wait, if there's a chance we can get in.'

'No problem,' Hammy said. 'I just need to find the weakest spot.' He began examining the sides of the shutters, where they met the brickwork, tapping and listening. 'Here,' he said, indicating a spot about halfway up. 'It's slightly buckled.' He set to work and Clare stood back to give him room. The woman in the tabard was back outside her shop now and a small crowd was gathering.

'Coupla lads tried to break into the pub the other night,' a young girl in a tracksuit said to her friend. 'Doors like that. Couldnae get past them.'

'Aye. Good doors, they.'

Chris joined Hammy and they worked together until they were able to wrench the shutters away from the brickwork at one side.

'Torch?' Chris yelled and Clare ran back to the car to fetch it. She returned and handed it to Chris, who had managed to squeeze himself between the shutters and the half glass door. Craning her neck to see past him, she saw the beam of the torch moving around and she heard him swear under his breath. He muttered something to Hammy, who handed him the crowbar. Seconds later the sound of breaking glass rent the night air and there was a murmur of conversation and a couple of cheers from the crowd. The music was loud now, The Boomtown Rats, Clare thought. But she couldn't remember the name of the song.

Chris handed the crowbar back to Hammy and he felt through the broken glass, trying to unlock the door. Hammy resumed prising the shutters further from the brickwork. Then he stood back to let Clare pass through.

'Keep them back,' Clare said to Cheryl, indicating the crowd, then she followed Chris through the gap. He found the handle and pushed the door open with a *ding*. Clare followed him inside, putting a hand up to her ear. The music was deafening now but, with the unit in darkness, she'd no idea where it was coming from.

Chris felt round for a switch and flicked it on. Two strip lights came to life, dazzling them after the darkness outside. The walls left and right were lined with shelving units, some with hooks holding all manner of electrical components, from packets of fuses to huge drums of cable. For a moment Clare thought of Theo, the life choked out of him almost certainly with a length of cable, then she scanned the rest of the room. To the back there was a long desk with an old chunky desktop computer and a tray overflowing with paperwork. A portable radio sat next to the tray, music blaring from it, and Chris moved to turn it off, the silence that followed a blessed relief.

A computer chair, its fabric worn at the back, was behind the desk and to the left of this was a door marked *Staff Only*. It was closed but there was no lock. Clare glanced at Chris, then she made for the door.

The smell hit her as soon as she entered – the noxious odour of a blocked toilet. Or was it more than that? Her heart pounding, she ran her fingers over the wall, flicking on a switch. The room was bathed in light and she saw it wasn't the toilet that smelled. It was the man lying on the floor, almost certainly caked in his own mess, his hands cuffed to a radiator.

Danny Glancy.

Chapter 48

For the second time in a couple of hours, Chris bent to check for a pulse.

'He's alive,' he said, taking out his phone to call for an ambulance. 'Danny?' he said. 'Danny? You're okay. We're police officers. We're getting an ambulance for you.'

Hammy appeared at Clare's back, gagging at the smell.

'See what you can find in the shop,' she told him. 'We need to get him off this radiator. God knows where Davis got these cuffs. It's a weird kind of lock.'

He disappeared and returned a few minutes later with a hacksaw, handing it to Chris.

'Hold as still as you can,' Chris told Danny, supporting his wrist, and he began working at the cuffs. 'We'll soon have you out of these.'

Danny's mouth opened a little but no sound came out. Clare moved to the sink and took a mug from the draining board. She filled it with water and bent, holding it to Danny's lips.

'Danny, it's DI Mackay – from St Andrews. I have some water here. I'll hold it to your lips. Sip if you can, okay?'

She held the mug up and his mouth began to move but he didn't seem able to drink. She dipped a finger in the mug and ran it round his cracked and broken lips. He winced and she apologised. 'Sorry. I know it must hurt. But if you can sip even a little…'

She held the mug to his mouth again and he made an effort to sip but most of it went down his chin.

'Well done,' she said. 'A few more sips like that and you'll be on the mend.' She carried on talking, trying again with the mug, as Chris sawed gently at the cuffs.

'Almost there,' he said, easing off with the hacksaw. Hammy bent to join him, a fine-nose pair of pliers in his hand. He snipped at the remains of the metal, finally breaking through, Chris supporting the cuffs to avoid tearing Danny's skin. As they eased the cuffs away, the sound of a siren split the air.

'That's the ambulance,' Clare said. 'Soon have you sorted.'

Minutes later the ambulance arrived and Chris directed them to back up to the front door. Then he led the paramedics through to where Danny lay, explaining how they'd found him.

'Severe dehydration,' Clare heard one of them say, and she stood back, giving them room to work. 'We'll hook a drip up,' he said to Clare. 'Get some fluids into him.' She thanked them and nodded to Chris.

'Let's get some fresh air.' They emerged through the gap in the shutters. 'I'll get someone out to see to this,' she said. 'Then we'd better have SOCO out again.' She sighed heavily. 'Raymond's going to kill me. And he knows how to get away with it.'

–

'I'll tell you this, Clare Mackay,' Raymond said when she finally tracked him down, 'I'll be bloody glad when you've tied this case up. We've a huge backlog, thanks to you.'

'I know,' Clare said. 'But I really do appreciate it.'

'Yeah, whatever.'

She heard the sound of conversation in the background.

'Clare, I have to go. But I'll send a team over now; and we should have some test results from Balunie Crescent soon – tomorrow, hopefully.'

She thanked Raymond and ended the call. The police station at Longhaugh Road in Dundee was half a mile from Sean Davis's premises and, within five minutes, six uniformed officers had appeared. The tabard woman had been joined by at least twenty curious locals and Clare directed the officers to set up a cordon.

'SOCO will be here soon,' she said, 'and they'll cover the entrance. Keep that lot back in the meantime.'

One of the paramedics shouted they were ready to leave and Clare directed Hammy and Cheryl to follow them to the hospital. 'He is not to be left,' she said. 'I'll ask some of the uniforms here to relieve you but stick with him in the meantime; and, whatever you do, make sure he and Sean Davis are not in the same ward!'

Chris watched them go, then he turned to Clare. 'I doubt there's anything else we can do tonight; and, to be honest, you look done in.'

She opened her mouth to protest but realised he was right. 'I am pretty tired.'

'Come on, then. I'll run you home.'

She climbed wearily into the car and sank back, closing her eyes. In all the excitement she'd been aware of the pain in her ribs but now she'd stopped the ache was all-consuming. 'Left my painkillers in the station,' she said, and Chris nodded.

'We'll stop on the way.'

–

Almost an hour later Chris pulled into Clare's drive. A volley of barking from within told them Benjy had heard the car. As she clicked off her seat belt, her phone buzzed with a message from Janey.

Danny and Sean in separate wards – 14 & 15. Dundee sent cops for overnight so me, Bill, Hammy and Cheryl are heading home. They've not been assessed yet but they've requested a psych consult for Sean. Unlikely he'll be fit for interview tonight. Dr thinks tomorrow doubtful.

J

Clare held out her phone and showed the message to Chris. Then she replied with a thumbs up, too tired to type more. She thanked Chris for the lift and climbed out of the car. The security light came on and, before she could reach for her key, the DCI opened the door, Benjy barking from somewhere within the house.

A delicious smell reached her nose as she wandered through to the kitchen. Benjy came over and raised his head for her to pat then he returned to sit by her father, who was engrossed in something at the kitchen table.

'Something smells wonderful,' Clare said, wandering over to greet her dad.

The DCI indicated a casserole on the hob. 'The last of your mum's curry – from the freezer.'

Her dad looked up. 'She'll bring some more when we come for Christmas,' he said.

Clare squeezed his shoulder and she saw he was using her iPad. 'Shopping?'

'Kind of. I was just thinking – if I'm not driving any more, maybe your mum and I could do one of those luxury coach trips. There's one on this website that visits different gardens. Your mum would like that.'

The DCI put a plate of curry down in front of her. 'Naan bread just coming.'

She sank down and gave him a smile. Then she turned back to her dad. 'That sounds like fun. Maybe there's one you'd like as well.'

A smile spread over his face. 'There is this other one – it tours cricket clubs.'

–

She wandered up to bed not long after her meal, bone-weary. The DCI followed half an hour later. She watched as he undressed, taking a hanger from the wardrobe for his trousers, placing everything else in the laundry basket. Then he bent to retrieve her discarded clothes from the floor.

'Once your ribs are better,' he began.

'Yes, I know, I know! I'll try to be tidier.'

'Promises, promises.'

He climbed in beside her and moved close so she could feel the heat of his body and she put a hand out, letting it rest on his chest.

'I didn't want to say in front of your dad,' he began. 'But I need to talk to you about work. As you know I had another meeting at Tulliallan.'

She was growing sleepy now, a combination of the events of the day and the curry. 'Sounds good,' she murmured.

'It might mean some changes, though,' he said, his hand stroking her hair.

It was an effort to form the words now. Sleep was overtaking her. 'That's fine,' she managed, and she let her hand fall from his chest and sank back into the pillows.

He lay propped up on one elbow, watching her, then he turned away and switched off the light.

Day 9: Wednesday

Chapter 49

'DNA results are in,' Chris said, as Clare waited for her computer to warm up. 'Some of them at least.'

'Yeah?'

'Leon Maddox, first of all – definite match with most of the victims in England. So he'll be charged with multiple counts of murder.'

She smiled. 'That is good news. Ben must be chuffed. Anything else?'

'Oh yes. That cold case Nita was on about – the one in Falkland Estate?'

'The thirty-year-old one?'

'That's it. It was pre-DNA but they'd stored samples from the body. They've only gone and matched it.'

'Leon?'

'Yup. So he'll be questioned about that as well. Charged, hopefully.'

'Didn't he have an alibi?' Clare said, her brow creased as she tried to remember. 'Nita was looking into it, wasn't she?'

'Yeah. Think so. She's not here, though.'

Clare picked up her phone. 'I'll send her a message. Anything else?'

'Yep. Positive match for Finn's blood at Balunie Crescent. Carpet fibres match traces from one of his shoes as well.'

Clare stifled a yawn. 'Good. That places him at the scene.'

'But that's not all.'

'Go on.'

'DNA for the McCarthy twins.'

'Seriously? They're the ones who assaulted Finn?'

'Looks that way.'

'Anything for Val?'

Chris sank down in a chair opposite. 'Sorry. I mean, we think Val was involved in this, but SOCO couldn't find her DNA in that house. If she was there I've no idea how we prove it.'

Clare sat back, thinking. 'The McCarthys – do they work exclusively for Viggo?'

'Don't think so. According to Hammy they're goons for hire. Work for whoever pays them.'

'Any chance we can we find out a bit more about them?'

Chris shrugged. 'Sure. Want me to do some digging?'

'Please. It might turn up something useful. Is that it?'

'Mostly. Raymond did say there was dog saliva on Finn's jacket. Apparently you asked about it?'

'I did.'

'Don't see how that helps. We already know there was a dog there. Finn told us. It's not like we can check the dog's DNA.'

Clare said nothing to this.

'Can we?'

'That's what I don't know. But I can't see why not.' She lifted the phone and dialled Raymond's number.

'I've not even started on last night's scene, if that's what you're asking.'

She laughed. 'I wouldn't dare.'

'I phoned through the results from the assault house this morning, though.'

'Yes – thanks. Got them. Chris says there was dog saliva on Finn Coverdale's clothing.'

'Yep. Mostly on his jacket and sweatshirt. Upper body.'

'Can you isolate a DNA profile from it?'

'For the dog?'

'Yes.'

Raymond hesitated. 'I mean, we can. But I'm not sure how much good it'll do you. We don't have a database of dodgy dogs.'

'But if we found the dog we think was involved you could tell us if it was the same animal?'

'I mean, I suppose. But my guess is the dog won't talk.'

'Very funny. It might help us identify the owner.'

Raymond agreed to extract DNA from the dog's saliva and Clare put down her phone.

Chris shook his head. 'I'm with Raymond, here. How do you propose to find the dog?'

She smiled. 'Think what we know. We have the McCarthy twins at the scene.'

'Or their DNA at least.'

'Yeah, I know.'

'They could argue they'd visited the house in the past.'

Clare shrugged. 'They could. No doubt their defence would advise that. But it's a start. And we also suspect Val Docherty was there.'

'Well, you do.'

She stared at him. 'What is it with you lot? You know what Val's like, and she's in this up to her neck. She's friends with Rhona and she's out for revenge. Val doesn't like to lose face. Having her friend's son murdered is losing face in her eyes.'

'Fair enough. But the dog?'

'Let's find out if either of the twins or Val has a dog.' She thought for a moment. 'Remember what Finn said?'

'About the dog?'

'Yes. He was sitting on a low-ish seat and the dog was almost face-to-face with him.' She opened her desk drawer and began rifling through it, clicking her tongue in irritation.

'Painkillers?'

'Tape measure.'

'Eh?'

'Do you have one?'

'Erm, at home.'

'Ask Jim, would you? He's bound to have one. Bring it to the staff room.'

'You want a tape measure?'

'Have you developed professional deafness? Go and ask him!'

He rose from his chair and went in search of Jim. Clare followed him out and made her way to the staff room. A minute later Chris appeared with a tape measure.

'I swear Jimbo has everything in that cupboard.'

'Probably.' She moved to one of the easy chairs and sat down. 'Okay, I'm Finn. I'm sitting on a chair like this. The dog's face is almost level with mine. Maybe it has to look up a bit. But I can feel its breath.' She indicated the tape measure. 'What height's its head?'

Chris extended the rule until it stretched from the floor to Clare's face. 'About seventy-five centimetres.'

'What's that in old money?'

He sighed. 'I don't know why you persist in using inches. It's not like you're in your eighties.'

'Just tell me.'

'About thirty inches. Maybe a bit under.'

'So we're looking for quite a tall dog,' Clare said. 'Benjy's much shorter and he's medium-sized.'

'Could be a cross,' Chris said. 'It's not necessarily a particular breed.'

Clare heaved herself to her feet. 'Yes, that's true. But it's a start. So let's get some local intel. Do the twins have access to a dog?'

'Does a bear shit in the woods? They're scumbags. They always have dogs.'

'So, find out what they have – or have access to.'

'And Val?'

'Definitely.'

They wandered back through to Clare's office. 'To be honest,' Chris went on, 'she strikes me as the type to have one of those fluffy toy dogs. Either that or a hulking great Rottweiler.'

'Either way, we need to know,' Clare said. 'And fast.'

'Wait, though,' Chris said. 'How do we get the dog's DNA? If it's as aggressive as Finn made out, I'm not keen to ask it for a cheek swab.'

'We'll cross that bridge when we come to it,' Clare said. 'Let's see what dogs they have and take it from there.'

Chapter 50

'Got something,' Max said as Clare entered the incident room.

She wandered over to his laptop and sat down beside him.

'I've found the McCarthy twins on Facebook,' he said. 'Their profiles are public so I can see all their photos.' He jabbed the screen with his finger. 'This is Brad's profile – and this photo...' He clicked on an image and a group of men appeared, grinning at the camera. 'He's the one holding up a pint of Tennent's.'

'And there's his signet ring,' Clare said. 'Well spotted. Can you forward that to Raymond please? It's a long shot but he might be able to match it to the bruising on Finn's face.'

Max noted this down.

'Any dog photos?' Clare asked.

He looked surprised. 'I didn't look. But hold on.' He clicked on *Photos* then groaned. 'Looks like hundreds, if not thousands.' He glanced at Clare. 'I guess you want me to check.'

'Yes please. And do the same for his brother. There was a dog involved in Finn's assault and we might be able to match it to the saliva on his clothes – if we find it.'

She headed back to her office but Chris forestalled her. 'Cops in Newport and Edinburgh are checking up on Val. They'll let us know if she has a dog.'

–

It was mid-morning when Clare heard Danny Glancy was well enough to be transferred to the hospital in St Andrews.

'He'll need a couple more days to recuperate,' Chris said. 'But Rhona requested the move. In the circumstances, they were happy to make a bed available.'

'Can we speak to him?'

'Yes. The doctor advised not tiring him out but he's much better.'

'Okay. Give me a shout once he's there and we'll head over.'

But it was almost midday before they heard Danny was safely installed in Ward One of the community hospital.

'I'll drive, shall I?' Chris said, dangling the car keys.

'I can't wait till I can drive again,' Clare muttered, following him out to the car park. 'If I have to suffer one more of your handbrake turns…'

He affected an injured look. 'I'll have you know I'm driving especially carefully so I don't hurt your ribs.'

'Hah!'

'Anyway, what's the plan for our Mr Glancy?'

'Just a straightforward statement.'

Chris unlocked the car and Clare eased herself in.

'You going to mention Millie Davis?'

She considered this. 'I'd prefer to speak to Sean Davis first. See if he told Danny who he was.'

'I can't see that happening any time soon,' Chris said. He pulled out of the car park, heading for the hospital. 'He's been moved to Carseview. Intensive Psych Care Unit,' he added.

'Not surprising,' Clare said. 'He must have been pretty disturbed. It's hard to imagine his state of mind. All that grief over his daughter – then his wife dies. He kills Theo and realises he's got the wrong man. It's enough to push anyone over the edge.' She shook her head. 'He must have been in hell.'

Chris took a left at the roundabout and turned into the hospital car park. 'I'd save your sympathy for Theo. Rhona and Ruby too. They're the innocent victims.'

'Sean Davis didn't do anything wrong, though,' Clare said. 'Except love his daughter so much he couldn't bear to live without her.'

'Apart from killing Theo and leaving Danny chained to a radiator.'

'There is that.'

Chris drew into a parking space and they made for the front entrance, following signs for Ward One.

Danny was sitting on a chair next to a bed in a cheerful ward. Clare showed her ID badge at the nurses' station and they walked across the bay to greet him. Superficially there was little sign of injury. But his face was pale and drawn, and his skin had a translucent quality. He looked up as they approached but said nothing. Chris went to fetch two chairs from a stack by the window.

'Hello,' Clare said.

'Hey.'

Chris placed a chair behind Clare and she eased herself down. 'You're looking better than you did last night.'

He shrugged. 'I'm all right.'

'Were you injured at all?'

His lips twitched, as though attempting a smile. 'My dignity, mostly. Bit embarrassing, like.'

Clare thought back to how they'd found him – the smell she'd initially thought was a blocked toilet. If he'd been chained to a radiator since Saturday night without access to one… She guessed he'd rather not talk about that and she gave him a smile.

'Maybe you could explain how you came to be there.'

His gaze dropped and he began worrying the cuff of his sweatshirt. 'I'm not sure, really.'

'Let's go back to Saturday, then. You left your mum's house, yes?'

He nodded. 'Needed to get back to the flat. Mum – she was doing my head in – not wanting me or Ruby to go anywhere, panicking in case something happened to us as well.' A wry smile played on his lips. 'Turns out she had a point.' He stopped for a moment, as if lost in thought then he went on. 'Val was there too. Couldn't get rid of her. Said she was supporting Mum but, really, she was trying to find out what had happened. It was driving me mental.' He raised his gaze to meet Clare's. 'I was gutted about Theo. Angry, too. But I needed a break, yeah?'

'Of course,' Clare said. 'We all deal with these things in our own way. So, you went back to your flat?'

He nodded again.

'Did you go straight there? Or stop off somewhere?'

'Tesco,' he said. 'Went to get a couple of things – sandwich and a paper.'

'And after that?'

'Straight over to the flat. Couldn't wait to eat my sandwich in peace.'

'Was there anything suspicious in the building? Or in your flat?'

'No. Didn't see anything. Parked my car round the back as usual and took the lift upstairs. Flat was pretty much as I'd left it.' He swallowed. 'Seems like weeks ago, now.'

'How long did you stay in the flat?'

'I was gonna stay all night. Order a pizza, few beers. But then I got this text.'

'From?'

'Fella I know. Malky Dennehy. Asking for a meet. I say Malky but it wasn't his number. He said he'd lost his phone. Must have got himself a cheap one from Tesco. Told me to use that number till he sorted it.'

'What time?' Clare asked, keen not to betray she already knew this. She needed to know if Danny was being honest.

'About eight. Bit later, maybe.'

'Where did he want to meet?'

'Up by the ice rink.'

'Is that usual?' Clare asked. 'Pretty dark spot, especially given what happened to Theo.'

Danny shrugged. 'Didn't think about it at the time. Malky's pretty sound, yeah? Sometimes—' He cleared his throat and Clare had the impression he was working out how much to tell

283

them. She waited and finally he continued. 'Sometimes you want to talk about something without other folk seeing, yeah?'

Clare glanced at Chris. 'What folk?'

He looked away. 'Just folk.'

'Viggo Nilsen?' Chris said.

He shot a glance at Chris but said nothing.

'Okay,' Chris went on. 'I get that. Viggo's a hothead. Maybe a bit quick at jumping to conclusions. Would that be fair?'

Again, he said nothing.

'Let's say it's fair, then,' Chris continued. 'So Malky asks you to meet. What happened after that?'

'Malky said to meet at Camperdown – behind the ice rink. I hadn't had my pizza so I thought I'd go by Maccy D's. Get a burger.' He stopped at the mention of the food. 'Don't suppose you guys could get me something decent to eat? Food here's okay but…'

Clare smiled. 'Let's see how we get on. So, you went up to McDonald's. What happened next?'

His brow creased as he thought back. 'I drove to the far end of the car park to eat my burger. That way I could see if anyone else appeared.'

'Anyone in particular?' Clare asked, but Danny simply shrugged.

'Never know who's watching. Anyway – I finished the burger then I sent a message to Malky telling him I was on my way. So, I locked the car, went up the side of the rink and into the park. Pretty dark,' he said. 'But after a bit I started to make stuff out. I mean, there's some lights. But you cannae see too far ahead. Then I hear Malky's voice.'

Clare and Chris exchanged glances. 'You heard Malky's voice?'

He stared at them, as if unsure why they were asking. 'Aye. He said my name and something like "over here". I started walking over and – I dunno. Think someb'dy must have hit me from behind.' He put up a hand and touched the back of his head. 'Had a right lump. Nurses said it'd been bleeding. I never realised.'

Clare picked up her pen. 'Can you go through that again, please? You went up the side of the ice rink and into the park.'

There was a look of confusion in his eyes. 'Yeah. Like I said, I went into the park. I'd sent a text to Malky so he knew I was coming. He must have seen me cos he tells me to come over—'

'You definitely heard his voice?'

'Definitely Malky.' He shook his head. 'Never had him down for a rat. Set me up. Good and proper.'

Clare glanced at Chris again. Then she looked back at Danny. 'I can't give you too much detail at the moment but it's a matter of public record that Malky Dennehy was in custody on Saturday night.'

Danny gaped. 'Malky – what?'

'He didn't send that message, Danny. Someone else had his phone. Malky was arrested on Friday afternoon. He was in a cell until Monday morning.'

His eyes widened, as though he couldn't take it in. 'Someb'dy had his phone? Who? Who the fuck did that to me?'

'As I say, we can't tell you much more at the moment. But Malky did not send that message.'

Danny's hand went to the back of his head again, probing the injury as if it would give some clue as to who'd hit him. 'But I heard his voice,' he insisted. 'It was Malky.'

'You're sure?'

'I've known Malky for years. It was him.'

Clare was quiet as she weighed this up. Could it have been Malky? Might he have been part of some sting operation she knew nothing about? Surely not? Even Ben wasn't that devious – or was he? She put this thought to the back of her mind. 'Let's leave it for now,' she said. 'What's the next thing you remember?'

His eyes closed for a moment then he opened them again. 'That place – where you found me. I'd no idea what had happened – why I was there. Thought it musta been someone trying to muscle in on Viggo. Hit him by hitting me.'

'Anyone in mind?' Clare asked. She knew Danny's abduction was nothing to do with Viggo but information was always handy. The corners of Danny's mouth turned up. The bump to his head clearly hadn't blunted his wits.

'Nah. Nothing to take over, is there?'

Clare suppressed a smile. 'Go on.'

'I was on the floor,' he said. 'Cuffed to that radiator.'

'Was anyone else there?'

'Not to start with. Thought there was – radio was on. Blaring. I yelled out but no one came.' He shook his head. 'The only thing worse than taking a beating is waiting for a beating.' He broke off, running his tongue round his lips. 'No idea how long I was there. Kinda lost track of time. Then I heard the shutters getting pulled up and a ding as the door opened. He pulled the shutters down again and in he came.'

'Can you describe him?'

'Not really. Big, though. Broad, yeah? He had the light on in the shop so when he opened the door I could see his outline.'

'Anything else?'

'Dark hair, I suppose.'

'Did he speak?'

Danny rolled his eyes. 'Did he ever. Thought the fucker would never shut up. Mind you, when he was talking he wasn't giving me a kicking so—'

'Can you recall what he said?'

Danny shook his head. 'Something about this lassie. Millie. How I'd killed her and he was gonna get his revenge. Raving loony.'

Clare stared at him. *Oh my God*, she thought. *He doesn't even remember.* She tried not to let her face betray her feelings. 'Did you know who he was talking about?'

'Eventually, yeah. He was pretty hard to understand at first – stomping about, yelling at me. And then I got it. This lassie

– we went out for a bit. But she got into the drugs scene. Went right off the rails.' His brow creased, as if he was trying to remember. 'I heard she died. Happens with druggies. Anyway, turns out this bloke was her dad – and he was blaming me for what happened.' He shook his head. 'Loony,' he said again.

Clare fought with her temper. There was no point in reacting to Danny's version of the truth. She had to know what else had gone on in Sean Davis's unit. 'So this man blamed you for the death of his daughter?'

'Yeah! Like it was down to me. I told him it was nothing to do with me. Said it wasn't my fault she got hooked on drugs. But he just kept yelling it was me who got her on the stuff.' His expression darkened. 'Complete bollocks. After a bit, he went away again. I shouted after him. Said he'd better let me go – that somebody would come looking for me, but he just went. Pulled the shutters down and away. Left that radio blaring as well. I started yelling for help but nobody came.'

'Did he come back again?' Chris asked.

'Coupla times. Brought me a bottle of water. No food, though. Just the water.'

'You managed to drink?' Chris said.

'Aye. Bit of a hassle getting the cap off with my hands. Spilled a bit but I managed. Asked him to let me use the toilet but he said I could piss where I lay.' His face coloured and he looked away. 'In the end I'd no option.'

'Did he speak to you when he came back?'

'Aye, a bit. I thought I'd try that Stockholm thing – get on his good side, yeah? I asked him some questions. Asked about his lassie but that just made him greet. So I tried fitba. Asked if he was a Dundee or a United supporter – you know? Anything to get him talking. But it was like he wasn't all there. He'd shout at me – ranting and raving. Then the fight would go out of him and he'd be greeting again. Sometimes he'd sit, staring into space. I tried everything I could think of but I reckon his mind was well away. I even said if he let me go we'd say no more about it but if he kept me here he'd be in a lot of bother.'

'What did he say to that?' Clare asked.

'Not much. Just there wouldn't be any trouble. Pretty soon neither of us would have anything to worry about.'

'What did you think he meant by that?' Clare said.

'Thought he was going to kill me. Stick a knife in, cut my wrists, maybe beat me to death with a brick. Either way, I didn't think I was getting out of there.'

'And he assaulted you?' Clare said.

At this, Danny's hands began to shake and he gripped one with the other. 'Just a few kicks. I was surprised, to be honest. Thought he'd really go for me. He killed Theo. You do know that, don't you?'

Clare glanced at Chris. 'He said that?'

'Yeah. Said how he'd been watching me. He knew my jacket.' He stopped, shaking his head. 'Poor Theo. All he did wrong was take my jacket.' He broke off for a minute. 'So I thought for sure he was going to kill me. I didn't know how but I thought he was stringing it out – make me suffer. But then…'

They waited.

'The third time he came he said he wouldn't be back. To be honest, I was losing the will. I'd had no food, just the odd bit of water. I was cold, tired. Part of me wished he'd just get on with it. Do whatever he was going to do.' He shook his head. 'Then he said he wasn't going to do anything. He was just going to leave me.' Danny ran his tongue round his lips. 'Said he'd leave me to die – like I'd left Millie. I yelled at him not to do it. Promised him money – anything he wanted. Said I'd get it for him. I told him how my brother had been killed and I knew how he felt. Said maybe we could put up gravestones for them both. Or a bench – you see them in parks. I was talking and talking – trying to keep him there but he went, closing the door behind him. I heard the shutters coming down and I thought that was it. I've no idea how long I was there before you guys turned up.' He flicked a glance at Clare. 'You saved my life. How did you even know where to come?'

Clare took a moment to answer. 'That's the thing about the police,' she said. 'We'll help anyone – no matter what they've done.' Out of the corner of her eye she saw a figure approaching. Rhona's face was lined with worry but she managed a smile when she saw Danny. Then her eyes went to Clare and Chris, and she stopped.

Clare pushed her chair back. 'Thanks for your time, Danny. We'll leave you and your mum in peace.' She walked across to Rhona, hovering at the entrance to the bay and she patted her lightly on the arm. 'He's fine,' she said. Rhona's eyes met Clare's and she saw they were brimming with tears. 'Honestly. He'll be fine.'

Chapter 51

'Jesus,' Chris said as they emerged from the hospital and walked towards the car. 'What a prospect – chained to a radiator and left to die.'

'Not that different from Millie Davis,' Clare snapped back.

'Yeah, I know. But chances are Millie died pretty quickly. Danny was there for days, knowing he was going to die.'

'But he didn't.'

'You due some painkillers?' Chris said, clicking to unlock the car. 'You're helluva snippy today.'

'Scumbags have that effect on me.' She eased herself into the car. 'Funny thing, though – Malky's voice.'

Chris shook his head. 'He's misheard. He was expecting to hear Malky so he heard him. Most likely Sean Davis heard Malky mouthing off in the pub, when he lifted his phone. Could be he shouted something like *over here* to the barman when he was trying to get a drink. Sean copied his voice. That's all.'

Clare considered this. 'I'm not so sure. Dark night, meeting in an isolated park. You'd surely be on your guard.'

'You're reading too much into it,' Chris said. He tugged on his seat belt and pulled out of the car park.

'Maybe. But Sean Davis—'

'What about him?'

'He's a sparky, isn't he?'

'You thinking he's done some electronic wizardry?'

She was quiet for a moment. 'I'm not sure.' She took out her phone and dialled the number for the Tech Support unit in

Glenrothes. Diane Wallace, who headed it up, was in a meeting but her colleague Craig took the call. Clare explained what had happened at Camperdown Park.

'And this Sean Davis had the lad Malky's phone?' Craig said.

'Yes.'

'And he's a sparky?'

'He is.'

'How did he get hold of the phone?'

'We're not sure yet. But we think he probably lifted it from him in a pub.'

'Hmm, okay. He'd need the passcode, but he could easily have looked over Malky's shoulder when he was typing it in. Or maybe Malky used his birthday. You wouldn't believe how many folk do that. Most likely his birthday's on Facebook as well. It wouldn't be difficult.'

'Assuming he could get into Malky's phone,' Clare said. 'What then?'

'Voice notes,' Craig said. 'Most folk use them. If it was me I'd listen to his voice notes. Isolate the speech I needed.'

'So if he'd said someone's name?'

'Exactly. He could select any recording where Malky's saying someone's name – or "come here", or anything like that. Then he creates a new audio file with all the speech he wants. You said he was in a park, yeah?'

'Yes. Camperdown Park in Dundee.'

'Plenty of trees, I'm guessing?'

'Lots.'

'Okay. He straps an audio device to a tree and operates it from his phone – or any other remote control. Piece of piss for a sparky.'

'So he could replicate Malky's voice? Make our victim walk towards the device—'

'…and he hits him from behind,' Chris finished. 'It fits.'

'And it wouldn't be hard. Not for a guy like that,' Craig said.

Clare's phone buzzed with a message from Max. She thanked Craig and switched to the message. 'Photos of the McCarthy twins with a dog, but it's a Staffy.' She glanced at Chris. 'They're not tall, are they?'

'Nah. Not tall enough for what Finn told us. Unless it's a cross.'

Clare squinted at the message. 'Max reckons it's too small.'

'Any word on Val?'

'Nothing so far. Come on – let's get back. I'm desperate for a coffee.'

—

Jim had left a message on Clare's desk and she clicked her tongue in irritation.

'Sup?' Chris asked, slurping his coffee.

'Seems we can't interview Sean Davis. He's been sectioned.'

'No real surprise,' Chris said. 'Not after what Danny told us.'

She sat thinking for a minute. Then she lifted the phone and dialled the number for Carseview, the psychiatric hospital. She'd almost finished her coffee when Sean's doctor came to the phone. She introduced herself and asked for an update on his condition.

'We suspect him of a serious crime,' she said. 'Is there no possibility of interviewing him?'

'Sorry,' the doctor said. 'He's in acute mental distress. Not only could it be dangerous for him, I'd have to put on record that anything he did say wouldn't be reliable.'

Clare thought for a moment. 'Is that likely to change?'

Her phone began to buzz with another incoming call but she tapped to ignore it.

'Hard to say,' the doctor said, 'but probably not in the next few days. He's been unable to speak about what brought him here so he's a fair way to go.'

'Are you aware of his history? His wife and daughter?'

'Actually, no,' the doctor said. 'I can see from his medical records he was prescribed zopiclone to help him sleep. But there's no detail. Whatever was going on, he's not confided in his GP.'

Clare related the story of Millie, and Sean's wife's subsequent death. 'Might that have a bearing on his present condition?'

'Undoubtedly,' the doctor said. 'He may be suffering from PTSD, following his daughter's death. Thank you. That's very helpful.'

Clare asked a few more questions but learned little and she thanked the doctor for his time.

'So he might never face justice,' Chris said when she'd ended the call.

'Possibly not. If I were his solicitor I'd recommend he pleaded diminished responsibility. But he might never be fit to plead.' She shook her head. 'I hope Danny Glancy realises the part he unwittingly played in his brother's murder.'

'Bit of a stretch.'

Clare shrugged. 'Depends on your perspective.' She glanced at her phone and saw the voicemail icon was flashing. A message from Nita. She clicked to play and put it on speaker.

'Boss,' Nita's voice said, 'that historic case in the Falkland Estate. Sorry I'm late getting back to you. I was caught up on another enquiry. Anyway, I got the records from archives. It seems Leon Maddox was questioned but his cousin gave him an alibi. Weird coincidence, though. His cousin's Val Docherty. She said he was with her all weekend around the time Charlie Thomas was killed so they had to let him go. It probably is a coincidence but thought I'd better tell you.'

The message ended and they stared at each other.

'Did I just hear that Leon Maddox is Big Val's cousin?' Chris said.

Clare shook her head. 'I can't believe it.'

'So she lied. He killed Charlie Thomas and she's lied to protect him.'

'Hold on,' Clare said. 'I want to nail Val as much as you – more, probably. But it's thirty-odd years ago. I doubt we can prove she lied – not after so long.'

Chris frowned. 'I dunno. It has to be worth a shot.'

She was about to reply when her door opened and Max came in, his eyes shining. 'Val has a dog!'

She stared at him. 'What kind of dog?'

A smile spread over his face. 'A German Shepherd – and a big one, at that.' He closed the door and pulled over a chair. 'A couple of plain-clothes guys sat in a car outside her house in Newport early this morning. She came out about nine and put the dog in the car. They tailed her, keeping well back. She drove to this park along the road – Kinbrae Park it's called. They stopped a bit further back and watched her get out with one of those tennis ball things you throw. They waited till she was in the park then they followed her in, laughing and joking, cracking on they were a couple of mates out for a walk. Anyway, bit of luck – Val throws the tennis ball a few times then she throws it too hard and it ends up in the trees. The dog hares in after it but can't find the ball. Our two lads head over towards the trees, one shouting to the other he needs a slash. In he goes and he finds the ball before the dog. Quick as a flash he takes out an evidence bag and picks it up.'

'Dog saliva! That's genius.'

Max laughed. 'They thought so.'

'Did she see them?'

'No. She went into her pocket and took out another ball. The dog ran after ball number two and the lads headed back to their car.'

'Max, that's brilliant. Where's the ball now?'

'They dropped it at the lab about half ten. Raymond said he'd rush it through.'

'Excellent. Is that it?'

He hesitated. 'It might not be relevant but Gillian's got a bit more on Brad McCarthy.'

'Go on.'

'Seems he's planning on settling down. Girlfriend's expecting. Word is she's told him to get a proper job. Doesn't want their baby growing up with a father in and out of jail.'

Clare sat back in her seat, twiddling a pen between her fingers. 'That's very interesting. Any word on what he plans to do?'

Max shook his head.

'What about his brother? He'll struggle without Brad, won't he? That's their USP: the scariest twins in town.'

'Good point. I'd guess Viggo will pair him up with another wall-puncher; but they're such a unit, those two.'

She sat thinking for a minute then she came to a decision. 'Let's bring in the McCarthy twins. Keep them apart. Get them solicitors.' She picked up her phone. 'I've a call to make.'

Chapter 52

'This had better not be about Val again,' Ben said.

Clare hesitated.

'You're wasting your time. Penny won't go for it. Unless you have something absolutely cast-iron.'

'Well…'

He sighed. 'Go on, then. Spit it out.'

–

She spent the next couple of hours at her desk working through a backlog of paperwork until her phone began to ring. Glancing at the display, she saw it was Raymond and she swiped to take the call.

'Couple of things for you,' he said, dispensing with the usual pleasantries. 'First of all, Sean Davis's DNA's on the handcuffs used to restrain Danny Glancy. It's also on Malky's phone; and Danny's phone was in a desk at the unit.'

'Pretty conclusive, then,' Clare said. 'Not that there was any doubt. But it's always handy to have the evidence.'

'How is he?' Raymond asked.

'Not great. He's sectioned at the moment. He may never come to trial. Erm, is that all?' Her tone was hopeful and it didn't escape Raymond's notice.

'I'll put you out of your misery,' he said. 'We rushed the saliva test on the dog's ball – tennis ball, that is.'

Clare laughed and, out of habit, put a hand to her ribs. They were definitely improving. 'And?'

'Bearing in mind I am not an expert in dog DNA, there is a clear match between the saliva on the tennis ball and the saliva on Finn Coverdale's clothes.'

'Enough to say it's the same dog?'

'I'd say so.' He hesitated. 'There is just one thing.'

'Yes?'

'Did you get consent for the dog's DNA sample?'

She laughed again but Raymond cut across her.

'I'm deadly serious. Clearly the dog couldn't consent. Did the owner?'

She was quiet as the implications dawned on her. 'We didn't ask.'

'In that case, it may not be admissible. Dog DNA has been used in a couple of court cases in the past but I'm not sure there's been one like this. I'd suggest having some other evidence up your sleeve.'

Clare sat on after the phone call, weighing this up. He had a point. Not only might the test result be inadmissible, but any evidence gathered as a result might also be struck out. She had to find another way of nailing Val.

And then she recalled her conversation with Ben and a smile played on her lips. They might just do it.

—

It was after six when she heard Brad McCarthy had been picked up.

'He'll be here in about forty minutes,' Chris said.

'What about the brother?'

'Nothing yet. But they're hopeful. Apparently he's either at his snooker club or the bookies most days. They're watching all the likely haunts.'

'We'll crack on with Brad, then. Can you make sure he has a solicitor please? I need to alert Ben.'

He arrived just after Brad, the duty solicitor ten minutes later.

'Any luck with Penny?' Clare asked when she'd closed her office door.

'In principle. But she insists we have signed statements from both twins before she'll sanction Val being arrested again.'

'Works for me,' Clare said. 'The last thing I want is to have to release her a second time. I'm not sure I could face that.'

'You and me both,' Ben said. 'Her complaint about the last arrest's come in already.'

Clare shook her head. 'She's an absolute chancer; and I reckon she lied to give Leon an alibi for that case thirty years ago.'

'As to that,' Ben said, 'we may not be able to prove it. But it's one to keep handy. Maybe use it to wrong-foot her.'

Jim tapped on the door. 'That's the lad McCarthy ready for you; and Janey phoned from Dundee. They've picked the brother up. He'll be here within the hour.'

'Thanks, Jim. Could you stick him in another room please? And get him a solicitor as well. I'm hoping this one won't take too long.'

Brad McCarthy was built like a wardrobe, his shoulders broad and muscular. His hair was closely cropped and he had a tattoo up one side of his neck. He sat, dwarfing his solicitor, a nervous-looking man in his late twenties. Brad's arms were folded across his chest but when Clare and Ben entered the room he put a hand up to his chin, rubbing it as though bored already. Clare's eyes went to a signet ring – the one she thought had left an imprint on Finn Coverdale's face. It was a hopeful start.

She began the recording then introduced herself and Ben. There was a flicker of something in the solicitor's eyes when she gave Ben's rank, and she wondered if he'd been expecting Brad's misdemeanour to be a minor one. If so, he was in for a disappointment. Brad, for his part, kept his arms folded, his jaws chewing rhythmically. He grunted to acknowledge the caution and the solicitor indicated his client would be answering 'No comment' to all questions.

'That's a pity,' Clare said. 'We may be able to help each other.'

Brad snorted but Clare pressed on.

'Where were you last Sunday?'

He muttered a 'No comment' and Clare continued.

'Late afternoon,' she added. Seeing he was determined to remain silent she went on. 'Were you in a car that stopped on Ninewells Drive, just after the roundabout?'

Again, nothing.

'I believe you were in a dark-coloured saloon car that stopped on Ninewells Drive. You and another man got out of the car and approached a young man, forcing him into the car. This young man was then taken to a house where he was held against his will. He was threatened, assaulted and was in fear for his life. These are serious charges, as your solicitor will confirm.' She paused for a moment to let this sink in. 'You're out on licence – correct?'

The first sign of uneasiness flashed across Brad's eyes. 'I've not done anything,' he said.

Clare regarded him steadily. 'Sure about that?'

He met her gaze then looked away, examining his nails and, again, Clare's eyes went to the signet ring.

'Let's move on, then. Are you familiar with Balunie Crescent in Douglas? It's an area to the east of Dundee.'

'I know where it is,' he said, a note of impatience creeping into his voice.

'You know people who live there?'

He shrugged but said nothing.

'Have you visited any properties in Balunie Crescent?'

'No comment.'

'Okay,' Clare said. 'Let's save us all some time. The DNA of the young man who was abducted was detected at a property in Balunie Crescent. Your DNA is also in the room where he was held.'

'I'm sure properties like that have multiple visitors,' the solicitor said. 'The presence of Mr McCarthy's DNA doesn't mean he was involved in the abduction or the assault.'

'It would be quite a coincidence, though,' Clare said. 'And, given Mr McCarthy would be returned to custody if we arrest him on this matter, I'd say it was in his interest to talk to us.'

Brad stared at Clare. 'No – comment,' he said, emphasising each word.

'Interesting ring you have there,' Clare said, and Brad's eyes narrowed. 'The assault victim sustained bruising to his cheek and there's a distinctive mark from what we believe was a signet ring.'

'Not uncommon,' the solicitor said.

'It all helps,' Clare countered. 'We have enough evidence here to arrest Mr McCarthy, which would see him returned to custody to serve the remainder of his current sentence. But – we may be able to avoid that.'

'I'm listening,' the solicitor said.

'The statement given by the victim confirms he was forced into the car by two men and, once in the car, he was blind-folded. But when he was taken into the house in Balunie Crescent another person was there. A person with a dog.'

Brad shifted uneasily in his seat, his eyes avoiding Clare's.

'This person used the dog to further terrorise the victim and we have now identified the owner of that dog – the person we believe ordered the abduction and encouraged the assault.'

A smile played on Brad's lips. 'You'll never get her,' he said, goaded out of his silence.

'I didn't say it was a woman,' Clare said. 'But it's interesting you think it was – and that you think we'll never *get her*, as you put it.'

Ben sat back, his posture relaxed, and Clare wondered if this was an attempt to put Brad at his ease – defuse the situation. 'My officers tell me you're going to be a father.'

Brad's jaw tightened and for a moment he didn't speak.

'Congratulations,' Ben said. 'When's the baby due?'

'March.'

He smiled. 'Nice time of year. You'll be making plans, yes?'

Brad shrugged again.

'Maybe thinking of changing your ways? A new start. Be good to give the wee one a stable home. New job, regular money, a good life.'

'I'm not sure I see…' the solicitor began but Ben ignored him.

'We know some people,' he went on. 'People down in England. It's a project we run, jointly with one of the local authorities. Government funding, too. It's only open to ex-offenders and it's completely new. Building houses.'

Brad's lip curled. 'Slave labour, by the sound of it.'

'Far from it. Yes, you'd be getting your hands dirty – brick-laying, plastering – whatever you fancy. Staff come in from the local college and train you. You learn a trade and, okay, the money's not amazing. But every single person who works on the scheme gets a share of the profits. Not a huge share, but the longer you stay, the greater the share. We help you find housing as well.' He paused to let this sink in. 'It would be a new start for the three of you – away from here and the likes of Viggo.'

Brad snorted. 'Shows what you know.'

'What?' Ben rounded on him. 'You tell me, Brad. What don't I know?'

There was the hint of a smirk on Brad's face and he studied Ben for a minute before replying. 'Guys like – well, let's just say some guys – naming no names, you understand. They don't let you leave. It doesn't work that way. You leave – you might be fine for a few weeks. You think you've got away with it. You let your guard down and you end up with a knife in your back.'

'We can protect you from Viggo,' Clare said. 'You'll be hundreds of miles away. Let's be honest, Brad – you're not exactly public enemy number one. As long as you're off his patch, Viggo won't come after you. He's too busy keeping everyone in line here.'

'We can even give you a new identity,' Ben said. 'You and your girlfriend. No links back to your old life. But it has to be worth our while. It's a lot of trouble and expense, so we need to know you're on board.'

He looked at them for a long minute. 'What do you want?' he said eventually.

'We want to know who ordered the abduction,' Clare said. 'And we want the name of the dog owner and details of their participation in the abduction and assault. We want a statement that will stand up in court.' She stopped for a moment to let this sink in. 'We'll shortly be interviewing your brother,' she went on, 'and we are authorised to offer him the same deal. If two of you go on the record, you'll face no charges; and there's every chance of a conviction.'

Brad began fiddling with the signet ring. 'If I give you lads a statement and I walk out of here I'll be lucky to see next week.'

'If you give us a statement that ticks all our boxes,' Ben said, 'you'll be on your way to England by morning. We can keep you here in a holding cell, bring your girlfriend in, put her in the picture. Then we'll send her home, put an officer on the door and the pair of you can be away by morning. You'll go to one of our safe houses in England while we set up a job and so on. This time tomorrow it'll all be a distant memory and you'll be on your way to a new life – one with good, hard graft and a bright future.'

Brad glanced at his solicitor, who took the cue.

'Perhaps we could have a moment?'

'You reckon he'll go for it?' Clare asked Ben as they waited outside the room.

'Hard to say. He'd be daft not to. The DNA and the ring – they're enough to send him back to prison.'

Jim approached as they stood chatting. 'That's the other twin here now. Solicitor's on his way too.'

Clare asked Jim to install Bruce McCarthy in another inter-view room then she saw Robbie signalling that Brad and his solicitor had finished their talk. They re-entered the room, Clare's eyes on Brad, trying to guess what he'd decided. The solicitor was sitting forward, fountain pen poised over his notepad. Clare restarted the interview and she asked the solicitor if Brad was prepared to co-operate.

'Mr McCarthy has agreed to give a statement with one qualification: if his brother does not give a similar statement, he will not testify in court,' the solicitor said. 'Further, if he does testify it must be by video link, behind a screen and not in the same building as the accused.'

'Agreed,' Ben said. 'So let's get that statement done.'

—

Bruce McCarthy proved a tougher nut to crack. He stuck firmly to 'No comment,' refusing to be drawn. It was only when Clare mentioned Brad's time in prison that his eyes flickered with interest.

'Must have been tough on you when Brad was inside,' she said.

He shrugged. 'I managed.'

Ben took up the thread. 'My colleagues in Perth prison tell me Brad had a pretty cushy time. King of the Wing, apparently.'

'Knows how to take care of himself,' Bruce said.

'And he took care of things on the outside as well,' Ben went on. 'So they said. He let it be known anyone messing with you would be sorry.'

Bruce said nothing.

'So you might be mistaken for thinking if we arrest Brad and he goes back inside you'll have nothing to worry about.'

Bruce shrugged.

'Only it's not going to be like that,' Ben said, folding his arms. ' 'Cause where Brad's going, he'll not be bothering about anything back here.'

The solicitor eyed Ben. 'Perhaps you could explain.'

Ben ran through the plan for Brad and Bruce to begin a new life in England. Bruce listened, his eyes on Ben. For a few minutes he didn't speak.

'You don't outrun these guys,' he said eventually.

'You think?' Ben reeled off a handful of names. 'Heard of them?'

'Aye. Word is they upset someone and ended up in the river – or the foundations of someone's house.'

Ben nodded. 'I know. I put those stories about.'

Bruce stared at him. 'You saying they're no' dead?'

'Alive, well and working on one of the projects I told you about. A couple of them have just bought their first houses. Kids in the local school, lives completely turned around.'

The solicitor cleared his throat. 'Can you provide some evidence of this?'

Ben shook his head. 'Afraid not. We've kept them safe precisely because they can't be traced. Not by anyone outside the senior team who manage it.' He looked back at Bruce. 'Think about it. You and Brad – you're not getting any younger. Do you really want to spend the rest of your lives knocking seven bells out of whoever's upset Viggo? Watching your back all the time in case someone takes a pop at you? And what happens when you get too old to throw your weight around? When someone younger and fitter steps in? You're going to be an uncle soon. A new baby, and Brad's signed up for this. He's going whether you go for it or not.' He glanced at Clare, then back at Bruce. 'We're authorised to offer you this chance. But we want a signed statement naming the person who ordered the abduction and assault; and we'll video you reading it. If we have to, we'll set up a video link for you to give evidence. Your identity will be concealed, of course, your image blurred. But hopefully a recording of your statement would be enough for a conviction.'

The solicitor indicated he wanted to speak to Bruce alone and they left the room.

'What do you think?' Clare said as they wandered through to the incident room.

'Hard to say. It's a lot to give up, his lifestyle. To start again, laying bricks or learning how to plaster. The pay would be a lot less than he gets from Viggo. But Brad's baby might swing it.'

Jim signalled they could return to the interview and they walked back, Clare hardly daring to hope Bruce would agree. Without him, they'd lose Brad's evidence. Granted, they could charge both with the abduction and assault on Finn. The DNA might be enough to convict them. But they'd be unlikely to give evidence against Val. Naming her could get them a modest reduction in their sentences but they'd still be going away for several years. Val could argue they'd named her out of a grudge. She might even say someone had stolen the dog to use in the assault. She was expert at wriggling out of charges. No. They needed both twins.

The solicitor opened his mouth to begin but Bruce forestalled him.

'How would this work?' he said. 'Can I take my stuff?'

'Not furniture,' Ben said. 'Some clothes, although nothing distinctive. Personal possessions. But no electronics. No phone, laptop – none of that. We give you the basics to get you started. A new phone – not fancy but it is a smartphone. We set you up in a rented property, give you a bit of cash until you start earning.'

He sat weighing this, his hands clasped on the table in front of him. 'When?' he said, eventually.

'Tonight. Or tomorrow night at the latest.'

'So soon?'

Ben adjusted his position, his manner brisk. 'Has to be. We'll keep you in custody here – with your agreement, obviously. You won't be near any other prisoners – just Brad. Then about three in the morning we take you to your house. We use old cars, unmarked, officers in plain clothes, dressed to blend in. You'll have a maximum of one hour in your house to gather your possessions – under supervision, of course. Everything goes in black bin bags so it looks like you're doing a spot of fly tipping. Then you walk away. It's likely your disappearance will be reported a few days later and we launch a hunt for you. But there's minimal publicity – no photos. After a decent amount of time we'll start a rumour you've died in some turf war – body never to be found. We'll even haul in a few of the usual suspects and interview them in connection with your disappearance.'

A smirk crossed Bruce's face. 'Pity I won't be around to see all the fuss. Do I get a funeral?'

'That might be taking it a bit far,' Ben said. 'So…' He glanced at Bruce's solicitor, then back at Bruce. 'Do I take it we have a deal?'

He sat silent again for a few minutes, his head inclined as if running through the consequences. Then he met Ben's eye. 'Ach, what the hell. Viggo's finished anyway. You've got yourself a deal.'

Clare sat forward. 'A name, please. Who ordered the abduction? Who was there in that house using a dog to intimidate the assault victim?'

The silence that followed was agonising. Clare watched as he seemed to be accepting the inevitability of the deal he'd been offered. Finally he sat back, crossing his arms again. 'It was Val,' he said. 'Val Docherty.'

Chapter 53

It was after ten by the time Clare made it home. The McCarthy twins were both in custody, Ben having made arrangements for the moonlight flit that night. Brad's girlfriend, Molly, had taken a bit of persuading, particularly given the urgency of the move. She'd been shocked at the seriousness of the charges Brad might face. But, when the shock had died down and the plan was explained, the prospect of a new life for them as a family was a strong enough temptation.

'It'll be a wonderful new start for us,' she'd said. 'I'm hoping there's a good nursery wherever we end up. Then I can find a job and we can really be a proper family.'

Penny had taken even more persuasion but eventually agreed Val could be re-arrested. 'But only after those two men have left for their new lives; and, once she's in custody, you can formally request a DNA sample for the dog.'

Clare thought there was a hint of amusement in Penny's voice and, not for the first time, she wondered where she got her information. Nothing seemed to escape her.

Ben drove Clare home. 'I'd suggest you come in a bit later tomorrow,' he said. 'It's been a very long day.'

Clare shook her head. 'I'd like to be the one to arrest Val. Soon as we get the word.'

He pulled into the drive at Daisy Cottage and jerked on the handbrake. 'Sorry,' he said. 'Penny's ruled that out. You can sit in on the interview but you're not to take the lead.'

'What? No way!'

' 'Fraid so. Penny's concerned it'll look like a vendetta.' His voice softened. 'Let's be honest, Clare – she has a point.'

The DCI, alerted by Benjy's barking, opened the front door, light streaming out.

'We'll chat about it in the morning,' Ben said. 'In the meantime, you're not to set foot in the station before ten at the earliest.'

She eased herself out of the car and walked wearily towards the DCI. He gave Ben a wave then he put an arm round Clare.

'Come on, you. I'll warm up some food.'

As she walked into the sitting room, the lights caught her eye and she smiled. 'I can't believe you've put the tree up. It's still only November.'

'Blame your dad,' he said. 'Anyway, it's December in a couple of days.'

They sat round the table, Clare eating warmed-up shepherd's pie, her dad's face full of concern.

'Do you always work so hard?' he said, and Clare shook her head.

'Just a tricky case.'

'Making progress?' the DCI asked.

'I think so.' She tapped the table with her fingers. 'I really think we've got Val this time.' She smiled. 'And we won't be letting her go.'

The DCI frowned. 'I thought you had your killer.'

She waved this away. 'Oh yes. We caught him; Ben's delighted. But if I could just put Val away…'

He eyed her. 'You're not letting this become an obsession, are you?'

She put down her fork. 'If being obsessed means wanting to see criminals put away then go on. Call me obsessed. But I for one will sleep easier in my bed knowing the likes of Val's under lock and key.'

The DCI's phone buzzed with a message and he clicked to read it. He scrolled through several screens then he tucked it back in his pocket without comment.

'I'm guessing you'll be going in tomorrow,' he said, 'if you're so determined to put Val away.'

She looked at him, wondering at his tone, his choice of words. *Determined?* She was starting to think he'd been away from front-line policing for too long. Had he forgotten what it was like out there, cocooned in his office on the third floor, writing reports on national policy, or whatever it was? Had he forgotten the frustration of seeing folk like Val escape justice time and time again?

'Don't worry,' she said. 'I'll call a taxi. Save you a trip.' His face fell and she felt a pang of conscience. She was being petty. She knew that. But she couldn't stop herself. He'd irritated her now and she couldn't let it go.

'It's fine,' he said, rising from the table. 'Just let me know when you want to go in.'

‒

She lay beside him, listening to his breathing, slow and regular, and she wondered about that exchange. Was he right? Was she becoming obsessed with seeing Val behind bars? Penny had used the word 'vendetta'. And now Al was suggesting pretty much the same thing. Maybe if her dad hadn't been around they'd have talked this through – those end-of-the-day chats as they warmed their feet in front of the woodburner. And then she remembered he'd said something about his own job. Something about some changes. What had he meant? Her last thought as she drifted off was to make time to talk properly.

Just as soon as this investigation was over…

Day 10: Thursday

Chapter 54

'Val's on her way in,' Jim said as Clare walked through the front office.

'Oh yes? Any reply to her arrest?'

'The usual – victimisation, personal vendetta by you. Nothing you wouldn't expect.' He smiled, but the smile didn't reach his eyes. 'I'm not sure what's going on here, but do you definitely have enough to hold her this time?'

She returned the smile. 'I think so, Jim. But thanks for your concern.'

He nodded. 'Ben arrived an hour ago. He said you wouldn't be in before ten so he's been using your office. But I'll sort him out a room now.'

She shook her head. 'Don't worry. We need to work together on Val's interview.'

Ben looked up as she entered. 'You look better,' he said. 'Good sleep?'

'The best. First night I've not wakened with these ribs.'

'Glad to hear it.' He eyed her. 'I hear a rumour Al Gibson's on the move. Quite a coup, that new role.'

She stared, not understanding. Was she missing something?

He saw her face. 'Oh, Clare – sorry. Ignore me. I've probably got the wrong end of the stick.'

But it was all starting to make sense. Al's job. She recalled him trying to speak to her a couple of times. All those meetings through at Tulliallan. It must be something to do with that.

With this case and her late nights, she hadn't picked up on it. And now Ben was sitting here in her office, assuming she knew about it. That must mean it was a done deal. But what was the deal? What had he signed up to?

She forced a smile. 'No, don't worry. We've just not seen that much of each other this past week. It's been…'

He smiled. 'Tell me about it! Anyway, sorry if I've put my foot in it.'

She waved this away and sank down in a seat opposite. Whatever it was, now wasn't the time. They'd Val's interview to prep for.

And then she remembered the McCarthy twins. 'Last night,' she began.

'The McCarthys?'

'Yes. Did it all go to plan?'

'Yep. They left about four a.m., all three of them.' He glanced at his watch. 'They'll be there by midday.'

'Long way, then?'

'Best not ask. The fewer folk who know the better.'

'And you have their statements on video?'

'Yep. Both naming Val, stating she executed the whole thing. Told them to lift Finn – take him to the house in Douglas and beat the shit out of him until he confessed to killing Theo. She watched as they assaulted him, egging them on.' He smiled. 'Two independent statements admitting their own involvement and Val's. I reckon it's more than enough for a jury to convict.'

'So – Val. Will you bring up Leon Maddox's alibi – the thirty-year-old case?'

He was quiet for a moment. 'On balance, I think we'll leave that out. For now anyway. It can always be resurrected later.'

Clare said nothing. If it had been left to her, she'd have thrown everything she had at Val. But it was Ben's call. 'You want to lead the interview?'

He nodded. 'It's for the best, Clare. But I am happy for you to sit in – if you want.'

She considered this. It was more important they nailed Val than she was there to do it, but after all these years… 'You really think we've got her this time?'

'Definitely.'

'And my being in the room – would that compromise the evidence?'

'Not at all. You weren't involved in the video statements the McCarthys gave us and we've now made an official request for the dog's DNA. As a suspect under arrest she can't object.'

'Then I'd like to be there.'

'Thought you might say that.'

Val arrived half an hour later, striding into the station with the confidence of a woman who did not expect to be long detained. Dermot Callaghan, her solicitor, was wearing a long raincoat with a deep vent in the back and it flapped as he marched about the front office doing his best to demonstrate his indignation.

'It's quite outrageous,' he announced to Jim, who responded with his most patient smile. 'Mrs Docherty has already been subject to police harassment and I can promise you we will be speaking to the media as soon as this charade is over.'

Jim led the pair to an interview room and went to let Clare and Ben know they'd arrived.

Ben gave Clare a smile. 'You've waited a long time for this.'

She rose from her seat. 'Makes it all the sweeter.'

'I really must protest in the strongest terms,' Dermot said as they entered the room. 'Mrs Docherty has suffered quite enough of this nonsense.'

Ben made no reply, waiting while Clare set up the recording. Then he delivered the caution, which Val refused to acknowledge.

'I've had to get my lassie in to look after the dog,' she said. 'And she doesnae have all afternoon, so let's crack on. You make your threats, I'll ignore them and we can all get on with doing something useful.'

'Where were you on Sunday?' Ben said, his voice smooth.

She stared at him. 'Here and there.'

'Let's try late afternoon.'

She shrugged. 'Cannae remember. I'm a busy woman.'

'Were you in a house in Balunie Crescent in Dundee? Let's say late afternoon to early evening.'

Dermot twiddled a fountain pen in his fingers. 'Mrs Docherty answered this question at her last interview. It's a waste of everyone's time to go over it again.'

Ben ignored this. 'We have evidence you were in this property. Not only were you there but we aim to prove your dog' – he broke off to check his notes – 'a German shepherd – was used to intimidate the victim, Finn Coverdale, following his abduction. Mr Coverdale, as you'll recall, was the sexual partner of the late Theo Glancy. Theo was the son of your friend and business partner Rhona Glancy. We believe you ordered Finn's abduction and assault because you thought he knew something about Theo's death. You had invested a great deal of time and money in Retro's night club and, with Rhona grief-stricken, you could see your investment dwindling away. So you arranged for Finn to be abducted because you had to get to the truth.' He sat back, regarding her. 'It's only ever about the money with you, Val. Isn't it?'

She opened her mouth to speak but Dermot put out a hand to silence her. 'What evidence?' he said, fountain pen poised.

Ben took a moment before replying. 'Sworn statements from two witnesses. Statements which confirm Mrs Docherty ordered the abduction, that she directed the house in Balunie Crescent to be used to detain Mr Coverdale, that she used her dog to intimidate him and that she ordered a sustained assault on him. And only when she was convinced he knew nothing did she arrange for him to be bundled back into a car and dumped elsewhere in Dundee, half unconscious in freezing temperatures. Frankly, Mr Callaghan, your client is lucky not to be facing a charge of murder.'

He didn't flinch. Barely blinked. 'Sworn statements? From whom?'

Ben took a moment, watching Val carefully. 'Bruce and Bradley McCarthy.'

Clare's eyes never left Val's face. There was a flicker of some-thing – a brief moment of clarity. A split second as she assessed her situation – as she took in the news the McCarthy twins had turned on her; and then it was gone. Her face softened and she reached into her pocket for a crumpled tissue. She dabbed at imaginary tears and her lower lip began to tremble. Then she held up a hand. 'If I could have a minute.'

'Of course,' Clare said. 'Take all the time you like.'

They sat on while Val sniffed and dabbed at dry eyes, Dermot fussing over her with exaggerated solicitude. Finally, Ben cleared his throat.

'If we might continue…'

Val gave one last theatrical sniff, then tucked the hankie back in her pocket. 'I need to explain.'

Clare glanced at Ben. 'I'm sure we'd love to hear it.'

Val shot her a look then she turned to Ben, the mournful expression back in place. 'Okay. I was there – in that room.'

Suddenly Clare's mouth was dry, her heart beating out of her chest – so loud she wondered if anyone else could hear it. This was it. They had her. After all these years, all the times Val had slipped through their fingers. They actually had her. She'd just admitted to being present when Finn was assaulted. How many times had Clare tried and failed to get to this point? How long had she waited for this moment? She was breathing faster now. She knew that and she pressed her lips together, drawing air in slowly through her nose, torn between savouring the moment and staying alert.

And then she collected herself. Val was speaking again.

'I was there,' she repeated. 'But I didnae abduct the laddie. And I wasnae involved in the beating he took. I was as scared as he was.'

Clare raised an eyebrow but said nothing.

'How did you come to be there?' Ben said.

'Phone call. Said to go to that house or – or they'd torch the club.'

'Retro's?' Clare asked, and Val nodded.

'Aye. Said they'd wait until Rhona was in it, and all. Block off the fire exits.' She shook her head. 'After what happened to Theo, I couldnae let them do that.'

'Who made the call?'

'No idea. But I've lived long enough to know when somebody's making a real threat.'

'Okay,' Ben said. 'How did you get there?'

'Drove.'

'What about the dog?' Clare asked.

'Took her along. Thought it might be an idea.'

'Because?'

'Protection. She's a helluva bark. Folk see her and they back off. Seemed like a good plan. Only it didn't work out like that.'

They waited to see if she would expand on this but she let her gaze drop to the floor, as if the memory was a painful one.

'So you went to the house,' Ben said after a moment, his tone brisk. 'What happened next?'

Val swallowed. 'I went in. And I saw them – the twins. The laddie – he was in a chair, blindfold on, and those two lunkheads were knocking lumps off him. Soon as we get in the door Bella begins to bark but one of them – Brad, maybe – he grabs the lead and he takes Bella over to the laddie. Tells him the dog'll rip his face off if he doesnae start talking.' Val shook her head slowly. 'The laddie – he was roaring and bubbling, saying he didnae know anything; and the more noise he made the more anxious Bella got.' She shook her head. 'It was horrible.'

Ben sat back. 'Are you saying they wanted you there purely for your dog?' He went on without waiting for an answer. 'It doesn't add up, Val. Aggressive dogs are ten-a-penny with these guys. They wouldn't have needed your Bella.'

A smile played on her lips. 'Aye,' she said. 'You're right there. The dog was a bonus.' She raised her gaze to meet Clare's, a hint of triumph in her eyes. 'It was me they wanted.'

Chapter 55

'She claims Viggo's after the club,' Clare told Chris as they waited for the kettle to boil. 'He reckons it's a genius idea. Sixties and seventies music's huge just now and it's perfect for the town. Viggo wanted in and she says what Viggo wants Viggo gets.'

Chris shook his head. 'You believe her? I reckon she's more than a match for Viggo. Maybe not herself but she knows people.'

'Exactly. Anyway, her version was Viggo planned to muscle in on Retro's. Keep Rhona in charge but edge Val out. Said he'd make Val an offer she couldn't refuse.'

'According to Val.'

'Indeed. But she said Viggo didn't want any trouble. Didn't want anyone coming after the rest of the Glancys. He had to know who was responsible for Theo's murder and Danny's disappearance. Val told him she'd no idea but he said that wasn't an option. She was Rhona's friend so it was down to her to find out.'

The kettle came to the boil and Chris began pouring water into mugs. 'It sort of makes sense,' he said. 'Theo and Danny – it was starting to look like a vendetta against the family.'

'But she didn't reckon on the McCarthys giving us statements.'

'Her defence will challenge them in court, though,' Chris said. 'It comes down to who's more credible in the witness box.'

Clare hesitated. She hadn't told Chris about Bruce and Brad's moonlight flit. 'Chris…'

His face clouded. 'What's going on?'

'Bring your coffee to my office. We'll talk there.'

He followed her through and closed the door. Then he waited.

'Look,' Clare began, 'I can't tell you everything. But – you know Ben? You know what he does, yeah?'

He was quiet for a moment. 'The McCarthy twins?'

She nodded.

'But we need their testimony.'

'And we'll get it. We have signed statements, written and on video. Plus they'll give evidence, remotely.'

His eyes widened. 'They're off the scene?'

'Yep. But that's all I'm telling you. So if at some point in the future we're asked to investigate their disappearance we treat it like any other missing person, okay?'

He shrugged. 'I mean, yeah. Sure. It's not right, though – these guys getting away with it. That lad was battered black and blue.'

'I know,' Clare said. 'But guys like the McCarthys are ten-a-penny – easily replaced. The Vals and Viggos of this world – they're the real prize.'

'Suppose.'

'Not a word of it goes outside this room. Not even to Sara.'

He sighed. 'It's as well I don't talk in my sleep.' He took a draught of his coffee. 'So Val?'

'We've charged her. With the McCarthys' testimony and Finn's statement I think it'll be enough. Penny reckons it's a goer.'

'Even though she didn't lay a finger on Finn herself?'

'Yep. *Art and part*, it's called. If she incited or encouraged any of it she's as guilty as the twins.'

Chris looked impressed. 'Every day's a school day.' He was quiet as he considered this. 'Finn's bound to be a good witness,' he said, after a bit. 'But keeping him safe could be a problem. The trial's likely to be months away. Even if Val's remanded in custody, I wouldn't put it past her to get a message to some of her meatheads.'

'I know. But he did say something about a cousin in Canada. Has a sawmill out there. Finn reckons he could head over. Work for the cousin in return for bed and board.'

'That would be perfect.'

'Just until the trial – unless he decides he likes it there. Maybe a new start, after what happened to Theo.' Clare drained her mug. 'Speaking of Theo, how do you fancy driving me over to Rhona's? I'd like to update her myself.'

'Can we get doughnuts on the way back?'

'If you're very, very good.'

–

Clare called ahead to relieve Wendy Briggs of her duty as FLO to the Glancy family.

'We're pretty much done now,' she said, and she related the events of the past few days, omitting the part about the McCarthys. 'If you could let Rhona know we're on our way over.'

They found Rhona and Ruby on their hands and knees, cleaning out kitchen cupboards.

'I'm better being busy,' Rhona said, getting to her feet. 'But I could do with a break.'

Ruby steered her mother towards the sitting room. 'I'll put the kettle on.'

They followed Rhona through and a few minutes later Ruby appeared with a tray of mugs. She handed them out and took a seat opposite Clare and Chris.

'The other officer – Wendy – she's gone now,' Ruby said, and Clare nodded.

'She can come back any time. But you may not need her.'

Rhona was quiet for a moment. 'What happened to Danny,' she said. 'Is that to do with Theo?'

'We think so,' Clare said. 'I can't tell you too much at the moment. But we believe the man who abducted Danny is the same man who killed Theo.'

Ruby moved to sit next to her mother and put an arm round her. 'You've arrested him?'

'Not yet. He's in hospital – not well enough to be interviewed. But, rest assured, we have a police guard on him. As soon as the doctors say it's okay, we'll speak to him. But' – she softened her voice – 'he may never be well enough for that.'

'Is he injured?' Ruby asked.

Clare hesitated. 'It's a bit more complicated than that. I probably shouldn't tell you, but he's been detained in Carseview.'

Rhona said nothing, her hands clasped round the coffee mug. Her eyes were on the floor and Clare saw the rise and fall of her chest as she tried to control her breathing; then she lifted her gaze. 'So it was never Theo, was it? It was always Danny he was after.'

'We think so, yes,' Clare said. 'I'm so sorry, Rhona.'

She shook her head. 'Danny's getting out this afternoon.' She looked up at Ruby, perched on the arm of her chair. 'There's going to be some changes. Danny – he's going to have to change. All this heartache – that Dundee lot – it stops right here.'

Ruby leaned in and kissed the top of her mum's head and Clare found she had a lump in her throat. They sat on for a minute, drinking in silence, then Clare put down her mug.

'There is one more thing.'

Rhona's eyes were full of fear.

'It concerns Val.'

'I tried ringing her this morning,' Rhona said. 'But she's not picking up.'

'She won't be picking up for the next wee while,' Clare said. 'She's in custody.'

'Custody?' Rhona gaped. 'Val? What's she done?'

'She's been charged with abduction.'

'Chrissake,' Rhona said. 'Who's she abducted?'

Clare paused for a moment, considering how much she could tell Rhona. And then she thought Val would be up in court the following day and the press would be all over it. 'The young man Theo was seeing – he was abducted and quite badly beaten.'

A look of confusion came into Rhona's eyes. 'Val – I don't understand. You're saying she beat up Theo's – his boyfriend, I suppose. Is that what you're saying?'

'We believe she ordered his abduction and watched while he was seriously assaulted.'

Rhona shook her head. 'But why? I don't understand.'

'She thought Finn – that's the young man – she thought he knew something about Theo's death. She was determined to get it out of him. Unfortunately for Finn, he knew nothing. But he'd taken quite a beating before Val accepted that.'

Rhona's head drooped now, her shoulders sagging. What little fight she had left in her had gone. 'I can't believe it,' she said. 'I just can't.'

Ruby patted her mum's arm. 'She was always a bit rough, though, Val.'

'The club – what'll happen to the club?' Rhona was crying now. 'What if Val's put away for years? What'll I do?'

Chris regarded Rhona. 'Val – she put up the money, yes?'

Rhona nodded. 'We agreed a payment plan. Nothing formal. Val gets a share of the profits. Quite a big share,' she added.

Chris gave her a smile. 'I wouldn't worry. The charges against her are pretty serious. She's up in court tomorrow and we're expecting her to be remanded in custody. There's a strong case against her and, if the jury believes it, she won't be collecting her share any time soon.'

'Give you time to turn a profit,' Clare said. 'Without worrying about paying Val back.'

'They're right, Mum,' Ruby said. 'You don't need Val to run the club. You know about bars and Danny can do all the heavy stuff. If we're not paying Val, we can afford to get some more staff in. It'll be fine – I promise.'

'But Theo…' Rhona broke off.

'I can do the computer stuff,' Ruby went on. 'And it'll be good for you to have something to think about. Theo – he wouldn't have wanted you to let Retro's go. He was so proud of you.'

Rhona looked up at Ruby again. 'Really?' Her voice was hoarse. 'He was proud of me?'

'He was. We all are. Me and Danny – I don't know where we'd be without you.'

Clare nodded to Chris and they got to their feet.

'We'll leave you for now,' Clare said. 'But I'm at the end of the phone if you need anything.'

Rhona made to rise but Clare waved her back down. 'Stay and enjoy your coffee. We'll see ourselves out.'

Ruby followed them to the door. 'Thanks,' she said. 'I mean, for everything, but especially for what you said to Mum. I never liked her dealing with Val. If she's locked up for a few years it'll suit us just fine. Mum doesn't need her. *We* don't need her.'

Clare gave her a smile. 'Look after her.'

They walked down the drive, Chris clicking to unlock the car. 'She's a nice kid,' he said.

'They all are,' Clare said. 'Well, maybe not Danny, but this mess – Viggo and Val – the McCarthys – maybe he'll take a look at his life, now; and Rhona obviously knows what's been going on with Viggo.'

'That reference to the Dundee lot?'

'Yep. I reckon she turned a blind eye to Danny's drug dealing. Hopefully this will be a new start for all of them.' She glanced back at the house. Ruby was at the window, watching them. She lifted her hand and Clare smiled back. 'I certainly hope so.'

Chapter 56

'I had a word with Hammy,' Chris said, rinsing his mug under the kitchen tap.

Clare eyed him. 'Look at you, washing your mug like a big boy.'

'Very funny. You want to hear what he said?'

'Go on, then.'

'He reckons no way Viggo's interested in Retro's. He makes a pretty tidy living from drugs and girls. Apparently he reckons it's a lot of bother for not much in return.'

Clare shook her head. 'What a scumbag.'

'No argument there.'

'It confirms Val was lying, then – her story about the assault on Finn. But I don't see how it helps us. It's not like Viggo would testify. He's hardly going to stand in the witness box and say he's too busy with drugs and girls to take over Retro's.'

'Fair point.'

'We'll just have to hope the jury believe Finn and the twins.'

'Amen to that, Inspector.'

–

By mid-afternoon, Clare decided to call it a day. She shut down her computer, grabbed her coat and headed for the incident room. Chris, Max and Sara were deep in conversation.

'Custard first,' Chris said. 'It's got to be,' but Sara was shaking her head.

'You put the custard next to the cream. Jelly goes after the sponge.'

'Glad to see you're debating the finer points of – trifle, I'm guessing?'

'I can't believe they put jelly in their trifles,' Max said. 'Sponge, fruit, custard and cream. That's it.'

'And sherry,' Sara said.

'Try Cointreau,' Max advised. 'It's so much nicer.'

Chris rolled his eyes. 'Doesn't much matter. Soon as that cat sees it, he'll knock it off the table.' His eyes went to Clare's coat. 'We going somewhere?'

'I was hoping for a lift home.'

Chris got to his feet. 'Anything's better than Trifle Wars. Honest to God, if I get to the other side of Christmas without my head exploding it'll be a miracle.'

–

Clare found her dad engaged in hanging decorations from the ceiling, Benjy observing from the sofa. She had a momentary panic, recalling her mother's story about him not setting the stepladder up properly but a quick glance told her the legs were locked in place.

'These look great,' she said, holding the ladder as he climbed down. 'Thanks, Dad.'

He stepped heavily onto the carpet, grasping the hand she offered. 'I'll just put the steps away.' She watched him for a moment, hefting the steps under one arm, assuring herself he could manage then she went into the kitchen. A movement at the window caught her eye and she saw the first flakes of snow begin to fall. 'It's snowing,' she said, turning as her dad came in behind her.

'Oh, I hope it's not too heavy,' he said. 'Alastair said he'd run me home tomorrow.'

She turned, surprised at this. 'You're going home?'

He nodded. 'It's time. I've enjoyed being here and it's helped me get used to the idea of giving up the car. But I need to get back. I don't like leaving your mum for too long.'

She took hold of his hand. 'It's been lovely having you here and, for what it's worth, I think you've made a good decision. Time to let someone else drive you around.'

They wandered back through to the sitting room and her dad put a match to the stove. 'I've brought some more logs in,' he said, indicating the basket. 'Keep you going for a day or two.'

The kindling caught and they sat enjoying the heat while the snow fell steadily outside. She wondered about her dad's decision to return home tomorrow. She had thought he might stay until the weekend when one of them could run him back to Glasgow. But now Al was taking him back in the morning. Did that mean he was off to Tulliallan again? He'd been through there a lot, lately. And did it have anything to do with what Ben had said? Something about a new role being *quite a coup*. More to the point, why had she heard about it from Ben?

She glanced at the window and saw the snow was heavier now. 'You might end up staying longer than planned,' she said. 'Both our cars are rubbish in the snow.'

As they sat, eyes trained on the window, the white flakes hypnotic against an inky sky, headlights swept across the room and the DCI's car appeared. Benjy immediately went into a frenzy of barking. Clare's dad rose from the sofa. 'You stay by the fire. I'll get the door.'

Day 11: Friday

Chapter 57

'I gather Sean Davis is still not fit to be interviewed,' Penny Meakin said.

Clare shifted the phone to her other ear and pulled the computer mouse towards her, running an eye down her Inbox. 'Unfortunately not. The doctor has said at least another two days before he'll consider it.'

'But you're confident he killed Theo Glancy?'

She thought back to the conversation with Danny at the hospital. 'Oh yes,' she said. 'A case of mistaken identity. If only Theo hadn't taken his brother's jacket.'

'Moving on, then,' Penny said, her manner brisk. 'Val is up in court this morning, yes?'

'Yes. We're opposing bail. I'll be surprised if she's let out, given the nature of the charges.'

'Good. Keep me informed,' and with that she ended the call.

Clare worked on steadily, catching up with a backlog of tasks she'd set aside while they'd investigated Theo's murder. She was trying to put Ben's remarks about Al's job to the back of her mind. He'd run her into the station that morning. She could have asked him then. But she wasn't sure how the conversation would go and she wanted her dad back in Glasgow before she raised the subject. So she'd confined herself to talking about the weather, her dad, Christmas – anything other than the elephant in the room – or the car.

She was wading through a report on sustainability and modern policing when Chris ambled in.

'Yes?'

He shrugged. 'Nothing really. Just thought I might nip to the shop, if you wanted anything.'

She studied him, trying to work out what he really wanted but, before she could ask, there was a tap at the door.

Jim came half into the room. He was holding a small white Jiffy bag. 'This was handed in. Got your name on it.'

Clare looked at the bag. *DI Mackay* was written in large black letters but there was nothing to indicate who it was from. 'Who delivered it?'

'Sorry,' Jim said. 'It was Zoe who took it in. The postie arrived at the same time with letters to be signed for and she can't remember who brought this one.'

She put out a hand to take it but Chris pulled her arm back. 'You've no idea what's in that.'

'Only one way to find out.'

'Wait, though – what if it's a present from Val – or Viggo? We've been dealing with some dodgy folk this week.'

She hesitated for a moment.

'At least put gloves on before you open it.'

She suppressed a smile. 'You don't think you're taking this a bit too seriously, Sergeant?'

'I don't fancy organising a whip round for your plastic surgery. Mind you—'

'Don't say it!' she warned. She took the Jiffy bag from Jim. 'I will take full responsibility for this,' and she peeled back the seal, holding it open for a minute before looking in. Then she put a hand in and took out a long pink tube, wrapped in plastic, squinting at the logo.

'What's a – a lip plumper?' She looked up, scanning their faces.

'Don't ask us,' Chris said. He went to the incident room door and Clare followed him through. Sara and Gillian were packing away laptops, no longer needed now the investigations were coming to an end. 'Oy! Womenfolk?'

Sara gave him a look and he held up his hands by way of apology. 'Our inspector needs some guidance here.'

They wandered out to the front office and Clare showed them the pink tube.

'Oh, it's a lip plumper,' Gillian said.

'Yes, I know that,' Clare said. 'But what's it for?'

'Erm, to make your lips plump.'

She stared at Gillian. 'Seriously?'

'Yeah. It's for folk who don't want to do Botox. I think it dilates the blood vessels, making your lips fuller.'

'What a time to be alive,' Chris said, dodging Sara's hand.

Clare reached into the bag again and pulled out a small card. 'It's from Ruby Glancy,' she said. 'A thank-you for helping the family.' She held it out for them to see. 'I can't accept this.'

Chris waved it away. 'It'll be one of her freebies.'

'I'll have it if you don't want it,' Gillian said. 'That's a really good make.'

Clare closed her hand round it. 'I'd better hang onto it.'

'I don't see why you can't keep it,' Chris said. 'They're victims, not perps. It could hardly be seen as a bribe.'

'Maybe.' Her phone buzzed with a message. Cheryl from the Bell Street station in Dundee. She scanned the screen and punched the air.

'Yes! Val's been remanded in custody.' She smiled round at them. 'That is a good day's work,' and she went back through to her office to resume reading the report.

–

It was late afternoon when she heard from Raymond – a quick message confirming the second dog DNA test was a match for the saliva on Finn's clothing. Not that it was needed, with Val admitting she'd been in the house at Balunie Crescent. Hopefully a jury would see her defence for what it was – a complete distortion of the truth. She glanced out of her office window. The previous night's snow had stopped after an hour or two but it was on again and she hoped Al had managed to take her dad back to Glasgow okay. Maybe she'd head home early – put the stove on – cook something. Have the house warm and cosy for him getting back. She ran an eye down her Inbox again and decided there was nothing that couldn't wait until morning – Monday, even.

She shut down her computer and wandered through to the incident room, looking for someone to give her a lift home. It was oddly empty and she wondered where they all were.

She saw the computer monitors before she realised they were standing just outside the door, necks craned to see her reaction. Someone had gone round every single computer and changed the screensaver to her official photo with a fish's mouth in place of her own lips. Someone – and she'd find out who if it was the last thing she did – had given her a trout pout!

Chapter 58

She lay on the sofa enjoying the heat from the woodburner while the DCI massaged her feet. He emptied the last of the wine into her glass.

'That was a nice curry,' he said. 'Lovely to come home to.'

'Gotta love Sharwood's,' she admitted. 'But I chopped that chicken like a boss!'

He laughed. 'So you did.'

They fell silent again, the knot in Clare's stomach reminding her she still hadn't tackled him about his new job – if that's what it was.

And then she knew it was time. She withdrew her feet and eased herself up on the couch so she was level with him. 'I hear you have a new job.'

She felt him stiffen, just for a moment, then he recovered himself. 'Well, I've been offered one. I did want to speak to you before deciding.'

She eyed him. 'Why did I hear it from Ben Ratcliffe? I felt a complete idiot not knowing anything about it.'

He sighed. 'I did try, Clare. Several times. But you had a lot going on. These investigations, those late nights, your ribs – then all the upset with your dad. It never felt like the right time.'

She was quiet, turning his words over in her mind. He had a point. She had been busy. Busy, in pain and downright narky. 'I'm listening now,' she said. 'Or is it too late? Have you accepted it?'

He didn't reply.

'You have, haven't you?'

'I've not actually signed anything yet. But they needed an answer so I've agreed in principle.'

She stared at him for a moment then turned and looked at the fire, flames licking round the logs. 'Congratulations,' she said, her voice even. 'Can I ask what it is?'

He turned to face her, taking hold of her hand. 'Of course you can. I wasn't trying to keep it from you. After the week you've had there's no way I could have hit you with it.' He took a drink of wine then put down his glass. 'It's a new role and they want someone quickly. Penny said it was mine if I wanted it.'

She said nothing.

'I'll be heading up a new cyber security unit at Tulliallan. Not the really secret stuff. That'll still be done at Gartcosh. But I'll be leading a communications and outreach team. It follows on from the work I've been doing. I pretty much wrote the job description.'

She tried her best to smile. 'It's perfect, Al. I'm so happy for you.'

'It comes with a promotion, too.'

'Superintendent?'

'Yep. So it's more money. We could book a bit of time off. Have a really fabulous holiday.'

'Suppose.'

'Only – I'll be based at Tulliallan.'

She frowned. 'That's a lot of driving.'

He didn't reply and she realised what he wasn't saying.

'You're planning to stay, aren't you? At the college?'

He nodded. 'There's a flat goes with the job. Pretty nice, actually; and I wouldn't be there all the time. I've agreed I'll go through on Monday mornings, come back Thursdays and work from home on Fridays.'

She smiled. 'Sounds like you've got it all worked out.'

'Only if you agree.'

'Al! How could I stop you? It's made for you.'

'It does feel that way.'

Benjy, asleep in front of the fire, began to dream, his tail thumping the rug, paws twitching. They watched him for a minute then Clare said, 'What will I do about Benjy? When you're away, I mean?'

He was quiet for a moment. 'You could ask Moira. Instead of her coming here to walk him maybe she'd let you drop him at hers while you're at work. Like a childminder. He'd love it and I think she would as well. You know she adores him.'

She considered this. 'Maybe. To be honest, I could do with a better work-life balance.'

'No argument there.' He put an arm out and pulled her towards him. 'There is another option.'

'Yes?'

'My job – the one I'm doing now. They'll have to fill it.'

She stared at him. 'Me?'

'Why not? You can't stay operational for the rest of your career – working all hours, getting kicked in the ribs. You're too good for that, Clare. You know you are; and Penny would back you. She pretty much said so.'

'Sounds like you have it all worked out between you.'

He smiled but said nothing.

She stared into the fire, his words running round her head. Was she ready to step back from her role? Leave Chris and Max? Jim and Sara? It wasn't something she'd ever considered. And could she do Al's job? Developing policies and strategies had never appealed to her but it would be nine-to-five. No more farming Benjy out overnight when she was stuck on an operation and Al was away. Stepping away from the desk after putting in her eight hours. It had an appeal.

And then they all came into her head, unbidden. Chris and his Wagon Wheels, Zoe with her hair, a different colour every week and Jim – solid, reliable Jim, the mainstay of the station. Could she walk away? Leave them all to shake down with a new DI? Al had a point. She didn't want to spend the next ten or twenty years grappling with people like Leon Maddox. But somehow it seemed an awful lot to give up.

She eyed her wine glass, empty now. Maybe the decision would be easier with a clearer head. She put the glass down and got to her feet.

'Coffee, Al Gibson. We need strong coffee.'

Epilogue

Eleven Months Later

THE SCOTSMAN – 22 October

Edinburgh Woman Convicted of Abduction and Serious Assault

By Ronald Jaffray, Legal Correspondent

An Edinburgh woman who ordered a savage attack on a man has been convicted at the High Court in Livingston following a trial which lasted nine days.

Valerie Docherty, aged 49, from Barnton, was found guilty of the abduction and serious assault on Finn Coverdale at a Dundee property in November last year. The court heard how Docherty concocted the plot that left the 29-year-old with multiple fractures and serious internal injuries.

Docherty's lawyers had argued a special defence of incrimination. But the jury rejected the claim after just two hours.

Mr Coverdale, who wasn't present for the verdict, had provided key evidence that led to Docherty's conviction.

Speaking outside the court, investigating officer DI Clare Mackay hailed the victim's bravery throughout the ordeal.

She said: 'Mr Coverdale suffered an unprovoked and sustained assault. I commend him for his bravery in giving evidence against Mrs Docherty.'

Judge Lady Darvell adjourned sentence until 19 November, warning Docherty she was facing a lengthy period of custody.

Acknowledgements

An old proverb tells us it takes a village to raise a child. Likewise it takes a huge team of people to bring a book to publication and there are so many lovely folk who helped bring *Dead Man's Shoes* to fruition.

There's nothing like planning a book to make you realise how little you know. Thankfully my wonderful friends seem to know everything about everything. In particular I'm so grateful to Peter Darbyshire, Persia Honar, Alan Rankin and Jonathan Whitelaw for filling in the gaps in my knowledge.

Throughout the writing of this book my incredible agent Elizabeth Counsell has been on hand with excellent advice and endless support. Thank you so much for all you do, Elizabeth. None of this would happen without your steady hand on the tiller.

Once the book reaches my publisher Team Canelo swing into action. Louise Cullen, Alicia Pountney, Thanhmai Bui-Van, Nicola Piggot and Kate Shepherd have worked tirelessly on this book and really are the best publishing team I could wish for. For their sage advice on edits and proofreading I'm so grateful to Becca Allen, Deborah Blake and Vicki Vrint. Thank you all for making my book so much better than the scrappy monster I originally submitted. The icing on the cake has been James Macey's stunning cover design. Thank you so much for such an atmospheric image, James. I love it!

My lovely friends in the writing community are always there to listen to my moans and groans and I owe them all so much for the support they have given me. Special thanks go to Sheila Bugler, Tana Collins, Jeanette Hewitt, Rachel Lynch, Angela Nurse, Francesca Riccardi, Victoria Scott, Daniel Sellers, Barnaby Walter and Sarah Ward. Thanks for being the very best group of friends I could ever wish for.

Finally, the biggest thank-you is to the many festival organisers, booksellers, reviewers and readers. You make this whole thing possible and I'm immensely grateful. Let's get together at *Retro's Club* for a drink!

ⓒ **CANELO**CRIME

Do you love crime fiction and are always on the lookout for
brilliant authors?

Canelo Crime is home to some of the most exciting novels
around. Thousands of readers are already enjoying our
compulsive stories. Are you ready to find your new favourite
writer?

Find out more and sign up to our newsletter at
canelocrime.com